THE MALTHUSIAN CONSPIRACY

A Mitch Stone Adventure

THE MALTHUSIAN CONSPIRACY

Dave Monroe

Writers Club Press
San Jose New York Lincoln Shanghai

The Malthusian Conspiracy

Writers Club Press
an imprint of iUniverse, Inc.

For information address:
iUniverse, Inc.
5220 S. 16th St., Suite 200
Lincoln, NE 68512
www.iuniverse.com

This is a work of fiction. All events, locations, institutions, themes, persons, characters, and plot are completely fictional. Any resemblance to places or persons, living or deceased, are of the invention of the author.

ISBN: 0-595-21481-9

TO: Rumi for all her help and constant support and for believing in my dream.

ASHES TO ASHES, DUST TO DUST

Contents

Acknowledgements

Special thanks to Chris Madere and everyone who gave the first draft a critical read and provided important suggestions to make it better.

PROLOGUE

*B*ill Totman had been a loyal employee for thirty plus years. He had met the man who would become the chief engineer of the project at the culturally historic Woodstock concert in 1969. The two would become friends and their friendship continued through the last years of college and into graduate school and beyond. Bill had decided that the new world that had been born in the sixties would be better served if he finished his engineering degree and worked to build a better world. He embraced the concept that the world should be more peaceful and that humans should be less destructive and more in harmony with nature.

He believed that he couldn't beat the system so he decided to join it and correct it from the inside so he vigorously pursued a background in engineering and after his fateful meeting with the future chief engineer of a major world recycling company he truly felt he was contributing to the betterment of mankind and the world. That philosophy would in the end be the undoing of Bill Totman. He had worked for many years mainly on a new developing nano technology which would revolutionize the fields of materials sciences and more importantly make recycling one-hundred-percent efficient and for his employers very profitable.

Over the years Bill had researched and developed applications for the new technology which would convert virtually any waste product, solid, liquid or gas, back into its constituent elements which then of course were sold at great profit back to manufactures for production into new products. He felt good about his job and his contribution to the planet.

After his graduation from graduate school he married his collage girlfriend and they set up housekeeping near his new employers main research labs in Dallas. He was finally promoted to chief assistant just beneath his old friend and he had started to work on the newest and to his employers, the most critical aspect of their recycling business. All his altruistic feelings changed then faded one day when he found out the true nature of his employers' activities.

He wrestled with his conscience for several months on whether to blow the whistle or resign. Each passing day though brought new stress and the pressure to do something increased with every successful test of the new technology and the proposed application. He just couldn't bear it any longer and one day for the first time in his life he called in sick to work. He then made a second call from his home phone. This call however, would have been completely against his principles except that the continued development of his project was even more against his principles.

He made the call and then agreed to the meeting. He agonized over his decision for most of the day and called in sick on the next day for two reasons. First he was making himself sick with nervous energy about what he had done. Second, he had made the meeting which was set for lunchtime in a very public restaurant near his house. His wife had gone to work as usual and he sat alone in the livingroom until it was time to go to the meeting. He drove the few blocks to the restaurant and waited at the table as he had been instructed. The meeting would take place at twelve thirty and he was a few minutes early.

While he was waiting for the two men he was to tell his story to a waiter stopped at the table and asked Bill if he wanted something to drink. Bill opted for a cup of tea and a glass of water. The waiter was very friendly and promptly returned with both. Bill sat and looked around the restaurant wondering if his two contacts would be on time. What Bill didn't notice was that the friendly waiter had left the restaurant immediately after serving him and was now sitting in a car across the street.

The former waiter watched the nervous Bill through a pair of binoculars and saw him take a long drink of water followed by a sip of tea. Just as Bill finished the cup of tea and took another swallow of water, the former waiter place a call on his cell phone. He watched Bill as the phone rang in his ear. The line answered.

"Village Green Restaurant, how may I help you?"

"Yes, I have a phone call for one of your patrons. Could you put him on the line for me?" the former waiter asked.

"Yes sir, what is his name?"

"It's Bill Totman and he's sitting at the small table near the front window."

"Yes sir, please hold." A few moments passed as the waiter watched Bill through the window. Then in the binoculars he saw another waiter deliver the phone to Bill and Bill picked up the receiver.

"Hello," Bill said.

"Yes, Mr. Totman. This is agent Phelps from the FBI. I am very sorry but our field office has been involved in a very delicate matter and our people are tied up on a case. I was wondering if you wouldn't mind postponing your meeting until the same time tomorrow?"

"Well, I, ah, would have to call in sick again but yeah, I guess so. All right," Bill said a little angered and disappointed at the sudden change of plans. Damn Feds, he thought. "Same time then?"

"Yes, sir. Same time."

"OK, fine," Bill said and hung up. He waved for the second waiter who couldn't understand how Bill had been served a cup of tea but presented a check which Bill promptly paid and left the restaurant. The former waiter hung up his cell phone and watched as Bill left. Bill took only a few steps down the street and he suddenly stopped and doubled over in pain. He fought off a wave of nausea for a few minutes and then continued on his way. The former waiter punched in another phone number and waited for the answer.

"Yes."

"The leak has been plugged with no sign of any collateral damage."

"Very good," the voice on the other end said and the line went dead. The former waiter started his car and drove away. He had to pack his things. He'd just been notified that he was being transferred to one of the company's newest labs and he was going to be the director of security.

Bill Totman managed to get himself home but not without some great difficulty. He vomited three times and nearly passed out in traffic. It was a monumental struggle for him to make it the few blocks to his house and then get up stairs. He needed to lie down, but first he had to use the toilet. In fact he had to go worse than he ever had and he was even in pain now but he stumbled over a shoe his wife had left on the floor next to the bed. He fell and by now was so weak he couldn't get up off the floor. As he approached unconsciousness his bladder released and he started to urinate until he succumbed.

That evening his wife returned from work at her usual time and went upstairs to change her clothes and check on her husband. She didn't find him in bed and figured he may have felt better and gone into work. What she did find and was a little annoyed at was a mess on the floor near the bed. It looked as though her husband had taken a shower in his clothes and left them in a heap. Not only that, she noticed a powdery substance inside the clothes that now looked like wet sand. She changed her clothes and started to clean up the mess. She vacuumed the wet sand like stuff up and picked up the wet clothes. They smelled like urine and she began to get concerned.

The next day when her husband's office called wondering where he was she really became concerned and after the second day that her husband didn't show up, she notified the police who came to her house and looked for some clues. They didn't find anything but, as a standard practice, they notified the FBI. The FBI was greatly interested in the disappearance of Bill Totman who they had had a meeting scheduled with, and who hadn't showed two days earlier. They took samples of everything in the house including the contents of the vacuum cleaner. They were never quite sure of what happened to Bill Totman but the contents of the vacuum cleaner gave them a list of chemicals that looked as if it was a list off of a vitamin supplement bottle.

CHAPTER 1

THE RELOCATION

980 A.D.

"*L*ars, welcome to my hall and hearth. Please be seated and I'll have one of the thralls bring us some ale."

"Most gracious of you sire, but I am uncertain why you honor me so by summoning me to your great hall."

"Please make yourself comfortable," the Chief said as he turned and called to one of his slaves. Though only seen when the master wanted something, a good thrall was never far from the master. A quick response kept the master happy and the slave somewhat free from torment.

"Bring us ale woman and be quick about it," he said in a manner denoting his status and authority. Eric the Bloodaxe had been the chief of most of East Anglica, as the natives called the place for nearly twenty years. His father before him had expanded the territory and was primarily responsible for the fact that Jorvik was the most prosperous of the western territories. His grandfather was the leader of the warriors who first conquered this land nearly ninety years earlier. Eric the Bloodaxe bore the name and the family reputation of many generations of great warriors and conquerors.

"I humbly beg your pardon but I am unworthy of such generous hospitality especially since I am but a mere farmer these days."

"Yes, yes, I am very well aware of your status in this kingdom, and as your name signifies you are the son of a Karl. You and your line are free born of our kind and are the masters of this land. As such, you have a sworn duty to answer the calling of your lord and master."

"Yes Sire, and I will faithfully follow you into any battle or conquest. Are we to do battle here? My clan and friends are at your service and are always ready to do battle."

"Patience, son of Karl, known as Lars. I have called you to do service for me. That is true, but it is not a battle against known foes."

"I apologize sire, I do not follow your words."

"Lars, I know of you and your clan. Your father fought bravely beside mine to subdue this land and the natives. I have kept an eye on you for most of your life and I am certain you are indeed a very brave and smart man."

"Sire, I am honored again, by your kind words."

"Lars, that is precisely why you're here. I need your bravery and that of your clan and men as well as that intelligence."

"Sire," Lars said as he started to genuflect from his seat directly to the floor.

"Lars rise and come with me for a walk. We must talk in private and although the thralls are out of immediate sight they have very acute ears when it suits them." Both men picked up a large mug made from the tusk of some distant and strange animal. The Vikings had trade connections to the far corners of the world and as with the mugs, they acquired many unusual items they did know the origin of.

"I certainly would not like to meet the beast that lost this great tooth in the dark some night," Eric said as they walked out the rear of the large hall into an open area behind the house beyond which Eric kept many of his personal horses and animals in an enclosed pasture.

"Yes, Sire," Lars said as he held up the hollowed-out tooth and tried to imagine what the former owner looked like. It was nearly as long as his arm and almost two hands wide at the brim. It held approximately a quart of strong ale, which was probably fermented from some of his own crops that he paid in tribute to the Chief each year when the leaves began to show fire. As they walked out into the early spring sunshine, Lars thought to himself and couldn't imagine what the Chief could possibly have in mind for him. He looked around and except for the two large men guarding the Chief's gate they were alone in the warming spring air.

The Chief stopped in the center of the large open space. Probably calculated to be out of earshot, Lars thought as he stopped about one pace away from his master and took another long drink from the tusk mug. He wondered again what the Chief had in mind. Certainly this much ale was meant for something more than a social drink. A lot of ale meant a great decision was to be made and he figured he was the one required to make that decision. The Chief was using the ale as a lubricant to make the wheels of Lars' mind roll easier and without hesitation.

"Lars, son of Karl. Freeman and descendant of great warriors…," the Chief began. Here it comes Lars thought through the ale induced haze that was starting to envelop his brain. What the hell he thought and took another long drink from the almost bottomless mug.

"I must ask you a favor of great importance but at the same time it must be a command that you serve me and our people."

"You have no need to command me Sire. I will follow you or do your bidding. All you need is say the word and I will comply."

"Good. I will always remember this and your dedication," The Chief said and hesitated for a moment. Lars took another drink and almost reached the bottom of the mug. His brain was now almost completely enclosed in the fog of the strong ale.

"Lars, we Vikings, the children of the Norse gods are in serious trouble here and elsewhere in our world."

"Trouble, how so, Sire?"

"Many reasons. We have spread ourselves very thin over this world. We reach far to the East and the South. That mug in your hand comes from a land far to the South. We have only reached the peoples on the northern fringes of that distant land and yet those peoples are more than a year's journey away. We Vikings are few in number but our appetites are great."

"Sire," Lars said still a bit confused and now really beginning to feel the effects of the Chief's refreshment.

"We are beginning to feel the stresses of overextending ourselves. Many of our men have become complacent in their new lands and lifestyles and in fact have begun to dilute our race with foreign bloodlines."

"Sire," Lars said again a little apprehensively. "I beg your forgiveness if I have offended you or the Gods by taking a wife from the island to the west. But it was done with your permission, Sire."

"Yes, yes, I am not making any accusations against you and I did not call you here on that account. What I mean is that our Nordic bloodlines are being mixed with all manners of peoples. You, Lars have a very comely wife and fine strong children, but I fear that is not the case among all our brothers."

"Yes, Sire. Thank you for your kind words," Lars said a bit humbled by the Chief's statement.

"Be at ease my young comrade. You are not the focus of my concern. You are the savior I believe." Lars just stood and looked incredulously at the Chief.

"What I am about to tell you must not go beyond these walls and lands until we are ready with what must be done." The Chief paused to gather his thoughts and Lars finished the last swallow of his ale. "For some time now," the Chief began, "there have been rumblings and dissension among the locals and I fear that there will be an uprising against our control of this land."

"I was not aware of this, Sire."

"Yes, well in any event you are now. These rumblings among the natives have caused some problems. The thralls are becoming more recalcitrant and even a show of force does not bring them into docility. Alas, my advisors suggest and I must concur that a full scale insurrection is in the offing and that it will happen soon. To our great disadvantage we do not have the men or the capacity to put down a revolt when it comes."

Lars stood erect and tried to show his pride. "My men and I shall join with you to quell any such insurrection."

"That will not be necessary. What I have in mind for you is not a battle with these primitives but a far greater and more dangerous battle against the forces here on this world and those that the Gods themselves may send to test you."

"Sire, command and I will obey."

"I know you will, but first hear my plans, then you may decide whether you will want to obey so quickly."

Lars took a deep breath and wished he had not finished the ale so quickly. The Chief was giving him a choice over a matter that certainly should have been a direct order. This was truly a sign of the Chief's good favor. The Chief was taking Lars into his confidence and giving Lars the right to make a decision. Lars smiled and eagerly awaited his fate.

"Lars, son of Karl, we Vikings must now seek out other more favorable lands to colonize and where we can maintain the traditions of our peoples. I have heard from our homelands that a great Viking sailor has discovered vast and wonderful lands to the distant west."

"Sire?"

"Yes, these lands are said to be bountiful, even more than here and they are populated by small bands of primitives."

"Children of the Gods?"

"Not sure, probably not but no matter, the information from the journey is that these primitives are few in number and hide in the deep forests like wild animals."

"Primitives indeed."

"Lars, I would like you to go to these lands and establish a new kingdom for the people of the North."

"Your Grace honors me and my clan with this command."

"No, Lars, I can't command you to do this. The journey is long and arduous. The previous travelers were absent from civilization for more than two full cycles of the seasons and lost more than six men in ten."

"I shall do better at keeping the men alive and make the quest successful."

"That is the true Viking spirit that I had hoped you still possessed."

"There is no greater honor for me than to both serve the Chief and lead men into new lands. I will not fail you my lord."

"It is more than me you serve. It is all of our people. And it is because of this that I give to you my best longboats and as many knarrs as you will need to transport your men and their farms and families."

"Families Sire?"

"Yes, you are to take everything and everyone you feel you will need to relocate our people in the far western lands."

Lars tried to focus his thoughts through the haze of the alcohol. "Sire, if I take everyone and everything as you say what will become of our great city Jorvik. I can't possibly take all of its citizens and their shops and farms."

"No, you can't but you can take the basic necessities to rebuild a community in the new lands. In addition you will have the entire contents of the domains' treasury. All of the precious metals and stones plus all of the rarities from our farthest trading routes."

"Sire, I am not worthy of this."

"Yes, you are and you will take the tools, goods and treasures of our lands here and deliver them to a new home where they can flourish. You will serve the gods and your people well."

"But the riches and the treasure, what will I need of such things in a new land?"

"You may find such things useful in dealing with the primitives. Even savages must appreciate such things."

"Yes. I will do as you command. When do you wish me to start my journey?"

"My advisors tell me that the weather improves with each day and that soon the God of Winter shall sleep and the warmth shall reign again. You must leave before the next full moon. Can you be ready?"

"It shall be done."

"Good your fleet will be ready in seven days. Serve your people well Lars and the Gods will reward you in the next world."

"I will Sire. Thank you for this great honor."

"I will have my advisors provide you with all the charts and information they possess on the far west. I bid you well Lars, son of Karl and leader of men."

Lars suppressed a prideful smile and bowed to the Chief. He also knew that if he succeeded he would be the Chief of a new land. If he failed, he would doom all his fellow travelers and fade into obscurity. He must not fail, he thought as a thrall led him from the Great Hall of the Chief.

The Chief was a man of his word and Lars thought, as he stood at the shore, that the Chief must be a very rich man indeed. There before him was a fleet of eight Viking ships. Six of them were longboats which could carry a hundred men with weapons and supplies enough to last for months. The other two were the much larger knarrs used for long distance trading and hauling cargo. From the size of the fleet Lars realized that he would be taking most of the freemen and their families with him to the western lands. Lars was at once proud of the great honor bestowed on him and apprehensive with the fear of failure to the Chief and so many people.

He stood and watched as the men, women and children loaded the ships with every manner of goods and animals. Whole farms and shops were being moved to the new lands. He called to the master of the largest knarr, "we sail in two days at high tide."

"Yes sir," came the reply and Lars was again proud and disquieted by what lay ahead. He went to his house to gather his life and family to join the pilgrimage west.

CHAPTER 2

THE MEETING

LAST WEEKEND

The boat tugged at its mooring lines as it bobbed gently in the wind propelled ripples moving across the small harbor. If the boat possessed emotions, it would have been jealous of the waves. Like the waves the boat too was wind powered when freed of the constraining lines that bound it to the dock. The ripples on the surface of the harbor were mere small samples of the wind's strength this day. The breeze was strong and steady and the sun was warming the moving air to a comfortable temperature. It was turning out to be a fine late spring day. If the boat were alive, it would want to show its stuff out in the open lake in the stiff breeze and warm sun. The boat was new to all of this but the boat's owner was a halfway decent weekend sailor. Not great by any means but having acquired enough practice to make sailing in most winds of less than twenty knots a very pleasurable experience.

The boat's owner stood on the dock for a moment and admired his new weekend retreat. He had waited more years than he had wanted for the chance to own a sailboat again, let alone a new thirty-two-foot gleaming white sleek beauty like the one he was now eager to test on its maiden voyage. The owner of the new fiberglass yacht, he liked to call it a yacht, stood proudly for a while and then snapped a few pictures with his newly purchased Nikon camera. It was nice to have toys, he thought. He was expecting the rest of the day's "crew" and he checked the parking lot to see if his friends had arrived yet. He walked the length of the slip to get a shot of the transom and he composed the shot, centering on the name he had given his new floating castle. The auto focus motors whirred turning the lens until the picture was in razor sharp focus. He looked at the name affixed to the transom for a moment and then gently pressed the shutter button. The screen went dark for a brief moment and then the name in three inch dark blue letters, reappeared in the viewfinder. 'Cold Fortune' was an appropriate name for the first thing he had purchased with the proceeds of his discovery last summer in this same lake. After the various governments and private agencies had decided who the final owners would be and after making a sizable contribution to the IRS and other taxing authorities he was able to pay cash for his new home away from home at the winter boat show. The boat had looked magnificent standing on display in the large exhibit hall at the state fair grounds. In the cold of February the only place for the display of summer toys was inside. He thought back for a moment at how beautiful this boat had looked even without its fifty-foot mast. It was propped up on a steel cradle and he had to climb a set of wooden steps nearly fifteen feet off the ground to step onto the pure white deck.

He had performed that ritual every February for the better part of a decade. He had been attending the winter boat show even when he had his older smaller sailboat. No harm in looking, he always said as he and Gary, his partner at the Sheriff's Department, made the pilgrimage to the largest indoor boat show in the Northeast. Even Gary, the perennial power boater, was impressed by this sailboat. Clean lines, lots of deck and cabin space and an aft cabin that would certainly qualify as a stateroom. The most important feature though was the queen-size bed on a thirty-two footer. That luxury sold him and after all of the years of telling the sales reps that he was just looking, he shocked them all when he said he would take it. Since the sales reps were also the same people that owned the marina he was now standing in, it was no major chore to have his new boat ready for action as soon as the ice left the harbor. That was two weeks ago and the demands of his job had kept him from getting a free weekend until now and the marina was beginning to fill up fast with the rest of the summer boat tenants.

He thought about the day he signed the contract for the boat. The sales reps were even more amazed. Flabbergasted is a better word. They about fainted when he changed from a regular want-a-be to a full-fledged owner. They were even more amazed when he made twelve consecutive payments of $9,999.00 each day for the next two weeks. He had paid cash but kept each day's total below the $10,000.00 threshold amount for cash transactions that would trigger the Federal requirement of a lot of forms, questions, and unnecessary scrutiny. No one needed to know how much of that long lost British gold was really recovered and how much remained obscured in his own personal hiding place. The proud owner took a couple of long shots of the graceful curves and the teak accents on the deck and then put the lens cap back on the 35-70mm zoom lens. He gently set the camera down on the seat in the cockpit and walked down the slip and stepped onto the main dock. From there he turned right and made his way up the dock walking in the center as much as possible to avoid the lines, cables and equipment belonging to the other boats that had been launched for the start of the new summer season.

He strode across the gravel parking area to his other new acquisition. In addition to the new sailboat, he had recently purchased his other dream toy. He inserted the key into the boot, as the builders called it, and popped the trunk, as he called it. For a two-seat roadster built in the mid-sixties, the car had a remarkably large trunk and he pulled out his duffle bag of clothes and personal items. With his free hand he grabbed one of the two large shopping bags, set it on the ground and retrieved the other bag. He set it next to the first one and gently lowered the trunk lid until he heard the lock click. He gave the lid a little tug with his fingers to see if had latched.

He started to pick up the two grocery bags and stopped and then set the duffle bag down as well. He looked up at the clear blue sky and thought for a moment about leaving the top down while he was out sailing and thought better about it. He didn't figure anyone would try to steal it or even try to damage it here in the marina, but curious people might accidently spill or drop something onto the interior.

It wasn't very often that people would see a perfectly restored 1967 Austin-Healy BJ-8 and no matter what he did, it would draw a crowd. An MGB was a fairly common sports car but it was designed for the young couple on a weekend road trip. It was a quick little car but the Austin-Healy was designed as a muscle roadster with an inline six-cylinder engine with 3000 cc displacement. A serious engine in a small car made the Austin Healy a road burner in its day and even now with all of the technological innovations in even the most basic of commuter cars, the Austin-Healy was still a car that could snap your neck a bit if you jumped on the accelerator.

No sence creating a problem, he thought and opened the trunk again and pulled out the folded cotton cloth. It was shaped like the car and had elastic along the edges. It looked like a fitted bed sheet with some extra cloth in the middle. He stretched it along the rear bumper and unfurled the car cover as he pulled it over the trunk and up across the cloth roof. He had decided to put the top up anyway, to protect the inside from a sudden change in the weather. The cover would be enough protection as long as it didn't rain. He maneuvered the cover up over the windscreen and down over the curved hood which the builders called the bonnet. He pulled the cover tight and slid the other elastic end over the front chrome bumper. There, he said to the car as if it were human too, all nice and snug.

Just as he walked to the back of his precious toy to pick up his bags, he caught sight of Gary's sport utility vehicle coming down the road from the main street of Smyth's Cove. He waited until Gary pulled up in front of him.

"Hey, Mitch. What's with the giant sock on that hot rod of yours?" Gary said trying to get a reaction.

"First of all you cretin, the car is a classic British roadster and secondly, that is not a sock it's a big pillow case." Mitch heard a giggle from the back seat of the S.U.V. and he bent over to peek into the rear window at the source of the chuckle.

"I don't know how you do it, Gary. The ugliest man on the planet, driving around in this uninspired piece of Detroit engineering and you still manage to pick up the two most beautiful women in the world." The young blond in the rear giggled again. "How is the lovely and talented Liz Faulkner doing this fine day?"

"Just fine. Thanks Uncle Mitch."

"And then there is of course the beautiful and…"

"Careful there old man. I might just get jealous," Gary chided.

"I'm fine Mitch," Carol Faulkner said. "Thanks for inviting us on your first cruise."

"No problem dear lady. A beautiful new boat needs a gorgeous crew." Lizzy as she was called giggled again.

"Mitch, why don't you use some of that charm of yours on some nice single girls and you'd have a permanent crew of your own."

"That's what's he afraid of Honey," Gary said as he looked around the lot for a spot to park.

"Oh, yeah, park right here next to my toy."

"It says Marina Staff Only."

"Don't worry. After the cash flow I provided them with this year they treat me pretty well."

"OK, if you're sure," Gary said and pulled into the slot next to Mitch's A-H.

"Hey Mitch," Carol started again, "I'm serious. Why don't you use your charm on some nice single girls? You must know a few, don't you?"

"He's afraid," Gary said as Mitch stuck his head into the 1990's version of the family station wagon.

"Uncle Mitch is not afraid of anything. Are you?" Lizzy yelled trying to maintain her presence in the adult conversation.

"You're almost right, Lizzy," Mitch said helping her out of the back seat. "I'm only afraid of one thing."

"What's that?" Lizzy asked, her eyes wide in disbelief.

Mitch looked around like he was a spy on a mission in the Kremlin and then said in a low voice, "women."

"Women," Lizzy said aloud and started to giggle again. "Women aren't scary. They don't even bite."

"Not according to Mitch, Honey," Gary said in response to Lizzy's statement. "According to him, they suck the life right out of you."

"Like vampires?" Lizzy added.

"Yep, just like vampires," Mitch said as he pretended to suck Lizzy's neck. She giggled and squirmed until Mitch set her down.

"Is that true daddy?" Lizzy asked as she ran to the rear of the truck.

"Careful how you answer that Dear," Carol said with a slight chill in her voice.

"Ah, no Honey. Mitch is just being silly."

"Good answer," Carol said, "but seriously Mitch I worry about you. You need a girlfriend."

"I need a woman like I need to be a couple of years older and a couple of pounds heavier."

Gary just chuckled as he unloaded the truck, but he thought he had better come to his partner's defense. "Mitch is just a little reluctant to get involved with women especially after the messy divorce."

"That was more than ten years ago. God Mitch, holding on to that kind of fear is not healthy."

"What's diborse?" Lizzy asked, again trying to stay in the conversation.

"It's something that happens between married people when they don't like each other anymore," her mother said.

"Are you and mommy going to get divorced?" she asked struggling with the pronunciation of the new word.

"Never. Right Dear?" Carol said with a glare towards Gary that would melt steel.

"Absolutely, right Dear. No, never. And on that harmonious note lets not talk about Mitch's love life…"

"Or lack of," Carol interrupted.

"Love life, any more. Let's go sailing."

"Yeaaa," Lizzy yelled in response to the first thing she really understood about the conversation.

Somehow they managed to unload the Faulkner's sport utility vehicle and carry all the stuff down to the boat in one trip. Even Lizzy managed to half carry, half drag her own duffle bag almost all the way, until Mitch set the groceries down and picked up both the child and her bag in his left arm.

"Thanks, Uncle Mitch."

"No problem. I like picking up young women."

"Not," came Carol's voice from the end of the slip.

"Hey," Gary said from the dock near the bow of the boat.

"OK," Mitch said trying to direct the conversation away from himself.

"Let's get this adventure underway," Gary finished and Lizzy clapped.

"Lizzy, would you do your poor old Uncle Mitch a favor and reach into that big bag and get the bottle."

"Sure Uncle Mitch, and I don't think you're too old."

"Thanks, I think," Mitch said as she handed him the foil-wrapped bottle. "All right folks, gather 'round. Carol would you grab my camera in the cockpit there and record this moment for posterity."

"Sure," she said and reached over the side and picked up the NIKON. "What do you want me to shoot?"

"I want you to record the moment Lizzy here, christens this magnificent craft."

"Sure great, but I think she'll need some help. Everyone gather 'round. Get close."

"Hey, hold it," came a voice from down the dock. "Here, let me take the picture so you can all get in."

"Ah, sure," Mitch said as he turned to look at the source of the silky sounding voice.

There on the dock, walking toward them was a strikingly beautiful woman. Her auburn hair cascaded to just below her shoulders and she seemed to be wearing a pair of faded jeans that were having an intimate relationship with her well-proportioned hips and thighs. Her old sweatshirt covered but didn't obscure the rest of her 5'10" frame.

Mitch stood for a moment and let his gaze sink deep into her emerald green eyes. Just as he was about to go under in the green pools, someone grabbed him and pulled him back.

"Ah, Mitch, hey," Gary said.

"Yeah, oh ah," Mitch sputtered. "Thanks. This is my new boat and this is its first cruise."

"Very nice," the emerald eyed goddess said, "for a blow boat."

"What," Mitch said feigning an insulted ego.

"Yeah, you know, blow boat, wind burner. Now I'll take power anytime. Go when and where you want at the touch of a button."

Gary couldn't resist the chance to throw a dig at his friend. "Well you know what Mitch here always says about any brain dead Neanderthal being able to drive a power boat." Mitch tried to talk over his obnoxious friend's contribution to embarrassment.

"I'm sorry I missed that," the beautiful woman said.

"Nothing important," Mitch said giving Gary an evil look. "Never mind, Gary old pal. Ah, here," he said and handed the camera to the woman. "Just aim and push the button, the camera will do the rest."

"Oh," she said, "just right for any brain dead Neanderthal to own," she said with a sly smile. Mitch started to blush and looked away. "OK, everybody ready," she said.

"Yes," Lizzy said as she held the bottle of champagne. "What do I do?"

"Just hit the point of the boat with the bottle and say 'good luck'."

"OK, here goes," she said and swung the bottle like a baseball bat. She hit the point of the bow and the bottle smashed sending champagne over the fore deck. Mitch heard the camera's motor drive click off a several frames.

"I hereby christen this boat 'Cold Fortune'. May she sail with great distinction."

"Yeaaa," Lizzy said clapping her hands.

"Congratulations," Gary and Carol said together.

"Yes, congratulations," the green-eyed beauty said as she handed Mitch back the camera. "I'm sorry but I didn't get your name," Mitch said holding the camera while she held the strap.

"Never gave it," she said "but it's Alicia. Alicia Carlsson. I'm new around here. That's my boat at the end there. I'm on the 'Viking Princess'."

"Interesting name," Mitch said still not completely taking his camera back.

"Yeah well, my family has some Viking blood in the past."

"Oh," Mitch said trying to show interest without staring too long into deep green eyes.

"What's your name?" she finally asked after and uncomfortable lull in the conversation.

"Uh, I'm uh, Mitch Stone and oh, ah, this is Gary and Carol Faulkner and this is…"

"Elizabeth Ann Faulkner, but you can call me Lizzy, everybody does."

"Glad to meet you Lizzy. Glad to meet all of you," she said but smiled broadly when she looked back at Mitch. She let go of the strap and Mitch almost dropped the camera. "Yes, very nice to meet you too," he said.

She waved and turned and Mitch took a nice long look at the curves and contours of the jeans as they walked to the end of the dock. "Oh Mitch. Earth calling Mitch, come in please," Gary said nudging him back to reality.

"Ah, I was ah…"

"Yeah, thought you'd forgotten how."

"Nice girl," Carol said, "really nice girl, huh Mitch."

"Not my type," he said trying to act like he was back in control.

"What do you mean, not your type? She's gorgeous, isn't she Dear?" she said to her husband.

"Oh, I hadn't noticed Honey," Gary said trying to avoid a potential marital landmine.

"And she obviously likes you," Carol continued.

"Powerboats," he said, "not my type. And besides she's probably married."

"I didn't see a ring,"

"Then she's got a boyfriend or two."

"You're impossible," Carol said and turned to start loading the things onto the boat.

"Carol's right you know," Gary said quietly to Mitch, "Ms. Carlsson is perfect. Maybe you should ask her out to dinner here in town."

"No thanks. You know what happens when I get involved with women."

"No what happens? It's been so long I can't remember and as old as you are I'm sure you can't either."

"Funny man. I've saved your life all those times so you can harass me like this."

"Ah, I saved yours the last time if you recall."

"Oh, yeah, well then you should be nicer to me. I've been traumatized."

"Bull shit. Lets get out on the water and see what this blow boat, as Ms. Carlsson called it, can do. She really was gorgeous, wasn't she?" Gary asked in a hushed voice hoping that Carol wouldn't hear.

"Who was gorgeous?" Lizzy yelled and popped her head up through the front hatch.

"Ah, your mother, Honey," Gary said.

"Good answer," Carol said. "Everything's put away. Are we ready?"

"That's stowed. Everything is stowed, and yes we're ready."

"Yeaa," came the excited voice from below deck somewhere.

Gary stepped aboard the boat and moved to the opposite side. "What can I do?" he asked.

"I'll need some help with the sails and the sheets. Then once we're all rigged you can handle the dock lines, all right?"

"You're the Captain, Captain," Gary said standing and saluting.

Lizzy popped up through the main hatch and saluted too. "What can I do?"

"You can get into your personal flotation jacket and stay out of the way until we are away from the dock, OK?"

"OK, Uncle Mitch," she said and disappeared below deck.

"What can I do Mitch?" Carol asked.

"Stow the sail bags below and help Lizzy with the PFD, OK? And any more discussion about me and women and I'll consider it mutiny."

"Aye, aye, Captain Bligh," she said and saluted too.

In the hour it had taken to load, christen and launch the 'Cold Fortune' the wind had died down a bit but the boat cut smoothly through the blue-green water. Mitch leaned back in the cockpit and recalled the events of the previous summer that led him to the discovery of the real cold fortune and in the process, save the United States from becoming the victim of the worst terrorist attack in history. The terrorists had managed to acquire sixteen medium yield atomic weapons and were using this very lake as the staging area for a coordinated attack on the major cities of the continental United States. Mitch and Gary had managed to discover the plot while trying to solve a murder case and they had thwarted the plan. Too bad though that the terrorists chose to die like that though, the trials would have been real crowd pleasers.

In the process Mitch had also managed to discover a sunken War of 1812 vintage warship, with the help of an old family diary. The ship had perished in a storm in the autumn of 1813 but it hadn't been just any warship. While searching for the lost ship Mitch had stumbled on the terrorist sub and the rest as they say was history. But history had also provided Mitch with a sizable retirement account. At the time of its sinking the warship was transporting several thousand gold coins, which at the time were worth more than a million dollars. The twentieth century value was substantially greater and although Mitch had been forced to turn over most of the treasure to the governments, he had managed to relocate a sizable amount to a place only he knew about. Mitch had to go diving more often than he used to, but each dive was now worth about $100,000 in gold coins. He thought of it as a tax-free savings account with the interest provided by the ever increasing value of historic gold.

Even though he had found the gold and was keeping the supply to himself, he wasn't exactly selfish with the riches. He had told Gary that he had inherited a large sum of money, which wasn't far from the truth, and he insisted over the protests from both Carol and Gary that he be able to share the wealth so to speak.

They had protested but in the end they had agreed to accept a generous contribution to Lizzy's college fund. Actually, she could just about buy a college with the amount of money she had in the bank but then nothing was too good for the daughter of the man who had saved his life and career so many times. Mitch never divulged the exact amount of his gift to Lizzy but told the Faulkners that they would not have to worry about her future education. On her eighteenth birthday he would hand over the bank book and show them the balance of $500,000 plus interest. Not too many eight year olds had that kind of money generating interest every day.

Relieved of the financial concerns for their daughter, the Faulkners were able to spend their two incomes on some things for themselves. Gary had bought a new fishing boat, albeit a powerboat, and Carol had purchased the sport utility vehicle. Gary had a car toy of his own though. He bought a new red Corvette.

Mitch gently caressed the wheel of the sailboat and turned it slightly to the left. The wind on the port tack slid over the lee side of the Dacron sail a little faster and the boat healed a little more to starboard. Mitch headed west with his close friends serving as crew on his new boat and the first day of his new life. Life was good once in awhile he thought to himself as he relaxed at the wheel and the let the warm spring breeze blow across his face.

CHAPTER 3

THE CRUISE

JUNE, 980 A.D.

The bow of the boat sliced through the light chop of the dark blue water. The sail was kept full by the steady breeze coming over the stern, which to the man at the helm seemed like a lucky break since they did want to head west and that made his job that much easier. The boat would stay on that course for a while and then when the signs from the gods left in the sky were right the heading would be slightly changed and the boat would nudge north and slightly west.

Lars held the long arm of the tiller which was tied to the rudder hanging over the gunwale on the right side of the stern. He took his turn at the helm as much to relieve the crew as to enjoy the feel of the boat gliding toward a new land and a new hope for the members of his expedition. Lars looked over his right shoulder and made sure the other seven boats were within a close distance from his boat. He didn't want to have any of the boats get separated and get off course. All the boats and people were indispensable to the success of the voyage and especially to Lars.

The two large knarrs could, under ordinary trading runs, carry fifty or more men and supplies for half a year and nearly a ton of trade goods from the distant corners of the Viking's vast sphere of influence. The six small boats were designed as long ships and used for raids on the lands and islands nearer the homeland. On this voyage the longboats carried the strong men and their families and the knarrs were designated for the personal belongings of his fellow travelers. The big knarrs had about twenty-five men each and the longboats carried approximately two hundred passengers each. All totaled, Lars was in command of and responsible for the lives of 1250 people including himself. He hoped and asked the gods each night that they would show favor on his group and make the voyage safe for the sake of his charges and the future of the Viking race. He sighed and his breath mixed with the wind from astern and he imagined it gave the boat an extra push to the new land. He had never been farther from any piece of land than the limit of sight but now as he looked back past the fleet of wooden boats he realized he hadn't seen land now for almost a month.

He stood at the tiller and took another deep refreshing breath of the sea air and said a silent prayer to the gods thanking them for their generous and gentle behavior for so long in the trip. There had been only four days of rain in the last thirty and when the rains had come they were sufficient to replenish the fresh water supplies of the fleet. When it didn't rain, the ships were blessed with gentle and steady winds and the fleet had only stalled twice when the wind had reversed direction.

The ships were rigged with a rectangle piece of cloth made from strips of wool stitched together along the vertical axis. This meant that unlike the sailing boats from the 1800's on, which could sail into the wind within an angle of about 45 degrees, they were forced to rely on a wind coming more or less directly from the stern to push them forward. The modern sailboats had the luxury and advantage of being able to sail in almost any direction regardless of the direction the wind was blowing. A modern designed sail boat could sail back and forth across the flow of the wind in a maneuver called tack-ing. This meant that a good sailor and navigator could start out and sail in any direction and reach an unseen destination in a generally straight line where the boats under Lars' command were at the mercy of the direction of the wind. They could get to an unseen destination but were more dependant on luck and a lot of course corrections.

In addition the modern sailor had the additional advantage of good global charts and an accurate compass and within the last ten years or so most ocean sailors had invested in a global positioning satellite system. The GPS as it is called could instantly pinpoint the location of a boat within a hundred yards or so of the exact location. The system depended on several satellites in a fixed Geosynchronous orbit around the world. Like the ancient sailors who depended on the heavens for navigation the modern counterparts used the enhanced heavenly bodies for guidance.

The Vikings' ships were limited by technology but still were making a trans-Atlantic crossing in the tenth century A.D. and Lars continued to thank the gods and pray for further help in assuring that the winds continued to blow from the east to push them to their new home in the west. It would be at least another millennium before the sail would be modified to act as an airfoil and in fact pull a boat through the water. Lars and his fellow voyagers were still at the mercy of the wind and depended on a steady and gentle push for their propulsion.

Yes the gods had blessed this voyage and Lars was thankful. "Where do you put our position, navigator?" Lars called out to the man on his left. The navigator was in fact more of a scribe and record keeper. He kept the log of the journey and the names and records of the passengers. He was also placed in charge of the ships stores and provisions. Part of his duty was to keep an inventory of the supplies and ration the meals. He was the jack of all trades and was given this important set of tasks because he could read and write. As for the task of navigation it was done mostly by the sun during the day and the stars at night. For the positioning part the 'navigator' counted the days and compared his count with the hand copied records of the previous explorations by other Vikings. He read and reread the historical accounts of the past successful crossings to the west and he compared their own progress to the past chronicles.

The navigator was one of only two people in the entire group that could read and write the complicated language of the Norse peoples. The other person who had the remarkable ability to was a young boy, whose parents had insisted that he apprentice with a navigator from an eastern trade convoy. The boy was nearly as good at the mysterious form of communication as their navigator. The both of them could look at the strange symbols and shapes on papyrus or animal hides and hear the voices of the people who made the marks. Not only could these two understand what was 'said' by the marks but they could make these marks themselves and their marks could talk to others.

When people first began to make and understand these marks some of the elders in the group had been afraid and said that the people who could listen to signs and symbols were possessed by evil spirits. Time and successful trading expeditions to distant lands year after year based upon the writings of these gifted people, proved all the skeptics wrong. Now every voyage beyond the homeland had navigators who could read and write and they read from the journals of past travelers and meticulously kept detailed records of their own.

Lars stood and admired the navigator and was more than a little jealous of his abilities. Too bad it took so long to learn how to do it, he thought, he might try to learn someday, if he had the time. The navigator looked at the journal from a past trip made in this direction nearly ten years ago. He was silent as he performed the miracle of reading. He looked at his own writings and seemed to compare them to the journal. Then he made some more symbols of his own and finally in response to Lars' question he said. "Sir, I put our position about two days to the south of the 'green land' that the prior expedition recorded. That means we are almost half way to the place they called 'new' land. If the gods of the air and water stay pleased with us, we should be at our new lands in a handful of days."

Lars was most amazed and pleased. He recalled that the previous travelers had taken nearly two full moon cycles to reach the eastern most point of the new found lands. Now on his first journey to sea and first as a leader of an expedition, his crossing time would be a few days less than the best time so far.

"That is excellent. Please make your marks in the records about our good progress and also mention to whoever may see those marks that we have been blessed by the superior services of our navigator."

"You are too kind, sir. I am pleased to be of assistance on this journey."

"You are most expert at your skills, and I would ask a very large favor of you," Lars said trying to appear as a friend rather than a superior to the navigator.

"Yes, sir. Ask me anything. I am glad to serve."

"As I said, it is a favor to me not a service to your king that I seek. I would ask that you teach me your special skills. I believe you call it reading and writing."

"Sir, I would be honored to show you this ability but I must caution you that it takes a lot of time and practice to learn the skill."

"I don't think that will be a problem in our new homes. Once we are able to survive the elements we all will have time to do many things."

"I will be glad to share my skills with you, sir," the navigator said smiling with pride.

Lars looked back out over the blue sea. The wind was stronger today and the blue water had white crests on the waves but the wind was still behind them and pushing them along in the right direction. Lars was smiling with pride as well. He was the leader of a large number of his fellow Vikings and the trip was so far uneventful with the major exception that they were many days farther west than the previous expedition. Lars was very happy with the prospect that they would be at landfall with several weeks of pleasant weather available to them so they could build good sound shelters before winter. Fewer people would suffer this winter and even fewer would perish.

Lars was very happy indeed, and felt even now, as the boats all moved over the waves in unison, that the mission would be successful, but Lars fell into the same trap that all men did once they gave into complacency. He would soon learn the folly of his presumptive pride. The gods were watching and they did not like men who were too proud. The gods began to set things right and although Lars and his people would not suffer the wrath of the gods immediately, they were going to sooner or later.

The voyage for the most part was the first time that any of the people in the fleet had been out of the sight of land for more than a day or two. In the early days of Viking explorations most of the ocean crossings were done within the sight of land. The early explorers would follow a coastline as far as they could and only venture beyond landfall if they had reliable information about land across the open water. If they couldn't find land after a few days they would retrace their route and return to the last known land.

The first westward trip across the great ocean had taken great amounts of bravery. The explorers had heard of and even met peoples from an island to the west which some called the land of ice and it took the early Viking sailors two weeks to reach. Once they had gotten that far they were more brave and ventured further west to find the land of green and finally the new lands, which Lars was proud to say was his destination and destiny.

The last few days of the voyage passed much as all the others had. The crews of the boats were alternating between handling the boats and maintaining them. Their days were fairly busy but routine. Part of the crew was devoted to keeping the boats moving and moving in the right direction. They were responsible for keeping their particular boat close to the others in the group. It would be nearly impossible to recover a boat if it was to become separated from the rest. It most likely would be lost and the crew and passengers with it. Keeping the boats close was a great responsibility for the crews and a great worry for Lars.

The rest of the crew was responsible for keeping the boats seaworthy. Prior to the journey each boat had been man handled up onto the shore and the bottoms were coated with the sap of pine trees. It was messy and sticky work, but the boats floated better and didn't leak as much. The non sailing crew was in charge of checking below decks to watch the integrity of the hull. A leak would be disastrous if not controlled. The water would endanger the ships and at the very least would contaminate the supplies stored below the loose plank decking and the hull.

In addition to the leak checks the crews had to maintain the sails. Even though they were made of wool and very strong, the strips of cloth were held together by thin pieces of twisted line. The wind would stretch the woolen sail cloth and the holes made for the lacings would expand and the sails would lose their tension and ability to catch the wind. Each boat had two sails. While one was in use, the other was constantly being repaired.

The passengers were not merely along for the ride, each of them was an integral part of the operation. Added to their responsibilities for the boats, each passenger was also responsible for their own personal possessions as well as the community supplies. Although the boats were fairly large, the number of people on the trip dictated the quantity of supplies being carried. The plan was for enough food and water for two cycles of the moon which would allow the voyagers ample if simple means of salted meats and gruel. Not exciting but life sustaining. The remainder of the limited space was crammed to capacity with all manner of supplies and equipment for the establishment of a new Viking colony. One of the ships even carried the components for a forge in the event their new home had a supply of ores.

Lars watched the crew and passengers on his lead boat and presumed that the other boats had the same activity aboard. The passengers were checking and securing the supplies. Tools, seeds, clothes, cooking utensils and enough dried and salted food for one winter. Lars hoped the new lands were as bountiful as the previous expedition had indicated. They would need to hunt and fish while they waited for the crops of wheat, barley and oats to be grown and then harvested next summer.

Watching the passengers stack and tie the large barrels of grain and water made Lars thankful that he wasn't on the boat which had the dubious honor of carrying the farm animals. Those poor souls had to contend with all manner of foul tempered and smelling beast. The fleet included not only the hearty Vikings but pigs, cows, chickens, sheep, and goats. There was even a dog and he had heard that someone had snuck a cat on one of the smaller boats.

Lars couldn't or wouldn't complain about that too much. He figured almost everyone had spirited something a little unnecessary or selfish on board. With that thought, he subtly moved his left foot and touched the collection of large wooden crates lashed to the transom. He had made it expressly clear to all aboard that these boxes were consigned to him by the king himself and that no one under severe penalty and punishment was to come near let alone touch any of them.

He hadn't looked in the crates himself but he knew that they contained the treasure that the king had told he would carry as an incentive in dealing with any of the natives in the new land. He was surprised at the size and number of crates and figured that nearly the entire wealth of the colony was now onboard his boat. He didn't look but he knew how important and valuable that part of the cargo was and he kept his most trusted man as a guard on the ten large crates that took four men each to carry on board.

Having assured himself for the hundredth time that the crates and everything else were all right, Lars stepped across the crowded deck to where the navigator was busy reading and writing and trying to make do with his very cramped space.

"Tell me Johhan, what it is that you are always writing?"

"Well sir," he said, "like our esteemed predecessors, I am recording everything I can about our trip. It will not only be valuable to anyone who may want to travel across this sea again, but I am also giving details of our experiences during the trip. And with your permission I would like to continue recording our story after we find new lands."

"Of course, permission granted," Lars replied, "and maybe you can teach me to read this epic."

"Of course, sir," Johhan said pausing briefly to look at Lars and smile. Lars was more concerned with his desire to read than with what Johhan was writing. In fact Johhan was very conscientious and detail oriented. The success of the trip and lives depended on his attention to details. To that point Johhan was very good and not only did he chronicle each and every event that he witnessed, he made detailed manifests of everything onboard the boat. He even recorded the ten large wooden crates and noted the posted guard and the standing orders of the leader. He wrote on parchment and when he finished a sheet he would roll it tight and place it into a leather bag that had been treated with animal fat and pine sap. He didn't want his diligent efforts lost to the sea or the weather. Once safely secured in the water proof bag he stowed the bag in his private trunk, which like all the rest, served as both personal storage and as seating for the passengers. Johhan made sure his writings and journals would last a long time. He just couldn't imagine for how long.

CHAPTER 4

THE CONFRONTATION

*M*itch and the passenger/crew of the 'Cold Fortune' had been out for nearly two hours. Two hours and decent winds and a half way decent skipper at the helm put the sleek fiberglass craft into the next harbor, southeast of Smyth's Cove. They were moving nicely along at about 6 miles per hour for a land vehicle and Mitch figured they were doing about five knots on the water and the knot meter on the bulkhead agreed with him. A high-tech meter and a low-tech drag device under the keel. A small plastic fin shaped finger stuck out into the water and as the boat moved, it was pulled back by the force of the water. The meter calculated the length of the movement into knots per hour.

In the two hours they had sailed about ten miles and were approaching the largest island in this end of the lake. When Mitch was a kid, which was now nearly a third of a century ago, the island belonged to a boys' and girls' club and was used for 'camping' trips. Camping was a liberal interpretation of the summer lifestyles of the kids and counselors. The island had its own plumbing system and sanitation facilities and every group of ten cabins had a bathhouse and latrine. Each cabin had electricity supplied by an underwater cable from the mainland, and even without TV, they were comfortable enough for a kid on a two-week vacation from mom and dad.

There was a large and well-equipped kitchen and cafeteria and the island was large enough to have several baseball fields and still leave enough woods for nature trails. Of course an island meant lots of water and virtually the entire island was a beach.

On the nature trail side of the island away from view of the mainland were some small secluded beaches where, as Mitch had only heard, anybody with a boat could go for a day of some natural swimming. Those were the days before the clubs had fallen on hard times and before the island had been sold to the current residents. In those days as now the island had been named Society Island, presumably because the boys' and girls' clubs wanted to make better citizens out of the summer denizens. The new owners had kept the name and most of the buildings but little else remained of the idyllic summer camp. The new owners had sealed off access to the island and had stopped all unauthorized landings. To that end the new owners had security patrols on shore in four wheel drive trucks and on the water in fast boats.

Apparently, security was a main concern of the new inhabitants. That was obvious by the existence of the guards and the fact that the guards were armed. As cops both Mitch and Gary were leery of civilians having guns and some authority. Mitch and Gary had both, but they also had several hundred hours of training and updates. No telling how much, if any, these armed guards had. In addition Mitch and Gary and every other sworn police officer were answerable to the Chief or in their case the Sheriff, and to the taxpayers. These guys weren't answerable to anyone except the guy who signed the paychecks and maybe an insurance company somewhere. That was the scary part and that made Mitch very nervous. Loose cannons with cannons.

He kept an eye on the island and the blue and white speed boat anchored about one hundred yards from shore. Guess that's the theoretical boundary line, he thought. Maybe he'd just check it out sometime. Not in his new slow-moving sailboat but in the nice big and very fast county police boat. It was fast, maybe not the fastest on the lake but damn fast anyway. He'd have to cruise right up close and see what the hired guns would do to two of the County's finest. Gary would love the challenge of testing some civilian rent-a-cops.

Mitch sat back against the starboard gunwale and steered a nice wide course away from the anchored guard boat and the island. He was just getting comfortable and was beginning to relax and savor his ice cold beer from the real refrigerator in the galley, instead of the old-fashioned ice chest, when his personal gloating was interrupted by a click and a whir sound. He focused his attention and saw Lizzy standing in the hatchway with ones of those self contained recyclable cameras.

"Got ya," she said giggling.

"Hey, that was my bad side," Mitch said.

"Daddy says all your sides are bad," she said back and shot another picture.

"Hey, you'll break the camera."

"No, its too tough. It's even water resistive."

"Resistant."

"Resistant," she repeated and ducked below deck again only to pop up a moment later through the forward hatch and start shooting pictures in all directions.

"Thanks for having us out today," Gary said and sat down across from Mitch after retrieving another beer for each of them.

"Yeah, thanks," Carol said from her reclined position just forward of the mast. She decided to work on a little color while the boys talked and Lizzy just had a good time. Mitch envied his old friend. Carol was every bit as beautiful and attractive as she was when he first saw her fifteen years ago. Mitch had wanted to date her but his divorce wasn't final and she refused to see a married man even if the marriage was only a technical term by then.

In the time it had taken to finalize the divorce Gary had asked her out and well, the rest was history. Timing was everything, he thought as he admired the view she now provided in her bikini.

"Hey pay attention to the water and not my wife," Gary chided kiddingly.

"I was, I was," Mitch protested.

"Sure and I'm six feet tall."

"Well your five foot seven anyway," Mitch shot back.

The banter was interrupted by the blast from an air horn and the sudden swaying form side to side. Mitch looked out to his left across the stern and saw a large power boat pass within fifty feet of them. The wake of the big cruiser bounced the sailboat from side to side several times and Mitch had to trim the sheets and change the heading to maintain headway.

"Sorry," came the voice faintly, just in time for Mitch and Gary to catch a glimpse of a beautiful auburn haired girl at the wheel of the cruiser shoot by.

"Damn," Mitch said resetting the sheets.

"Yeah, nice suit too," Gary said.

"Oh, yeah, that too."

"Like you didn't notice, you pervert."

"No, I didn't notice. I was busy, ah, ah trying to sail."

"Sure. Right. Anything you say."

"Notice what?" Carol asked. "And can you two seamen keep this thing steady. I'm trying to relax up here."

"Yes Dear," Gary said.

"Yes Dear," Mitch parroted. "Where the hell was she going in such a hurry?" he wondered out loud and pulled on the port side sheet to trim the sail and maintain a constant heading on the starboard tack.

"I don't know," Gary said trying to take another sip of beer as the boat stopped bobbing, "but she handles that big cruiser pretty well for a swimsuit model."

"She's no model, but yeah, you're right she does handle it well," Mitch said. "I wonder what she does in real life when she's not buzzing poor defenseless sailboats and looking really nice doing it."

"See you did notice her," Gary said.

"Notice what. The boat, the boat had great lines."

"Yeah, the boat, sure," Gary said not believing his friend one little bit.

"Hey, you two seamen. Can we like stop or park or something? I'm getting hungry," Carol said, now making her way across the deck and down into the cockpit. She did look nice in her two-piece suit that would make even high school girls blush.

"Ah, yeah, we can anchor if that's what you mean and we can have a floating picnic."

"Yeah, a picnic," Lizzy yelled as she stuck her head up through the main hatch. She had a pair of Nikon Marine Binoculars hanging around her neck and just as she started up the steps, Mitch heard the disheartening thump as the precision optical instruments met the teak steps in the pendulum swing on the strap that was too long for an eight-year-old girl.

"Ah, Lizzy, can you give those glasses to your mom?" Mitch asked pointing to the expensive binoculars being bounced off the hard wooden stairway.

"Oh, I'm sorry Mitch. She didn't mean anything."

"I know, no problem, but could you just hold them for her before they get knocked around too much."

"I hope they are OK," Gary said as he reached out toward Lizzy and took them from her.

"I was just looking at all the boats out front and waved at that pretty girl Mitch likes, but she didn't see me. I guess she was too busy with all her friends."

"What boats?" Gary asked Lizzy.

"What girl?" Mitch asked almost at the same time.

"Those boats and you know the pretty girl from before. The one Uncle Mitch likes but doesn't say so."

Gary crossed over the cockpit and Mitch compensated for the weight shift with a small adjustment on the wheel. Gary held the glasses up to his eyes to take a look and to make sure his darling daughter hadn't inadvertently messed up a $500.00 pair of binoculars. He focused on the group of boats about one thousand yards in front of the sailboat and slightly to port. The sail had obscured most of the view but Gary moved up on top of the cabin deck and wrapped his arm around the mast for a stable view through the glasses and for a hand hold in the event Mitch hit a wave or had to change the tack. He focused the glasses and looked over each of the boats. One was indeed the 'Viking Princess' and he held the view of the beautiful captain in her very well fitting white swimsuit.

Ms. Carlsson was not so happy it seemed and the reason as Gary saw was that her boat was surrounded by four blue and white security boats with a larger boat about fifty yards off between the group and the island. Gary watched for a few moments as an armed crewman from each of the boats near hers boarded the 'Princess'. He could see Ms. Carlsson protesting and waving her arms. Although he couldn't make out what she was saying from that distance he could hear the shouts and could guess what she was yelling about. He watched as two of the men talked to her and tried to distract her while the other two appeared to be searching the boat.

"Hey our nice looking lady friend seems to have some unwanted suitors."

"Yeah, I can just see the boats under the sail. What's going on? Can you tell?"

"It looks like she's being hassled by those rent-a-cops and she's none too happy," Gary said still looking through the binoculars and giving Mitch the minute by minute description of the action. "You bring your piece with you?"

"Yeap, never leave home without it. You never can tell when you might run into some marine lowlifes. OK folks, I'm going to change tacks here in a few minutes and I need everybody to be ready. I need to see this group of marine misfits and I'm putting us on a port tack."

"Sounds good to me," Gary said, "where's your piece?"

"Down in the aft cabin, top drawer of the dresser. I have the key to the trigger lock in my pocket. Just bring the case up here and I'll get it ready."

"Come, Lizzy," Carol said, "we need to go below for a while."

She knew that as police officers both Gary and Mitch carried weapons even when off duty. She also knew what 'get the piece' meant and had seen the boats that they were now concerned about surrounding that girl from the marina. Carol knew what it was to be married to a cop and she never interfered when he thought duty was involved. She just reacted and went into the 'protect the child mode'. Gary came back up from below deck carrying both his weapon and Mitch's pistol case. Carol ushered a protesting Lizzy below deck but as soon as Lizzy saw the looks on her dad and Mitch's faces she cooperated with her mother and went below.

"Find a comfortable spot in the bow and hold on, I may have to do some fancy maneuvering in a minute," Mitch said holding the wheel with his knee as he unlocked the pistol case and removed the trigger lock. With Lizzy on board he had double locked the weapon to keep it safe from inquisitive little hands. Normally it was just sitting in the drawer ready to go.

"You still got that old piece of shit wheel gun," Gary chided as he checked over the magazine of his Smith and Wesson stainless steel 9mm. "When are you going to get into the twenty first century?"

"Hey, I like old reliable stuff. Just like me. This suits me just fine and with a couple of speed loaders I have just as many rounds as you do and twice the fire power."

"Yeah, yeah, but that antique is just too slow and big for my taste."

"I thought all your taste was in your mouth."

"Nice," Gary said, "you call the shots Captain, I'm all set here." He put an extra magazine in his pocket from the duffle bag and set the weapon inside the open bag within easy reach. Mitch collected his two extra speed loaders and his reliable revolver and set it into the compartment in the gunwale. Not the best place but hopefully the weapon would be back in its case shortly.

"What's the plan, man?" Gary asked.

"Not sure. We have to play it by ear," Mitch said getting ready to come about. "I'm coming about so watch your head and keep an eye on our friends up ahead." Mitch turned the wheel hard to port and released the sheet in the port cleat. The momentum of the boat carried it through the wind and for a brief moment the boat was only coasting along until the wind caught the opposite side of the sail and the airfoil took shape again. The boat responded with a new forward surge and Mitch cleated the sheet with his right hand and made a small adjustment on the wheel. Now the thirty-two-foot sailboat was heading directly between the large cruiser and the four other patrol boats surrounding the 'Viking Princess'.

"What are they up to now?" he asked Gary who was watching the activity on the cruiser through the binoculars again.

"Same as before. She's very pissed and they are giving her boat a major tossing."

"OK, we go to the rescue and be ready to repel boarders."

"From hers or ours."

"Maybe both," Mitch said. "Now here's what we're going to do and I'll need your help to pull it off," and he proceeded to give Gary the details of his plan.

"No problem," Gary said ready for a little off duty action and he listened as Mitch spelled out the plan to rescue the nice girl. The nice thing about a sailboat was it didn't make any noise and with the nice steady wind the stealthy boat was approaching the floating boats rather quickly. In fact the 'Cold Fortune' was within one hundred yards and closing before anyone even noticed. The two crew members on the lone boat were preoccupied with the activities of their fellow mercenary security guards and didn't notice the sudden intrusion of a ten-meter sailboat into their private meeting.

Once the lone boat's crew members realized they had more company, they started yelling to the other boats and at Mitch and Gary as the 'Cold Fortune' sailed gracefully between the boarding party and the picket boat closer to shore.

Mitch stood at the helm and held it steady as he guided his boat between them with about fifty feet to spare on each side. Mitch could see the looks on the faces of the two crewmen on his right and he just smiled as he cruised by. "Sounds like they said something about what the fuck are we doing," Mitch said to Gary who had moved closer to the bow and had one leg over the pulpit rail and looked ready to jump.

"Yeah, that's what it sounded like to me," he said. "I think we should stop and tell them just what the fuck we are doing."

"Sounds good to me," Mitch said and just as he had explained earlier to Gary he cranked the wheel hard to the left and the boat immediately fell of the wind. Almost as if on cue, Gary had moved from the pulpit rail to the mast and was gathering in the main sail at the moment Mitch uncleated the halyard from the cam-cleat on the top of the cabin near the cockpit. The sail dropped into Gary's arms and he quickly gathered up the loose Dacron cloth and wrapped the sail around the boom and secured the not so neatly bunched sail with the stretch cord called a centipede because of its many loops and hooks radiating along the length of the line.

"All secure here," Gary said.

"Good lets talk to these gentlemen," Mitch said. "Get ready to come along side to starboard." Just as he released the main halyard Mitch had started the Yanmar diesel engine and the boat was now under power and he could maneuver it like any other, well almost like any other. A sailboat was a displacement hull design and the engine was only large enough to move the boat into a slip or out of the harbor. Even with the rudder all the way to port the boat took a very wide turn and at the last minute, Mitch had to make a correction to avoid a collision with the five boats floating together. Gary saw that they were going to miss the approach on the starboard side and quickly moved the fenders to the opposite side. Even though the maneuver hadn't been the prettiest, it had distracted the security people long enough for Ms. Carlsson to give one of her tormentors a good hard shove over the side and the second one, who had been in her face, a swift and effective kick in the groin, dropping him to his knees. She moved like a cat and pulled out the guard's gun just as he fell onto his side still clutching his wounded manhood.

The other guards waiting in the patrol boat were now concerned about a pending collision and were too busy watching their own patrol boats for the moment to worry about the girl who was now holding a gun on the guard with the groin injury and his two buddies. The guard who had been searching the boat emerged from below deck to find out what all of the commotion was about, only to find the great pair of legs and nice body in the white swim suit pointing one of their own .38 specials at them.

"Can we play too?" Mitch asked as he cut the engine and grabbed for the side of the patrol boat. The guards had recovered their poise and started to reach for their weapons, not knowing who the new intruders were.

"Not necessary boys," Gary said pointing the stainless steel 9mm semiautomatic toward the first guard.

Mitch joined in with his big revolver and hooked a deck cleat on the patrol boat with a looped end on one of his dock lines. He used his left hand to make a couple of loops around the aft cleat of the patrol boat. "Can you hold us in tight?" he asked Gary.

"Sure," Gary said stepping down off the cabin and doing the same thing Mitch had just done with a line at the bow. Now there were three boats tied together. The 'Viking Princess' and the patrol boat were facing in the same direction and the 'Cold Fortune' was bow to stern with the patrol boat.

Mitch stepped onto the cockpit seat and then up onto the deck walkway and took a couple of steps toward the bow. Mitch was a bit surprised and pleased that his boat was at least ten feet longer than the patrol boat and he was able to step onto the rear cruiser from the middle of his boat. He looked at the auburn hair and the white suit and smiled but not so Gary could see. "Hi, can we join the party?" he asked across the two boats to Ms. Carlsson.

"Yeah," she said a little indignantly which Mitch perceived as frustration.

"I guess so, but I can't be a very good hostess and introduce you to the other guests since they have been rather rude and failed to tell me who the hell they are."

"Well maybe we can help with the introductions then," he said as he pulled out the folded leather case he kept his badge in. "I'm Deputy Stone from the Sheriff's Department and this is Sergeant Faulkner," he said gesturing to Gary behind. Mitch made sure every one of the guards saw the badge and the gun just to keep any of them from doing something really stupid. He held the badge up high over his head and repeated his statement so the guards on the other boats would stay put and not try to interfere with guns drawn. "Now just so there won't be any mistakes that might force me to do some paperwork on my day off, let's all of you security people just set your weapons on the deck until we find out what's going on."

Just then the large cruiser that had been floating in the distance pulled near the flotilla. "Who the hell do you think you are?" came the surly voice.

"Well I think I'm a cop and so does my friend here," Mitch said holding his weapon a little higher and nodding over his shoulder toward Gary who was now pointing his weapon at the new arrivals. "And unlike you and your buddies here we are the real cops."

"Oh," was all the reply Mitch got.

"Now let's all talk and see why ten men are harassing one lady on open water. Let's see some ID from everyone along with the pistol permits and guard licenses."

All the uniformed men moved simultaneously and produced the demanded documents. Mitch took the cards from the guard in front of him and stepped up onto the patrol boat's gunwale and then stepped over to the 'Princess' and then down onto her deck. "Hi," he said to the beautiful woman who was holding the gun on her unwanted guests, "Nice to see you again." His eyes couldn't help checking her out at close range.

"Yeah, I'll bet," she said noticing him notice her. "How nice of you to drop in. Does everyone on the lake just think my boat is open territory? I don't recall inviting anybody."

"We just can't resist a good party but I'm afraid I didn't know it was a theme event. What's with all the uniforms?"

"Looks like shift change at midnight, doesn't it, Mitch," Gary called from the top of the cabin of the 'Cold Fortune'.

"Yeah, sure does. What's up?" he asked Ms. Carlsson.

"Not sure she said and handed him the .38 she had not so gently removed from one of the guards. "I was just out for a ride and these guys stopped and boarded me."

"Not exactly," the guard who was kicked said now trying to stand. He couldn't quite stand fully upright yet.

"Oh, and what's your story then?"

"Perhaps I can answer that Deputy." The voice came from the larger lone boat. "I'm Security Captain Pierce and these are my men. We are working for Millennium Eco-Technologies and we have instructions to keep boats away from the island. Apparently our bosses are doing some secret work and don't want any trespassers. You can understand that Deputy, I'm sure."

"Yeah, I understand that part just fine and even the use of armed patrols maybe, but I just can't figure out why ten men wanted to stop and board a boat driven by one woman. Care to elaborate?"

"I'm afraid we made a small mistake. We inadvertently stopped this young lady and we extend our apologies. We were under the mistaken belief she was an industrial spy and was trying to gather information from our employees."

"Yeah well as you all have noticed and not too subtly at that, I'm hardly dressed for espionage."

"I'd tell you anything dressed like that," Mitch whispered to her. She gave him a dirty look.

"Yes, we seem to have made a small error. We hope we didn't cause any harm over our misunderstanding."

"Misunderstanding my ass," she said and everyone looked in her direction. Gary snorted a half-concealed laugh.

"OK, gentlemen," Mitch said after everyone returned their attention back to him. "All the paperwork seems to be in order. In the future, Captain, try to keep in mind the right to privacy and try not to search any boats especially by mistake."

"Certainly," the guard Captain said disdainfully, "but doesn't the right to privacy also extend to private corporations as well as citizens?"

Before Mitch could answer, the guard Captain motioned to his subordinates and without saying a word, they all began to untie their boats from the 'Viking Princess'. The boat between the 'Princess' and Mitch's seemed to be trying to pull out without untying so Mitch handed the guard with the sore groin his paperwork and gun and started back to the 'Cold Fortune'. "Will I see you again?" he asked the rescued damsel.

"Probably," she said with a Mona Lisa smile and she turned and started her engines. The guard left the boat and tried to regain his composure on his own craft. Mitch stepped across the patrol boat. "You're luck it was her you boarded. All you got was a kick in the nuts. Try boarding me like that and even the detectives on my department won't be able to find your body," Mitch said just loud enough for the one guard to hear and no one else. He smiled at the others and stepped back onto his own boat and turned back to the security boat. He smiled again as he untied the stern line and Gary released the bow line. The guards pushed their boat out from between the two bigger cruisers. Just as the patrol boat's stern cleared the two boats, the guard at the helm started the engine and gave it full throttle. The resultant churning of the water caused both stationary boats to toss back and forth.

When the patrol boats had pulled far enough away from the scene of the encounter with the local law, Captain Pierce motioned for one of the boats to pull along side his. "What did you find in her boat?" the Captain asked the guard that had searched below a deck.

"She has a lot of lab equipment and testing gear down there. Looks like one of our labs only in a smaller space."

"See anything that might tell us who she works for?"

"Nope but the way she handled herself and the gun she removed from our guy, I'd guess she's a cop."

"Guesses we don't need. The boss will want answers. But you're probably right although she's not with the locals though."

"Fed?" the guard who had done the searching asked.

"Fed," the Captain said and the boats parted.

"The boss won't be happy the Feds are this close," he said to the other man on the boat. "We'd better get in and let him know what happened." The other man revved the engines and pushed the gear lever forward. The boat headed back to the island's dock.

"Shitheads," Mitch mumbled as he tried to maintain his balance. "Hey, Ms. Carlsson, he called over to the auburn haired beauty. "Want to join us at the marina later for a drink or dinner or…?" he said running out of choices.

"Or something," she answered with that museum smile again. "Maybe I'll see you later."

"Ah, great," Mitch said as the boats started to drift apart.

"Smooth as a pothole in winter my friend," Gary said, "real ladies' man."

"Hey you're the one who said I should try to get to know her, remember?"

"Yeah, but your lines are for dorks. She wants charm and sophistication not some tongue tied geek."

"It's been a while, OK. Now as your ship's Captain let's hoist the sail and try to rescue the rest of the day."

"Aye, aye," Gary said with a mock salute again and went to the mast to haul on the halyard. As soon as Mitch had gotten back onboard, he had secured his weapon and placed the duffle bag back below deck. Mitch had unloaded and locked his back in the pistol case and set it in the locker under his seat. Gary took his position at the mast and was ready to haul up the sail. Mitch got ready to steer the boat into the wind to make Gary's job easier. It was nearly impossible for one man to raise the sail until the boat was pointed straight into the oncoming wind. If the wind caught either side of the sail it would flap and act like a very large balloon with no easy way to control it.

Mitch started the engine and turned the bow into the wind as indicated by the vane on the mast head. As soon as the bow headed up, Gary started pulling on the halyard and the huge sail crept up the fifty-foot mast. Mitch was pulling the trailing end of the halyard back into the cockpit and had it wrapped around one of the coffee grinder winches. As soon as Gary had the sail most of the way up Mitch would winch in the rest of the line drawing it up tight and then force the line into the cleat where the tension would work against a double set of toothed cams. Once the sail was secured and taught, Mitch cut the engine and turned a bit to starboard to establish a port tack and the boat was back running on just the power of nature with a little guidance from man.

"Hey guys how about a couple of beautiful female crew members joining the fun?"

"What beautiful crew?" Mitch asked smiling and feigning naivete.

"Us, Uncle Mitch. Can we come up now?" Lizzy called from below.

"Yeah, everything OK up there?" Carol added.

"Everything's fine. What do you think Gary, should the women be allowed on deck?"

"Very funny, Mr. Stone," Carol said.

"Ah, this is your battle," Gary said and tried to ignore his partner's efforts at goading his wife and daughter.

They didn't wait for any further invitation and both appeared in the cockpit. Carol had put on a T-shirt and shorts much to Mitch's chagrin and Lizzy was wearing long pants and a jacket because she said she was cold now.

"What was that all about?" Carol asked not really sure if she wanted to know.

"Just some impolite men making advances at Mitch's girlfriend, that's all."

"Silence you or you'll be chained below with the other rowers," Mitch said trying to sound like the tyrannical master of a slave ship. Everybody laughed except Lizzy who asked "What's happening now?"

"OK," Carol said, "I'll find out later. Let's just enjoy the day."

"Yes ma'am," Gary said bowing.

"Yes ma'am," Mitch said and copied his partner's actions.

"Yes mom," Lizzy said and giggled.

Mitch looked around and caught a glimpse of the 'Viking Princess' as it disappeared around the far side of the private island. Hope she stays out of their way, he said to himself.

CHAPTER 5

THE DEVICE

"**B**ase to all units," the radios in the boats crackled. "Base to all units."

"Unit One."

"Unit Two." Each Patrol boat called back to acknowledge the radio traffic. After the last of the active patrol units called in, the base broadcast the message. "Report to Administration in one hour."

"Unit One, received," announced the first patrol boat and all the other answered in order and the radio was silent again.

"Shit," the guard who had been kicked said, "this just isn't my day."

"What do you mean?" his junior partner asked.

"I mean we're going to get reamed, big time."

"Why?" the younger man asked, still not comprehending the meaning of the message nor his partner's voiced despair.

"Ad-Min is where the big bosses are and they don't call in the whole shift for pizza and beer. We're going to get chewed out for the little water ballet today. That's what I mean. Now shut up and let's head in. We might as well start on some of the paperwork before the ass chewing starts."

"Yeah," was all the younger man said and he began to grasp the seriousness of the whole affair. All the patrols seemed to have the same idea at the same time and the dock was turned into another disaster as each boat tried to get in line to fuel up while trying to avoid collisions with the other boats. Usually the patrols set out at ten minute intervals and ended in the same time pattern to avoid the mass confusion. This allowed for nearly constant coverage and for the unencumbered access of the fuel dock.

Not today. The mess on the water and now the order to report to Ad-Min meant everyone's day was ruined and no one would be leaving at their regular quitting time. "What a cluster fuck," the guard with the sore groin said.

"Yeah," his junior partner agreed.

After a wait of about forty minutes and several near misses and a few bumps by their fellow boats waiting for the fuel dock, the older guard tied up to the fuel dock and started to fill the boat's twin hundred gallon tanks. The one good thing he could think of about the whole day was that most of it had been spent with the engines off so he only needed to pump in twenty gallons to top off the tank.

"Good," he said lets get this thing tied up so we can get a good seat at the bitch session.

"Gentlemen and Ladies," the Security Chief said trying to be politically correct even though all but two of his staff were male and then only because his corporate bosses took research grant money from the Federal government. That made every department comply with the government's regulations on hiring. He didn't like it but his bosses paid him well enough to not to complain to much about the political necessities. "As you are aware," he continued, "there was an incident on the south side of the island only a few hours ago. Officially, we were well within our rights to search that and any other craft within five hundred yards of shore. Apparently several of the patrols stopped and boarded a cruiser and were confronted by some of the local police authorities. Even though they were on a private boat and out of uniform they displayed identification and weapons which our personnel were prudent in not challenging."

"That's for sure," the younger guard said to his partner who had engaged the boat's owner up close and more personal than the rest.

"Shut up and listen," the other guard said in a whisper that didn't obscure his anger. "And don't mention our contact with that girl again. Understand!"

"Yeah, sure," the junior guard said and leaned back on the other arm of the conference room chair.

"Although I am not at liberty to discuss the complete nature of our employer's activities on this island," the Security Chief continued, "I can tell you all, that they are very protective of their company secrets and are most concerned about leaks of information and industrial espionage. Now the events of this afternoon are going to be discussed further between myself and the participants as well as the Vice President of Operations for this facility. The personnel involved today will be notified of the meeting."

"Oh shit, we're in for it now," the junior guard said.

"Look Daryl," his partner said, "we just do the job and follow orders. We were doing just that this afternoon. We shouldn't be in any trouble because we were doing just as we were told. Now shut up and listen."

"OK, Chuck, but we're guarding some high tech garbage dump here and now we run into the local cops. I just don't like the feel of it, That's all."

"What did you say?" Chuck asked under his breath.

"I said we ran into some…"

"No, not that, the other part."

"Oh," Daryl said, "Yeah, I heard that this place is just one big garbage dump but that these science guys are making some kind of secret device to eat the stuff."

"What are you taking about?" Chuck said. "And where did you hear that bull? It sounds like science fiction to me."

"Yeah, me too," Daryl said still whispering but just a little softer now that Chuck seemed to be paying attention. "I heard from one of the kitchen girls that I'm trying to date, that she heard some of the science guys talking about this thing that can be told to eat only garbage and then stop automatically."

"You're full of shit, and this chick is just filling you up with more."

"Yeah, OK, but why are all those dump trucks coming across the causeway full of all kinds of trash and garbage? They leave empty but there's no place on the island to bury the stuff and they don't burn it. Not only would we smell the smoke but the locals and the Feds would pitch a fit over the pollution."

"Yeah, I guess you're right. I just never paid any attention. Besides it's none of my concern and shouldn't concern you either."

"Just think about it though," Daryl went on, "a machine that eats only garbage. You could get rid of almost anything without worrying about where to put it."

"I have just one question. If you can get rid of anything why just stop at garbage? Now shut up and listen," Chuck said again, "and just forget whatever you have heard or thought you heard and just do what you're paid to do."

"Yeah," was all Daryl said and sat back in the almost comfortable chair. Neither he nor Chuck noticed the dime sized black button on the back of the chair in front of them. Had they noticed, they would have kept very quiet indeed and they would have just listened to their boss. You didn't get into trouble just by listening. You didn't even get into trouble for just thinking. What you did get into trouble for was when you put those thoughts into words which is just what the small round microphones disguised as buttons were able to pick up nice and clear and send to another room in the facility where the real security was handled.

"These guys you hired are certainly not professional security people. They are more like professional idiots. These two here in the back. The ones we just recorded discussing the company's work here.

These guys are complete idiots. When either one of their IQs gets to 50 they should sell," the first dark suited man said as he zoomed the overhead camera in close enough to read the two guards' name badges.

"Hey what do you want for ten bucks and hour, spooks and shadow operations guys just looking for something to kill time between real world assignments?" the other dark suit said.

"No, but maybe a few retired guys would be nice. You know, more like us and less like them."

"You know our kind doesn't come cheap and the people calling the shots around here are nothing more than egg heads and bean counters to the 'nth' degree. Look at what it took for them just to cough up the cash for our services. They'd never foot the bill for a whole section of real pros."

"Yeah, and that's what makes our problems even bigger. These two yahoos just caused me to lose the first full weekend off in six months. They will have to pay dearly for their interruption of my fun time."

"You'll just have to make the payback that much more…" the second suit hesitated to choose the right word, "interesting and color-ful."

"I like your style," the first man said and he wrote down the names of the two new problems as the badges came into focus on the monitor. "Charles Ratiglio and Daryl Evers. Sounds like the members of a punk rock band."

"I hate punks and rock," the second man said.

"Yeah. Me too," the first one said and slipped the piece of paper into his pocket. He'd burn it once he had pulled up the two guards' personnel files. "Keep up the monitoring of our children," he said to the second man sitting at the video monitors. I have to do some damage control as usual and these guys are in need of some serious control. Let me know if anyone else has any spontaneous thoughts about our employers."

"Sure no problem," the second man said and returned his attention to the wall of TV screens. "I'll call you if I hear anything that might need your special attention to detail."

"Thanks," the first one said and he stepped out into the small hallway and headed down the hall to the offices of the administrative staff. He would find a nice quiet computer terminal to run the checks on his two new problems. He'd search the records from one of the secretary's terminals and no one could trace the search back to him if anyone ever decided to start asking questions about Mr. Ratiglio and Mr. Evers. The trail would start and stop at a nice innocent location.

Daniel Conners was a twenty plus year veteran of several intelligence agencies both part of the government alphabet soup of agencies and also part of some that had no name or alphabet letters that ever appeared in any reference or budget hearing. Most of his career he had operated out of offices of legitimate American business but he himself had no title or job description other than trouble shooter. He would find the word shooter amusing at times especially when he worked for some major high tech companies. He hadn't actually shot anyone in a very long time although he still carried a gun. It was more of a habit from the old days than of any real necessity now. He had access to some very fatal toys and now he could make the problems of his employers disappear without any trace and more importantly without recourse.

Conners had been recruited for his current employment when he was a problem solver for a large high tech company in California with major government contracts and therefore major money. One day he had found a telephone number in his locker and he had placed the call. No names were exchanged but within a week he had received a generous severance package and a relocation allowance. For all he knew he was working for the same company or the government for that matter but he didn't care. He just went where the money told him to go.

Even though he had never actually received a government paycheck he never really left government service and just worked from one front company to another. If a situation needed to be resolved that normal agencies couldn't or wouldn't handle, then he'd receive a phone call, meet an incorporeal voice somewhere obscure and come to an understanding about what needed to be accomplished and what the remuneration would be. Dan had more than a few identities and consequently multiple legitimate financial accounts as well as a few very private ones in countries that took great pride in keeping secrets even from themselves. He would mention a number between one and a hundred which was understood to be a designation of how many million dollars it would take for the problem to be rectified and then he would mention a bank's name and an account number. He'd done that dozens of times and now had a nice retirement fund under several names in as many banks.

So far this job had been more like a vacation. Until today the problems had been few and far between. From the time he had been flown across the country and driven to this island in a dark and very private limo, he had been treated very nicely and his new employers were keeping him in a lifestyle that didn't require him dipping into his previously arranged retirement contribution. Life was good and even the weather was beginning to improve over the island. Today's little problems were the first real demands for his special brand of resolution and he was actually rather pleased that he could now do what he enjoyed even though it meant cutting into some of his personal time. He'd even keep his talents sharp in dealing with these two idiot security guards. He laughed to himself again at the thought of these cretins knowing anything about security. Daniel Conners had breached, broken into and bypassed more security in his various assignments than these two guys had kissed girls.

The uniformed guards were nothing more than babysitters and did all of the boring and tedious leg work. For the most part they managed to keep the civilians away and did an adequate job of keeping the perimeter secure. The real security was handled by himself and his partner. Their jobs were to keep the secrets of the company within the company and everyone else out of the company's business. They were hired to keep the secrets secret and he and his partner Jeff were just doing their jobs.

Conners liked Jeff. They'd only been working together on this site since it opened a couple of months ago, but from the way Jeff talked and handled himself, Conners figured he had the same kind of resume'. Conners didn't ask. That was one question you really didn't need or want an answer to.

He proceeded down the hallway of the Administration building and stopped in front of the door to the secretarial pool. As the real Director of Security at the island complex he had keys and access codes for every door in the place. On the weekend he fully expected the office to be locked and empty and since no one had been passed through the gate security post he knew the room on the other side of the door was free from prying eyes. He opened the door with the coded pass card looked up and down the hallway and stepped inside. He used his small portable radio to call Jeff in the video booth. "Jeff, I am doing some systems checks in the Ad-Min office and I want you to take the surveillance system off line in this area while I do a manual inspection."

"Sure, no problem. More damage control?"

"Yeah," was all Conners said as he watched the light go out on the video camera in the corner.

"Your off line," Jeff's voice announced through the radio in Conners' hand.

"Thanks, I'll be done in a few minutes," Conners replied and went to work.

If anyone ever asked he always had the excuse that he was checking for security breaches and Jeff would always back him up on anything he ever said or did. As expected the room was empty but just incase some curious employee or the real occupants of this office showed up, he grabbed a chair from a table in the middle of the room and wedged it under the door knob. No since being interrupted and creating more problems to be fixed later. If someone wanted to get in, the chair would stop them long enough for him to exit any computer files and make some excuse for the door being stuck. No one would question the Head of Security too much.

Once secured in the fact he would be alone for a while he looked around the room. Now lets see, he said to himself looking over the large office space segmented by the ubiquitous portable walls, who will be the lucky curious secretary this time? He decided purely at random and sat down at one of the secretary's desks. He didn't even pay attention to the name on the cubicle wall. He turned on the computer, waited for the system files to load and then he typed in the password he had "borrowed" from one of the system's engineers. The moron, he thought, shouldn't have left it taped to the bottom of his keyboard. No telling who might use it. He reminded himself that there was another problem that needed fixing sometime soon. Anyway now Conners would appear on the system log as an engineer doing a diagnostic or some other maintenance program. He never used his own password to log onto the system. He didn't even remember what it was. He much preferred to use someone else's in the event that questions were ever asked. He could plausibly deny everything.

There were so many users on the system and he had managed to acquire most of their personal passwords either by overseeing the codes when some careless user logged on or by just "finding" them as he had with the one used today. These people were so stupid it was scary, he said to himself as he set up a new e-mail file. He typed in the private address he knew belonged to the Vice President of Operations, who was his boss and who he suspected was the real boss of the entire complex. There was a President and CEO somewhere who spent most of the time glad handing local politicians and raising cash and business somewhere. The V.P. was the man who called the shots on site and Conners had the rare distinction of having a direct contact with him and therefore his personal ear. Conners was the expediter to other people's whims and desires as well as the person who made problems into solutions.

He finished his message to his boss and pursuant to standard operating procedures he made it cryptic enough to foil any eavesdroppers, yet not so cloaked that the V.P. would misconstrue the meaning. This time he was logged on as an engineer and he made the message sound as engineering as possible.

"Background noise detected in equipment. Interference beyond specifications. Request permission for source adjustment." He hit the return key and the mail was posed. He waited for the answer which came back in a few minutes. Damn, he thought. The V.P. must be just sitting at his desk waiting for someone to talk to him. The response was just what Conners had hoped. An equally cryptic message to any outsiders but one he fully understood.

"Permission to rectify or reconfigure any equipment found to cause the interference, granted. Use lab assets. Assistance guaranteed in all aspects. Use system code Omega Zebra." Conners didn't write down or even print the e-mail. Years of field work had developed a great short term memory and he could forget the message as soon as he completed his work. He read it twice and then deleted it. He smiled and logged out of the system. He liked working for a company that took the maintenance of their equipment seriously.

He made sure the office was just as he had found it. Easy for a man with an eye for details and he even put the chair back precisely over the indentations it had made in the carpet. He brushed the marks out of the carpet in front of the door with his shoe until it looked like it did when the occupants had left the previous day. All was back to normal and he hadn't left a trace of his interoffice communication.

Conners walked down the hallway back to his office which was designated as the Supervisory Oversight Area. He unlocked the door and stuck his head inside. "Hey Jeff. Everything OK?"

"Yeah, the Captain is talking up a storm just as we instructed him to."

"OK," Conners said, "signal him to keep up the spiel for fifteen more minutes and then have him send those two TV stars to the briefing room."

"OK," Jeff said, "damage control?" It was a rhetorical question. He already knew the answer and he knew Conners would answer anyway.

Conners just smiled and left the room again locking the door behind him. He walked down the hallway and checked the status of the doors as he went by. He was the Director of Security after all and he was checking to see if all the doors were secure. He also kept in mind the various offices he could use if he needed to send some more memos on an innocent computer terminal sometime. He rounded a corner at the end of the long hallway and climbed a single set of stairs. He turned right and walked through the double doors into the white walled lab room and stood before the closed steel doors with wire mesh laminated between two thick pieces of glass.

The signs on the door in bright red on white lettering proclaimed that the lab was a clean environment and that only properly attired personnel with the highest level of clearance could enter. He had the clearance but didn't want to be bothered with all the clean room regulations. He pushed the button under the speaker of the intercom mounted on the wall to the left of the doors and under another large window and waited until one of the lab people appeared in the glass and a voice spoke to him.

"Mr. Conners?" the voice half asked half stated.

"Yes."

"I'll be right out."

Conners dispensed with any further comments and didn't even say thanks. He watched as the man in a spotless white lab suit stepped into a glass tunnel and closed the lab side doors tight. Conners felt the pressure change in his ears and he swallowed hard as he saw the man inside the tunnel now almost get knocked to the floor from a blast of air. The man's clothes and the mask over his face were pressed tight against his body as he was buffeted by the dust suppression system in the glass tunnel. The man in the white clothes walked through the doors on his side of the wall and then the pressure changed again and the white suited man stepped out into the vestibule. Conners cleared his ears as the pressure changed in the small space.

"I received the instructions only a few moments ago but the password gave this the highest priority," the lab technician said.

"Is this for Omega Zebra?" Conners asked. He hesitated to reach for what the technician was carrying.

"Yes. Per instructions this has been programmed for Calcium and Sodium Chloride. Just be careful that you don't get any on your skin and for God's sake don't ingest any of it."

"Ah, Yeah, sure. No problem," Conners said.

"Oh, yeah, and as per the instructions, that should be enough for about four hundred pounds of material. We also gave it an expiration period of forty-eight hours. If it isn't used or if the material isn't all processed by this time on Monday the solution will go inert."

"Yeah right," Conners said and cautiously took the glass bottle filled with a murky blue liquid.

"I never saw you," the technician said and went back inside the glass tunnel. The doors closed and Conners felt the air pressure change again.

That's OK, Conners thought, I don't know you either. Nice touch with the mask too. No face to remember that way. Conners carried the bottle carefully in both hands. He wasn't 100 percent sure what was made or done in the complex or on the island although he had heard the rumors. Even though the lab was restricted, it was more to keep contaminates out than dangerous materials in. After all, he said to himself as he held the bottle a little tighter and a little farther from his body, they weren't building biological or nuclear weapons. At least he didn't think so, or rather he hoped so looking at the bottle of blue gel.

His imagination must be playing games, he thought as he felt the liquid moving on its own. Get a grip he told himself. You've handled much worse things than this blue stuff. Nevertheless, he didn't waste any time heading to the briefing room. He arrived with about five minutes to spare. The Captain was reliable if not the most competent and he would end his little talk at precisely the time Jeff had told him. Then he would make his way to the two guards with the running mouths and tell them to meet someone important in the briefing room and in about two or three minutes depending on how fast the guards hustled, they would indeed meet the real Director of Security. Conners was their boss and they didn't even know it and in about twenty minutes they wouldn't be able to tell anyone about their meeting or about what they have ever heard about what happens on this island.

Conners set the bottle of blue liquid on the table and pulled out a pair of latex surgical gloves from his coat pocket. He wasn't concerned about handling the sealed bottle so much as he was worried about any splashes or drips when he poured the stuff. He carefully unsealed the bottle and poured the contents into coffee urn hoping that the heat of the coffee would not destroy the effectiveness of the liquid. He knew the guards would always take a cup of coffee when offered and he hoped they were real thirsty.

CHAPTER 6

THE TEST

T he coffee pot ready light just started to glow when there was a knock on the door and the two guards, still in uniform, entered the briefing room.

"Please sit down gentlemen," Conners said motioning to the two chairs on one side of the table. The men sat down and Conners did the same on the opposite side of the table. "Thank you for coming so quickly," he said. "Can I get you two a cup of coffee?"

"Sure," the younger one said. Conners knew him to be Daryl Evers.

"Sounds good to me," Ratiglio said.

Conners got up and walked over to the coffee pot. This is too easy, he thought to himself and carefully poured two cups. He returned to the table and handed the men the cups being very careful not to spill any on himself. He didn't know what the solution would do and he didn't want to find out first hand.

"Cream and sugar?" he asked the men.

"No thanks," Ratiglio said.

"Nope none for me either," Evers added.

Too easy, Conners thought again, and sat back down across the table from the two unsuspecting guards. He handled a cup of his own to make a show that he was drinking coffee too. His was empty though, but the prop worked. The two guards drank theirs quickly and Conners had them help themselves to more. All the time Conners was feeding them some more bullshit about how important their work was and how well they did their jobs today. Conners just kept up the meaningless praise and the men just sat there and nodded their heads and drank all the nice fresh coffee Conners had made. After about twenty minutes Conners figured they had about finished the pot and he told the two men how pleased management was with their performance and dismissed them brusquely. They looked at each other, finished their coffee and left.

"What was all that about and who the hell was he?" Daryl asked after they had walked a few steps down the hallway.

"No idea and I don't care," Chuck said. "He said he was happy with us and therefore I'm happy. Not only that but we just racked up another hour of O.T. at double time for spending our precious Saturday listening to hot air from the suits."

"You're right," Daryl said. "Ah, can we move it along? All of a sudden I really have to go to the john. Must have been all that coffee I drank?"

"Yeah, me too," Chuck said and both men hustled down the hall to the locker room. Daryl got to the door first and rushed inside and as his luck would have it all the stalls and urinals were in use. The entire shift had just finished changing after the meeting and was by some misfortune of fate using all the spots. Daryl was now in pain. Coffee never had this effect on him and he hadn't had all that much. Hell he'd drunk that many before lunch and only used the head on the patrol boat once all shift.

Chuck was right behind him through the locker room door and by the strangest coincidence one of the stalls nearer to Chuck suddenly became available. Chuck pounced on the opportunity. "Sorry man," he said to Daryl who was doubled over clutching himself, "it's really bad."

"Yeah, you shit. Tell me about it," Daryl said dancing around now with a grimace on his face. "Damn, the kidneys must be working on overtime too," he said just as his bladder succumbed to the intense pressure and released the muscle tension holding in the liquid. "Ah, shit," Daryl said.

"Now what," Chuck asked still emptying his bladder.

"Damn. I just couldn't hold it and now I can't stop it," Daryl said partially embarrassed at wetting himself and beginning to become concerned at the amount of liquid he couldn't staunch. "What's happening?" he asked as he tried to hide his loss of control. Finally a spot opened and he rushed over to continue his discharge of fluids. The other guards in the room all began to stare at Daryl and most of them chuckled at the two men's predicament.

"Hey guys, this isn't funny. This really hurts now and I can't stop."

"Yeah, sure," one of the hecklers said. "Even my three-year-old doesn't piss herself anymore."

More of the audience laughed and continued the catcalls and remarks as they left the room.

"Hey Chuck, I'm getting worried here."

"Forget about those assholes," Chuck said.

"Not them, I can't stop and it really hurts now."

"Yeah, me too. What's up with this?"

"Don't know. Too much coffee I maybe?"

"Nah, we've had twice as much as we just had and gone all shift standing a post and never had to go like this. And I'm in pain. That's never happened before no matter how much we drank," Chuck said holding himself steady with his left hand against the bathroom wall. He was still urinating as was Daryl. Both had been going for several minutes and suddenly Daryl's knees buckled and he collapsed into a lump on the floor. Chuck wasn't feeling much better and he just stood there for a few seconds and watched his friend go into convulsions and start thrashing around on the floor. He was still urinating and now he was rolling around in the ever growing puddle.

Chuck screamed at the top of his lungs both out of fear and out of concern for his friend. "Hey, I need some help in here. Somebody help," he yelled. That was all he could do. He was still releasing fluids and couldn't move to help his friend. He just stood there and watched helplessly and just as soon as the convulsions had started, they stopped and Daryl laid there motionless in the large puddle he had made.

"Daryl, hey Daryl, you OK?" Chuck asked between yells for help. Daryl wasn't OK and Chuck would never find out what happened either. After one more weak yell for help he too collapsed and his convulsions began. Daryl was dead and Chuck was only moments away. He died just as someone entered the room in response to the shouting.

All the people, who saw the bazaar shapes on the floor, could say was that Chuck and Daryl were healthy and looked OK that day. Now they were both just lifeless forms on the floor. All the people in the room just stared at the bodies and tried to figure out what had happened. Bodies was a description that could only be applied because the people who worked with the two dead guards could recognize the uniforms. That was all that could be recognized though, since under the urine soaked uniforms was nothing that resembled the original features of the deceased owners.

Dan Conners joined the medical team and tried to keep as many of the gawkers out of the area as possible but they were all pushing and shoving each other in morbid curiosity. Finally he just gave up and decided to have what was left of the two men removed to the clinic. He would have to decide how to dispose of them so that no one would ask too many questions in the future.

This was the one time he had hoped that there was a security camera in the locker room instead of the hallway outside. The union had fought its installation on the grounds that no one needed to know what happened when people were changing their clothes and this was one of the few places that didn't have a camera. Damn he would have liked to see these two die though. The hall camera would have to do as a record of the people in and out of the room for later damage control but he would have liked to see the two piss themselves to death.

As it was the limp and nondescript lumps of flesh told most of the story. Except for the fact that some of the hair and most of the skin blemishes were still apparent there wasn't much else that gave the forms the distinction of being human. There were no bones left and the head had collapsed like a deflated balloon. The faces looked like flattened masks. It was gruesome but he would have to remember what that stuff he had gotten form the lab was. Programmed for Calcium and Sodium Chloride, huh? Nice stuff and fast too, he thought.

Almost too fast. He should have waited until they left the site for them to die. Now he would have to explain things to the staff and probably to the local authorities. Oh well, he said to himself, nothing ever works as expected and with this stuff he didn't really know what to expect anyway. Nice stuff, he said to himself again, fast, easy, and efficient.

Conners went back up to his office as soon as the bodies had been removed. He punched in the code for the door lock and entered the room. "Did you get all the people in and out of the locker room on tape?" he asked Jeff who was sitting on the console drinking some coffee of his own.

"Where did you get that?" Conners asked pointing to the cup in Jeff's hand.

"Just made it why?" Jeff asked, "there's some in the pot over there."

"Oh, yeah, thanks," Conners said, "did you tape the action downstairs?"

"Yeah, what happened?"

"Seems two of our uniform guys had a nasty accident. Got all pissed off and then died."

"Died. From what?" Jeff asked.

"Not sure. But I guess we'll have to inform the locals. We'll have to give them the 'guided' tour to the clinic then back to the main gate."

"You want me to stay around and give them the no sight seeing tour?" Jeff asked.

"No, I'll do it. I want to see what kind of local talent there is around here anyway. My guess is that most of the local cops are good old boy rednecks who got the job because they voted for the right guy."

"Yeah, maybe," Jeff replied, "but some of these small departments have some very sharp officers."

"Yeah, like those two heros who interrupted our search and seizure. They just flashed a badge and a couple of guns and thought they had the world by the ass."

"OK, OK," Jeff said, "I see what you mean. I'm off in twenty minutes anyway. I'll put everything on automatic. The tapes are brand new so they'll last until 9:00AM."

"Thanks," Conners said and went out to find an empty cubicle again.

"Lock up and I'll see you tomorrow," he said to Jeff as he closed and coded the door. He decided to use the 911 number to make the call to the police. Even though it wasn't an emergency he didn't want to wait around all the rest of the day for the locals to make the trip out to the complex. He picked up the phone and punched in the three numbers and waited for an answer.

"911 Operator," the female voice said, "what's your emergency?"

"It's not an emergency," Conners said, "but this is the Director of Security at Millennium Eco-Technologies on Society Island."

"Yes sir, how may I direct the call? Is this for police, fire or ambulance assistance?"

"Police, but like I said there isn't any emergency now. I need to report an accident at our facility."

"Do you need an ambulance?"

"No they're dead."

"Dead. What's the nature of the accident?"

"Everything's under control. I just need to report it to the police. We have a doctor on site and he'll do all of the necessary medical reports."

"Yes sir, but we need to have an officer investigate."

"Yes, I know, that's why I'm calling," Conners said frustrated at the quality of help the taxpayers and therefore his employers were getting for their money.

"I'll have an officer there as soon as possible," the dispatcher said.

"I need to know exactly when. This is a highly secured facility and I'll have to meet the officer at the main gate to escort him to the medical center."

"I'm not sure, sir, all of our cars are tied up at the moment. I'll send someone there as soon as I can get a car free."

"What if this was an emergency, wouldn't they have to come quicker?"

"Yes sir, but you already stated this wasn't an emergency."

"Yeah, right," he said with a touch of sarcasm.

"The best I can do sir, is call you when the patrol is on its way."

"Fine but make it quick will you. I don't intend to wait all night for one of your local good old boys."

"Yes sir," the dispatcher said coldly.

Now Conners was even less impressed with the lack of quality in the personnel of the police agencies in the area. It shouldn't be much of an exercise for his brain to dazzle whoever showed up. The site doctor would certify the cause of death as anything Conners told him and the local should be just another fat, stupid, and happy ticket writer. No investigation, no fuss no muss. Just a little goodwill cooperation with some of the overpaid and under worked county cops. This would be very easy he thought. Now if the guy would only get here in a reasonable amount of time.

CHAPTER 7

THE CONNECTION

$\mathcal{M}$itch steered the thirty-two-foot sailboat through the channel buoys and toward the harbor. Although the water was fairly deep this time of the year Mitch wanted to stay as close to the center of the narrow waterway as traffic would allow. Even with the spring water levels very high this year and the fact that his new boat had a wing keel instead of the more traditional fin that drew more water, he didn't want to steer over any submerged obstacles and test the draft of his new boat. At five feet from the waterline to the bottom of the keel he didn't want to risk finding a rock with only four feet of water clearance. He moved slightly to starboard as a small day cruiser was making its way out of the harbor. Mitch hadn't yet dropped the main sail. He had reefed it one point and Gary was just now working the jib sail into its canvas sail bag. The female members of the crew were busy preparing the fenders to be hung over the sides at the dock.

"Get ready on the mainsail," Mitch told Gary who had just fin-ished with the jib sail.

"OK, say when," Gary said as Mitch uncleated the main halyard from the cockpit. Gary held onto the line and wrapped it around the mast-mounted winch for some leverage and control over the descent of the Dacron main sail.

"Anytime now," Mitch said and tried to steer the boat a little closer to the wind to keep the sail from blowing around too much once it was released.

"OK, I got it," Gary said as he worked the halyard with one hand and tried to gather in the sail with the other.

"Carol, just drop those fenders over the side. Just make sure they're tied to something first."

"OK," she said and both she and Lizzy pushed the large blue foam tubes over the guidelines. The tubes were hung just above the water but occasionally a wave crest would catch the bottom of a fender and there would be a gentle thud against the hull.

Another great sailing day in the books, Mitch thought to himself. "Hey, Carol can you give Gary a hand with the sail. Use the centipede to hold it around the boom until we're in the slip."

"OK, Mitch," she said, "Lizzy, you sit in the back with Mitch until we're at the dock, OK?"

"Sure Mom. What's a centipede?"

"It's that long springy rope with the hooks to hold the sail tight," Mitch said.

"Oh," Lizzy replied still not sure of the word yet. She did as her mother told her and sat in the cockpit and tried to stay out of Mitch's way. It wasn't easy though. Mitch was standing at the big wheel and moving from side to side which forced Lizzy to tuck in her feet every few minutes.

"What are you doing, Uncle Mitch?"

"I'm trying to see both sides of the boat to make sure we don't hit something. I have to keep it in the channel here between the buoys."

"Huh?"

"Those are buoys," he said pointing to the red balls floating on either side of the boat. "They are anchored to the bottom at the edge of the channel. On the other side it is too shallow for boats and especially for most sailboats."

"Oh," she said and started to look along the side of the boat like Mitch was doing.

Mitch held the helm steady and guided the boat through the channel and made a right turn into the harbor. He nudged the throttle down to the last position before it would stall the engine. The twenty horsepower diesel revved down and the boat slowed to a gentle glide just barely moving against the subtle current in the harbor. Mitch didn't want to take any chances with his new toy and was taking things very slowly. He had to make another right turn to head into the main marina area and then a sharp right into the row where his slip was. That was the tricky part and the part that made him the most nervous. Several years earlier when he'd had his old sailboat he had been trying to back out of his slip and backed into another boat tied up in another row. Although there was nearly one hundred feet between the ends of any boats in the two adjacent slips, there wasn't much room to maneuver when the wind and the current worked against the direction the captain wanted to go.

To compensate for the wind and water forces sometimes you needed more engine power and if the wind died or shifted the boat could lurch. Brakes were not part of the equipment list on boats and inertia was. Collisions happened once in a while but at a slow speed they wouldn't do much damage. Mitch's collision resulted in about $200 worth of repairs to a boat's gel coat and a couple of six packs to placate the owner. He didn't want to repeat that incident and was concentrating on balancing the forward motion against the effects of the shifting wind. So far so good and he had Gary on one side of the bow and Carol on the other. Both had boat hooks to fend them away from any hard objects. Especially expensive hard objects.

The slip was on the port side and Gary's job was to step off onto the dock just as the boat started into the slip. He could then catch the bow and help guide the boat into place. Carol's job was to toss him the bow line and try to hold the boat close to the dock with her boat hook. Mitch had the trickiest part. He had to maintain steering until Gary could get to the dock. He also needed to get the engine into reverse just as the boat started into the slip in an effort to reduce the momentum to little more than a slow crawl. He had to do all this while he tried to hook onto the dock cleat at the stern of the boat so the rear end wouldn't swing away from dock and toward the big cruiser in the neighboring slip.

This is why he sailed with a crew whenever he could. It usually took at least two and preferably more to get the boat in and out of its parking space. If the wind was blowing hard across the marina, it would sometimes be difficult for even three or four people to get back into the slip. Fortunately for the most part other boat owners would always appear on the dock to help position and secure the boat. Mitch was never sure if it was done out of kindness or self pres- ervation. Help the guy and protect your own boat was the way Mitch had figured it. Like most other days, today was no exception and there on the dock was the tall attractive girl with the auburn hair. She was still wearing her white swim suit but now she also had on a pair of very tight jeans. Mitch tried not to pay any attention to her while he was trying to hold his stern close to the dock and handle the helm and the engines.

"Hi," he said to her, "thanks for the assistance."

"No problem," she said a bit coldly. "I wanted to talk to you any- way." Her voice had a bit of an edge to it.

"OK," he said trying to do all of the necessary movements to dock the boat. "Can it wait until we get secured here?" he asked.

"Yeah," was all she said and Mitch got the impression that she didn't seem to be in very good humor.

It took about fifteen minutes to pack the sails and tie off all the lines and reconnect the shore power and water.

"We're going up to the restrooms," Gary said giving Mitch and Alicia some privacy.

"You're not leaving yet are you?" he called after them.

"No, we'll be right back."

"OK, what's up?" Mitch asked as soon as the Faulkners were out of ear shot. "Come on board."

"No thanks," she said, "I just want to know where the hell you two get off with that macho bullshit out there today?"

"Ah, well it looked like you needed some help," Mitch responded a little shocked and insulted by her statement and attitude.

"I was doing just fine and didn't need you two to come thundering in acting all tough and throwing your weight around."

"Woah," Mitch said getting a little indignant at her comments. "First of all I've been trying to lose some weight and secondly we didn't thunder in we arrived on a sailboat which is very quiet I might add. As for the other part it looked like you were having some problems with all those hired guns around your boat and in fact even boarding your boat."

"I was doing just fine. I didn't need or ask for your help," she continued.

Mitch stood there and looked at her with a surprised and amazed expression on his face. Neither of them said anything for several seconds.

"Well?" she said in a huff.

Just as he was about to give her a juicy retort his cell phone chirped.

"There," she said, "Maybe somebody really does want your help." She didn't seem willing to end her tirade yet and she just stood there on the dock with her arms folded sort of hovering and waiting for the next chance to strike.

"Excuse me," he said trying to retain his composure by being overly polite. He forced a smile and held it as he went below to catch the phone. What the hell was that all about, he thought, trying to keep calm as he answered the phone. "Hello," he said in as neutral a tone of voice as he could muster. "Yeah, I know where it is. In fact we had a run in with a couple of the hired hands this afternoon," he said, "no, no major problem but the Lieutenant may be interested in how they conduct business. I'll put something on paper for him and the boss." Mitch listened as the dispatcher gave him the details of what she had called him about. He went over to one of the ports in the main cabin and peered out at the temper tantrum disguised as a gorgeous woman. He sighed and shook his head. "No, that wasn't at you Connie. It was for a little problem at the marina here. Yeah, I understand, I'll head that way in about twenty minutes or so as soon as I close up the boat. They expecting me?" he asked and listened to the response from the dispatcher. "OK, but I hope they have a sense of humor about this afternoon. I'll call when I get on the site." He pressed the end key, set the phone down and took a deep breath before he went back topside to face the heat and the warm spring day.

Mitch returned to the cockpit and felt as though he had entered the twilight zone. Alicia was standing there smiling and instead of continuing to vent her misplaced anger she said, "I'm sorry I lost my temper but I just don't like it when men think I'm helpless. I can handle myself pretty well."

"Yeah, I saw that," Mitch said throwing in a bit of sarcasm. "My mistake," he said, "I guess I didn't grasp the fact that you were handling things when those two goons were searching your boat."

She smiled but Mitch could see she was forcing herself to refrain from jumping back into the argument. She also hated it when men tried to bait her. She was still smiling but Mitch could see it wasn't easy for her. "I couldn't help but overhear your end of the phone conversation," she said, "your not going back to that island, are you?"

"That I'm afraid, Ms. Carlsson is private business of which you are not privy. I'm sorry but now it seems I'm in a bit of a hurry and must cut this pleasant conversation short." He was smiling now at his own sarcasm and she just stood on the dock for a moment with a glare in her eyes. She turned and stomped off. Mitch took a brief moment from his boat duties to watch the near-perfect figure in the tight jeans and white swimsuit march down the dock towards her own boat.

He shook his head and reminded himself of how lucky he was not to be involved with a woman like that again. Just a lot of pain and agony waiting to happen, he thought as he finished stowing the gear and securing the main sail. Just as he was about to lock the main hatch and leave for his sudden new assignment, his portable phone chirped again.

"Hello."

"Mitch, this is Lieutenant Anderson, you're headed over to Society Island on that death call, right?"

"Yeah, I'm just finishing up and was ready to head there. It should be about twenty to thirty minutes, why?"

"Ah, I just got a call from the FBI and…"

Mitch cut him off in mid sentence. "What the hell do those leeches want?" he asked now not trying to restrain his anger.

"Listen, Deputy," the Lt. said. Mitch knew it was serious now. The Lt. only used the rank designation when he was pissed and/or when he was about to give an order which no one would like.

"Yes sir."

"The FBI just called and they asked or rather insisted that we take along one of their people when you check out that island. They were very insistent if you read me on this."

Mitch paused and looked at his phone in disbelief. "I thought you wanted me to take care of this matter soon. I'm on my day off and the damn Fibbies will take better than an hour to get here. It'll be dark by the time I get out there." Mitch felt his composure going right out the window and the Lt. finally got a word in.

"Look I don't know or care what your personal problems are with the FBI, but they asked for our cooperation on this and I was glad to help and now so are you. Got it!"

"Yes sir," Mitch replied a little contritely.

"Now that you have vented your spleen, let me tell you what's going to happen," the Lt. said in his authoritative voice.

"OK," Mitch said trying not to piss the Lieutenant off any further.

"First of all you will give the agent all of your cooperation and you will be friendly about it. Understand?"

"Yes," Mitch said. He hated being on the receiving end of the Lt.'s wrath especially when the Lt. was giving orders. He always asked if you understood them like you were some kind of moron.

"Second, you shouldn't have to wait very long. The field office said they had an agent working on something in our area and that the agent will meet you at your location shortly."

"What is the FBI working on up here especially without our knowledge and how does anyone know where I am?" Mitch asked.

"Look Stone, everybody on the Department knows you have a new boat and where you keep it. And this is your day off as you have reminded me. That's why I'm the Lieutenant. I can figure these things out. As for what the FBI is doing, I didn't ask since they obviously didn't think to include us."

"OK," Mitch said, "I'll wait here until the agent shows."

"And cooperate."

"Yes, I'll be nice," Mitch said. "Hey what about that day off thing you said?"

"Yeah, well put in for the compensation time."

The phone clicked off and Mitch stood there and sighed again at his less than good fortune of having to work on his day off and having to work with some Federal agent. At least he got a full day of sailing in before the call back to duty. He was doing the Lt. a favor by taking the call he thought. They could have sent someone else like one of the on call Detectives.

It didn't take long for the news to go from bad to worse. Just as Mitch finished checking the dock lines for the last time, Ms Carlsson showed up at the end of the slip. "Still pissed or did you think of something else to complain about?" he said sardonically.

"Nope," she said with a smile on her face showing both victory and relish in something Mitch was suddenly sure would cause him an intense pain in his derriere. In the same place the Lt. always found for his chew outs. Here it comes, he thought. "I'm going with you to check on those two deaths at Society Island."

"How do you…?" he stopped in mid thought. "Don't tell me you're the Fed who's come to bother me?"

"OK, I won't tell you as you have so quaintly phrased it. I'm here to participate in an investigation which by the way I believe your Lieutenant assured my office that you would happily cooperate in."

"He never said happily," Mitch grumbled.

"True, but you should be happy. You're with one of the best people the bureau has in the field of molecular biology."

"I thought the Fibbies were lawyer accountant types. What's with you and micro biology?"

"It's molecular biology and I'm not really with the FBI, exactly."

"Oh gee," Mitch said feigning amazement, "now there's something for the six o'clock news."

"Just a minute, asshole," she snapped back, returning to her angry mode. "I work for the CDC in Atlanta and I have been temporarily assigned to the FBI to assist in an on going investigation."

"What kind of an investigation?"

"I can't say, it's classified," she said.

"No shit, another news bulletin," he shot back not even trying to hide his contempt and frustration this time.

"Look, it's classified to keep the press out of the loop until the authorities can get a handle on what's causing the problems and how far the problem has expanded. I'd tell you if they'd let me but right now it's strictly on a need to know basis."

"And I don't need to know, right."

"Yeah, well for now, yes," she said showing a small amount of guilt at not being able to tell him anything. She knew cops hated surprises especially in a new investigation. A lot of cops liked the satisfaction of knowing things other people didn't and maybe never would and she sensed this cop was no different and always knew what was happening. "I'm sorry," she said, "But if this isn't something related to my case I'll just disappear and leave you to whatever local case you may have. But…" she paused, "but if it is something connected with my ongoing investigation, I promise to talk to my people to bring you and your department into the loop. That's the best I can do for now," she said smiling trying to thaw the block of icy tension.

Mitch saw that both she and the smile were sincere. He still didn't like being kept in the dark, but he would try to start off on the right foot. At least she was an attractive Fed. He could have been saddled with some old guy ready for retirement. He forced a nod and an "OK." They walked down the dock and up into the parking area. "We'll take mine. It's the one under wraps over there," he said pointing to the covered Austin Healy.

"Sure," she said, "another macho institution. The man always wants to drive."

"Yeah, something like that." He snarled back. "It's just that I'm the one that got the call and I'm the one that works in this county, OK?"

"Sure, anything you say, for now," she replied and headed for the car.

"Hey Mitch, what's up?" Gary asked as he was returning to the dock.

"Yeah where are you two going?" asked Lizzy with a smile on her face.

"Company business," Mitch said, "probably routine but I'll fill you in on it later," he said to Gary but trying to answer both questions at once.

"Oh, Mitch that's to bad," Carol said, "but we had a great day on the boat."

"Yeah, thanks Uncle Mitch," Lizzy said.

"No problem. We'll do it again, soon," he said.

"Next week," Lizzy half asked half insisted.

"Maybe Lizzy," her mother said, "Mitch might have plans of his own."

"Oh," Lizzy said, as her mind started to formulate what those plans might be.

"No," Mitch assured her, reading her devious little mind. Lizzy smiled and giggled.

"What's the company business that allows civilians along?" Gary asked nodding toward Ms. Carlsson who had walked over and was standing next to the covered car.

"She's not a civilian," Mitch said, "she's a Fed."

"No shit," Gary said a little astonished.

"Yeah," Mitch responded, "I'll fill you in later, but the Lt. just called on this one. Sounds like a routine unattended death and all our cars are busy. He asked if I'd do a quick look and report."

"Oh," Gary said with an expression on his face that said he understood enough for now to drop the conversation. "OK then. Yeah, thanks for the great day Mitch. I'll hear from you about T.S. soon, right."

"Yeap," Mitch said as Gary shepherded his wife and child toward their own car.

"Thanks Uncle Mitch," Lizzy yelled loud enough for most of the Marina to hear.

"What's T.S.?" Alicia asked.

"This shit," Mitch said as he started to unhook the car cover from the A-H.

"What's T.S.?" Lizzy asked her father.

"This stuff," he said and backed out of the spot and put the S.U.V. in gear. The whole family waved as the truck passed Mitch and Ms. Carlsson.

"Do you think they have a date?" Lizzy asked.

"I don't think so," Gary said knowing Mitch's chronic dislike of Feds. "I don't think so," was all he said again, and the Faulkners returned to middle America and Mitch folded the cotton flannel car cover carefully and set it in the boot of the British roadster.

"Wow! What kind of car is this. It's gorgeous," she said.

"Thanks. It's an Austin Healy. A 1967 BJ-8 with an inline 3 liter six cylinder engine." Mitch was always happy to give the details of his favorite toy. Why not, it took years of waiting to be able to afford one and well now he could.

"In its day it ran with the best European and American sports cars and even now more than 30 years after it rolled out of the Layland factory she still tops 125."

"Very nice," she said as she slipped her gorgeous frame into the car's. "Let's go," she said, "and let's go fast."

Mitch smiled, started the engine and after checking all of the gauges to make sure the oil and water pressure were good, he put the car in gear and slowly backed out of the parking spot. He put the gear shift into first and slowly let out the clutch not wanting the tires to spin in the loose gravel of the lot and kick up stones that might chip the original paint job.

"We going to a funeral or for a ride in this sports car you said was fast?"

"Wait for it," he said with a big grin on his face like a kid with a new bike at Christmas. As soon as he pulled out of the marina and onto solid pavement he put the car back into first gear and this time let out the clutch quickly. The tires squealed and the big 3 liter propelled the car down the street with little effort. Since he had been the local cop in this village as well as a Deputy for the county, he didn't want to show Ms. Carlsson all of the car's power while the locals were milling around on the street. As soon as he was on the main highway he'd show her just what a real drophead sports car could do.

The A-H passed through the small village as Mitch kept the car at the posted speed limit. No sense pissing off the locals and having one of them call the Lieutenant and complain. Everybody seemed to know how fast a car was going except when they were driving.

Alicia just sat in the seat and appeared to be enjoying the ride in the roadster. Mitch tried to keep his eyes on the road but couldn't help looking at her. Her hair was streaming out behind her and she was still wearing the tight jeans over the perfectly fitting white swim suit. She had however, taken the opportunity to put on a shirt but had only tied it around her flat, firm stomach. It was still open and unbuttoned in the front and Mitch could still enjoy the view.

"Better watch the road, Deputy. Wouldn't want you to wreck your beautiful car."

"Humph," Mitch grunted and now consciously refused to look in her direction. Once he was out of the village and on the main highway Mitch wasted no time in getting the A-H into high gear. They were cruising along now at 60 mph. A little over the limit but not enough to draw the attention of some citizen with their phone's speed dial programmed to the office and certainly not the attention of the State Troopers who might be on the way back from checking ID's at the beach.

"Now that's more like it," she said with her hair now fully extended behind her and blowing in the wind. Mitch gave her another "Humph" and didn't look at her. He couldn't see but she was now smiling with glee. He though he'd ask the obvious while she was in a good mood.

"So what's the connection with the Feds and this local unattended death? And don't give me any of that administrative shit about need to know. You're here on a local case and that's why I need to know."

Alicia didn't say anything for a few minutes then tried to answer Mitch without giving away too much information.

"Look, what I said is true. What I am working on is very classified at the moment and you really don't need to know about it yet. But I can tell you that we have been watching and investigating the activities of that company for almost a year now."

"This company. Millennium Eco-whatevers."

"Yes, Millennium Eco-Technologies."

"Wait, wait. They've only been set up here for a few months."

"That's here. They have been in operation in several major cities for almost two years. We've had a file on them starting last summer. We think that they are connected to some very strange disappearances and losses of property. We managed to get close to a techno geek a few months ago in the mid west. Near as we can tell he was working for an environmental group trying to develop nature friendly recyclable products. Seems he got all liquored up one night and started spouting off about how the world would be less crowded and there would be a much simpler life soon once the numbers were reduced."

"What the hell was he taking about?" Mitch asked not following any of this.

"No one knows. Somebody called us anonymously and said this guy was linked to an eco terrorist group."

"Was he?"

"Don't know. When we went to his house to talk to him, he had disappeared without a trace. All we found was a hand written note with the name of our company here and a pile of dust on the floor near his desk."

"Dust, what kind of dust?" Mitch asked trying to keep the information stream flowing.

"Pure chemicals. Carbon, calcium, a few trace minerals, that's it."

"Sounds like he just dried up and blew away," Mitch said jokingly.

"Yeah," she replied seriously. "We are working on the Millennium Eco-Technologies link to find out what happened to the guy."

"So what's your connection with all this. I mean what's a molecular biologist doing working an eco-terrorist/missing persons case for the FBI?"

"Mitch I've said too much already but I think you should know what we might be up against here. It could be dangerous."

"Thanks for your concern but I have been in dangerous situations at least once or twice in my career you know."

"Not like this. I'm taking fatally dangerous here. We don't believe that environmental engineer is missing. We think he was right there."

"Right there, where?"

"The dust. We think he was the dust. What was left is exactly what you get when all of the water is removed from the body."

"What the hell are you saying. You think those guys out on the island can reduce a guy to dust. Oh, come on."

"Mitch, look at the facts you already have. They open up a waste treatment facility, truck in tons of garbage and trash and no one ever sees them bury it or burn it. You tell me where it all goes."

"Ah, maybe they have ten thousand goats eating the stuff, I don't know."

"Well we don't either but if they can do what we think they can, everybody on the planet is in for a lot of serious shit."

"OK, so what's your part in all this, then?"

"I was assigned to try and get close and see if I could make the science connection to prove our theory. I was trying to get close enough this morning, to see if I could find out anything."

"That's when you were stopped and we came in," he said.

"Yeah like gang busters. I thought they'd be even tighter on their security after that and I'd lose any chance to get close. That's why I was so…"

"So cranky, so obnoxious, so nasty…"

"So annoyed at you and your buddy there. I was closer than I had ever been and then you showed up and flashed all that cheap tin around."

"Hey my badge isn't cheap, we have to eat a lot of candy to get one you know." Mitch said trying to defuse the argument that was taking shape. She laughed and relaxed a little.

"Anyway I thought I was getting somewhere and then all hell broke loose. I figured I had lost any chance of watching that island up close until you got the call about some death investigation. I quickly called my boss who I guess called yours and the rest, as they say, is history."

"That's fine for how you got here on this with me, but I still want to know why."

"That I can't tell you yet."

"Oh yeah, need to know," Mitch said holding in the next pissed off comment.

"Look Mitch, if these guys are involved in something that pertains to my case then you'll be brought up to speed on the whole thing. If not, then I just stand by and watch a master at work with his dead body case. I go back to my investigation and you stay here with the local law stuff, OK?"

The rest of the ride was in silence and fortunately it only took twenty minutes to reach the causeway connecting the mainland with Society Island. Mitch pulled the A-H up in front of the guard gate and yelled over to the guard in the shack.

CHAPTER 8

THE EVIDENCE

"*D*eputy Stone, to see the Security Chief. I'm expected."

"Yeah," said the guard either unimpressed at the arrival of a police officer in a classic British roadster or just acting like what he was, an underpaid rental cop. "Go straight and turn left at the first stop. Mr. Conners will meet you in front of Building B. It's on your left, painted white."

"OK," Mitch said and let the clutch out just enough to engage the transmission and squeal the tires.

"How come he didn't even ask about me?" Alicia said a little indignantly at the snub.

"Maybe he didn't see you," Mitch said half jokingly.

Now it was Alicia's turn to respond with a "humph" and she wriggled in the bucket seat to show a little more of her figure under the loose shirt. "Think they'll see me now," she said as she ran her hands down her stomach and legs.

"Nah," Mitch said matter of factly and pulled the A-H up to the stop sign and then made the left. He didn't even look at Alicia now and he knew or rather hoped she was now just sitting there with a scowl on her face.

"Here we are," he said and pulled the A-H into a slot directly in front of Building B as the gate guard had said. And as the guard had said a man was waiting for them.

"I'm Deputy Stone from the Sheriff's Department. They sent me here to take a report on a couple of deaths."

"Yes, I've been expecting you, but I wasn't aware they were sending two officers, and I wasn't aware that female officers were so attractive." The tall muscular man said and reached out to shake Alicia's hand first. "My name is Conners, Daniel Conners and I am the Chief of Security here."

"Oh, I'm sorry, Mr. Conners," Mitch interrupted, "Ms. Carlsson is not with my Department, she's…"

"I'm with the Coroner's Office," she said cutting Mitch off and taking Conners hand. She smiled at Mitch and then gave Conners an even bigger smile.

"The Coroner. I didn't think that would be necessary. Our own physician will certify the Death Certificates and make all of the final arrangements. There's really no need for any involvement from the Coroner Office," Conners said displaying a look of suspicion under the toothy smile still aimed at Alicia.

"Oh, this isn't official," she said, "I was near by when Deputy Stone was dispatched and I just tagged along. That's all right isn't?" she asked and brushed back her hair and returned the toothy smile.

"Yes, of course," Conners said, "this way please." He still held onto Alicia's hand and escorted her up the steps and through the double doors of Building B. Mitch followed behind a little annoyed at the sudden change in dynamics and at the lie made by Alicia who now made this investigation a team effort. Maybe she'd write the reports too, he thought as he followed the two through the doors.

Once through the doors it was like entering into some kind of science fiction movie set. The exterior of the building like all the others on the island was plain and the buildings could easily have been twenty or fifty years old. In fact Mitch knew some of the history of the island and its inhabitants over the years. When he was a kid, his parents would take him fishing near the island and tell him about the Navy during World War II using the island for some kind of secret research. The Navy had kept all the buildings nondescript which explained the exteriors but this interior was beyond explanation. This stuff was a long way from the days of the Navy's occupation and certainly from the days when this was a children's summer camp. If he didn't know better he swear, he was inside a government facility now with all of the latest equipment just out of the boxes.

"What are you people doing here?" Mitch asked as they walked past the glass enclosed labs. "It looks like a cross between a computer geek's fantasy come true and a set for some major science fiction movie." Mitch walked along behind Conners and Alicia and looked in amazement at the rooms full of computers and high tech equipment.

"Well, what we do here is somewhat secret. I mean we are very concerned about industrial espionage and losing our edge in the development of some of the technology you see here," Conners said over his shoulder not really looking away from Alicia who now had her arm wrapped around his.

"OK, but I'm not working for some company," Mitch said, "I'm here to investigate two deaths and I need to know the basics of what goes on here."

"Yes, well of course," Conners said stopping and turning. He was looking at Mitch now. "We are in the recycling business." That was all he said and turned back to admire Mitch's new partner.

"Wait," Mitch said, "that's it. Just, we're in the recycling business. That doesn't tell me anything."

Conners turned to face Mitch again, "Precisely. I answered your question, though."

"Look smart guy," Mitch said, his temper beginning to flare which wouldn't be good for either of them. "What kind of bullshit double talk is that? I asked what goes on here and I get some chicken shit answer from a rental cop. Now, once again. What the hell goes on here?"

Conners glared at Mitch. They were almost the same height but Mitch was a bit taller. Conners' temper was almost at the same boiling point as Mitch's and he didn't appreciate some country bumpkin cop reading him the riot act, but he was able to control himself, for the moment. "No disrespect Deputy, but that is all we do here. We recycle everything and recover lots of useful chemicals and minerals from people's waste, which we then sell for a profit. I'm afraid I can't go into much detail, but I'm not up on all this high tech stuff. I couldn't explain much even if the company allowed me to. I'm sorry I seemed a bit curt but I really only know that this facility is one large recycling station."

"OK, sorry," Mitch said. The guy's apology seemed genuine enough, he thought but then again he looked like he wanted to get right into Mitch's face. That would be interesting, Mitch thought and leered at the back of Conners head as he resumed his macho act with Alicia. Mitch wondered if the guy's story was real or if the guy had been a professional liar all his life. The three of them continued to walk past a large transparent vat in the center of another lab surrounded by dozens of computers each manned by a technician in a white lab coat and hat.

Mitch paused for a moment and watched as a conveyor belt carried up an assortment of old electronics parts and circuit boards. At the top of the conveyor the junk electronics were dumped into the large vat and sank slowly into a thick blue colored gel. He glanced at Alicia and Conners as they continued to walk arm and arm down the hallway and hoped to be able to get a few more second's look at the vat and the lab or with any luck ask some of the lab guys a few questions. Just as he was about to check for a door he heard Conners call his name without even looking back.

"This way Deputy Stone, we're almost to the medical section."

Mitch looked at the machine and then noticed that the whole place was full of similar machines but each one had a different collection of junk being dumped into it. He saw one had plastic bottles and another had old metal appliances that looked to have been cut into foot square pieces.

"This way, Deputy," came Conners' voice which now didn't seem too friendly.

"Yeah, sure, sorry," Mitch said and hustled toward the door now being held open by an impatient looking Conners.

"I'm sorry we don't have time for a tour now,' he said with a hint of sarcasm, "perhaps some other time."

"Yes. I'd like to see more of what you call recycling," Mitch said.

"Then we will be happy to show you around then," Conners said, "but only if Ms. Carlsson comes along," he said smiling at her.

"Absolutely," she said smiling back.

"Yeah, sure," Mitch said trying to disguise the annoyed sound in his voice.

"This way then," Conners said leading them through the door marked 'Clinic'. "We have one of the best private clinics in the area and are able to handle most situations that an ER can and maybe even more."

"Then why do you have two dead employees, if your clinic is so wonderful?"

"Yes, well not even the best hospitals save everyone, Deputy," Conners said.

"So what happened here then?"

"Well, our physician thinks it was some exposure to some of the chemicals we use to facilitate the recycling process."

"What kind of chemicals?"

"I'm afraid I can't answer that, Deputy."

"Oh, more secret bullshit."

"No. Actually I really have no idea what some of these chemicals are, but I assure you that all regulations as to use and storage are closely maintained. These two seemed to have ignored the warnings, which I can say are well posted and they came into contact with some hazardous materials."

"A leak, maybe?" Mitch was fishing for some indication of what went on.

"No, no leak. We've checked every storage and disposal site on the island and everything is secure."

"So how did two of your employees get this exposure?"

"As I said I don't know, but I assure you we are investigating and we will find the answer. Meanwhile, our physician will preform the necessary inspections of the bodies and will sign the certificate which relieves you two of any further responsibility. It is my understanding that you are here only to tacitly report on the circumstances."

"Yes. That's right just a courtesy call, if you will," Mitch said smiling, but I'll make a brief report about what I have seen here today."

"Of course, and Ms. Carlsson will notify her superiors in the Coroner's Office that all is proper and official."

"Yes, I will be glad to report how efficient this whole thing is here," she said still smiling at Conners.

"Fine, now that we have all the preliminary small talk out of the way," Mitch said, "Can we see the bodies?"

"Yes, but I'm afraid there isn't much left," Conners said, "the chemicals have really done a job on them." He pulled back the sheet covering one of the corpses. The sight was horrific and Mitch forced a swallow of his stomach contents as he saw the withered and desiccated body of what Mitch could only guess was once a male employee of this strange company.

At the sight of the pale shape that resembled a large white prune, Alicia did a 180-degree turn and bent over. She wasn't quite as good at holding the contents of her stomach in their place and promptly heaved them all over the lab floor. "Oh my god," she gasped, and grabbed Mitch by the sleeve and pulled him down with her.

"Gees, what a mess. I don't really think I needed to see your puke this close."

"Listen you shit," she said and gagged again. "I need a sample of that guy, so get one from that mess will you?" she asked and coughed again. Conners asked, "you OK, Alicia?"

Kind of friendly, Mitch thought.

"Yeah, but," and she gagged again. Conners moved over to see if he could help. She pushed Mitch toward the table and the disintegrated body.

Mitch got the not so subtle message and moved toward the table as Conners bent over and held Alicia. Mitch couldn't hear what they were saying but the conversation was punctuated by coughs and moans and gags from Alicia.

Mitch looked furtively around the lab for something to collect a sample in. He noticed a small plastic bag on the counter behind the table and started to move around the body and noticed Alicia peeking at him between her legs. She nodded between coughs and heaved up some more of her last meal. Conners bent over farther to help and Mitch walked around the table and grabbed the bag and then moved back in front of the table in one quick movement. Alicia added some more to the puddle on the floor and Mitch wondered which smelled worse, her last meal or the dead guy, but he pulled out his lock blade knife and cut a piece of skin from the buttocks of the deceased and hoped no one would notice until they were safely off the site.

Not wanting to touch anything that had been in contact with a dried up dead guy Mitch carefully placed the piece of skin into the bag and then dropped in the knife. He sealed the bag as well as he could and placed it carefully in his back pocket not wanting to have the knife puncture the plastic. He'd have to be sure to wash both the knife and his hands before he touched anything important. He was finished and figured Alicia was about puked out. He cleared his throat and asked "you OK, now?"

"Yeah, fine, thanks," she said and smiled at Conners who had offered her a tissue. "Can we go now, I've seen just about all I care to?"

"Ah, yeah me too. Thanks, Mr. Conners. You're right, your physician can handle all of the paperwork. Just send me a copy of the reports when they're done."

"Of course and I'm sorry about, ah, Ms. Carlsson's reaction to the body."

"No problem," she said, "I just wasn't expecting that sight, that's all."

"I presume the other one is in the same condition," Mitch asked knowing what the answer would be.

"Yes, I'm afraid so," Conners said. "Would you like to see it too?"

"Sure," Mitch said enjoying the prospect of seeing Alicia lose it again.

"No," she exclaimed, "that's OK."

"No, then we've had, I mean seen enough. Thanks for your cooperation Conners. We can find our own way out."

"I'm afraid that would violate company policy and my own rules," Conners said. "This way please." He led the way back down the hallway.

Mitch bent over so he could speak to Alicia who it seemed was being ignored by Conners after her display in the medical lab. "Hey nice diversion," Mitch said.

"Obviously you didn't notice or weren't paying attention, but that was no act," she said with an angry scowl on her face. "Did you get the sample?"

"Yes, and I think we were on TV."

"Are you sure?" she asked suddenly concerned. "How do you know?"

"Well, when you were genuflecting, I caught a glimpse of a small video camera in the wall and that's why I waited until you started your stomach opera."

"You're a shit you know that," she said scornfully, "So did you get a good sample or not?"

"Yeah, I got a nice piece of the guy's ass, but I think someone saw me."

"Conners?"

"No, but whoever Conners has on a leash somewhere. That's why we need to move out of here and quickly. You all right now?"

"Yeah, and getting better all the time," she said as Conners' cell phone rang.

"That's for us," Mitch whispered to Alicia as they hurried past Conners who had stopped to answer the hand phone.

"Hey wait you two," Conners called after them and then spoke into the phone. "Yeah, what?! When? No shit. OK they're mine then," he said into the phone." Hey you two, stop I want to talk to you," Conners was now yelling at Mitch's and Alicia's backs as they sprinted toward the door and out across the front yard of the building to the A-H. Mitch grabbed the plastic bag with the sample and his knife inside and tossed it into the back seat of the car.

"Get in and buckle up," Mitch said as he leaped over the closed door and slid into the driver's seat. In nearly one movement he had started the car and as soon it turned over he had it in gear and was backing out of the spot.

"Hey stop," Conners yelled and spoke into his phone again.

Alicia was a step behind and opened the door just as the car started. She hopped in and grabbed the windscreen and the door at the same time just as the car started to move. She fought to shut the door just as Conners made a grab for it. Mitch managed to coax the A-H into kicking up some stones and dust on Conners as the car bit into the ground and sprang around the corner pointed at the main gate. Mitch glanced at Conners in the rear view mirror and saw that he was still talking on the phone. Probably to try and block our exit, he thought and shifted gears to move the A-H toward the gate a little faster.

Just as Mitch had thought, Conners had managed to contact the guard and now the gate was down in an attempt to block their escape.

"Hold on," Mitch said nonchalantly to Alicia, "and keep your head down."

"You're not thinking what I think you're thinking," she exclaimed.

"If you're thinking about dinner on my boat later with a nice bottle of wine, than yes I am thinking the same thing."

"No, not that, about the gate."

"Oh, that," he said, "yeah well I think this car will fit under the arm."

"You think," she said peeking up over the dash.

"Yeah, I think," Mitch said and shifted the A-H into one lower gear. The engine revved and the car leapt at the obstruction and just like in the movies the guard who thought he would stand in the way, had to jump out of the way just in time. The A-H went under the gate and except for the top inch of the window frame cleared the obstruction. The thud caused Alicia to let out a scream and then look back at the broken gate arm.

"Think we'll be invited back?"

"Not very likely now," she said trying to ignore the attempt at humor.

"Shit," Mitch said.

"What now?" Alicia asked showing that worried tone in her voice.

"That's going to be expensive," Mitch said pointing to the dent in the window frame near the top edge.

"That's all you're worried about. A dent in your precious car. We could have been killed," she screamed at him.

"We wouldn't have been killed on that," he said assuringly, "but I think your admirer and his friends may be trying for another chance," he said pointing over his shoulder and looking into the dash mounted rear view mirror. She looked back and let out a gasp as she saw a big S.U.V. pullout of the gate and follow them at a high rate of speed.

"I think we made them angry. Maybe you should have told Conners you would go out on a date with him."

"I did," she said emphatically.

Mitch took his eyes off the road and gave her an incredulous look. "What?"

"Never mind that just watch the road," she said in a tone of voice that sounded like an order. "This old fossil can out run that truck, can't it?"

"Ah, probably not on a straight road, but then not all the roads in this part of the world are straight."

"Good," she said, "let's get moving then," and she reached into her bag and pulled out a small automatic pistol.

"I do hope you have a permit for that."

"Nope just a badge like you," she replied and held the pistol like she had lots of practice with it.

"Walther?"

"Huh."

"Walther PPK, it looks like."

"Oh, yeah. The punch of a 9mm but smaller."

"Yeah. Would you mind getting mine out of the box please?"

"Sure," she said and opened the glove box and let out another gasp. "It's a big one isn't it."

"Yeah," he said and reached over the pulled out the Smith & Wesson .45 auto.

"Promise you won't tell Gary I have this gun. He still believes I only like wheel guns. He'd never let me live it down if he knew I had an automatic."

"Why is it that guys always go for the big ones?" she asked smiling and adjusting her open shirt over the white swimsuit.

"It's a guy thing, I guess," he said and put the pistol between his legs.

"Ooh," she murmured and smiled.

"Ah, yeah, well we need to focus on our friends back there and try to get back to the office and get that sample checked."

"No need," she said looking back at the rapidly approaching truck.

"What?"

"No need. Just get me back to my boat. I have a complete lab set up on board."

"No shit," Mitch said.

"Nope. Just get us there in one piece."

"OK, hold tight."

She did and Mitch dropped one gear again and as the engine revved, he made a sharp left turn. The A-H whined and the tires squealed at the sudden stresses but the A-H made the near 90 degree turn, while the S.U.V. didn't. Alicia watched out over the trunk as the large truck just couldn't maneuver and the driver jumped on the brakes to halt the two tons of inertia. The truck's tires let out a horrendous sound as they took the brunt of all of the energy of the vehicle decelerating in a short period of time.

"Are they going to follow us?" she asked.

"Probably but this is the little harbor next to Smyth's Cove and there are a lot of cottages and marinas in town. They won't try any rough stuff but I don't want to let them get close enough to test that theory before we can get some help."

"What are we going to do, then?"

"Just wait and watch," he said and with that he turned the car sharply again and pulled into a parking lot and darted behind another S.U.V. "Good thing these land barges are everywhere," he said as he pushed himself up out of the seat just far enough to peer over the door of the truck between them and the road. Mitch looked through the truck's windows and waited for a few moments and just as he expected the S.U.V. driven by the unfriendlies drove slowly past the lot and down the road.

"Are they stopping?" she asked.

"No, but my guess is they'll be back, if they think we can't out run them."

"What now then?" she said growing impatient.

"Well for one thing we need some help and you need to make a phone call."

"No, I don't."

"Yes you do and you need to make it right now," he said insistently and took out his wallet and fished out a business card. "Here. Call this guy right now and tell him to bring his special car and meet me. Tell him I told you to call."

"OK, but who?"

Mitch cut her off. "Just do it. OK?"

"What are you going to do?" she asked.

"I'm going to keep the car running and watch for your boyfriend and his buddies. If they show, I'll flash my badge or something. Now move."

She looked at him for a moment and then reached for the door to get out. "I don't have any change for the phone."

"Tell the owner I sent you. His name is Jack Hanson. Gary and I solved a burglary here last year and recovered most of his property. He's always willing to help us out. Now get going."

"Yes sir," she said a little indignant at his sudden show of authority. She ran into the side door of the bar which was called the Mariner and felt as if she had stepped into what looked like a collection form every old sea movie that had ever been made. She asked for Hanson and explained her story and as Mitch had said he was more that happy to assist an old friend like Mitch. Hanson let her use his office phone and told her if she needed anything else to just let him know. She thanked him and ran back out to Mitch in the A-H just as the S.U.V. drove past the bar again.

"Shit," she yelled at Mitch, "I think they saw me."

"Yeah, no shit, get in. Did you get through on the call?"

"Yep."

"And?"

"And, the guy said he was on his way."

"Good. I hope his timing is right." Just as Mitch said that the S.U.V. pulled into the lot and stopped in the entrance way. Conners got out of the passenger side in front and two other guys got out, one from the driver's side and one from the rear. The driver was wearing a uniform like the all the other guards but the other guy was wearing a jacket and tie like Conners. Mitch guessed that he was the one who had been watching the TV.

Mitch started to put the A-H in gear just as Conners rounded the parked truck next to them. He walked up to the driver's door and leaned over to talk to Mitch.

"It seems that you left in such a hurry we didn't say goodbye," he said and looked at Alicia, "and by the way it seems that you may have inadvertently picked up something that belongs to us."

Mitch looked over at Alicia who just shrugged and had a blank innocent 'who me' look on her face.

"I don't think so," Mitch said.

"I do," Conners said now trying to sound intimidating.

Good, Mitch thought, maybe he'll do something stupid and I'll get to play bad cop with the guy. Mitch didn't have to wait long to play the tough cop all over Conners.

"Well I don't," Mitch repeated. "Now why don't you take your want-a-be rent-a-cops and go back to your island playground before something bad happens to all of you out here in the real world."

"Look you local…" Conners started to say as he grabbed for Mitch's shirt. Mitch saw it coming and quickly opened his door and pushed as hard as he could shoving it into Conners' knee caps. With that Conners collapsed onto the gravel parking lot and clutched both his knees. Mitch jumped out of the car and pointed the big .45 at the uniform and Alicia aimed her PPK at the other jacket. Both men stopped where they were and didn't move. Mitch walked over to

Conners and bent over to say something so no one else could hear. "Look shithead, I may be a local cop but you're in my local. Next time you talk to me or one of my fellow officers, it's 'sir' and don't even think about touching one of us. Got it!" Mitch said in a low voice but placed emphasis on the last part.

"Yeah sure," Conners said still shaking off the pain in his knees. Mitch stood and noticed that the cavalry had just arrived.

"Hi Mitch," the huge police officer said as he unfolded himself from the car that he seemed to be wearing instead of driving. "Got a frantic call from some woman said you might need my attention."

"It wasn't frantic," Alicia chimed in, "it just had a sense of urgency that's all."

"Yeah, well," Mitch replied, "we seem to have had a small misunderstanding with some of the rent-a-cops from the island and I was just coming to an agreement with Mr. Conners here. Right Mr. Conners?"

"Yeah, right, no problem here," he said and suddenly remembered Mitch's last words and added "sir."

"That's good Mr. Conners. I see we understand each other now," Mitch said smiling as Conners got to his feet and limped back to his vehicle.

"This won't be our last meeting," Conners snarled, "and next time I suspect my cavalry will arrive first. Good day Mr. Stone and to you as well Ms. Carlsson." And with that parting statement showing his contempt for Mitch, Conners slowly climbed into his truck and it pulled out of the lot recklessly enough to force the street traffic to stop suddenly.

"Want me to chase him down and give him one of my special invitations to court?" the local officer asked Mitch.

"No let him go, but thanks anyway."

"So what was that all about?"

"We just came from the main lab on Society Island and we found two rather strange looking corpses. He seemed to take offense at the fact that we borrowed a sample from one of the stiffs."

"Is that all? Hell, I thought you got caught with his wife or something."

"If you two big deal lawmen are through I'd like to get back and examine that sample, if you don't mind too much."

"Oh. I am sorry," Mitch said, "Alex Brady this is Alicia Carlsson. She's with the CDC and is here doing some kind of investigation that she hasn't told me about yet. And Alicia, this is Alex Brady. He's the local Police Department here in the harbor and he's about the only cop in the county even larger than me."

"How nice for the both of you," she said, "nice to meet you Mr. Brady, but can we please hurry it up."

"Same here," Alex said and reached out and engulfed her hand in his. He shook her hand and her whole body moved. "Anything else I can do for you Mitch? I need to get back home. I've in-laws over."

"No thanks, Alex. I appreciate your help as always."

"No problem," he said and he folded himself back into his car. "Oh, and Mitch if you need some help leaning on those island types, let me know. The locals around here keep calling me with all kinds of weird complaints and they all want to blame those people who bought up Society Island."

"Oh yeah, what kind of complaints. I haven't heard any at the office," Mitch said as he stepped closer to the car.

"No, the locals are kind of funny about it and they wouldn't call your office and sound like weirdos. They'd rather call me at all hours."

"So what are they calling about?" Mitch asked bending down to look into the car's window at Alex and to keep their voices low.

"Well," Alex began in a low tone of voice, "it seems the company that bought the island started going around to everybody's place in town and told them they were in the recycling business."

"Yeah that's what we know about the operation," Mitch said.

"Yeah, that's what they tell everybody and that's what is one of the weird things."

"What's so weird about a company actually trying to recycle trash? Sounds like a good program to me," Mitch said.

"Yeah me too but…" Alex hesitated for a moment and looked around in a gesture like he thought somebody was listening.

"Yeah what?" Mitch prompted and bent closer to the door in a reflex motion to Alex's gaze around the parking lot.

"At first they went door to door to solicit business for the recycling operation. It all seemed innocent enough and the only ones complaining then were the regular trash haulers. They made noise but nobody listened and even the Town Counsel jumped on the band wagon. They saw an easy out of the landfill problem. They figured just let somebody else recycle or do whatever with the trash and garbage."

"Sounds good to me. Where's the problem?" Mitch asked.

"Well almost everyone in town signs on as customers to have their stuff recycled or whatever. I mean this company wants to recycle everything they can get their hands on. Garbage, trash, all of it. Even old appliances and junk. At first they came around and picked up truck loads of junk and trash and carted it all off to their island there. They were hauling stuff around the clock."

"So, no problems that I can see yet," Mitch piped in.

"Yeah that was at first. Then about two months ago they stopped hauling the stuff away."

"What happened they go out of business?"

"No, I don't think so but that's when the calls started."

"Like what?"

"Like one guy from out on the old highway told me they were able to take care of all his old cars."

"No shit, how?" Mitch asked.

"Don't know but that's where it starts getting weird."

"Why?"

"The guy says yes and they leave. The next day all his old cars are gone along with everything else he had thrown away."

"I'm still not seeing anything weird in that," Mitch said.

"I didn't either until the guy says he never heard or saw a truck of any kind come and get the stuff. I mean he had six or eight old junk cars and a pile of stuff that would need a dump truck to haul away and he says he never saw or heard a thing."

"Maybe they came at night."

"Yeah, maybe, but no one else has seen any trucks in a month or so and for that matter anybody ever collecting any trash or junk, but it all seems to just disappear."

"How the hell does that happen?"

"That's part of what's weird but for a while nobody complained. They were just wondering out loud how it was happening."

"OK," Mitch replied, "so where do the complaints come in?"

"Like I said all the junk and stuff in town just disappears almost overnight with no sign of any collection efforts. Then about a couple of weeks ago maybe three, I get a call from old Mrs. Conroy over on the other side of the harbor there. She's kind of eccentric but still a nice lady. She keeps cats and a couple of dogs as pets and I've been out there a few times to talk to her about the animals. Seems they get into the neighbors' trash and then I get complaints. I go and talk to her about it and she keeps them at home for a while but, you know how it is."

"Yeah, she lets the animals out and they have a mind of their own. But I still don't see a problem. Sounds to me like typical small town police work."

"Yeah, I thought so too until she called me and complained about someone stealing or even killing her animals. Seems they were out one night and never came back."

"So maybe they just ran away."

"Yeah, I told her that, but she insisted the animals wouldn't go very far especially the older ones, so I asked a few of the neighbors if they had seen any of the animals."

"One of them take care of the problem, maybe?"

"That's what she thought and I kind of agreed until one of her neighbors said they saw the dog in their trash. She was going to call but decided to let it slide."

"What's the big deal then?"

"The neighbor said she started for the phone and it rang. She answered it and talked for about five minutes and when she went to see if the dog was still there she saw the can was empty and the dog was gone."

"Problem solved then," said Mitch.

"Maybe, but she said the can was empty. I mean everything. Paper, plastic, bones, everything. Dogs only eat the food scraps and leave the rest spread all over the lawn. She says the can was completely empty except for a kind of powder or something."

"What about the dog?"

"Well she wondered what happened and why the full can was now an empty can and she followed the footprints of the dog until it disappeared."

"It, you mean them, the footprints right?"

"No, I mean it, the dog. She said the prints were in the soft dirt and just stopped. No more prints and no more dog. Nothing except she said the prints had the same powder in them that she noticed in the can."

Mitch just stood there and thought about what Alex had just told him and what Alicia had told him earlier.

"I'm sorry man, " Alex continued, "I know it sounds like everybody down here is way around the bend but this isn't just our small town way of fighting the boredom."

"Yeah, I know," Mitch said trying to calm his friend.

"That's probably why no one has called your office or the State in on this," Alex said a little embarrassed at his story. "The folks down here just don't want to be labeled as nut cases or even worse have the news vultures get wind of it."

"Anything else, old buddy?"

"Well, yes I guess. At first I thought the dog disappearing bullshit was just that. I figured it was a coverup for the fact that the neighbor really just shot and buried the mutt. Until the other calls started coming in."

"Like what or shouldn't I ask."

"You shouldn't but I'll tell you anyway," Alex started but was interrupted by a blast from the horn of the A-H.

"Hey you guys, I've got work to do and I think it's a little more important that your local troubles. Let's go Mitch."

"Yeah, hold on."

"Gee, she seems nice," Alex said sardonically, "maybe you should marry her or something."

"Or something," Mitch sneered. "So what else do you have on this recycling company. You started to say."

"Not much on them only nobody ever sees any pickups any more and all of them tell me about this powder in their yards or cans. Everywhere they leave the trash the next day it's gone and all that's left is this powder stuff."

"Got any of it?"

"Thought you might ask," Alex said and handed Mitch a small plastic bag with about a half inch of light grey powder in the bottom. "You know what it might be?" he asked as Mitch looked over the contents of the bag. "Be careful, you may not want to touch the stuff. It could be dangerous."

"Yeah, I'll check it out," Mitch said, "but it seems everybody in town has been in contact with this stuff and except for the dog story have you heard of any problems with this?"

"None that I know of. The only illness that I know of in town recently is Billy Weber. He lives over near the causeway on the mainland side. Got really sick a few weeks ago and now he's down in University Hospital being treated for a mineral deficiency."

"So?"

"So he's ten years old and I heard he has only about 10 percent of the normal amount of calcium in his bones. He can't stand and seems to be dissolving away."

"Dissolving."

"That's what I heard."

"Birth defect?" Mitch asked to rule out that possibility.

"Nope. He was an all star in the Little League last year and now he can't even lift a ball. It's like he's got the world's worst case of that old folk bone disease."

"Osteoporosis."

"Yeah, that's the one."

"Any idea how he got so bad?" Mitch asked.

"None. I saw him riding his bike about a week before they carried what's left of him to the ambulance. Seems whatever it is, took only a few days to do the job."

"Thanks, Alex," Mitch said tapping his hand on the car door. "Oh, just one more thing. Billy wouldn't have been playing near the island by any chance would he?"

"Don't know for sure, but living that close and being a kid, probably. Why?"

"Just wondering, that's all. Thanks again, I'd better get the Federal princess to her lab before she calls in the army or something."

"OK, Mitch, let me know what turns up on that stuff. Maybe your girlfriend there can have a look at it if she has the time."

"Sure, and thanks again for your assistance with our friends."

"No problem, see you around," Alex said and backed his patrol car out of the lot and into the empty street. Mitch waved at his friend just as the A-H's horn sounded again.

"Hey, anytime. I'd like to examine this sample before it gets any older. I need to do my job you know."

"So do I and for your information my job is just as, if not more important, since it deals with the daily lives of a lot of nice people," Mitch said as he handed her the second plastic bag.

"OK, I'm sorry," she said still frustrated at the delay, "What's this?" she asked looking at the bag of powder.

"If what you have told me is even half true and from what Alex just told me while I was doing my job, my guess is that is what's left of a family dog."

"No shit," she said giving the bag a squeeze.

"And while we're comparing the relative importance of our respective jobs just what is it that you do, and why are you giving me so much shit?"

"It's…"

Mitch cut her off by raising his hand like he was directing traffic. "Don't even begin to give me any of that secret government crap. I've worked with government types before and seem to get nicely involved in all kinds of shit with no idea what the underlying problem is. I want the straight story the first time or you're on your own and I'll recommend that our department refuse to extend any further courtesy until we get some answers. And before you make your decision just remember you do need me in on this. I just may have found your science link to the island of trash out there."

She sat back in her seat and didn't say anything and didn't even look at him for a long moment. "It's a matter of national…"

He cut her off again, "Uh, uh, what did I just tell you?"

"If you'd let me finish," she hissed back at him. "As I was going to say, it is a matter of national security and you must swear never to discuss the details with anyone except me. Understand?"

"Yes, so what is it?"

"First of all I didn't tell you all about myself."

"No surprises there, go on," he said.

"Can we get back to my boat now we'll talk on the way."

"Oh, yeah sure," he said and gave the A-H some gas. The deep throaty sound was music to his ears and once the oil pressure peaked he couldn't resist the urge to give the car some gas and rev the engine. He let it idle down and pushed in the clutch and slid the gear lever into the first position. The A-H pulled smoothly out of the parking lot and down the road. Mitch worked through the gears and was back cruising with an attractive although cranky woman in the passenger seat. Her hair was flowing out behind her and she pulled it into a ponytail before she started giving Mitch the details of the national security matter that he now seemed to have found himself in the middle of. Mitch didn't push the car on the trip back. He wanted to have lots of time to hear the story from Alicia. It took her a minute before she started and once she did it didn't stop for most of the ride except for the questions Mitch interjected.

"So tell me about this engineer guy. What's his connection with all this?"

"Like I said. We, the FBI and the CDC, have been investigating some strange occurrences around the country."

"Like?"

"Like whole buildings disappearing off the face of the planet. Not falling down, not blowing up. Disappearing. So far it has only been abandoned ones in some of the inner cities and nobody really pitched much of a fit. A lot of old eyesores vanished and the mayors just went on the news and told everybody that it was a new urban renewal project."

"Sounds OK. Doesn't it?"

"No, it doesn't," she said. "When you think about it, what's to say the next building that disappears won't be some office building or the Congress or even the White House."

"Oh."

"Yeah, oh, and that's where the FBI entered the picture. They were trying to find out how all these huge buildings just disappeared. All they ever found was some powder just like this. That's when I got the assignment. My job is to help them with the high tech science. As for the engineer geek, we had gotten close to him and were using him to get inside the Millennium facility in the Midwest. He woke up one day and had a sudden urge to clear his conscience and walked into our field office with this science fiction story. No one believed him until he predicted when and which old building would disappear. We were going to meet with him to get his notes and set him up to work with us when he goes off on a drinking binge one night. The next morning his wife reports him missing. She's in the bedroom vacuuming the floor when the police arrive."

"Don't tell me. She sucks up the dust from the bedroom floor and you guys think it's her husband."

"Yeah, that's about it. She doesn't know and officially the case is an open missing persons matter with the local police."

"OK, so you get the transfer from the CDC to the FBI. I'm sorry but I thought the Fibbies were just full of science whiz kids, why you?"

"As I said, I haven't told you everything about myself. When I said I was a molecular biologist I was a little misleading."

"News flash!" he shouted.

"You want to hear this or not?"

"OK, sorry couldn't resist."

"Try harder. Now as I was saying I'm not a molecular biologist. I'm nano-biologist."

"A none biologist?" he asked not sure of what he had heard.

"Nano. The science of life and mechanics on the atomic level."

"Lost me."

"Look we can manipulate our environment and that is one of the signs of intelligence," she paused and looked at him, "and in your case the only sign I suspect."

"Funny lady."

"Payback. Look we change our environment by shaping and forming chemicals on the molecular level. We make this car by using huge pieces of steel and then bending and cutting that steel into the shapes for this car. Then it is welded or bolted or in this case tied together. We build things in big chucks and after awhile when we're through with the stuff, we pull those things apart in big chunks. With me so far?"

"Yeah. We build things and take things apart in big pieces. OK, so?"

"So the rest of the physical and biological world doesn't do it that way. The rest of the world builds things and takes things apart one atom at a time. Take a cow for instance."

"Boy or girl?"

"Doesn't matter."

"Does to me and where am I going to take this cow?"

"Could you stay serious here for just once?"

"Sure go on," he said smiling.

"Thank you. Now take a cow, a girl cow. That cow eats grass all day every day yet produces milk and in some cases steaks. Grass gets turned into proteins in the form of meat and milk. How do you suppose that happens?"

"You're the scientist," he said trying to follow her explanation.

"It happens one atom at a time. The biology of the cow takes the atoms of the grass apart and recombines those atoms into protein and milk and bones and teeth and skin and…"

"OK, I get the picture. The cow builds things using atoms."

"Yes and so does every other organism on the planet. You, me, the dog everything works one atom at a time multiplied a million times or more but it happens that way every day."

"OK, now for this dumb old country cop, who got all his science from the B movies of the fifties, make the connection to why we're here being chased by trash collectors."

"What if somebody figured out how to duplicate the process on an industrial scale. You said that you think the stuff in this bag is what's left of a dog. What if you're right. What if someone, like the people on that island have figured out away to reverse the building process and can disassemble things one atom at a time. Pull out the hydrogen atoms and all the water disappears and you get dust."

"Just like your engineer guy."

"Just like him."

"OK, so what about those buildings? They don't have water holding them together," Mitch added.

"No, they don't, but what if the island folks there could make their nano-machines react to specific chemicals."

"Then you'd have the world's nastiest and least traceable weapon," Mitch said suddenly grasping the big picture.

"I think the problem just got very serious. If this is true and it gets into the hands of the wrong people."

"Sounds like, with this stuff, everybody's hands are the wrong hands."

"Terrorists."

"What?"

"Terrorists. They'd have the ultimate weapon of mass destruction. Just pick a target and it turns to dust."

"You think that's what happened to those two guards we saw today?" Mitch asked. "They didn't look like they turned to dust."

"I don't know maybe they got into the stuff by accident. Maybe they found a test batch or something."

"Yeah, or maybe they were handed the right stuff. Something to remove their bones and leave a trace for future reference or attitude adjustment for the rest of the employees."

"Calcium," she said in an inspiration.

"Huh?"

"Calcium. That's what bones are made of. If you take away the calcium, the bones dissolve."

"Like Billy."

"Who? What?"

"Billy Weber. Alex was telling me about this kid in town that looks like he has osteoporosis."

"That's a calcium deficiency disease."

"Yeah, just like our two dead guys."

"So how does this nano-machine stuff work and how does it get into people and trash and buildings?"

"I don't know yet but we need to get back to my lab on the boat, and quick."

"Yeah," Mitch said and pressed the accelerator a little closer to the floor.

CHAPTER 9

THE LOSS

AUGUST, 980 A.D.

The days all seemed to blend together and some of the passengers were becoming bored and anxious with the lack of activity and the monotony of the journey.

"How long until we reach our destination?" Lars asked Johhan.

"A few more days," Johhan said, "depending on the wind and the current of the sea. If the wind stays behind us, we should see land by the end of seven suns."

"Let us hope so for the sake of our passengers and our destiny," Lars said.

The small fleet continued on its journey pushed by the wind and the currents. Several more days passed and with each, the passengers became more and more restless. None of them ever expressed their concerns or frustrations directly to Lars or the crew but the mood of the group was understood by Lars and he wasn't happy about the mental state of his fellow travelers.

That evening things turned for the worse. A monstrous storm blew up from the southwest and engulfed the fleet. The waves, which only that morning had barely rippled the blue ocean, now rose and fell at the height of the mast. The tiny boats were bobbed about like corks and the terrified passengers were clutching their provisions and each other in panic. Lars was helping Johhan hold the rudder trying to keep the boat moving with the waves rather than across them. The sail had long since been ripped from the mast by the ferocious winds and now the only headway was at the mercy of the monstrous walls of water.

Lars and Johhan held on and desperately tried to save the ship and Lars could only hope that the other boats were being handled in a similar manner. Lars only held that thought for a moment as another wave lifted the boat by the stern and sent the poor soles sliding to the bow clutching desperately to their family members and meager possessions. The screams thankfully were drowned out by the roar of the water on all sides of the boat. The boat surfed along at the crest of the giant wave and Lars and Johhan held on for dear life. They only had a brief moment of rest before the next wave grabbed them and the harrowing ride began again. They stayed in the clutches of the terrible storm for what seemed like an eternity but unknown to them was in reality three days.

When the wind subsided and the ocean returned to the peaceful ripples, Lars and Johhan relinquished their death grips on the tiller and surveyed the damage and hopefully the survivors. They began a head count. As they worked their way forward Lars felt the heavy burden of responsibility and loss. Each step brought a new discovery of misery. One family had lost all of the children and the next only had the children left. At each position in the boat Lars found people missing or lashed to the deck dead. Of more than two hundred soles that left Anglica, only twenty-eight remained alive and of those only nine were healthy enough to assist the others. Lars stood and was flooded by sorrow at the sight of the broken and battered bodies and at the loss of more than 80 percent of his crew and passengers.

He set the able bodied to the task of caring for the injured and he returned to the stern and gazed out over the now placid ocean. He wasn't used to failure especially when lives were the price he had to pay. After a long moment of reflection and battling the guilt, Johhan stepped up to his side with the log book in his hand.

"Sir," started Johhan, "I fear we are in great peril unless we are able to reach land soon."

"Yes, I know. Where are we?"

"I won't be certain until we are able to see the stars tonight."

"Let me know when you have our position."

"Yes sir," Johhan said and left Lars to brood over his failure and the loss of so many lives. He was deep in his personal anguish when he heard a clamor from the bow and shouts that he couldn't believe. He heard the words the voices were saying but his brain wouldn't allow him in his grief to believe what the words were telling him.

"Land, there I see it, over there," one of the passengers was saying and pointing as he stood and leaned over the gunwale on the port side.

"Yes, I see it too," another called.

"We are saved, The gods have decided we should be blessed," cried another as even the weakest survivor struggled to see the sight of their salvation.

Lars stood for a moment and stared incredulously at the faint apparition of land just peeking over the horizon off the port bow. He smiled and raised his head skyward and thanked the gods. Once he had made peace with the divine masters he walked to the bow to join in the revelry at the prospect of being on dry solid ground again. He didn't labor on that wonderful thought long before his thoughts were turned to a more pragmatic matter. "Johhan," he called and the wise navigator appeared with his beloved log under his arm.

"Yes sir."

"We must head for that wonderful land of deliverance that our gods have provided for us, but I fear we are at the mercy of one of those gods who has already caused us so much pain and sorrow."

"Yes, sir, we are at drift in the sea and our sails have long since been stolen by the angry gods. I am afraid we will not make that landfall on our present course and without a sail we cannot alter that fact."

"Exactly what I was thinking. Can we delay our progress in the current for a while until we can fashion a new sail?"

"I suppose so, but how are we to craft a sail when most of our stores have been ravaged by the sea?"

"Wise Johhan, if you can impede our progress, I believe I can provide our craft with a means of propulsion. Just watch. With that Lars began to confer with the able-bodied survivors as Johhan pondered the proposal. After a few moments watching his leader move between the groups and families he set out to work on his aspect of the solution. Lars talked to every remaining member of the crew and passengers and all of them eagerly began to implement his plan. Even the injured wanted to help and some even refused the personal care by family members in order to free up the hands for Lars' plan.

Johhan was busily at work finishing up his end of the plan when Lars returned to the stern and took his place at the rudder. "Are we ready to make our headway and release ourselves from the grip of the currents?"

"My end is ready," declared Johhan, "but how are we going to replace a whole sail?"

"Well we can't replace a whole one but I can give us a half of one." Lars gave the signal to several of the remaining passengers who had the strength left and they hauled and strained at the lines and in a few minutes a patchwork sail was flying over the deck once more.

"Brilliant," exclaimed Johhan, "you used spare clothes and bedding to fashion a sail."

"Yes but I am afraid that the shapes of the garments leaves large gaps in our new sail and we only had enough material to make one to raise halfway up the mast."

"That will be better than nothing and as you can see we have not drifted much in the last few hours."

"Yes, you're right. I've been so involved with my part of the project I had forgotten about yours. How did you accomplish it?"

"I took several of the large trunks, opened them and tied a rope around the hinges. Then I just through them into the water and they drag along behind us catching the water in the top and bottom. They act like sea anchors and the water keeps them open. They are what's been keeping us in place."

"You are a genius, Johhan and you must enter that in your log. As the leader I even order it."

"Yes sir," Johhan said smiling, and the two men stood at the tiller and admired their handiwork.

"Your anchor seems to allow us more control over the direction with the reduced sail."

"Yes we may suffer a loss of speed but we are better able to maneuver."

"Good we will surely make the land now."

They watched the passengers turned crew tend to the new sail and ultimately to the injured and they watched the distant land grow larger and more inviting. It took several hours for the battered boat and the decimated passengers to reach the land and as they got close enough to see the beach and the individual trees they noticed they were at what they believed to be the head of a large bay and they could see the opposite shore now that they were closer.

"We seem to be blessed by providence after our ordeal at sea," Johhan said as the two men maneuvered the battered boat slowly into the embrace of the two shorelines.

"I do not see the back shore of this bay," Lars said straining to see the curve of land joining the two protruding shorelines. "Have we discovered a pair of islands instead of the new lands described in your book?" he asked Johhan who was also attempting to see a continuous shoreline connecting the two points of land they had sailed between.

"No sir. These are no islands, they are the opposite shores of a great river. Somewhere ahead we will find the source of the river and fresh water. See here, the water is changing color from the blue of the sea to a greenish brown. This is because the river water is mixing with the salt water. This is most fortunate sir. We will have an endless supply of fresh water and even food once we are farther up river and beyond this estuary. Here the water is fouled by the mixing of fresh and salt. We couldn't drink it and I don't know of many fish that would live in such a mixture. We would be better advised to proceed up river until we can find only freshwater."

"From the size of this opening that may be a long way off and our people are tired and suffer from many injuries. I can't ask them to stay aboard this boat in the face of dry land just a short distance away."

"That is true sir," Johhan said, "but we cannot be sure of our survival if we do not have a source of fresh water, and easy food and I believe it lies up river."

"Yes," Lars said and looked out at the two opposite shorelines now almost in line with the boat. He thought about what Johhan was saying but also held the concern for the injured. Most passengers needed rest and time to recover from their ordeal and the fresh water of the river could be many days ahead.

"Fellow Vikings," he said at last, "we have traveled a great distance and even though we have suffered the rages of the gods of the wind and the sea other gods have blessed us with being delivered to this land we see before us," he was interrupted by cheers and clapping hands. Even the injured were trying to rejoice. "Our expert navigator Johhan and I believe we are at the mouth of a great river and that it continues for a distance inland. We feel that there should be a good source of fresh water and ample food once we get past the estuary here, but I also know most of you are tired and those that are injured can't be expected to travel any farther."

"What are we to do then?" came a voice from a woman who was tending to her injured husband.

"I propose to land on the shore to the southeast and establish a base camp. I will take the boat up river and search for a suitable location for a permanent settlement. If I find one, I'll send back for the rest of you."

"You say you'll do this, but what about the rest of us?" came another voice.

"As I said, we'll set up a base camp and make sure it is provisioned with as much as possible from the ships' stores and from whatever we can scrounge from the land. I ask only for volunteers to join me on the search up river and must caution anyone who might want to join me that we will travel with minimum provisions."

"What about the other boats? Did they survive? How will they know where we are?" the first woman asked in rapid succession.

"Yes we need to hope that they are as fortunate as us and that they are following our path here but that is another reason we must set up a camp at the mouth of the river. Those who stay must set and maintain signal fires to serve as a beacon for our fellow travelers."

None of the passengers had any further comments or questions for their leader and all returned to their own tasks. Lars spoke to Johhan for a moment and the boat was turned slightly and the small sail was adjusted for the new direction of the wind. They were headed for land finally after so many days at sea.

"Recover the anchors," Lars told Johhan who went to the transom without delay and began the arduous task of pulling the open trunks against the drag of the water and the force of the boat's forward movement. He tugged at the line but only succeeded in making the flesh of his hand raw against the rope. "We must drop the sail if we are to retrieve the anchors," he cried to Lars at the tiller.

"Can't we just cut them loose?"

"No, we may need each and every piece of gear and material we can get our hands on to survive in this new found land." Lars ordered the sail to be lowered and went to help Johhan with the trunks made into sea anchors. After several long minutes and a lot of effort they managed to pull the trunks over the transom and onto the deck. Lars returned to the tiller and without saying anything his new crew had raised the sail again and they headed toward dry land.

It took several months after their landing before Lars and a few of the remaining healthy passengers set out to explore the mighty river. The able bodied, constructed shelters from the abundant trees on the new found land and the injured began to recover. A few died and were buried near the beach where they first set foot on land. One job became an obsession with the settlers. They never allowed the signal fire to die out. They kept it burning night and day with the hope that the others that started out with them would see the plumes of smoke or the glow at night and be able to find them. They would never know if anyone would ever follow their arrival to the new land.

By the last days of the summer of that year Lars and Johhan were ready to embark on the up river expedition. All during the summer the people had been so busy building shelters and searching for food and water that none of them paid any attention to the boat that had carried them across the sea and kept them alive in the fierce storm two months earlier. Lars was thankful for their unconscious over-sight. He had kept the trunks filled with the treasure the king had entrusted to him, safely on board and below deck. For the sea jour-ney most of the passengers ignored the numerous trunks believing them to be nothing more than ballast for the boat. Others thought they were the personal possessions of Lars and they gave deference to him as the leader. Now after nearly two months it seemed everyone had forgotten about the trunks stored below the wooden deck. Lars would leave them just where they were. The king had entrusted him with personal care over the treasure and Lars would continue to personally watch over those trunks filled with the gold, silver and jewels from the far corners of their old world.

It took several more days to prepare the boat for the trip up river. Along the gunwales the new but smaller crew had affixed wooden posts at regular intervals. They had been busy cutting and crafting long oars from the trunks of young trees and had fashioned enough to allow ten men to row if the wind failed to cooperate. Now they would use the posts as oar locks and they could row while standing. Finally, thirty six days after the celebration of the summer solstice, Lars and twelve of the most healthy men plus Johhan as the navigator and keeper of the log, set out from the small encampment and headed into the mouth of the river and alternatively rowed and relied on the newer and larger make shift sail. They rowed and sailed in a diagonal path to offset the effects of the current and made excellent headway.

"This river is still very wide," Johhan said to Lars.

"Yes, maybe we should continue for a few more days until it marrows. Then we can utilize both shores to catch fish and even expand our settlement once our numbers recover."

"Yes, I agree and maybe our fellow travelers will join us and we can share both banks of this great river."

The boat and its crew pressed farther up river for several more days until early one morning they rounded a bend in the river and beheld a magnificent sight.

"The gods have blessed us once again," Lars exclaimed in awe at the splendid scene unfolding before the boat as it cleared the bend in the river. There before the travelers turned explorers was still the wide river but now it was dotted with numerous islands of all sizes and shapes. Some were only small points of land in the green blue river and only managed to support a solitary tree. Some were larger than many of the towns in their old lands. Each was covered with trees and grass and now in the waning days of summer some of the lush greenery was dappled with the first colors of autumn.

Each man was overcome by the endless beauty of the scene before them and they now rowed with a renewed vigor. They continued up stream and with each passing hour counted more and more of the islands spread out across the broad river.

"How many so far?" Lars asked.

"More than all the people in Jorvik," Johhan said, "I think there may be ten times a hundred of these magnificent islands."

"Then we have found our new home," Lars said triumphantly.

"It is here and we will bring our families and build a new Viking land. We have found our heaven on earth."

"We have been blessed again by our gods," Johhan said, "Let's hope the others will find our encampment before we return. It would be wonderful if we all could live in such a beautiful place as this."

"Yes, indeed," Lars said in agreement.

The men rowed with new life inspired by the surroundings and the wishful thinking of a new life. They were speculating and exchanging their thoughts and fantasies about each one of them having a whole island of his own. They were rowing hard and Lars was at the tiller. He too was doing some day dreaming of the bright future that lie ahead. He was completely oblivious to where they were going but his concentration was focused not on steering the boat but rebuilding a Viking community.

Suddenly his attention was dragged back to the reality of the moment and the general euphoria of the afternoon was extinguished by the sudden jolt that brought the boat to a complete stop and knocked all the crew to the deck. Lars was bent double over the tiller when the boat halted its momentum and he let out a gasp of breath. As soon as he caught his breath again, he asked if everyone as all right. Unanimously they were all without injury but equally surprised by the sudden stop. They looked around and to their amazement they were several hundred feet from the nearest piece of land and all agreed that they were still in the middle of the river. A quick check with a weighted line proved otherwise. It seemed that the river was capable of deceit. Although it was beautiful on the surface, the tranquil waters disguised a dangerous spirit that had reared up and grabbed the boat. They had propelled themselves onto a shoal and the rocky bottom had torn a large hole in the hull of the wooden boat. Lars and Johhan restrained their panic but several of the crew began to voice their nervousness aloud.

The men were now on the horns of a dilemma. Even with the hole in the hull the boat was in no immediate danger of sinking as long as they stayed on the shoal. The worst that would happen was some water would leak into the hold. Lars didn't think the gold, silver, and other valuables would suffer much from the fresh water. His concern was now focused on the problem of extricating them from the shoal and keeping the boat afloat long enough to get it to shore. If they stayed on the shoal they might not lose the boat but they'd be trapped like flies in a web. Alive and aware of their plight but unable to do anything about it.

Lars paced at the stern of the boat and every time he stopped he heard the disquieting sound of water flowing into the area beneath his feet. The crew heard it too and soon were clamoring for him to do something and soon.

"Fellow Vikings," Lars began, "we seem to have run afoul of the gods again just as they have given us this wonderful new land. I must tell you now the rest of the story of our journey. Before we left our homes, the Chief entrusted me with a small portion of his treasury so that we could live comfortably and in the event we encountered any natives, we would be able to buy provisions for our community. My sense of duty led me to keep that treasure on board this boat."

The crew let out a unified gasp of amazement. Johhan was vigorously recording this precious bit of information in the log book. "We must now make some decisions regarding our immediate fate and our ultimate survival," Lars continued.

The crew talked among themselves for a time and Lars heard snippets of the conversations and wasn't too surprised when he heard the men's suggestions.

"Sir," one of them began, "couldn't we off load the treasure and make the boat lighter. We could then row to shore and make repairs and return for the treasure once we have a sound boat."

"Yes," Lars said, "that is what I have been considering as well but alas we are some distance from a convenient place to off load the cargo."

"Sir," Johhan chimed in, "we could just set it over the side here in the water. If we mark it somehow and carefully record the location using fixed points of reference on these opposite shorelines," he continued pointing to several rock out croppings and large trees, "we would have no trouble locating this place again and we could simply pull up the boxes one at a time and be on our way again."

Lars thought for a moment as the men gathered closer and the expressions on their faces seemed to indicate that they had made up his mind for him, Lars didn't have much of a choice nor much time to work out an alternative. "OK," he said after what seemed to be a very long time, "we will place the cargo over the side in shallow water. Johhan please make very accurate notations in your book about our exact location. This is the most important navigation you have done in your life."

"Yes sir," Johhan said as he was already diligently taking down the notes of the proceedings and making and recording his observations about their position.

"All right then, it is settled," Lars continued, "first we must devise a method so that we may easily spot our treasury in the water." Lars thought for another moment as he set the crew to the task of retrieving the cargo from below the wooden decking. Johhan was busy moving from one side of the boat to another and making notations in his log. He made his observations and notations then rechecked them several times to be absolutely certain he could find the exact spot again. Rather than site on trees he used only rocks and points of land figuring they would last longer than a tree that might get toppled in a storm.

The crew worked hastily and soon had all of the boxes and trunks loaded with the treasure of a Viking kingdom spread out on the deck. As suspected some of the boxes and trunks were wet from the river seeping into the hold but Lars didn't care at this point. The plan was to drop them over the side to save the boat.

He had devised a plan to locate the treasure even with the aid of Johhan's extensive notes. Lars had the men set the boxes and trunks onto the remains of the sail and when all of the cargo was brought up from below they began to lower it over the side. The first box was used as an anchor point. Lars had the men tie off a length of rope through the handles and around the large trunk. They gently eased it over the side and slowly lowered it to the bottom. Since the boat was aground, they knew the water was only as deep as the bottom of their hold and that was only half again the height of the tallest among them.

The heavy treasure chest settled on the bottom and the men threaded the free end of the line through the handles of the next box and pushed it over the side into the water. This one dropped quicker but the men used the line to control the decent. The rope acted like a brake around the box as it slid through the handles. It took some work but finally the last of the trunks was ready to be lowered over the side. Lars had the men wrap the last chest in the battered and ragged sail as a bright flag to locate the sunken treasury.

The men protested at the thought of losing the sail but Lars calmed them be reminding them that for most of the river trip they had been rowing and then he mentioned the fact that the current downstream would replace any aid the small sail had given them. They lowered the sail clad trunk over the side and set it down next to the others. Just before they released the line Lars had them tie a large loop in the end. "We'll be able to snag it with a grappling hook when we come back," He said and the men nodded in agreement and did as he said. They threw the rope in after the trunk and watched as the loop drifted slowly down out of sight.

What the men and Lars were not aware of, because they couldn't see the bottom, was that the trunks had passed through a layer of sediment and silt before settling on the rocky bottom. Each box was now sunk down into the soft material and was nearly covered. In addition each subsequent trunk had stirred up the bottom and when it settled again it further coated and obscured the trove of chests and boxes. Lars and his crew would never again see the treasure of Jorvik. In fact the treasure would remain hidden for nearly a millennium but it would be discovered long before Lars and his crew. The gods would abandon the Vikings one last time.

"OK men we must now find a way to save the boat and ourselves," Lars said as the rope disappeared in the green water. First of all gather all the cloth you can find and stuff it into the hole. We'll start bailing out the water once the inflow is slowed."

The men jumped to the task even before Lars had finished but fortune was not on their side. As soon as the additional weight of the cargo had been removed, the boat did become more buoyant and had floated free of the submerged rocks. None of them had noticed including Johhan who had been diligently logging the activities. Once the boat had floated free of the rocks it began to fill at a rapid pace. The rock had punctured the hull but had also acted as a cork and the water had been only seeping into the hold. Now with the stopper removed, water was gushing in.

Before the men could get organized and stuff the hole the hold had filled and the boat had drifted back into the main channel. Even a frenzied effort to stem the flow failed and soon the main deck was awash and the boat began to list to starboard. Lars was speechless as was the crew for a brief moment before the boat rolled on its side and then slid beneath the cold water. Lars and the men found themselves floundering about trying to grab onto anything that stayed floating. The two trunks Johhan had used so effectively as sea anchors now provided small rafts for several of them to hold onto. Some of them were beginning to panic. Although they lived on or near the water most of their lives, several of them couldn't swim and were struggling to stay above the surface. One had already gone under and not returned. A couple of his friends searched frantically to no avail. "Lars," Johhan gasped trying to hold his precious log out of the water and swim with one hand. "We are doomed."

"Yes, I'm afraid so. I have failed the men and women of our group and I have failed our Chief."

"You are not to blame but we are finished."

"Yes, we must try to make the far shore though. We might succeed yet," Lars said trying to regain his composure and boost the dashed spirits of the remaining men. "This way," he commanded and started to swim.

"Wait, wait," Johhan begged, "we must protect the log. Maybe we will make it and we'll need it to return to our treasure."

"Yes, of course," Lars said trying not to inhale any more water. "Put it inside one of these trunks. At least it will float and stay reasonably dry."

Johhan struggled to right the floating trunk and open the lid. He managed to accomplish the feat once Lars swam over to steady the trunk. Johhan placed the log book into the trunk and noticed a small amount of water in the bottom. He closed the lid again.

"There our record is safe. We can find our way again."

"Thank you for all you have done," Lars said. The two men looked at each other for a moment without saying anything then began to swim for shore. Some of the crew were helping the others who shouldn't swim well. They swam in silence to the shore and the unknown. Both Lars and Johhan knew cold weather was not far off and Lars was sure the others knew as well but weren't saying a word.

The trunk holding the log book floated for several days until it too filled with water and sank. It was however, closer to shore and settled into the soft bottom only twenty feet from shore in about eight feet of water. The cold and the sediment would protect the contents from decay for the next ten centuries. Lars and his small crew would soon starve and perish before the winter solstice. The Vikings at the encampment at the mouth of the river would die one by one through the winter and by spring only the shelters and a few possessions remained. The other Viking boats that survived the storm at sea would find land farther to the southeast and establish a colony that would last two years. Disease would take its toll and the survivors of that band would sail for home and tell of the hardships and losses. They would be heros. All ten of them would live and die as Vikings in their home country.

CHAPTER 10

THE CONSPIRACY

"This is totally unacceptable," the CEO said in a tone of voice evincing her anger and frustration at hearing the report from her security chief. Not only that but she had just been on a plane for the last three hours and was not happy about being called back to her office from a vacation trip to hear about a problem after only six months of operation. "What the hell am I paying you for?" she nearly screamed at Conners who merely stood there and passively listened to the tirade. "Our entire operation is now in jeopardy and it's all because of some goody-goody woman in a tight swimsuit. You said all your high-priced watchmen were completely stymied by one woman. What is the problem and what are you going to do about it?"

"Well ma'am, we have her under surveillance along with that local cop that butted in."

"Yes, and that's another thing. Now we have the police involved," she said starting to build her rage again.

"Not a problem. He's only local and as far as we can tell has no clue to what she is doing here and in fact seems to want no part of her or her operation."

"Let's hope that is the case for your sake," she said regaining some composure. "We must keep him and his department out of this matter and we must see that she does not discover the true nature of what we have started on this island."

"Ah."

"Ah, what," the CEO said nearly biting Conners' head off.

"Well both of them were on the island today."

"What?" she said now completely livid at the news.

"Yes, we had an accident with two of our guards."

"Yeah, I heard, so?"

"So we called the locals to report the deaths. Standard ops."

"OK, continue."

"So this local from the boat incident shows up and has her in the car with him. She gives me this bullshit that she's with the Coroner's Office but I can't very well call her on it with the cop right there."

"Go on," she said coldly.

"So I give them the quick look at the bodies and they leave."

"I sense you're not giving me all the good news."

"No. They took a sample from one of the bodies."

"Shit. I can't believe I am actually paying for this level of incompetence. Find her and the sample, take care of the problem. Fast. We can't let the true nature of this operation get out until everything is ready for deployment."

"What exactly is that, Ms. Landry?" Conners asked knowing what her answer would be.

"That is not your concern. It shouldn't hinder you doing your job whether you know what our goals are or not. Just see that no one else knows either."

"Yes ma'am," he said, "how far am I allowed to go to protect this secret?"

"Do whatever you have to do. Use our field resources. I believe you already know how to use them," she said, "just so that nothing comes back on the company. Is that clear, Mr. Conners?"

"Perfectly," he said and headed for the door.

"No one must know," she repeated after him.

"Understood," was all he said and left. "Bitch," he said under his breath as he closed the door.

"Moron," she said as the door closed. She waited for a few seconds. "He's gone you may come out now," she called out to the empty office. A panel in the wall slid to one side and several people entered the room including the V.P. of Operations.

"You're the site manager, how in the hell did all this happen?"

"It started this morning when this woman approached the island. We sent out patrols to stop her and search her boat to find out who she's working for."

"And?"

"And we were interrupted."

"By the local cop Conners mentioned?" she answered for him.

"Yes. Then a couple of the guards involved started to talk about rumors they heard around here and Conners used some of the company assets to fix the problem."

"Yeah, great job. Seems he invited more trouble. That's when the local and our mystery girl got access to the facility?"

"Yes," he said sheepishly.

"Then they need to be removed from the equation, don't they?"

"Yes ma'am," the V.P said.

The rest of the people in the office began to talk among themselves. They were wearing outfits that were more reminiscent of a flower child convention in San Francisco rather than a meeting in a corporate board room.

"This Mr. Conners seems to be difficult to control," one of the new age hippies said.

"Yes, are we sure we can trust him? He seems too uptight and not at peace with himself," another one said.

"Look I don't care if he's so uptight he cracks, he has his orders and he'll carry them out," the CEO said, "besides we need to get a handle on this mess before it bites us in the ass."

"We aren't cool with the prospect of people getting hurt to protect our movement," the first neo-hippie said.

Mary Landry had worked for these "60's" leftovers for several years and in fact whole heartedly embraced their concept and long terms goals. Especially when she figured she had an inside tract to be one of the chosen few to survive their plans. When they had contacted her with their proposal she at first thought they were all suffering from some chemical induced dilution, but after several meetings and months of research she began to like the proposal and finally with the inducement of an unlimited budget, she joined their cause. They set up one of the most advanced bioengineering laboratories in the world in an abandoned recreation camp on an island in the eastern end of Lake Ontario. They also had several other smaller labs located throughout the country but this one was the largest and until this morning the most secret.

She had managed to recruit the world's top bio and mechanical engineers to work on the project, that the hippies called the Malthusian Prophesy. She had to look up what they meant by Malthusian though. Seems that in the 18th century a clergyman wrote an essay claiming that the earth could only support so many people and that eventually an equilibrium would be reached between the resources of the planet and the population. If the population increased at a rate faster than the resources, then war, famine, and disease would enter the equation and reduce the population back to the equilibrium. Mary Landry didn't fully understand at the time what that had to do with the hippies and the state of the art lab but they paid well and let her run the operation.

Now these leftovers from Woodstock were questioning her decisions. "Listen, you long-haired freaks. You hired me to run this operation for you and to get the job done. Now that I know what it is you're planning to do, I don't want to hear any whining about hurting people. It seems a bit hypocritical of you to worry about a few people getting hurt when your plans call for the elimination of six billion people to fulfill your Malthusian Prophecy as you call it. You flower children want to turn everybody on the face of the planet to dust along with everything ever built. I just better be one of the blessed hundred thousand left, that's all."

"Yes, but that's for the advancement of mankind as a species friendly to the world. What you're advocating is murder," the first hippie said.

Mary laughed at that last remark. "If you kill off billions it is for a good cause, but if you kill a few to keep it a secret you call it murder and you can't handle it. It is all the same folks and I'm just protecting your investment. Just remember our arrangement. I'm to be one of the chosen few, right?"

There was a pause and no one said anything. "Yes, of course Mary, we will honor our commitment to you."

"Good, just see that you do. And in case you have any lapses in memory just remember what happened to those two guards today. You all might not like the next glass of fruit juice you drink or herbal tea or whatever."

"We will not be threatened like that."

"No, well think about what happened to your bio-engineer hippie buddy in Texas."

"He's been listed as missing," said one of the old hippies. "You had something to do with that?"

"We did a field trial of your blue gel. It seems to work as you have expected. It will act on a chemical specific basis and can be programmed for a specific amount. Seems your loud mouth friend was only about one hundred and sixty-five pounds of atoms when he 'disappeared'. Fortunately we conducted the field test before he was able to compromise our plans by talking to the Feds."

There was a murmur of conversation between the small band of new age radicals. "You used the NANOs on him?"

"Yes and quite effectively I might say. You people have invented a nice little doomsday device."

"All right, Ms. Landry, it's not a doomsday device and we won't quibble over semantics between your problem solving and murder, and we assure you again that you will be one of the remaining hundred thousand after we deploy a full scale release of the NANOs."

"And my methods to protect our operation?"

"We agree that the project should be protected," the spokesman paused and looked back at his associates, "by any means you deem appropriate."

"At all cost," she said rather than asked.

After another moment's hesitation the spokesman replied, "Yes."

"Good. I'm glad we understand each other. Thank you for your continued support," she said callously. "Now let's get back to the business at hand."

The small band moved around the table and each one took a seat. "Shall we begin?" Landry said.

"Yes," they replied.

"First of all, I'd like to report on the progress of our devices in Europe and Asia."

"You have deployed the devices already?" the apparent spokesman said in amazement mirrored by his associates. "We were under the understanding that only research and development would be permitted. You were not supposed to deploy until the time and place we all agreed on."

Now Landry was getting really angry at the spinelessness of her benefactors, but she fought to maintain her composure. "Yes, that was the initial understanding but I took the liberty to extend the development to a few field tests. We needed to know if the devices could perform in an uncontrolled environment. I had no intention of usurping the authority of this committee."

"I see," the spokesman said and the others nodded in agreement, "we are just concerned that any full scale deployment would alter our time table. We must prepare our regional and local committees for the moment of equilibrium. They must take precautions against the devices. Our project must survive the release and that release will be on the autumnal equinox. Is that clear Ms. Landry?"

"Yes, perfectly clear," she said. She detested being admonished by these people.

"Good then," the spokesman said, "we are back on track then. It is absolutely imperative that our projections and schedules are strictly adhered to. Our computer model shows that the human race can be self sustaining in an agrarian society or by hunting and gathering with a world wide population of one hundred thousand. We have carefully calculated this number and it is one that can live in harmony and balance with nature and not place any stress on the planet's ecosystems."

"Just remember that I am one of the chosen hundred thousand."

"Yes, of course," the spokesman said, "as we assured you earlier you and most of your staff here at the lab will be included in the final group. We need to be certain that the devices deactivate as designed after the shift to the natural equilibrium."

"Of course," she repeated in the same flat tone of voice, "and as long as we're discussing our mutual understandings let's discuss mine. Your people, the committee, and your followers believe the human race should be reduced to one hundred thousand to be in balance with nature."

"Right," they all said.

"OK, what if there are more or fewer survivors that number?"

"Then there will be no balance. We would have to reduce the excess population or encourage growth to maintain the point of equilibrium."

"You advocate murder to cull the herd so to speak?" she asked.

"Not murder as an act of violence but a sacrifice for the good of the whole," one of the others said.

"Good," she said, "we all have to make sacrifices."

"Of course," the spokesman said. "Now what about the precautions against the termination devices?"

"We have been working on that simultaneously with the chemical selective units," she said. "We have developed a prototype that can be programmed as HK units that will neutralize any of the termination devices."

"HK?" one of the committee asked.

"HK, hunter killer, like our submarines looking for enemy subs to destroy. Same principle only much smaller of course."

"Oh," they all said in unison.

"How will these HKs be used to protect our project members?" the spokesman asked.

"Just before the final deployment your people will be given an injection of the HKs in a saline solution. The HKs will only be programmed for the termination units and will not react with any other chemicals or minerals. None of your people will ever know they are there until after the Autumnal Equinox."

"How will they know then?" one of the committee asked.

"Because they will still be alive," Landry replied coldly.

"Oh," was all the member said.

"Now what about the infrastructure, the buildings, all the technology?"

"Well that is what our field tests were going to tell us," Landry said with an ingenuous smile. "We were working on a deployment method that would be target specific."

"Our project calls for the complete elimination of all technology and infrastructures. There is to be nothing except what can be made from nature."

"That's part of the problem we were working on," Landry shot back. "Just because it doesn't happen to be growing at the moment you need it doesn't mean the atoms aren't the same. A wooden house is still made of trees and our nano-machines can't be that selective. If you program for cellulose, they will go after houses, trees, paper, anything made from wood. You wouldn't want the entire planet to dissolve would you?"

"No but," the spokesman started.

"No but, nothing. That's why we were working on the field tests. We were trying to make the nano-machines target selective and allow us to reduce a building to its basic elements and then have the devices self destruct as it were."

"How are they going to do that?" they all asked again.

"Obviously your computer model didn't project this contingency. If we had universal deployment of unlimited NANOs, the whole planet would be reduced to dust in six years and 294 days. Your Malthusian utopia would disintegrate under your feet. Now we can't have that," she said rhetorically, "and I suggest that you retract your statement about the field tests."

"I'm sorry, I, ah, we didn't know," the spokesman said contritely.

"Good. Now we have an understanding," Landry said flexing her authority. "Since we only have 135 days until your scheduled deployment date I suggest you return to your communes or whatever and make your final arrangements. The lab will distribute the HK serum on September 1 in plenty of time for you to send it out to all your members."

"Very good Ms. Landry," the spokesman said, now showing his support of her methods. "You have done well. Carry on."

"I will," she said smiling again. "I will."

"Then we are finished, " the spokesman said and they all rose and headed for the door. "We assume you have everything under control and we won't interrupt you again," he said as they filed from the room.

"Thanks for your endorsement," she said as they all left and the door closed. As soon as the door shut, Landry pressed a button near her desk and a man walked in from another door. "Did you hear that drivel from those middle-aged flower children?"

"Every word," the man said.

"What about Conners," she asked.

"He's a loose cannon and should be cut from our list," the man said.

"I agree, but not yet," she countered, "we need him to tie up the loose ends and then we'll use him for one of our field tests. I think the calcium NANOs would suit him well, don't you?"

"Yes, he used them on those two guards. It would be a fitting coincidence."

"How are the field tests proceeding?" she asked now focusing on her own agenda.

"We have launched chemical specific nano machines in Asia and Europe and parts of Africa. The machines have multiple programs and have succeeded in destroying the crops of several populous countries. The beleaguered governments are blaming drought for the crop failures but the new generation NANOs are multi phased units. First they convert any free water molecules to its base elements. Then the NANOs reprogram themselves and attack the plants and reduce them to piles of carbon. We have shown great success in keeping the NANOs active only against plants and not seeking out humans, yet."

"Very good," she said, "I never thought those hippie freaks had a very good idea about reducing the human population down to a subsistence level."

"I agree," the man said, "why do that when we can control segments of the population and ultimately countries. It is much more profitable to sell the use of the NANOs."

"Or have the governments pay for the privilege of not being a target of the devices," she said smiling. "Malthus was right though, equilibrium will be reached between humans and resources. Like the old saying, everybody has their price." They both laughed at that comment.

"Yeah," the man said, "about $10,000 per head I figure." They laughed again.

"Good then we are on schedule. We'll deploy on September 1 and our first targets will be those new age nuts. We'll use the calcium NANOs in their 'protection' serum. They'll piss themselves with excitement," she said with a snide chuckle. "Now what about our infrastructure field tests here?" she asked.

"We have one scheduled in forty-eight hours. We are testing a multi phased unit that will seek out calcium which is one of the key elements in the calcium carbonate of the cement, and iron as the base element in the steel."

"Sounds lethal," she said.

"It will be to the dam and power project at the Seaway locks. The NANOs will reduce the cement to calcium and then attack the steel superstructure and reduce the entire facility to a few thousand pounds of wet powder."

"Are we testing the self limiting features as well?"

"Yes, after the NANOs recycle one hundred thousand tons of material they will stop and the dam should be sufficiently eroded to be useless. The seaway will stop functioning and we will use it as an example of our power when we are ready for full deployment."

"How will the NANOs be disbursed?" she asked.

"We have programmed them to be chemical specific as I said and we will release them from a small boat that will be sent down river to the locks. Once within a few hundred yards we'll release the NANOs and the river current will carry them into and through the dam. They'll know what to do then," he said.

"Good, very good," Landry said. "How will the self destruct mechanism know when to stop them if there are so many of them?"

"As I said, we programmed the hoard for one hundred thousand tons of material and we will release a couple of billion, but we've thrown in a few billion extra just in case some of them get lost in the currents. Each one is programmed to stop functioning after it processes thirty-two ounces of material either, calcium in the cement, or steel in the support structures."

"Billions of devices. Won't you need a large ship to carry them all to the site?" she asked still not completely understanding the science involved in her plot.

"No, not really," he said, "as you're aware we have been developing new technology. Until our successful tests on the crops in Asia and Africa and some other more isolated experiments like a few old buildings and a couple of problems, humans have only been able to build or dismantle things in chunks if you will."

"OK, that part I follow," she said as she walked over the large window in her office and looked out over the blue green lake and watched the dozens of pleasure boats plying about in the harbor across from her island. "And what about the stragglers? What do they do?" she asked not overly concerned.

"They wander around the river currents and find lunch wherever and whenever. A fish, a dock, a swimmer."

"I see, now tell me how these little things can be so destructive," she said continuing the conversation. She really wanted to understand how something supposedly microscopic could cause so much damage.

"OK," he said continuing, "we as humans have only been able to manipulate our world in pieces. I'll admit in the past twenty years those pieces have gotten smaller and smaller but pieces none the less. These pieces are made up of thousands even millions of atoms. We merely cut, mold, form these big chunks of atoms into more convenient shapes like tools, cars, buildings, whatever."

"That I know, so what are we doing then?"

"We have discovered the holy grail of materials science. We can now make things the exact same way our bodies and every other creature on earth does. We can build things one atom at a time."

"Huh," she said a little confused. "I knew our project was working on ultra-small machines but you're saying atoms."

"Yes, that's right," he continued. "We have developed a series of atomic sized machines that can duplicate biological construction techniques."

"OK, fill me in," she said, "but keep it simple."

"I'll try," he said, "now as I said, every biological creature, us included, takes in material, food, and processes it one atom at a time and transforms that food material into bones, blood, brain cells, skin, whatever."

"So far so good," she said nodding.

"Take a cow for example. It eats grass. Grass is for the most part water and carbon atoms attached to each other in a certain pattern. The cow eats the grass and through a process, which we have duplicated, turns that grass into among other things a steak. We in our primitive ways wait for the cow to change the grass into protein and then go in and hack off a big piece and call it dinner."

"Then our bodies do the same thing with the meat," she said forming an understanding of the new science her company was developing.

"That's right," he said, "every living creature or plant does this each and every day of its life and does it one atom at a time. We have now emulated this with our nano-machines. They are ultra-small devices which can be programmed by a computer to seek out a particular atom, say carbon, and either stack the atoms together in a preset pattern or as in our filed test cases, take those atoms apart from each other."

"Like disassembling a puzzle one piece at a time," she interjected.

"Exactly," he replied, proud of his explanation. "Now these machines are only about one hundred or so atoms in size themselves and therefore, to answer your question, we can fit billions of them in a space the size of a few quart jars. It won't be any problem delivering the necessary quantities of NANOs to the dam. In fact we have them all programmed and ready to go and waiting in about twenty plastic jugs the size of a gas can."

"Gas cans?" she uttered in amazement.

"Yes, it's made of plastic and not on the NANOs diet today. All we need to do is dump them out in front of the dam and leave. They'll have lunch and then shutdown."

"You said the machines can be programmed to build things too?"

"Yes we just set up the atomic matrix and provide the raw materials and a pattern of the shape we desire and set them loose in a tank of a suspension medium."

"A what medium?"

"A suspension medium. We found water works well. They just need some way to work in three dimensions."

"Oh," she said.

"Then we just wait and out comes whatever we programmed."

"Like what?"

"Like those water glasses over there on the table."

"They're glass, so what?" she said unimpressed.

"Not exactly. They are made of carbon in one of its more valuable forms. We recycled the carbon out of some of the garbage we have collected from around here."

"You mean," she said, her eyes growing wide as she hefted one of the sparkling glasses.

"Yes, those are diamond water glasses each weighing about two hundred carats."

"My god think of what we could do if we just made diamonds."

"Relax. Diamonds are just carbon and the only thing that makes them valuable is the fact that the diamond merchants regulate the supply to force up the prices. We've been making diamond everything for almost a year now. Most of the windows in the lab are diamond. Better transparency than silicon-based glass."

"No kidding," she said awed by the revelation. "What else can we make?"

"Everything and our front business is providing us with an endless supply of raw materials and the people are even paying us to haul it away as well." They laughed.

"Amazing," she said, "I didn't have any idea as to the potential. What kind of time frame are we looking at after the machines are released at the dam?"

"The canisters have a timing devise on them and will be set for between five and twenty minutes after release in the water. We want our people to get clear in the event the NANOs go after the steel in their boats' engines. After that the dam and locks will be sufficiently compromised and begin to leak in about six hours from release. Within twelve hours we expect complete failure and the river and lake will begin to drop. We expect NANO termination between twelve and eighteen hours after release."

"Excellent," she said, "Then we'll commence with the notification of the world governments and present them with the price list of their assets. What's a dam worth these days?"

"About ten billion dollars or so," he said smiling.

"Ten billion to prevent the next one from turning into atomic dust particles. Very good," she said, "you've done a remarkable job. You were the perfect choice as director of the project."

"Thank you," he said, "will that be all?"

"No, not quite. Here's a list of some people I'd like to see…" she hesitated to search for the right words. "I'd like to see recycled."

"Very well," he said taking the list and reading it over. "These are the members of the committee."

"Yes that's right. They did say I should take every necessary step to protect the project."

"Yes they did," he said smiling and turned to leave the room. He stopped at the door before opening it. "What about Conners?"

"Ah, yes, him. Tell him to take care of that local matter and give him whatever assistance you deem appropriate from your lab."

"Understood," he said with a sly smile.

"And once the problem is resolved to your satisfaction then treat Mr. Conners and his associates to one of those NANO cocktails of yours."

"Certainly," he said and left the room.

Landry stood for a moment then walked over to the table and picked up one of the diamond drinking glasses and returned to her desk. She held the glass up to the light and watched the spectrum of colors in the facets of the huge diamond. She thought for a long time about what to do with all the money she was about to extract from the world governments when she could have diamonds the size of footballs made as easily as dinner from a cookbook. No matter, she thought with money would come power and that couldn't be made even by her machines. She'd get the power by not using them. She smiled at her diamond drinking glass.

CHAPTER 11

THE SEARCH

This weekend had turned to shit, Mitch thought as he set out the dinnerware on the small fold out table in the middle of the main cabin of his new sailboat. By day it was part of the sofa, by evening it was his dinning room table and at night it could be reconfigured to form a double bed for any guests that might be on an overnighter. That made him think about the fact that he hadn't had anybody spend the night on this double bed let alone his almost queen sized bed in the aft cabin. All this nice new room and no one to share it with. Oh well, he thought it was peaceful and it had been his dream for a very long time.

He set the table for himself and then, went around the counter to the galley and started to cook his meal. The doctor had told him to drop a few pounds and the sheriff had made a point to mention that his uniform was getting a little tight. The heck with the uniform, he thought, they always made larger sizes. The uniform was one thing but he was beginning to get out of breath even with basic daily exertions. His SCUBA diving would really suffer this year and that could be dangerous to both him and Gary. The harrowing experience under the ice a couple of winters ago had convinced him to drop a few pounds and eat better in the process. He'd been trying to eat more vegetables and fruits and tonight's meal was a tasty low calorie stir fry.

He cut up the bunch of broccoli into two-inch pieces and started them boiling in a small pan of water. While the broccoli boiled, he opened a can of his only vice and took a long drink of beer. Some things would never change, he said to himself as he tested the broccoli with a fork. A few more minutes, he thought. While he waited, he cut up a couple of cloves of garlic into slices and poured a couple of tablespoons of olive oil into a frying pan. When the oil was just getting hot, he added the garlic and some sliced red pepper and started to cook the tasty veggies in the pan. He drained the broccoli after one more test with the fork and added it to the browned garlic and peppers. A dash of salt wouldn't kill him, he said to himself as he sprinkled in the sea salt. He stirred the mix until all the broccoli was covered by the oil and garlic and cooked it for another minute. There he said to himself, a nice quick meal and reasonably healthy too. He finished the first can of beer and reached into his real electric refrigerator for another. He was just getting ready to sit down at the table when her voice pierced his solitude.

"Hey that smells good. Got enough for two," she said coming down the steps into the cabin. "You did say something about dinner as I recall when we were fleeing for our lives."

"Stress of the moment," he said and looked up without taking a bite. She had changed shirts and was now wearing a loose-fitting T-shirt with the emblem of the FBI across the left breast. He couldn't tell what she had on underneath and guessed she had ditched the tight white swimsuit. "Don't you FBI types knock?" he asked as she appeared in his home.

"Nice to see you too," she quipped, "and no, not unless we have a warrant."

"Funny," he said and tried to compose himself, "yes I do have enough for two if you'd like some but I don't suspect that's what brings you to my boat unannounced."

"Not really, but thanks for the dinner invitation though. It does smell good. What is it?" she asked reaching out to pick a piece of broccoli from his plate and popping it into her mouth.

"Hey."

"Mmm, this is good, did you make it?"

"No, my personal servant did. Who do you think made it and I'll get you your own dish?" he said and got up and moved back to the galley to get her a dish of his culinary creation.

"I didn't know you could cook," she said somewhat amazed at the revelation.

"Quite well actually," he said, "but I don't suppose that's what brings you here now, is it?"

"No, but I'm lucky I made it for dinner."

"Would you like beer or wine?" he asked as he set the plate down in front of her. He noticed she had taken a spot next to where his dinner was instead of across the table.

"White wine would be nice," she said smiling. Mitch opened the small refrigerator and pulled out a chilled bottle of domestic champagne. She let out a startled squeal when he popped the cork.

"Oh, my, a champagne dinner on a sailboat. How…interesting."

"Yes. So what brings you here?" he asked in as much of a business tone of voice as he could muster.

"Well if you insist on talking business."

"I do."

"OK, I've been analyzing that sample you got from the lab since we got back and I'm really puzzled."

"Oh," he said feigning disbelief.

She ignored his mock surprise. "Yes and that's what I want to talk to you about. You took the sample from the dead guy right?"

"You were there. I cut a piece of him off his ass."

"That's what I thought."

"So what's the deal? What did he die of?"

"He didn't exactly die. He dissolved."

"What are you talking about? He was laid out as dead as I've ever seen."

"Yes, well technically he died but not in the ceasing of his bodily functions."

"OK, now in English for us nonscientific cop types," he said taking a bit of his dinner and a swallow of his beer. She followed his actions with a bite of her own and a sip of wine. "Very nice," she said, "my compliments to the chef."

"The dead guy, how did the die?"

"Yeah, like I said he didn't die in the strictest sense of the word he just dissolved away."

"What kind of shit is that?"

"He wasn't, but he was close. He was nothing more than a pile of elements in a sack of goo."

"Not a very nice thing to say but then aren't we all?"

"Yeah but we are put together in a specific way. In normal people both living and dead those elements are put together into shapes and organs like bones and blood. This guy has no shape at all except for the uniform he was wearing. He is just a pile of chemicals like wet sand at the beach."

"I'm lost," Mitch said taking another bite and washing it down with the remains of his beer. "I thought we were looking for things turning to dust. He didn't look very dusty to me. Oh, can I get you some more?" he asked as he got up for another beer.

"You shouldn't drink so much, it's not good for your performance."

"What performance?"

"Never mind," she said, "and yes I'd like some more. Anyway all I found was some crystals of calcium and some carbon dust once I dried out the sample. If I didn't know better I'd say all his atoms just let loose and he fell apart. I think whoever runs the show over there can change the way these nano-machines process things. Sometimes they work one way sometimes another"

"So how do these things do what they do?"

"I have no clue other than what I told you earlier today. Either this guy got digested by something big enough to swallow him or somebody has figured out how to build and program a whole batch of different nano machines."

"Any other ways to dissolve a person down to atoms?"

"Sure but it would take a lot of energy or heat."

"Like an atom bomb?"

"Yeah, but he wasn't cooked, he just came unglued. And besides an atom bomb isn't exactly a personal weapon," she said finishing her meal.

"So how do we find out how this guy died and make the connection between him, the buildings, the dog and the islanders?"

"I sent some of what's left of the guy to Atlanta for them to look over, but I'm not hoping for much from their end."

"I know how we can find out what happened," Mitch said working on his third beer.

"How?"

"Go back and look around some more."

"Are you crazy?" she blurted out. "Didn't you see how pissed off that Conners was at you? I don't think he'll be very happy or friendly if we go back."

"I just love a challenge," Mitch said and leaned back in his seat.

"So do I," she said and reached over and kissed him.

Mitch did find out what was under the T-shirt. In fact she wasn't wearing anything and to his surprise she was wearing underwear so small he called it butt floss. Between interruptions they discussed their crazy scheme to revisit the island and get answers to the mystery of the disintegrating man.

"What would you like for breakfast?" Mitch asked as he rolled over and got out of bed.

"Just toast and coffee," she said into the pillow.

He slipped on a pair of shorts and headed for the galley. "No coffee, just tea, OK?"

"Fine," she said as she sat up in bed holding the sheet over her bare breasts.

"I must say I would not have believed that I would spend the night with you."

"Oh," he said from the galley.

"Yeah, we just don't seem to get along that well."

"We did last night."

"Funny," she said and appeared in the doorway wearing only her T-shirt. Mitch assumed that was all she was wearing.

"We do make a very good team."

"As long as we work together," he reminded her.

"When are we going to try to get to that lab?"

"How about tonight," he said placing the toast on a plate and handing her a cup of hot Earl Grey tea.

"I thought I'd get breakfast in bed."

"You're not in bed," he said.

"I could be," she said smiling. The tea and toast were cold when she finally ate it and Mitch was on deck when she got dressed.

"What's up now?" she asked.

"We're going for a sail just like a nice normal couple and then tonight we'll try to get onto that island. How are you at diving?"

"Done it a couple of times, why?"

"That's how we get on the island. In the mean time while I get the boat ready to go, why don't you get whatever you need for the day and later tonight. Dark clothes for our little adventure."

"OK, I'll be right back."

Mitch finished preparing the boat for a nice day of sailing. He untied the small lines holding the boom. He checked to make sure all the lines and halyards were free of knots and ran unencumbered through their guides. Just as he was stowing the sail bags Alicia appeared on the end of the dock. This time she had on very tight nylon bike shorts and a microscopic bikini top that didn't leave much to Mitch's imagination.

"A little risque, aren't we?" he asked staring at the tiny piece of cloth.

"Not for a normal day on the water just cruising around. Wait 'till you see the bottoms."

"I'm sure," he said still admiring the new view. "What about later?"

"Oh yeah, I have a black one piece I think you'll like."

"Probably, are we ready to go?"

"Just tell me what you want me to do."

"That'll be a first."

"Smart ass."

Mitch piloted the boat out of the harbor and into the main part of the lake and set the sails for a port tack. He planned to sail back and forth and gradually work the boat close to the island and wait until dark and slip the boat quietly close to shore. He had never tried to sail at night but there was a first time for everything.

They spent most of the day just sailing and relaxing. For the most part Alicia was on the foredeck showing off her assets in the micro bikini. A couple of times they worked their way down to the main cabin while the boat drifted. At dinner Mitch prepared a salad from spinach, onions, garlic and bean sprouts.

After dinner Alicia pulled Mitch into the aft cabin and they killed an hour before darkness set in. While she changed into something more practical for the night's activities, Mitch was back at the helm trying to bring the boat close to the island.

"Kill all the lights," he whispered to Alicia through the open port hole. The boat went dark and when she appeared back on deck in her black swimsuit, Mitch could only see her outline against the darkening sky.

"Nice suit, I think," he said, "as soon as I set the anchor we'll head in."

"OK, I'll get the gear ready."

"All taken care of," he whispered.

"Very efficient," she whispered back.

"You OK with this?" he asked as she started to get into the diving gear.

"Yeah fine, I've just never done this at night, that's all."

"Just relax and make sure you hold tight to the rope."

"Can't I hold your hand instead?" she said.

"Of course. I didn't have time to get you a wet suit so the water will be a little cold."

"No problem as long as we don't waste any time getting to shore," she said and tested her mouth piece for air flow. Mitch finished getting his gear and stepped through the opening in the transom and sat on the swim platform. As soon as he put his feet in the water he let out a gasp. "Shit this is cold. We'll have to move quickly."

"OK, so let's go already," she said impatiently.

Mitch hit the inflate valve on his vest and let a little air from the tank into the flotation vest. He slid into the fifty-degree water. "Damn," he gasped bobbing in the cold water.

"Baby," she said as she sat on the platform and repeated his actions. She slid off into the water and gasped too. "Damn," she said.

"Baby," he replied.

"Next time let's get the wet suits before we try this."

"Yeah, you ready?"

"No, but let's do it and fast," she said. With that they adjusted their masks and bit down on the mouth pieces. Each took a breath and gave the OK signal with their hands. They both released the air from the vests and dropped beneath the surface. The blackness enveloped them and Mitch reached out to find Alicia's hand. She was frantically moving it back and forth in the inky blackness and when she felt Mitch's hand she grabbed hard. They didn't want to risk detection so neither of them had lights but Mitch had an illuminated compass and he set off toward the island leading Alicia by the hand.

They swam quickly in the direction shown by Mitch's compass. They didn't want to stay in the frigid water any longer than necessary. Finally as the chill of the water was beginning to get uncomfortable, the bottom began to rise up and Mitch felt the bottom in front of him with his outstretched hand. He guided Alicia's hand to the rocky bottom and she let go of his hand and pulled herself up the slopping bank until her head popped up out of the water. She quickly looked to the right and spotted Mitch who now was standing on the bottom and removing his fins so he could walk better along the rocky bottom. She stopped and did the same and both of them maneuvered over the rocks and up onto the beach. They sat for a moment and got out of their gear and stashed it behind a large rock near the waterline.

"What next?" she asked in the hushed voice. "You think they saw us?"

"Not sure, to the first question," he whispered back looking around to try and see anything, "and I don't think so," to your second question.

"Wrong again Deputy Stone," the familiar voice said in a condescending tone as the flashlights were trained on the two intruders. "Seems you've made several mistakes tonight Deputy Stone," Conners said with a sarcastic emphasis on the title of Deputy.

"Mr. Conners," Mitch said mocking Conners' tone of voice, "what an unexpected surprise."

"Yes. I'm sure it is," Conners replied. "OK, bring them to the Director's Office," he ordered to his men who promptly grabbed Alicia and Mitch. Mitch tried to pull away from the grasp of one of the guards but was met with a baton to the stomach which caused him to clutch his middle section and drop to his knees on the sharp rocks.

"You bastard," Alicia exclaimed and struggled to get free from her escort to assist Mitch but to no avail.

Several of the guards shown their lights onto Mitch as he tried to catch the wind that had been knocked out of him. Conners strutted over to the doubled over Mitch and bent down and spoke in a barely audible voice. "Now, Deputy, we are even for our little discussion in the parking lot yesterday, Oh, and by the way you're in my locale now and my cavalry has arrived and well, yours is nowhere in sight."

"Don't count on that shitbag," Mitch said between breaths. Conners didn't respond to Mitch's remarks except to snap his fingers. At that signal Mitch was grabbed again but he didn't resist this time. He was half dragged half carried over the rocks and through the woods. Alicia was trying to kick her guards and struggled with them every step of the way until they were brought to a large office and ordered to sit in two uncomfortable metal folding chairs in front of a large wooden desk.

Mitch was regaining his posture but the pain in his abdomen from the jab from the night stick was making sitting difficult at the moment. Alicia was at regular intervals trying to stand and being pushed back down by her two guards. "Relax," Mitch said to her finally, "save your energy. Let's find out what these scumbags want."

"I agree," came the voice, "except for the scumbag part."

"Who are you? I've met the security department already," Mitch said sitting a little straighter.

"I am the Director of Operations here at this facility. My actual title is Vice President but I'm sure that means nothing to you."

"I'm sure," said Mitch.

"As for what we're doing here, we are just a business conducting lawful research."

"Yeah, but it is the unlawful application of that research that we're interested in," Alicia said.

"I thought we were looking for the reason two of their people ended up looking like prunes," Mitch said.

"Yeah and the disappearance of a lot of crops and buildings. I told you about the buildings, Mitch but I also think these shitballs are involved in the disappearance of crops as well. I think they are trying to cause world wide famine but I can't figure out the reason for all the infrastructure disappearances," she said to Mitch hoping the new face in front of them would help her fill in the blanks.

"You didn't say anything about any crops before."

"We weren't sure there was a connection. We thought it was some kind of disease but we couldn't pin it down. One farmer's fields would be totally destroyed and his neighbor's would be perfectly fine. When we investigated all we ever found was normal soil. Now I think the crops were converted back into their base elements. Isn't that right Mr.?..."

"It's Dr. Brandon Lindquist, and yes that's correct, Ms. . "

"Carlsson," she said.

"Carlsson. And who is this?" Lindquist asked Conners.

"This is Mitch Stone. Oh I am sorry, Deputy Stone. He's with the local sheriff's department."

"A little far from ticketing people for parking, aren't we Deputy?" Lindquist said.

Mitch ignored the remark and Lindquist returned his attention to Alicia and her observations.

"You're very well versed on our process, Ms. Carlsson."

"Thanks," she said, "but I don't get it, what's the big plan for all this technology? Is this what you call the Malthusian Prophecy? Sounds more like a plot to me."

"The what?" Mitch asked now completely lost in the conversation.

"Very clever, Ms. Carlsson, I suspect you know nothing more than that and any other information about our plans died with that informant before you could get to him."

"Are you two talking about the dust guy?"

"Yeah," she said, "now we know these guys had something to do with his death but I still can't figure what this Malthusian Prophecy is all about."

"I think I know," said Mitch, "they plan on controlling the world's population according to the writings of Thomas Malthus."

"Very good Deputy Stone."

"Yeah, how did you figure that one?" she asked.

"I read and I have a history degree."

"Well that was the original plan of some very strange and misguided individuals who saw themselves as the founding fathers and mothers of a new world utopia. They had the crazy idea that the world would be better off with only one hundred thousand of their hand-picked followers as occupants."

"And that is the Malthusian Prophecy?" she asked.

"Yes, but the plans have changed somewhat."

"Sounds like a conspiracy to just take over the world to me," Mitch said.

"Call it whatever you want Deputy," Lindquist said, "but the plans have changed. We are less concerned about controlling the populations with our technology and we certainly do not want to establish a new world of tree huggers and environmental nuts."

"No of course not. I'll bet you guys want to resort to good old fashion extortion and blackmail. Develop the ultimate destructive weapon and charge people not to use it."

"Deputy, straight to the point. We much prefer that over the use of the devices. It's better that way as long as they pay we keep our machines in the lab."

"Blackmail," Mitch said.

"Terrorists," Alicia said.

"No," Lindquist snapped, "not terror, just business."

"So what happens to us now that we have been let in on your little secret conspiracy?"

"Well, our secret will stay that way?"

CHAPTER 12

THE RESCUE

"**M**y people know that I'm here. They will be looking for me" Alicia exclaimed. "And Mitch too. He's a cop and they just don't disappear without a lot of questions."

"That's right," Mitch said.

"First of all," Lindquist started, "I don't think Ms. Carlsson's people even know she's here. If they did, they'd have been here long before now. I think they have no clue about our operation and as for Deputy Stone here well disappear is the right word. Your office will look for you and unfortunately they will never find even the slightest trace."

"Remember no body, no crime. Isn't that right Deputy?" Conners said enjoying the turn of events.

"What did he mean by that," he asked Alicia?

"I think we are going to get a first hand look at their process."

"Very good Ms. Carlsson, you two will be one in a series of field tests for our new technology. Don't forget that we are in the recycling business."

"And we're going to be recycled."

"Very good Deputy Stone. Who said cops were dumb?" Lindquist asked.

"Yeah, well a little slow on the uptake, but…"

"A little slow?" he was interrupted by Conners.

"That will be all for now Mr. Conners. Please wait outside with your people. I don't think they will cause much harm. It doesn't appear they are armed," he said referring to them in their swimsuits. "I'll buzz if I need you."

"But," Conners started to say.

"That will be all Conners," Mitch repeated.

Conners gave out a snarl and threw Mitch a glare but didn't say anything else. He motioned to the four guards to follow and they all exited the office. Once the door shut Mitch stood and Alicia followed.

"Remember Deputy, Conners and his men are just outside."

"Relax, Lindquist. Just stretching my legs. Now as we were discussing. It seems that no one is going to give a shit about some crops or old buildings. In fact you probably did the building owners a favor. What's going to make a government pay you any money much less even answer your phone calls?"

"Funny you should ask that, Deputy. You're absolutely correct. No one would even give us the time of day if we made a threat and used the wheat fields as an example. We had something more impressive in mind to get the proper attention."

"What would that be if you don't mind saying?" Alicia asked. "You going to destroy the White House or something?"

"No, not the White House," Mitch said. "If they did that, they would have played their high hand and no one would give in after that. Their plans work only if they maintain the threat."

"Exactly Deputy. We need to keep certain targets in our sights even though we don't really want to destroy them."

"OK, so what's a high profile target that isn't at the top of the list?" Alicia asked again.

"Aside from the fairly remote nature of this island, we chose it as the location of our facility because of the proximity to a large and visible public works project."

"The international bridge?" she said a little puzzled.

"No, Alicia, I don't think he's talking about the bridge. My guess is the power dam and locks farther down the river."

"Very good Deputy Stone. Now you may go to the head of the class."

"But why that?" she aked.

"Because it controls our fourth coast and most of the food exports from the Midwest. Plus the power plant supplies most of the Northeastern U.S. power grid. A lot of people will notice for a long time."

"Very good again, Deputy. Conners would never believe you had it in you."

"Yeah, OK, so you plan to destroy the dam and the locks. By the time you're even half done the Feds and everybody else will be all over you. It'll take months if not years to dismantle that site."

"I don't think so Mitch," Alicia said, "the crops and buildings disappeared in less than an hour."

"No shit?" he said in amazement. "Care to explain that Lindquist?"

"Since you two won't be able to do anything about it, of course. Our new technology involves nano-machines."

"So we figured," Alicia said.

"Very good Ms. Carlsson, you two seem to have all the answers."

"Not really," Mitch said, "how do you deliver these nano whatevers to the target?"

"We have several methods but the most obvious for the buildings and the crops is a spray. We just cover the target with a vapor and the machines go to work."

"And now you're going to destroy something that affects tens of millions of people," she stated.

"Yes, and to answer your next question, it will happen in about ninety minutes."

"How? You going to spray the whole dam? It does have a security force of its own you know."

"Deputy such an obvious question. You can't possibly hope to thwart our plans."

"No, I guess not. Just curious then."

"Of course not, and we are aware of the security people. No, this time we have sent several containers of NANOs programmed for the components of the dam, down river. They will arrive at the dam in about an hour or so and then they will be released into the water by timers on each container twenty minutes after that."

"Your mother must be very proud," Alicia said but Lindquist ignored the remark.

"One more thing before we have to go," Mitch said.

"Yes?"

"Ah, you've got a nice collection of old books here. Where did you get them?"

"He's going to destroy a huge dam in ninety minutes and you're interested in some old books? I don't believe this," she said incredulously.

"Now, Ms. Carlsson. Indulged the man in his last moments."

Mitch turned and winked at her as Lindquist moved from behind the desk to the shelves and display case holding a particularly interesting volume. "This is my most prized book," he said proudly.

"Yeah, what is it?" Mitch asked trying to stall for time.

"It seems to be a log book from an ancient Viking ship. As near as I can translate it, the Vikings managed to cross the Atlantic and work their way down into the river here and quite a way upstream."

"No kidding," Mitch said and looked over at Alicia who was standing there bewildered at his sudden change of mind.

"Yes, but I question both the translation and the reliability of the author."

"Oh, why?"

"It seems that the author was the navigator of the boat and kept the log. Towards the end he says the boat went aground and sprung a leak. They jettisoned the cargo to free the ship but it must have sunk instead. There's no further entry after the part about them dumping the cargo."

"So what's the big deal then?"

"He says the cargo was the treasure of an entire colony in Old England and was entrusted to the ships Captain to establish a Viking colony here in the new world."

"Interesting. Where did you come by this book?" Mitch asked looking over the old parchment and leather book.

"I happen to have found it in a trunk stuck in the bottom of the river. I was fishing and it caught on the end of the line one afternoon just a short time ago. I thought I had better enjoy the recreational aspects of the river before it was drained dry."

"Yes, of course," Alicia said still bewildered.

"So as far as you can tell it is authentic and it was found in the river here, right? What else does it say?"

"Yes, Deputy I believe it to be authentic. It seems they dropped the chests of treasure over the side and covered one with the sail so they could find it again after they repaired the boat."

"This navigator didn't happen to say where this all happened, did he?"

"Not in so many words, but he records the journey up river and says that it took them ten days from the mouth of the river until they went aground. The author describes what I believe to be the Thousand Islands but I can't find any of his reference points. And believe me I have tried every free moment I've had. He just didn't make very accurate note about his bearings."

"Too bad," Mitch said, "I love historical things."

"Yes and too bad for you Deputy. Under different circumstances I'd love to work with you on this project. Maybe between us we could solve the mystery and discover the lost Viking treasure. You seem most interested and your background would have been valuable in my search."

"But," Mitch spoke for him.

"But, I'm afraid you must be made a part of our research and development. We can't afford to have any loose ends now, can we?"

"I guess not," Mitch said.

"What the hell are you doing Mitch? This nut case wants to separate our atoms and you're chatting it up about some old books and Viking treasure bullshit."

"It seems that Ms. Carlsson is growing impatient," Lindquist said and returned to his desk and pressed a button near the phone. Almost instantly Conners and the four guards popped through the door. "Yes sir," they said half hoping to find trouble.

"Relax, Mr. Conners, our two guests are ready for their tour, if you please."

"With pleasure," Conners said smiling with perverse delight. "This way," he said waving his arm toward the door and with that cue the guards took both Mitch and Alicia by the arms and led them out of the office into the hallway.

"I am sorry that I won't be able to give you the tour as Lindquist called it, myself personally. I have other duties to attend to but these gentlemen will escort you. I can't say that I'm sad to see your demise Deputy Stone," he said almost spitting out Deputy, "but you should have stuck to barking dog calls and whatever else you small timers do out here."

"Yeah, right," he said to Conners, "just remember you're still in my county."

"You won't be able to say that for much longer Stone and well I don't think the cavalry will appear to help."

"Whatever you say shit head," Mitch said trying to provoke Conners. Conners let it slide.

"As for the lovely Ms. Carlsson. It has been a pleasure seeing you again, especially in such a beautiful form. I do regret your end. We could have been good together."

"Fuck you," she said.

"I appreciate the offer, but there just isn't time for that and I prefer not to mix pleasure with business."

"Don't flatter yourself," she replied acidly.

Conners smiled at her, "yes, we would have been good together. I do like a woman with spirit."

"Ah, could we get on with this," Mitch said. "I'm getting sick of all this mutual admiration here."

"Yes," she said, "I can't stand the company."

"Then I must bid you two charming people good-bye," he said and turned and walked down the opposite hallway.

"Good riddance," she said.

"Never mind him," Mitch said as the guards pushed them down another hallway. "Just follow my lead."

"Huh," she murmured. "Ah yeah, OK."

When he was sure Conners was long gone, Mitch made his move and hoped Alicia would, and more important, could follow. The guards weren't holding him tight. They seemed more like they were just leading him along. He slowed for just a second and before either of his escorts reacted to the change of pace, he stomped his right heel down hard on the top of the right side guard's left foot. Mitch simultaneously yanked his arm free and as the guard on the right hobbled to a stop and clutched his aching foot, Mitch planted his left foot and pivoted hard to the left and drove his right knee into the other guard's groin.

As that guard doubled over holding his family jewels, Mitch brought his right knee up into the man's nose, which punctuated the moment with a crunching sound and an explosion of blood from the flattened facial feature. He returned to the first guard who was trying to stand on one foot and grab him. Mitch blocked the attempt and planted his right elbow in the guy's throat. The man gasped for breath and Mitch grabbed him by the hair with his left hand and took the guy's belt with his right and ran him head first into the wall. The guard crumpled to the floor.

As soon as his two escorts were incapacitated, Mitch quickly turned to help Alicia with hers. He stood for a moment and took in the scene before him. One of the guards was doubled up in a heap on the floor, apparently suffering from the same groin malady as one of his. The other was still standing and Mitch watched as Alicia hit the guy in the chest with a very nice karate kick that bounced him off the corridor wall. He slumped to the floor and didn't move.

As the unconscious guard's head thudded on the floor, Mitch just stood for a moment in awe. "Where did you learn to fight like that?" he asked.

"FBI Academy," she said, "and you?"

"South Side Academy," he replied.

"Huh?"

"Public school in a tough neighborhood."

"Oh."

"Now let's wrap these guys up and get out of here. Get their cuffs and we'll hook them all together back to back in a circle," he said and started dragging the limp guards together. They looped the guards' arms together behind their backs and latched the cuffs.

"There," he said, "Now stuff their ties in their mouths."

"Good," she said, "now let's get the hell out of here."

"Mitch."

"What?"

"What about the security cameras? They've probably seen us and someone's on their way here right now. We've got to get going."

"OK, but one stop first. I don't think the cameras are being monitored all the time. They are just on video."

"How do you know they are just on video?"

"Because no one has come running around the corner in the last few minutes since we took care of these guys."

"What?" she almost screamed at him, "Are you nuts? I mean I thought you were, back in the office shooting the shit about some old book but we need to get out of here, not stop to look around."

"We will, but we also need to stop whatever those machines are from destroying that dam and maybe killing a lot of people."

"Let's just get out of here and call the FBI or somebody and let them worry about this."

"You're with the FBI and we're here now and we're going to try."

"Shit," she said.

"I'll take that as a yes, now head for the lab, I think it's that way," he said pointing down the hallway.

"What are you going to do?"

"I've got an errand to run. I'll meet you in the lab in ten minutes."

"Ten?!"

"OK five, now go," he commanded.

"Yes sir. But what am I supposed to do?"

"Get to the computers and find out how those things are programmed. Maybe we can unprogram them some how."

"The lab will be full of people. I don't think they'll like me just walking in there and asking to use one of their computers."

"Wait for my signal," he called over his shoulder as he ran back the way they had just come.

"What signal?" she yelled at his back. "Shit." She turned and cautiously worked her way down the hall toward the main lab. She bumped into another guard as she turned a corner but he quickly joined the realms of the unconscious. Now she figured she had better move faster. She didn't want to be out in the open if someone found the guards.

She made it to the lab without any further incidents but hesitated to enter the room. What signal, she asked herself. Just as she completed that thought the fire alarm system activated and the alarms began their loud warnings. She covered her ears against the din and didn't have to wait long as the lab doors opened.

Fortunately she was behind one and none of the lab workers even noticed her as they hurried down the hall leaving the lab empty for her personal benefit. Guess that was the signal she said aloud to the now empty corridor and stuck her head into the lad and looked around for any stragglers. She hoped Mitch's guess about the TV cameras was accurate.

The lab was clear and she hurried in and closed the doors. The techs wouldn't be gone long, she thought and quickly started the search of the computer's hard drive unit. She had just accessed the file on the NANOs when she heard the door open and she ducked under the desk. She waited anxiously until she saw bare legs and feet standing in the middle of the floor.

"Mitch," she whispered.

"Who else?"

"Over here," she said crawling out from under the desk. "Damn, you scared the pants off me."

"Nice thought," he said with a grin.

"Not now, we have to save that dam remember."

"Oh, yeah, right. Did you find out anything?"

"I think so but you interrupted me."

"What do they have?" he said not responding to her last remark.

"Seems the machines are only about one hundred atoms in size and they can be programmed to process a specific amount of material. Once that preset amount is reached they self terminate. Safety mechanism, I'd guess."

"Great. Now how do we stop them once they've been released?"

"I don't think we can. They have to be programmed here at the source but once released they're on their own," she replied.

"No way to call them back or shut them down?"

"Nope. They're the ultimate weapon. Just set and forget."

"Well we've got to do something. What about a diversion?" he asked.

"To what?"

"To another food source," Mitch said grasping at straws.

"Not likely. Says here the batch was programmed for one hundred thousand tons of material."

"Shit," Mitch said. "I hope Gary got my message then. We need to get to the dam before those machines do. Maybe we can just pull the containers out of the water before they open."

"Good luck and what's this about Gary? And how are we going to get thirty miles across the lake and down river in less than ninety minutes on your sailboat?"

"We're not. It's good for most things on the lake."

"That's for sure."

"But once in a while we need some speed. Hopefully Gary is bringing the Department's patrol boat. With the twin 200 horse-power engines it should get us there with some time to spare. I hope," he added.

"What about all this stuff," she said pointing to the lab. "We won't be alone for much longer and we need to get back to the beach."

"Right," he said looking around the large room filed with computers, large tanks and all kinds of pieces of equipment he had no clue about. "Ah, can you down load some of that info fast while I take a quick look around?"

"Yeah, I guess so," she said returning to the terminal and loading a disk into the Zipdrive storage system. She moved the cursor and hit a couple of keys and moved the cursor again to start the down load.

Mitch walked around several counters and work tables and tried to figure out what all the stuff was used for. "Uh, how many of those machines do you figure they'd need to deconstruct something the size of the dam and power project?"

"I'd guess a few billion or so," she said looking up from the computer screen.

"How would they make so many in such a short time?"

"Probably like cells grow. Each unit would be programmed to make two copies of itself and after thirty days you'd have hundreds of billions of them. Then it would be easy to reprogram them for any element or compound you wanted to target. Their internal counters would start running and the devices would shut down after recycling the preset limit."

"Yeah, I got that part, but only, hasn't anybody discovered those things before?"

"You mean me?" she said a little indignant.

"Oh, ah sorry," he said.

"Well one reason is that at one hundred atoms in size they'd be just barely visible under a very powerful optical microscope. Two, I was looking for more conventional biological or environmental pathogens not some army of atoms sized robots."

"Oh," he said still wandering around the lab. "Could you reprogram these machines after the initial programming?"

"I suppose so. If they were all together in one place, hadn't reached their preset limit and I knew how they worked."

"Humm," he muttered.

"Done," she said, "Let's go."

"This way," he said waving her toward the door at the far end of the lab. They reached the exit just as the workers were returning from the fire alarm. "Quick hide," he said and she ducked under another desk. Mitch wasn't so lucky and came face to face with two lab technicians followed by Conners.

"Shit," she said to herself as Mitch was surrounded by white coated workers.

"Once again you amaze me Deputy Stone. Amazed but not impressed. It would appear that I will have to discipline several members of my staff since you seem to be missing your escorts. Oh, and where is the lovely Ms. Carlsson?"

"Hopefully back on my boat calling in the cavalry," he lied.

"No matter. By the time anyone arrives, if at all, you will be nothing more that a pile of wet powder. Even the best forensic lab in the world will never identify what's left as you."

"No body, no crime," Mitch said taking a step toward Conners before the workers grabbed him.

"Exactly. The perfect method to dispose of one's personal problems and other minor annoyances," Conners said with a small laugh. "Gentlemen," he said to the assembled lab staff, "Deputy Stone here has expressed an interest in our work and I think he needs a first hand demonstration of our product. Place him in the tank and program our devices for, oh, lets say, iron."

"Iron, yes sir," one of the lab techs said and two of them left the group and went to a computer near a large transparent tank in the center of the lab.

"Then as the good Deputy begs for his life with his last breath, reprogram them for carbon. We'll rearrange his atoms into a nice diamond coffee table for my office."

"Very nice touch," one of the lab workers said with a smile.

"I'll piss on your grave before you drink coffee off of any table made out of me," Mitch said trying not to let his fear show. As the lab techs started to lead him toward the tank he made the same moves on them as he had done earlier on the guards. He managed to break free this time and headed for the door at the far end of the lab as fast as he could. The lab techs chased him but it was Conners who caught him first and drove a knee into the middle of Mitch's back as they crashed to the floor. Conners gave Mitch a second thrust with a knee and Mitch let out a moan. Conners grabbed Mitch's hair and yanked his head back.

"Very amusing, Deputy Stone, I guess I over paid my debt for our meeting in the parking lot. Do forgive me won't you."

"I guess I'll have to reciprocate soon," Mitch grunted.

"Not very likely Deputy Stone," Conners said mater of factly, and wrenched Mitch's arms behind his back and cuffed them. "Now there is a sight for you, gentlemen. A cop in cuffs."

"Your turn is coming," Mitch said as he was lifted to his feet.

"I hope your not a gambling man, Stone. I wouldn't exactly bet on that last statement. OK, get him into the tank," he said to the lab workers who were standing there watching the show. They all held on tightly and marched Mitch to the tank and up the steps. They nudged him and he sat down and then two of the workers grabbed him under the arms and lowered him into the tank.

Alicia hadn't seen the rough treatment of Mitch at the hands of Conners nor did she see him standing in the glass tank handcuffed and unable to do anything. She had guessed Mitch tried the escape stunt even though he knew it would be futile, just to create a diversion for her. As soon as all of the men were on the other side of the lab dealing with Mitch she dashed out the exit door and prayed that no one saw or heard her.

She didn't look back nor did she waste any time running across the parking lot and into the small wooded area that separated the beach from the lab. She bolted through the woods and felt the branches scrape her bare legs and one of them snagged her swimsuit and pulled a hole in the nylon near her butt. She got untangled and ran on and popped out onto the beach but stopped in near panic. The boat was gone. She looked right then left and her heart returned to normal and she let out a sigh of relief. Mitch's boat was at anchor near the curve of the island about five hundred yards down the beach.

She carefully worked her way over the rocky beach feeling her way in the darkness and as she got within two hundred yards of Mitch's sailboat she stopped suddenly and crouched down behind the biggest rock she could find. Shit, she said to herself, they've found the boat. She watched as a second boat worked its way next to Mitch's and tied off. She watched for a few moments and only saw one person moving on board. She took a chance and worked her way along the shore again until she was even with the two boats. Then she ducked back into the woods for additional cover and escape if she had guessed wrong.

"Gary," she whispered as loud as she dared. Nothing.

"Gary," she said again cupping her hands over her mouth to project the sound. She took one more chance and just yelled. "Gary."

"What," Gary replied, "and keep your voice down. We don't need to announce ourselves."

"Yeah sure," she said to herself again and walked to the waterline. "Hurry up, Mitch is in deep trouble and we've got to help him."

"He's always in deep somewhere," Gary called back.

"Not funny. They're going to reduce him to a pile of dust."

"Relax," Gary said, "he needs to lose some weight anyway."

"Not all of it. Let's go," she said getting tired of Gary's dry humor.

"OK, OK, hold on," Gary said and lowered an inflatable raft over the side of the big patrol boat. Gary rowed the raft to shore in two minutes and pulled it up out of the water and tied a line from the raft around another rock.

"Hurry up, he needs us now," she said already into the woods.

"I'm coming but I have to get my survival kit out of the raft here." Gary grabbed a small duffle bag and flung the strap over his shoulder. "OK, now let's go," he said and they both ran back through the woods to the lab.

"What's in the bag that's so damned important?" she called over her shoulder as they ran across the parking lot.

"Just tools of the trade," he said reaching the main entrance two steps behind her. "Where did you learn to run so fast?" he asked slightly out of breath.

"FBI Academy," she said, "and you?"

"Soccer league," he said, "my daughter plays and I help her practice. Now where's our friend?"

"In the main lab, through here," she said, "follow me."

"Whoa, not so fast," he said grabbing her by the arm to stop her for a second. "There may be some baddies that we don't need to meet," he said opening his little bag and pulling out a canister about the size of a beer can. He also pulled out two small masks.

"What's all this?" she asked.

"New stuff I borrowed from my Army Reserve Unit. It's a fast acting sleep agent but can cover a room about forty feet square and works in about five seconds."

"I had a date once that did that," she quipped.

"Mitch?" he asked smiling.

"Government secret."

"OK," Gary said getting back to the business at hand, "first we send in our friend here then we go in and rescue old Mitch."

"On three," she said.

"Three," Gary said and opened the door and heaved in the canister that started hissing as soon as it hit the floor. The lab workers were startled by the clanking sound but they no sooner looked in the direction of the noise then they were dropping to the floor. "Put on the mask," Gary said through his and he burst into the lab holding his service weapon out in front of him.

"Hey where's mine," she asked.

"Ah, I forgot to bring one," Gary said, "anyway you need to help Mitch. He's over there," he said pointing, "and he looks pretty bad. How long have they had him in there?"

"About five minutes," she exclaimed as she ran to the tank to get a closer look at Mitch. He was lying on his back covered with a light blue gel and was desperately gasping for breath. He seemed to alternate between spasms and near unconsciousness. Alicia wasn't sure if it was the color of the gel or not but Mitch was cyanotic and was going out fast. Alicia was near panic with fear and Gary came over to bolster her nerve. "Hey, coming apart now won't save him so let's try and do something quick."

"What?" she said almost in tears. "You just gassed the only ones who know how those things work."

Gary stood for a second and didn't say anything he just turned and started calling up the different screens on the nearest computer terminal.

"Hey I'm sorry," she said, "I just lost my head that's all."

"OK, but Mitch is in there and he's going to lose a lot more very quickly," Gary replied showing no ill effects of Alicia's outburst.

"Hey, what are you doing?" she asked watching Gary surf through the unfathomable programs that flashed on the screen.

"I'm looking for the off switch," said Gary, "you said they were machines so I figured they must have an off button."

"No," she said pushing him out of the way, "they don't but we had a little meeting with the director of this place and he said they can be programmed for any element. He said they can build as well as deconstruct," she said, and started looking for the specific programs. "Here, this is it," she said with a little pride, "this will let us repro-gram the damn things."

"Can we save Mitch though?" asked Gary.

"Yeah, give me a minute," she said.

"I don't think he has a minute," said Gary as the dark blue remains of Mitch convulsed on the floor of the tank.

"I'm working at it," she said and called up several subprograms and typed in new commands. "I think that did it," she said looking hopefully over at the nearly dead man. "A few more minutes and those things were set to start on carbon."

"Let's just hope we got to him in time. He looks like shit now," Gary said. They both stood and could only watch Mitch as his body continued to twist and turn in the blue gel. They had no way to know nor could they tell if Alicia had managed to reprogram the NANOs to assemble rather than disassemble.

"What did you do?" asked Gary.

"I, ah, think I told them to put iron back into his system. Iron is the main element in hemoglobin and when those evil machines remove the iron your body can't process the oxygen. Mitch is suffocating in air. It's like he's drowning but the brain reacts to the CO_2 and keeps the lungs pulling in the air."

"But he can't use it," said Gary.

"Right. He just keeps breathing until all the hemoglobin is destroyed and then the brain dies."

The two rescuers just waited and watched and didn't notice when one of the lab workers struggled to his feet and staggered out of the lab.

"Damn," Gary said as he heard the door close. "We seem to have lost one of our guests. He'll bring back the reinforcements. How long will this take?"

"At least as long as it did to pull all of the iron out of his system. Five minutes I'd guess."

"Not good," Gary said picking up his duffle bag and heading for the door.

"When he comes to, help him to the boat. I've got some more toys to share with anyone who might come our way."

"What about you?"

"Don't worry. I'll be at the boat, just get him out of there and on board."

"OK," she said to Gary's back as he stuck his head out of the door and then left.

"Come on, Mitch," she pleaded through the glass of the tank. "You can do it." Whatever force or entity that Alicia called for help or whatever magic she performed with the computers, something seemed to be working. Mitch rolled over on his back again and Alicia watched with joy as he took a deep breath and some of the horrible blue color changed to pink. "That's the boy Mitch. Come on," she cheered as more and more of his normal color returned to his face and extremities.

Mitch's body started another spasm but this time some of the blue colored gel was expelled from his lings and more of his natural color returned. He rolled over onto his stomach and spit out some more blue gel and took a couple of restorative breaths. He struggled to his feet and stumbled into the side of the tank and almost face to face with a very delighted Alicia who had tears of joy and a smile for him as he caught his breath and found his footing.

"All right Mitch, you're back. You OK?" she asked and ran up the steps to help pull him out of the tank.

"Yeah," he said a little hoarse and between coughs to clean out the blue gel. "What am I covered with?"

"I think it is the stuff the NANOs need to move around in."

"What happened to them? The last thing I remember was being sprayed with this stuff and a couple of minutes later it felt like I was drowning even though I was able to take nice deep breaths."

"Yeah, the NANOs were programmed for iron and they dismantled all your hemoglobin. You could breathe but your blood couldn't move the oxygen around. Another minute and according to the computer they'd start on your carbon."

"Yeah, that was Conners' idea. He wanted to make my carbon into a diamond coffee table. Thanks for getting me out, but how?"

"Gary and I took the workers out and reprogrammed the NANOs to put the iron back into your blood."

"What did you do with the handcuffs?"

"What handcuffs?"

"The ones that Conners put me in."

"I don't know. I didn't see them."

"You said me and Gary. He's here, where?" he said looking around for his old friend.

"He got your message and the patrol boat is tied up next to yours but he said he had some toys to show the people around here."

Mitch coughed and spit out some more blue goo. "I guess I'd better go find him and give him a hand."

"No," she said holding his arm, "He said we were to get to the boat and he'd meet us there. He said it was an order."

"An order huh, well then I guess we'd better get to the boat."

Mitch was still a little weak and Alicia helped steady him. They walked to the exit and she stuck her head cautiously out the door. "All clear," she said.

"Yeah, no kidding," said Mitch admiring the new rear view in Alicia's suit.

"Is that all you think about? Five minutes ago you were near death and now you're looking at my ass."

"Everyone needs a hobby. Besides your cure seems to have given me all kinds of energy suddenly."

"Good then you can use it to run to the boat. Now let's get out of here."

Alicia started for the door and Mitch suddenly stopped. "Wait," he said.

"What's the matter now?" she said turning around and showing concern on her face.

"Nothing, I just forgot something," he said.

"What?" she asked impatiently.

"Something I found," he said looking around the floor of the lab. "Here it is," he said picking up a knapsack and putting one of the straps over his shoulder.

"What the hell is that," she exclaimed.

"Just some souvenirs," he said smiling, "a few things I picked up along the way."

"You were near death a moment ago and now you're worried about some junk."

"Yeah, and your swimsuit."

"Men," she said exasperated, "let's go now!"

"After you," he said smiling at her as she led the way. "After you."

She ignored him and pulled open the door and ran down the hallway. They cleared the building and headed for the boats. They ran as fast as their bare feet allowed on the pavement and through the woods. For some reason Mitch seemed to run faster this time and didn't seem to even breath heavy once they reached the beach.

"What's gotten into you?" she asked a little out of breath.

"I don't know. I seem to be feeling pretty good all of a sudden. Like I'm supercharged."

"I don't know either but we better get on board. Gary tied a raft up over there." They carried it into the water and they climbed in. Mitch's new found energy had them at the boats in only a few strokes of the oars.

"OK," he said, "we'll fire up the engines. Gary will be arriving on the run with a lot of baddies on his tail. In fact, go below and grab two of the shot guns and a couple of boxes of 'OO'. You can use a shotgun I hope?"

"Can you?" she snapped back.

"Stupid question," he said and started the twin engines. He let them idle so they would be able to respond with full power as soon as Gary arrived. Alicia returned from below with two pump action shotguns and handed one to Mitch. They dumped out the two boxes of shells into one of the seats so they could reload quickly. Then they chambered eight rounds into the tube magazine and racked one into the chamber. Both of them set the safety on their weapons and waited.

"Here put another one in the magazine," he said handing her another three-inch shell.

"Oh, yeah."

They didn't have to wait very long. Off to their left they heard what sounded like someone crashing through the woods.

"Here he comes," Mitch said and held the shotgun ready. A figure they hoped was Gary appeared on the beach as a silhouette and started running toward them along the shore. Suddenly he stopped and disappeared from their sight.

"What's he doing now?" she asked.

"Watch," Mitch said, "and get ready to fire. Aim about four hundred yards to the left of where he disappeared."

"OK, but I don't see," she was cut off as a half dozen silhouettes emerged from the woods and started walking down the beach toward Gary's hiding spot. The men fanned out and walked in a line stretching from the water's edge to the woods.

"They're doing a line search," Mitch whispered as he took aim. Alicia did the same and braced herself for the recoil from the gun. "Wait for Gary to make the first move, we'll give him cover fire."

"OK, just say when," she said holding the gun and keeping an aim on the six shadow figures. "You think one of them is Conners?" she asked hopefully.

"Wishful thinking, but probably not. He doesn't seem to like it much when others have weapons. He's probably close though."

Mitch no sooner finish his vocalized thoughts when Gary made his move. He had waited in hiding and prepared some more of his toys and now popped up from behind the rock and threw three more canisters in rapid succession at the advancing line of men. Before they could react first to Gary's sudden appearance and second to the sound of metal hitting on stone, the first of the canisters exploded with a bright flash.

"Shit, cover your eyes for a minute," Mitch said as he tried to focus his eyes after the first flash. The guards were doing the same and could just about see Gary when the second and third canisters went off with an even brighter flash. The six men were now holding their faces and screaming in pain and Gary just stood there laughing. Finally he took off his welder's goggles and ran for the boat carrying his duffle bag. Just as the men stopped screaming and started to regroup, Mitch said "when" and both shotguns fired simultaneously. The first volley went over the heads of the scattered men but they all ran for cover still not completely able to see but certainly able to hear.

"Hey, where's my raft?" Gary called out.

"Ah, right here, come and get it," Mitch said as he and Alicia gave the shore party another two round blast into the trees.

"Hurry up you old fart," called Mitch as he bent over the side to grab the duffle bag Gary was carefully trying to keep out of the water while he swam with one hand.

"Old fart may ass," grunted Gary as he climbed up the boarding ladder.

"Usually," said Mitch.

"Ah if you two are through with the joy filled reunion, we'd better get out of here."

"Ah, what about my boat though?"

"We'll tow it out past Lighthouse Island and anchor it in Wilson's Inlet. It'll be safe and out of harm's way," said Gary.

"And besides it's on our way," Mitch said.

"Our way where?"

CHAPTER 13

THE PROJECT

"*T*o the dam," Alicia said, impatient as always.

"The dam on the river," Gary said in surprise.

"The one and only," said Mitch. "Give them another blast," he said to Alicia, "while we get my boat ready for towing."

She let go one round and followed it with another. "This is fun," she said.

They pulled up the anchor on the 'Cold Fortune' and tied her bow line to the stern cleat on the patrol boat and pulled away slowly until the sailboat was gliding along behind the big power boat. The shore group finally recovered their night vision enough to fire a few frantic rounds at the escaping boats.

"They don't want to punch any holes in my new boat," Mitch threatened as they cleared the island and headed toward the head of the river.

Wilson's Inlet was on the north side of Lighthouse Island so named for the warning light and early19th century wooden keeper's house. It had been there since the first shots of the War of 1812 and was built then to guide the returning U.S. Naval ships into the harbor at Smyth's Cove. The lighthouse had been maned until 1950 when it was converted to automatic. Gary piloted the big patrol boat around and into the inlet while Mitch waited at the stern to catch the bow pulpit of his sailboat as it drifted toward the rear of the patrol craft.

"We don't have much time," Alicia reminded both of them.

"How much?" asked Gary.

"Not much," replied Mitch. "According to our tour guide we had about ninety minutes before those nasty micro machines were activated and that was about 30 minutes ago."

"Nano-machines," Alicia corrected. Micro machines would be about a million times bigger.

"Micro, nano, whatever," Mitch said not happy about being corrected or really caring about the technical differences.

"OK, you guys, I get the picture anyway, so let's get this tub of yours anchored and get moving," Gary quipped trying to separate the two dynamic personalities.

"Hey not so nasty, she's sensitive."

"Who me?" Alicia asked not quite hearing the conversation. Mitch caught the bow of the sailboat as it glided in and he pushed it off to stop the movement. He grabbed the rail and hoisted himself on board and opened the anchor bay. Alicia came to the back of the patrol boat and held the bow of the sailboat close to the patrol's stern.

Mitch dropped the forty-pound anchor into the water and let out enough line to give the boat a little slack so it wouldn't pull the anchor loose if a wave bounced the boat. "There," he said cleating off the line and climbing back on board the power boat. "Let's get up to the dam, ASAP. We'll need as much time as possible to even locate all the NANO containers."

Gary gently pushed the throttle forward to get clear of the anchored boat and once Mitch gave the word he pushed both of the handles fully forward and the patrol boat roared to life and speed off. At full speed the boat covered the thirty miles in less than fifty minutes and all three of them were putting on their dive gear when Mitch held up his hand and said "hold it. Didn't Conners say this batch was programmed for iron and calcium to disassemble the building components?"

"Yeah, so?"

"So. I just went through a very bad time with these things looking for iron. Not only are we carrying around some of the same target elements but these old dive tanks are steel not aluminum. If these NANOs get loose we're all done for."

"What are we looking for anyway? What are these NANOs?" Gary asked.

"Very small machines about one hundred atoms in size and programmed to pull out atoms of iron and calcium from the dam here until it is nothing but powder flowing down stream," Alicia said.

"So, how do we find things that small in the water in the dark?"

"They're in containers about the size of gas cans somewhere underwater and probably at or very near the dam by now," Mitch said. "The containers are timed to release the NANOs in about," he stopped and looked at his watch. "Hey, my Omega is gone."

"Was it made of steel?" Alicia asked, "and those missing cuffs. Were they made of steel too?"

"Yeah, both stainless, why?"

"The NANOs dissolved them when they were looking for iron atoms. Maybe that's what saved you. They went after the steel first and not the iron in your blood. Oh, my god," she exclaimed, as the thought hit her, "That's why you feel so much more energetic. I reprogrammed the NANOs to replace all the iron is your blood. They used all the iron from the watch and the handcuffs. It would be like taking a thousand iron supplements all at once."

"Will I be OK?"

"Probably."

"Probably?" Mitch repeated not comfortable with her answer.

"After all this you should see a doctor for a blood test."

"Yeah or a scrap dealer," Gary threw in.

"Not funny old buddy."

"OK, these NANO things," Gary said trying to get serious again.

"Oh, yeah," Mitch said, "we'll just have to chance the dive gear and hope they like cement and steel better than human bones and blood. We'll never find them otherwise."

"So what are we going to do with them if we find them?" Alicia asked.

"Shit, good question," Gary added, "we sure as hell don't want them on board if they get released."

"What else can we do?" Mitch wondered out loud. "Hey this boat is originally sold for fishing isn't?"

"Yeah."

"Then what about the live wells? They're made of fiberglass just like most of the boat. No calcium or steel in there. If we find the containers we shut off the timers and place them in the live wells. They hold the cans and keep the NANO goo confined if it releases."

"OK," Gary said. "I guess that'll work, I hope" he added. "Oh, wait, I've got some of those plastic garbage bags down below. Remember from our recovery of all that stuff from the sub last summer?"

"Yeah," Mitch said, "that'll work. We'll put the canisters in the plastic bags and then into the live well. Now let's hope we can actually find those things."

"What sub?" Alicia interrupted.

"Long story. Another time and place," Mitch said and put on his dive tank.

"Maybe your place then," she said doing the same.

"Am I interrupting something, I hope?" Gary interjected, "I mean we do have work to do, you know."

"Yes, right," Mitch said and swung his legs out over the side and slid into the water.

"Right, yes," she said and climbed up onto the transom and stepped in.

"Yes, right, yes, what," Gary said to no one and followed the other two into the water. "Oh my god this is cold," he gasped, bobbing in the water between Alicia and Mitch.

"Baby," they both said as they shivered.

"Alicia, you check to the left," Mitch said.

"OK," she replied and put the mouthpiece in her mouth and released the air in her vest. She disappeared in a circle of bubbles.

"Gary, you've got the right."

"OK," he said and did the same thing and disappeared.

"Mitch, you've got the center."

"OK," Mitch replied to himself and sank below the surface. Even with the powerful handheld lamps, he couldn't see either Alicia or Gary and for that matter he couldn't see much more than ten feet in any direction. He checked the time but realized again that his favorite watch had been recycled by the NANOs and all he had was the rubber coated compass. He got his bearings and kicked hard toward the dam. Fortunately, they had anchored only thirty feet away and he was facing the concrete wall in about ten kicks.

He felt the surface. Everything felt fine and as far as he could see everything looked fine. He pivoted in the water and held the light out to illuminate an arc. Nothing he thought, just as he felt something bump his leg. He recoiled from the sudden touch and held the light down toward his fins. He hoped it wasn't something big, alive and hungry. Wait a minute, he thought trying to get a grip on himself, there's nothing in the river or the lake that would attack a person and the only thing of any size might be a salmon or a sturgeon, neither of which are particularly dangerous to people. He probed the gloom and caught site of what had startled him.

There in the blackness was a plastic five-gallon jug. He bent at the waist and swam down to get a better look. It was just a big plastic container with a growth on the top. He grabbed it and looked at the device with a timer attached to one end. The readout was digital and the countdown had begun. The timer said 10.02, then 10.01, 10.00, 9.59 and Mitch guessed that didn't mean hours. Shit, he thought, less than ten minutes to round up who knows how many of these things. Maybe Alicia and Gary were able to locate some of the cans. He hoped so and took the one he had to the surface as fast as he could. He swam as fast as his dive gear let him and climbed over the side and placeed it in the plastic bag. It would be easier and faster of they could do this in the water but they have to wrestle a bunch of plastic bags in dark water and try not to lose both in the dark.

Mitch looked over the device and the timer trying to find an off switch. No switch. Damn, he thought no way to stop these things. Those island shitbags must have saved money and only provided an on switch. Guess they figured no one should be able to stop their plans. Mitch watched the timer as it lost a few more seconds and just stuffed it in the bag. Just as he was tying the bag, Alicia popped up a few feet from the boat and spit out her mouth piece. "I've got…" she gulped some water and coughed, "two," she said, "help," and she swallowed another mouthful of the river. Mitch slid back in and swam over to her and inflated her vest. With that keeping her above the water she stopped trying to drink the river.

"Thanks," she said and handed him one of the canisters.

"Alicia we can't stop those timers so we need someone on board the boat to handle putting these things in the plastic bags before they go off. You want the job?"

"Not really, but I guess it would be warmer. All right," she agreed.

"Good, I'll help you aboard and then get these cans into the bags fast, we don't have much time. The one I had said less than ten minutes."

"One of mine said three and the other said fifteen."

"They must have staggered the release in case someone found a few."

"Yeah, like us," she said, "and one of these is almost ready to pop."

"Oh shit," he said looking at the one in his hand. "14.20"

"This one," she said, "how do I shut it off?"

"Can't. We have to get it in the plastic fast," he said and grabbed it from her. He swam as fast as he could and climbed up over the stern and tossed it into the first bag he found. "Damn, that was too close. Now you better get into the boat and get ready to take these things as we find them."

"OK," she said working her way out of the water as fast as her dive gear would allow. Mitch helped her on board and she grabbed one of the bags before she even took her dive gear off. Just as they got all three of the cans wrapped tight, Gary popped his head out of the water and immediately cried for assistance.

"Hey, help. I've got three of them tied together with my swimsuit draw string."

"Very clever," Mitch said.

"Not really. The suit is down around my ankles and one of these damn things is now under a minute."

"Shit," Alicia said grabbing a bag. "Bring it here quick!"

Mitch swam over to help Gary and they kicked back to the boat and loaded the one container into the bag Alicia was holding over the transom.

"Twenty seconds," Mitch called out, "get it tied and into the well." She managed to tie a knot in the bag just as the timer hit '0' and then there was a sound like a balloon bursting. She let out a startled shriek. "Hey, you all right up there?" Mitch called.

"Yeah, what happened?"

"The last one just released."

"In the bag I hope," Gary said.

"Yeah, and I got it into the well now." The next one popped and filled the clear plastic bag with blue goo. "Shit, there goes the next one," she said and carefully lifted the bag into the live well.

"Mitch," Gary said bobbing in the water, "we're never going to find all of these things in time and we don't even know how many there are."

"I know, but every one we do find is one less batch of those NANOs eating away at the dam."

"Some of them must have popped by now if the ones we have just did. And didn't you guys say they would go after iron, like in our tanks and us?'

"Yup," Mitch said reflecting on the thought. "OK, let's see if we can find a few more. Just watch your pressure gauge and if it starts to drop, dump the tank and get back to the boat, fast."

"Ah, Mitch," Gary asked again, "aren't those things going to do to us what they did to you back in the lab?"

"Let's hope they like the tanks more than us," Mitch said and dropped back beneath the surface. He didn't hear Alicia call over the side and neither did Gary.

"Hey you guys, those NANOs won't cause a slow leak of air, they'll compromise the tanks so that they'll explode under the pressure." There was no answer and she looked over into the water and only saw bubbles. "I hope they figure it out before they blow up."

Both of them swam as quickly as they could back to the dam and even in the limited range of the flashlights they could see some obvious changes in the surface of the dam. Instead of the smooth surface that Mitch had felt only a few minutes before, there was a large area of cement missing. It looked as if a whole big section had broken loose and fallen out. Mitch guessed that it was the first batch of NANOs attacking the calcium in the cement. He hoped the NANOs would decide to feed on the dam first and not their bones. He looked over to Gary and made a facial gesture trying to show that it was too late. Gary nodded in agreement and signaled for them to get out of there. Mitch nodded back and gave one last look at the cavities in the dam. The one they saw first was now a foot wider and six inches deeper in just a few moments. They shone their lights along the dam in both directions and were shocked at the sight. As far as they could see the dam was pock marked with various sized holes and the holes seemed to grow larger as they watched. Gary tugged at Mitch's arm and they both turned and kicked away from the disintegrating dam as fast as they could.

Both popped up at the rear of the boat and Alicia stuck her head over the back as soon as she heard the two men.

"Any more?" she asked.

"No, it's already started. We're too late," Mitch said.

"The dam is being eaten and at the rate it's happening. I figure there will be at least one breach in about two hours," Gary said pulling himself up the boarding ladder and handing Alicia his fins.

"Yeah, and we need to warn the Power Authority that they'll lose dam integrity shortly. Maybe they can save a few people down river." Mitch hoisted himself up the ladder and doffed his gear.

"Gary, can you raise the Authority and tell them what's going on?"

"Sure."

"OK," Mitch said, "now that our friends at Millennium Eco Technologies have committed a crime, I guess we'd better pay them an official visit."

"Whose jurisdiction?" she asked.

"Ours," he said sharply and hit the throttles on the twin 200's. She was nearly knocked off her feet when the boat accelerated. "Hang on," he said and headed back up river toward the lake and Society Island.

"Hey, what's the rush?" Gary called from below. "I'm trying to make a call here."

"Duty calls too," Mitch snapped back as Gary came up from below. "Did you get through to someone at the Authority?" Mitch asked still pushing the boat as fast as it would move.

"Not exactly. I called our friend Mike Kelly and he said he'd make all the necessary contacts."

"Who's he?" Alicia asked.

"He's a retired State Trooper who now works for the Authority. He does speed checks on the big ocean freighters. His is the only number I knew."

"Good," Mitch said, "let's hope they can warn enough people." He kept the throttles pushed all the way to full.

"Ah, Mitch. We need to think this one through," Gary said.

"Yes, Mitch, we just can't go storming in there half cocked," she said.

Mitch finally looked at her after that statement but didn't say anything.

"You know what I mean," she said, "I agree with Gary. We've got to do this right."

"Listen," Gary started again, "I want these shitbags as much as you do but we've got to do it right if we have and hope of making them pay."

Mitch reached over and pulled back on the throttles, and the bow of the bow dropped back into the water and now the boat just cruised along. "OK," Mitch said, "we'll do it the right way, but if they get away with this I'll be really pissed."

"Deal," said Gary, "you can be pissed."

"Not what I meant."

They headed through the channel flanked by some of the islands between the dam and the lake.

"I've never seen these islands in the day time," she said, relieved that Mitch wasn't going to exact revenge that very minute. "I hear they are quite beautiful."

"They are. We'll have to come up here in the boat."

"Soon?"

"Probably," Mitch said smiling at her, hoping that she could see it in the darkness. "Gary?"

"Yeah."

"We don't want any of the cockroaches to flee before we can bring in the exterminators."

"You're right," he said, and punched in the numbers on his cell phone. He spoke for a few minutes. "OK," he said as the phone peeped. "The cavalry is on the way. They'll seal the place until we can get in and look around all legal like."

"Great," Mitch said a little more relieved that the people responsible would not get away.

"Now that we're not going back there."

"Yet," Mitch added quickly.

"Yet" she acknowledged, "where are we headed now?"

"Back to the office to work up the paperwork and get a warrant," Gary said.

"Good, I can call my office to get some help in on this."

"No," Mitch said emphatically. "Absolutely not."

"Mitch, take it easy," said Gary.

"What's your problem?" she asked.

"In case you hadn't noticed and obviously you haven't this is and always has been an FBI investigation."

"I knew it," he said, "just when we do all the work up pops the feds to steal the show."

"Mitch it's not that way," Gary said trying to reign in his friend.

"That's right, Mr. I Can Do It All Cop. Your department was asked to cooperate with my office and up until now I thought that's what we were doing. I don't want to push you out of this case, I only want to get my office up here and get the experts in to go over that lab. Now, are either of you familiar with what were dealing with here?"

"Familiar yes, up to speed, no," Mitch said.

"Oh, yeah, sorry," she said.

"No problem. OK, call your people but we're in this together right?" he said relenting on his initial rejection of her office's involvement.

"Absolutely."

"I've heard that before," Mitch said and looked away.

Alicia was a little hurt at Mitch's attitude towards her office and she took the hint to drop the matter for now. She went down below into the cutty cabin to be with Gary for a while and to let Mitch cool off.

"I think he's still stressed about being left to dissolve," she said still upset over the altercation.

"Yeah, probably those machines are still chugging around in his brain," Gary said.

"What's with him? Every time someone mentions a little help from the FBI he gets all bent out of shape."

"Long story."

"You two seem to have a lot of those."

"Well this one goes back a few years when we were both working the same shift."

"I've got all night, let's hear it. What gives?"

"OK," he said closing the hatch. "Like I said, both Mitch and I were working the same shift but I fell and broke my knee working a moonlight gig. Mitch was temporarily assigned to the Detective Division and he was working on a missing person's file that turned into a homicide."

"Sounds pretty straight forward," she said.

"Not really. It seems the missing guy's wife had just been served with divorce papers when suddenly her husband disappears."

"Who called the police?"

"She did but none of her story made much sense. She says he had planned to go to Mexico but somehow she knows he never got there."

"Huh?"

"The plane is delayed but she couldn't know that. She calls the police to report him missing before the plane actually lands in Mexico. She knew he never got there."

"OK, so where does Mitch and the FBI fit in?"

"The Sheriff figures the investigation may be international and he calls the FBI for help."

"So far so good."

"Yeah," he said, "but they take a couple of days to get an agent up here. You know a guy named Niederham?"

"Heard of him. They sent him?"

"Uh huh, and he comes in here like J. Edgar reincarnated and he starts making all these pronouncements and giving all these orders."

"He took over the investigation?!"

"Big time. Made it sound like all us locals were just too dumb to figure it out."

"Where were you during all this?"

"I was on disability but Mitch and I would have a few beers after his shift. He would vent his anger as it were."

"I can imagine," she said nodding her head toward the cabin hatch.

"Yeah, well anyway, Niederham is running around giving all these orders and trying to run the show."

"Didn't your boss step in?"

"Naw, he loves the FBI, so we were stuck with the mess."

"So what happened?"

"Well, Mitch works the case on his days off and comes up with a few leads. He finds the guy's car not at the airport like the wife said, but right in town. Some guy bought it from the wife only two days after she reports him missing."

"No shit. What did Niederham say?"

"He just about ignores it and then gets Mitch removed from the case for running a private investigation."

"Now I see why Mitch is so pissed."

"Not yet you don't, there's more."

"Ooh," she said leaning closer so as not to miss any of the details.

"So Mitch is back on the road working the graveyard shift and he stops this car for DWI. The driver turns out to be an employee of the missing husband. Mitch had talked to him early on in the case."

"And?" she prompted, the curiosity getting to her.

"And he starts to talk to the driver and do some field sobriety tests on him. Mitch has him out of the car and the driver's buddy is still in the passenger seat."

"OK, so what happens," she asked eagerly.

"Well apparently the passenger gets nervous. He figures the driver is telling Mitch about his missing boss."

"Was he?"

"No, but the passenger doesn't know that and he jumps out of the car and goes after the driver with a bat."

"What does Mitch do?"

"Mitch draws on the guy but now he's chasing the driver around the car, trying to hit him. All the time the driver is yelling and screaming, 'he did it, he did it, he killed the husband,' and the passenger with the bat is screaming 'I'll kill you, you fat bastard. You did it, you shit.'"

"So what did Mitch do?"

"He steps in front of the guy with the bat and rams his pistol into the guy's nose. He arrests them both and both start saying the other one killed the husband."

"No shit," she said, now riveted to the story. "What happens next?"

"During the mutual finger pointing, Mitch takes the driver aside and he tells Mitch to look in the front yard of his parent's summer place up in the mountains east of here?"

"Did he?"

"Yeah."

"Where was the body buried?"

"All over."

"Huh?"

"Yeah, whoever killed the guy cut him up and buried him in about twenty holes. Head in one hands some place else."

"Geez," she said.

"Yeah, well Mitch goes up there with a warrant and after a couple of hours digging in the mud, he and another detective uncover the missing husband."

"Where does Niederham fit in though?"

"He shows up and starts a press conference at the end of the driveway while Mitch is still bagging and tagging the body parts."

"Yeah?"

"Well Niederham tells the press how it was his personal investigation that solved the case and how the FBI had used all this wonderful forensic lab work to piece together the clues and locate the body."

"Oh," she said beginning to understand now.

"Wait it gets better," Gary said. "Mitch comes down the driveway escorting the ambulance. He's all covered in mud from digging all day and one of the reporters asks Niederham about the local cooperation."

"Oh, oh."

"Yeah, he doesn't see Mitch yet and he says that the local agencies contributed a small measure of assistance to his investigation."

"Oh shit," she said, "what an asshole."

"Yeah, Mitch thought so too and he grabs Niederham and punches him in the nose."

"Oh no."

"Yeah, the whole bloody scene is on tape if you want to see it. Ask Mitch, I think he has the only copy though."

"What happens then?"

"The Sheriff makes Niederham retract his statement and give due credit to the Sheriff's Department. He does it on TV with his nose all bandaged. Looked good," Gary added and laughed.

"What about Mitch?"

"Mitch gets suspended for thirty days with no pay for hitting the pompous ass but he says it was worth it. He had to file bankruptcy though. He owed a lot of child support and couldn't pay."

"I didn't know."

"Not many people do, but now you know why he despises your office so much and why he's so sensitive about joint investigations."

"OK, but I'm not like that and for that matter neither are most of the others in my office."

"I know that, and I'll talk to Mitch. He'll be all right but just be careful about pushing the cooperation thing too hard."

"OK," she said now looking up at the hatch and thinking of Mitch beyond with a little more sympathy.

"Hey you two, how about a hand up here?" Mitch called through the closed hatch.

"Sure," Gary said and went back up on deck followed by Alicia who now was smiling at Mitch.

"Have a good chat?" he asked Gary.

"Just some old war stories," he said.

"Whose war?" asked Mitch.

"Ours," Gary smiled.

"Oh," Mitch said and didn't press the issue. "We're almost at my boat. I need you two to help get this close."

"Sure. What can I do?" Alicia said, seeming to Mitch to be a little more friendly.

"Ah, I'll cut the engines and we'll glide in but I need you to catch the stern while Gary holds the bow."

"Sure," she said picking up the boat hook and waiting near the transom.

Mitch cut the engines and they coasted along the side of the moored sailboat. Alicia wondered how Mitch could afford it after the story Gary just told but she decided to wait for just the right moment to ask Mitch. After this mess was finished, she thought and reached out with the long pole and hooked the stern cleat on Mitch's boat. She pulled the two boats together and they gently nudged each other.

"Gary, have you got it?"

"Yeah, no problem."

"OK, I'll take my boat back in the morning and meet you two at the office. Our patrol boys will keep everyone in place until we can make a formal call."

"Yeah, good" Gary said.

"Hey, what about me?" Alicia asked.

"You can go with Gary and make whatever calls you need to get your people on board."

"That can wait. I thought we were going for an all day sail. I still have a few hours left in the day."

"Can't argue with that old buddy," Gary added as he took over the patrol boat's controls from Mitch.

"But."

"But nothing," she said and hopped over the railing of the sailboat and sat in the cockpit.

"I guess we'll see you in the morning," Mitch said to Gary.

"Yeah, first thing."

"Ah, about noon. I'm on the wind remember."

"Use the force of the power man."

"Yeah, forceful and powerful," she said trying to get Mitch's attention directed to something else.

"We'll be there," he said and stepped across to his own boat. "OK, cast off." The two boats drifted apart and Gary started the engines and pulled away slowly.

"Hey," Mitch called out as the boats separated, "put all those things in ice chests. We may need them for something."

"Like evidence," Gary stated.

"Yeah, like evidence, or something."

"I don't think I want to know what the something else might be," Gary said as they continued to drift apart. When he was clear he gave the throttles a push and the boat sped away and Mitch and Alicia waved at their parting friend.

"What was your talk with him all about?"

"Never mind for now," she said, "I need to get out of this suit."

"From what I saw earlier, you're just about out of it now."

"That's what I'm talking about this time," she said taking his hand and leading him to the hatch.

"Wait," he said.

"What, Mitch Stone being coy."

"No. I locked the hatch and now it's open."

They both took a step back in surprise as Conners pushed open the hatch cover and stepped on deck. He held a large automatic pistol and pointed it at Mitch's chest. "I can't say that it is nice to see you Stone, but I always enjoy seeing a beautiful woman again."

"Fuck you," she said.

"Again with the requests. Don't you keep her happy, Stone?"

Mitch took a step towards Conners but was stopped by the gun now pointing at his head.

"Please don't make me shoot you, Stone. It would mess up my plans."

"We couldn't have that now could we?" Mitch said. "How did you get on board? You're too slimy to walk on water."

"Not very nice, but if you must know, my incompetent staff followed you after you left so abruptly. In fact here they come now."

Mitch and Alicia both looked of the port bow and saw another power boat pull along side. This one however bumped the sailboat hard enough to knock the three of them around.

"Hey you fucks, watch the fiberglass. It's new you know."

"I wouldn't be too concerned about this boat, Stone. Neither you nor it will be around much longer."

"What are you talking about?" asked Alicia.

"Well it seems that your boyfriend here has managed to survive his first encounter with the NANOs, no doubt with your interference," Conners said as three of the men from the power boat boarded the sailboat and held Mitch and Alicia tight.

"No doubt," she said trying to pull free but with no success.

"As I was saying, both of you will now have the opportunity to see our little friends at work. On this boat."

"Fucker," Mitch snarled.

"Always the flatterer aren't you, Stone? Take them below and make sure they are fastened securely."

"Yes sir," one of the guards said and pushed Alicia hard toward the hatch. Mitch reacted and kneed the guy hard but the two holding him promptly brought their batons down on his head. Mitch slumped to the deck, and now the two guards merely picked him up and dumped him down the hatchway where he landed on the cabin floor in a lump with a loud thud.

"You bastard," Alicia hissed and tried to kick Conners.

"Get her below before I give her the same treatment."

"Just try it you piece of shit," she snarled. The guard shoved her through the hatch and she had to grab the bulkhead to prevent herself from falling on top of the motionless Mitch.

"Mitch, Mitch," she called as the guards followed her below and grabbed her arms. They pulled them hard behind her back and she yelped. They pushed her to the floor and wrapped her arms around the mast and cuffed both her wrists.

"Make sure they are nice and tight. We wouldn't want her to pull loose," Conners said as he stepped off the bottom step onto Mitch and then onto the floor.

"You'll get yours," she said to Conners who was now sitting on the couch right in front of her. She tried to kick him but he just batted her foot aside and laughed. "Futile, Ms. Carlsson. Just like all of his efforts to stop us," he said pointing to Mitch who was a heap on the floor.

"He's not finished yet and neither am I."

"I don't think I need to worry much, since for the both of you, yet is a very short time. Bring him over here and prop him up against the mast. Make sure he's really cuffed tight."

Alicia heard the cuffs click several times then once more.

"Check hers too." They did and got another click out of the cuffs.

"Ouch, you bastard."

"You won't feel anything in a few minutes Ms. Carlsson," Conners said.

"What are you going to do?" she asked.

"Well as you are probably aware we can program our little devices for almost anything."

"So."

"So we've programmed them for the main component of the fiberglass resin in the boat. They'll just turn the hull into mush and well…" he paused for effect.

"Well," she prompted.

"Well it just won't be watertight any longer, will it."

She spit in his face. He slapped her hard enough to leave his hand print on her check. She fought back the tears. "You'll pay for that, Conners, and I'll be there to collect."

"Not likely," he said and stood up. "Alas, parting is just that," he finished. "We won't see each other again. I'm afraid." He motioned for the guards to leave and he followed them up the ladder. "Oh, one more thing Ms. Carlsson, we'll be towing this tub into deeper water so that it will have a nice long way to sink." He closed the hatch and Alicia heard the latch click shut.

"Is he gone?" mumbled Mitch.

"Mitch darling, you're OK?" she asked.

"Ah, not OK, I think I badly bruised a couple of ribs, but yeah, I'm still functional."

"How long have you been conscious?"

"Long enough," he said, "I had a hard time restraining myself when he slapped you."

"One thing," she said, "if we get out of here, he's all mine, OK."

"Yeah, I guess you deserve the first shot."

"And the second, and the third and…"

"I get the message now let's get out of here before he messes up my boat."

"Get out of here? In case your brain is still out of service we're handcuffed back to back around the mast. I don't know about you but this situation doesn't fit with 'get out of here.'"

"Oh, yeah," he said, disgusted with their situation, "but remember the little altercation on deck before I was clubbed?"

"Yeah."

"Well I managed to liberate a set of keys from the belt of one of the guards. I don't think he'll miss them for a while and even if he does, he won't say anything for fear of Conners."

"Mitch you're wonderful," she said.

"Save it for later, we need to get loose before were missing at sea."

"Lake," she corrected.

"Lake, right. Now can you move around to my left and grab the key?"

She started to inch her way around. "The other left but OK, keep going. See if you can get the key from my hand. Hurry, my hands are getting numb. They cranked down on these cuffs."

"I heard. I'm trying," she said and grunted as she contorted herself around the mast between the bulkheads. "Not much room here on the floor."

"Not made for a game of Twister," he said.

"Me or the boat?" she asked.

"Ah…, the boat of course. Now come on, work with me on this key."

She wriggled and squirmed, and a couple of times she put pressure against Mitch's arms and he groaned in pain as his wrists were bent in the tight cuffs. "Sorry," she said, "but, I can't get around far enough."

"Shit," he said, "we've got to keep trying."

Suddenly the boat slowed and drifted to a stop. "Guess this is where we're supposed to go down with the ship."

"I'd rather not," she said still struggling to get her hands near his, "you could try and help you know."

"Not without a lot of pain."

"Baby," she said in a frustrated tone of voice.

"Believe me I want out as much as you do. Even more. They're going to dissolve my boat, remember."

"Sorry, I'm just really scared."

"Me too," he said and tried to find her fingers with the key. They heard foot steps on the deck and the latch pop open.

"Oh, good, your both still here," Conners said as he shown a bright flashlight in on them that temporarily blinded them. "A present from some of my men. They tell me you like bright lights at night."

"Tell them to eat shit," Mitch said blinking and turning from the light.

"Not very friendly, Stone but no matter, you won't live long enough to get to be pals with my men." Conners came down the ladder carrying a canister like the ones they had pulled out of the river earlier that evening.

"Here you go folks. Some nice fresh NANOs all programmed for the resin in your boat. They'll eat this blow boat down to the waterline and turn it into a glob of goo. A non floating glob by the way."

Mitch and Alicia just sat and watched as Conners placed the container on the floor next to them and set the timer for three minutes.

"That's all the time you have before they'll get out and start to work on your boat, Stone. Enjoy your last moments together." There was quiet on the boat. "Nothing more to say. Too bad. Good bye then," Conners said and left. He clasped the lock.

"By the way," she asked Mitch, "How did he get the key to your boat?"

"Must be he picked the lock and found the spare I keep on the boat for myself just in case. Maybe he was going to keep the boat for himself when I was gone. Well at least he won't get it now."

"Never mind that," she said still struggling to get her hands next to his.

"We've got two minutes and ten seconds before the NANOs are released to figure a way out of this."

They both moved and stretched and tried every possible way to hand off the key. Then Mitch tried to reach the lock on her cuffs but couldn't bend his wrists far enough.

"I can't reach your cuffs, "he said.

"Wait, why not just set the keys on the floor. I'll try to pick them up. I've got a little more room in these."

"OK," he said and let them drop to the floor.

"Shit, they're out too far, can you slide them over more?"

"I'll try," he said, "how's that?"

"Nope, not quiet. And damn we've got only ninety seconds left." They both froze as they heard a boat approach and then the sailboat rock as someone stepped aboard. Then they heard the footsteps on deck.

"Here. Down here," they both yelled. "Help, we're down here," they called again.

"Mitch?"

"Gary, is that you?"

"Yeah, but the hatch is locked."

"Break it we're cuffed to the mast and a can of NANOs is going to be released in a minute and ten seconds."

Gary kicked the hatch several times but the teak and plexiglass door just absorbed the blows and won't break.

"Shit, Mitch. It won't even crack."

"Get something heavy. We've only got fifty seconds before these things start on my boat."

"OK," Gary said, "hold a minute." "Oh sorry," he added thinking about what he said and jumped over to the patrol boat and then back to the sailboat and hooked the bar under the hasp and lifted. It pulled the screws out of the teak frame and he flung the hatch cover aside and leaped down the stairs to the cabin.

"Glad you could make it. Now get those off my boat," Mitch commanded just as the timer counted down to '0'. "Shit" was all Mitch could say as the canister popped and the blue gel seeped out of the container and down the sides to the floor. "Damn that Conners, now he's made me mad. He's messed with my boat."

"Remember," Alicia said, "he's mine first though."

"Nope. All deals are off. I want him now, in the worst way. Once for the slap and once for my new boat."

"Do you two even argue over getting even?"

"Yes," he said.

"No," she said.

"Great," said Gary as he unlocked the cuffs on Alicia's wrists.

"We've got to get that stuff off the boat," she said staring at the blue ooze spreading out on the floor.

"Too late," Mitch said sadly, rubbing his wrists and flexing his fingers to get the circulation back into his hands. "That stuff is already starting to work on the resin. Look. The floor is sagging. A couple of more minutes and the whole hull will be compromised."

"I'm sorry," said Gary watching the floor melt and bubble, "if I was just a little quicker maybe…"

"Don't worry," Mitch cut him off.

"We've got to get out of here. We've got bigger things to deal with."

"Yeah, like that scumbag Conners," she snarled.

"Yeah, and the dam and the lab," added Mitch trying to control his rage over the sight of his brand-new boat rapidly dissolving before his eyes like a clump of dirt in water.

"C'mon, you guys let's get out of here," Gary said pulling an arm on each of them.

"OK," Mitch said in resignation of the facts spreading out in front of his eyes and as he watched the floor and now the cabin walls start to soften and melt. The blue gel was still foaming out of the container and Mitch just couldn't pull himself away from the sad sight. "He'll pay for this," Mitch muttered as Gary and Alicia climbed the steps.

"C'mon, Mitch," she called down to him, "there's nothing we can do here."

"Yeah, OK," he said. "Just a minute, I want to get a few things off first."

"Well hurry. From the looks of that stuff they work fast."

"Yeah, all right." Mitch went into the cabin and retrieved his personal weapon and his clothes and stuffed them into a large duffle bag. He did a quick glance around the cabin and decided everything else could be replaced easily. He started to step out into the main cabin and held back his foot. The floor in front of the port side door was almost gone. He looked at the creeping blob of NANO jelly and in places he could see the exterior hull and the bilge.

"Shit," he said.

"What's the matter, what's wrong," called Alicia.

"You OK Mitch?" Gary asked.

"Ah, yes. Just that these damn things are really eating my boat fast."

"Get out of there then," she exclaimed, "remember, if they are after the resin, it's basically carbon and so are you."

"I know, I know," he snapped back. He shot over to the starboard side door and cut through the main head and back to the cabin. The NANOs were almost at the ladder and Mitch wasn't. "Hey, catch this stuff I need some of my charts," he yelled up to the two on the deck.

"Hurry up," came the united voices.

"I am, I am."

"OK, toss up the bag and get out of there," Gary called down.

Mitch heaved it up and out with a grunt.

"Ah, any time Mitch," she insisted.

Mitch ignored her and climbed up onto the navigator's station and started looking through his charts. Where is it, he said to himself.

"What did you say?" asked Alicia sticking her head down through the hatch. "Damn Mitch the whole floor is gone and so are most of the interior walls."

"Bulkheads," he corrected.

"Uh, huh!"

"Hey, either of you see that knapsack I had from the lab?"

"Yeah, I think so," Gary said, "why?"

"'Cause I need it. Have you seen it for sure?"

"Yeah, it's on the patrol."

"Are you sure?" Mitch said losing his patience.

"Yeah, yeah, but hold on, I'll look," he said and jumped over to the patrol. "Tell him it's right here," he told Alicia.

"He's got it, now come on, get out of there," she said to Mitch.

"OK," he said and grabbed a couple of the charts and crawled back toward the hatch. The NANOs had dissolved the floor under the ladder and now it just hung there by a couple of small hooks with no support at the base. The floor usually carried all the weight and the hooks only kept the ladder from sliding out of place. Now the small brass hooks would have to carry Mitch's weight.

He tossed the charts up on deck and leaned over and grabbed the ladder. He stretched out a foot and tested the ladder for strength. It seemed to hold and he swung his other foot over to the step and started up the ladder. He was nearly at the top of the six steps when the small hooks bent and the ladder fell away and onto the nearly dissolved floor near the cabin door.

"Wow," he said trying to keep his dangling feet out of the voracious goo. "Ah, a little assistance here," he called.

Gary and Alicia grabbed hold of his arms and pulled him up onto the deck. "Don't say it," he warned, "I know, I know. You told me so."

Both grinned at him and then they just shook their heads.

"What's so damned important?" she asked.

"And what is in the old sack?" asked Gary holding it up as if it was rotting garbage.

"Just some souvenirs," Mitch said, "and these are some charts for some research," he said gathering up the rolled pieces of paper. The melting boat lurched to the starboard side and threw Alicia into Mitch's arms.

"Well I thought we'd wait now that my boat is disappearing."

She gave him a playful swat. "Not in front of the children she said nodding over toward Gary."

"Huh, what?" he said with a snicker. "You two love birds about ready to abandon ship?"

"Yeah," Mitch said mournfully. He helped Alicia across to the patrol and then stepped across himself. Gary fired the patrol boat's two big engines and Mitch and Alicia undid the lines. They pulled away slowly and Mitch just stood at the stern and watched as his boat suddenly shifted again. He could hear water rushing in through the breached hull.

"It won't be long now," he said.

Alicia came over to him and put her arm around his waist. "You'll have another one soon."

"I hope so," he said, "I still owe you a quiet night at anchor somewhere."

"Is that all you think of?"

"Yeah, that and I was thinking about turning some of those NANOs loose on Conners, just for fun mind you."

"I don't know about that, but let's go and get our case together and nail the son of a bitch."

"OK, but what about the other thing now?"

"Well, if you're really worried, I have a boat too, you know."

"That's right," he said and put his hand around her waist. "Gary, crank it up we've got shitbags to stomp."

"You got it." The engines revved and they had to hold on as Gary steered the patrol boat toward home. They were out of sight and missed the final agonizing death of the graceful yacht. It sank below the surface and all the that remained for a few seconds was a foam on the surface from the air escaping the cabin. Mitch's dream summer home was gone and Mitch was not about to let the man responsible get away with this indignity.

The three sped back to the marina and Gary dropped Alicia and Mitch off on the main dock and Mitch carried his knapsack and the rescued charts like they were made of gold.

"I'll go and secure the boat," Gary said, "and then I'll pick you up."

"What for?" Mitch asked, "it's 2AM and we can't do anything more tonight. We'll meet you at the office first thing in the morning."

"You're right," Gary said on second thought, "our patrols will keep them bottled up until morning and we can all use some sleep. Right?"

"Yeah, right," replied Mitch.

"Right, yeah," added Alicia.

"OK," said Gary, "8AM at the office."

"Ah, 10AM and I'll bring the fat pills."

"Deal," Gary shot back and pulled the boat away from the dock to take it back to its spot at the other end of the marina.

"Fat pills?" she asked.

"Donuts, but all they really do is add on the pounds. Take two a day to gain weight. They should prescribe them."

She chuckled and took Mitch's hand and they walked toward her boat. "So what's in the knapsack you've been dragging all over the place and that has almost gotten you killed twice. And for that matter what's with all those old charts. I've got new ones which are probably a lot more accurate on my boat."

"I'm sure, but I'm just a lover of history I guess."

"What about a lover of young things?" she asked pulling him onto her boat and down into the cabin.

"Hey, this is kind of ah…"

"Professional?"

"That too," he said. "How do you live down here and where do you sleep?"

"In the V berth," she said and headed forward as Mitch stood in the middle of the cramped cabin and looked over the assembled equipment. She had all kinds of instruments and microscopes and computers crammed into the interior of the cruiser.

"What do you do with all this stuff?" he asked.

"Analyze and research," she said, "and try to find out what makes those things tick if I could get a sample."

"Shit," he exclaimed.

"What?" she called from behind the half-closed cabin door.

"We left all those NANOs on the patrol boat. You'd have all kinds of samples there."

"They should be all right until we can get a look at them in the morning," she said, "they were programmed for iron and calcium, remember."

"Yeah, but what if someone finds them? That's what people are made of too, right?"

"The boat will be locked up won't it?"

"Yeah, your right," he said still admiring the gear and then she stepped out from behind the door and Mitch set the knapsack and charts down right where he stood. She was standing in the doorway completely naked. "Did you find my equipment interesting?" she asked seductively.

"Yes, as a matter of fact, I was just admiring your micro…"

"Careful, mister."

"Scope," he finished and moved close to her. They embraced and both fell into the berth and it didn't take long for Mitch to show his full appreciation of Alicia's well-equipped boat. After about an hour

Mitch found he couldn't sleep. He glanced over and saw that Alicia was fast asleep and all wrapped up in the sheets. He quietly slid out of the bunk and donned his underwear and softly closed the cabin door. He found the main cabin lights and turned on the lamp over what was once the navigator's seat. Now on her floating lab it was a combination desk and dinner table.

He cleared the dishes and set them in the galley sink. Then he unrolled the two old charts he had managed to rescue from his now destroyed boat, and spread them out on the table. After that he picked up the knapsack and unzipped it. He pulled out the large bundled wrapped in newspaper and gently set it on top of the old charts. Mitch carefully unwrapped the newspaper from around the rectangular object and tossed the paper onto the floor. After the last piece of paper was removed Mitch sat back for a moment and gloated and grinned at the ancient and slightly decayed book. Liberating it from that scumbag bent on world domination didn't seem to bother his conscience nor conflict with his sense of duty as a cop. Besides he really only borrowed it and would return it after he discovered its secrets.

Seems to be in fairly good shape, he thought, and he gently lifted the cover to inspect the first page. He just stared in amazement as he contemplated the significance of the book and of the fate of the author and his shipmates. He sat there and wondered and thought for a few moments then carefully re-wrapped the old manuscript. He placed it gently back into the sack and pulled out a large envelope. Inside was a stack of numbered pages with what he hoped would be a typed transcript of the book and some drawings and notes from the translator.

He wasn't sure but he wondered if Lindquist had done the translation or if he'd had it done for him. Mitch guessed that Lindquist wouldn't trust anyone with the information so he probably did it himself. Hope he was good at it, Mitch thought and started to read through the English version of the 10th century log book. He also tried to match the translation with the original text to get a feel for the language himself. He figured he might be able to at least make an educated guess at the structure and substance of the words. Remarkably some of the words looked to be old English or German in origin and he made a mental note to look for a dictionary of pre-Norman English.

CHAPTER 14

THE CONFRONTATION

*M*itch had just finished the transcript and placed it back in the envelope when Alicia appeared in the cabin in the same condition she had been in earlier.

"Damn, woman have you no shame," he said as he tried to stuff the large envelope back into the sack.

"Having trouble getting it in?" she asked teasingly.

"Not until just this moment," he said finally replacing the envelope and zipping the knapsack.

"What are you doing out here?" she asked more seriously.

"Just more research. It's a hobby of mine and I couldn't sleep. I didn't want to disturb you."

"I wanted to be disturbed," she said taking him by the arm and leading him back to the front berth.

"Oh," was all he could say in response. Her alarm clock went off at 8:30 and both of them unwound from each other's embrace and tried to force themselves fully awake.

"I would make breakfast, but I'm afraid I don't have much in the refrigerator."

"That's OK. I've got to get the donuts anyway. What time is it?"

"8:32."

"We'd better get moving," he said and started to get up.

"You sure," she said and grabbed his arm.

"Yes, we told Gary 10:00 and he'll be pissed if we're late."

"OK," she said throwing off the sheet to expose her still naked body, "if you say so."

He looked and smiled. "Sorry we just don't have the time." He got up and headed out of the small cabin before she changed his mind. "Ah, why don't you shower here and I'll use the facilities at the marina office," he said.

"Naw, I use the showers there too," she said appearing through the door in a T-shirt and shorts.

"OK, let's go, but before we do that let's go by the patrol boat and get you a sample of those NANOs to analyze."

"Good idea. Maybe we can figure out how to stop them once they've been released."

"You seemed to know how back on the island."

"That was comparatively easy. The NANOs were in an enclosed space and still hooked up to the programming computer. Once they are released, it isn't that simple."

"I see what you mean. OK, then we definitely need to have you take a look at those things in here," he said and finished getting dressed.

They climbed up onto the deck and she turned and locked the door. Mitch was already off of the boat and he helped her step from the swim platform onto the dock. "Thanks," she said still holding his hand. They walked down the dock and up onto the solid ground of the marina. Mitch liked it here. The marina had been built on the site of an early 19th century naval base. During the War of 1812 the U.S. Navy had used this harbor, and in fact this very spot, to construct most of its Great Lakes Fleet including the largest ship of the time. That ship never got wet though and met the same fate as Mitch's boat last night. The British invaded in the summer of 1813 and burned the ship to the ground before it was launched.

"Do you know the history behind this place?" Mitch asked as they walked to the other end of the marina where the locked boathouse, holding the Sheriff's patrol boat, was located.

"No."

"It's a long story. I'll have to tell you it sometime."

"Another long story," she said a little sardonically.

"You'd like my stories."

"I'm sure if you'd ever tell me one."

"I will," he said, "when I have the time."

Mitch and Alicia turned the corner and walked out onto the dock along the side of the boathouse. The marina provided a slip in the secured boathouse for the patrol boat and only Mitch, Gary, and the Patrol Division Lieutenant had the key to their designated area. Even though the boathouse was shared by about twenty other boat owners the county had built a wall and a private entrance into the slip where the patrol was docked. They had taken about ten steps along the dock when suddenly Conners appeared out of the boathouse and stood right in front of them blocking their path.

"Where the hell did you come from?" Mitch asked.

"One might ask you two the same question. You're supposed to be at the bottom of the lake chained to whatever was left of that poor excuse for a boat."

"That reminds me, Conners, the insurance company will be contacting you."

"Only if they can find me," he said.

"Just turn over any rock. That's where all the slimy slugs are always found," Alicia said.

"Charming as always, Ms. Carlsson, but again we won't be able to share any quality time together."

"Ooh, lucky me," she said.

"Yes, well now that we have exchanged greetings again, we must conclude our reunion."

"One question, Conners, how did you get into a locked boat-house?"

"Quite simple. Your neighbors don't seem to be as security con-scious as your department. They just hook the lock in the latch and don't even close it. Very careless of them wouldn't you say? After that we just climbed that feeble attempt at a wall. Too bad you won't be around much longer. You could do an Officer Friendly on crime pre-vention."

"I'm not that friendly," Mitch said and lunged for Conners. "Run Alicia," he said just before Conners pulled out his 9mm pistol and fired directly at the charging Mitch. The bullet hit Mitch and he dropped to the dock at Alicia's feet. Alicia had stopped at the sound of the shot and she turned just in time to see Mitch crumple to the dock.

"You bastard, you've killed him," she screamed and bent down to help Mitch.

"He tried to attack me. It was self defense."

"He wasn't armed, you shit," she yelled. She was trying to help Mitch who was bleeding profusely from a large wound in his upper face over his left eye.

"That's not how my witnesses saw it, is it men?" he said to the two uniformed guards now standing formidably behind Alicia.

"No sir, he came at you with a knife and you acted in self defense."

"There, you see, Ms. Carlsson, they saw it just the way it hap-pened."

"That's not what I saw nor what I'll report to the police."

"No, Ms. Carlsson, I'm afraid you won't be reporting anything to the police or anyone else."

She grasped the meaning of his last statement and from the crouched position over the wounded Mitch, she pounced at Conners and went straight for his throat. His reflexes were not quite fast enough this time and she managed to rake her finger nails down his check and then clutched his throat with her fingers tightly around his Adam's apple. "Then you'll pay right here and now," she screamed.

"Get her off of me," he tried to yell to the guards and at the same time trying to break her strangle hold. Her fingers were almost to the first knuckled deep in his throat and the nails were starting to draw blood. His voice was more of a raspy gasp. The two guards managed to pry her away from Conners but not before she scored with a lucky kick to the groin. He doubled over and when he was able to stand upright again he felt his clawed face and gouged neck and then stared at his blood-covered hand.

"You bitch," he said and backhanded her across her mouth and jaw with the pistol in his right hand. She slumped unconscious into the guards' arms.

"Throw her in the boat and then toss in the corpse here too," Conners said kicking Mitch in the ribs. The guards dumped her into the back of the patrol boat with a dull thud and returned a moment later with the blood soaked body of Mitch. They tossed him in on top of Alicia.

"No more screwing around with those high tech toys," Conners said wiping the blood from his face with his handkerchief.

"She did a number on you, didn't she?" one of the guards said just before Conners punched him.

"You didn't see anything, understand?" he said to the guard getting back to his feet. "You neither," Conners said to the other one. "Just remember those two in the locker room a couple of days ago."

"Yeah, sure," they both said in unison.

"Good now, let's just finish this the old-fashioned way. Empty out the gas tanks and make sure you cover the whole boat."

"Yes sir," they both said together and they both jumped into the boat and pulled loose the fuel lines from the portable gasoline tanks. They poured out the contents all over the interior of the boat but since they were standing over Alicia and Mitch they managed to avoid getting any on the two unconscious victims.

"Pour the rest down into the cabin," Conners said and the two guards emptied their cans into the front cabin.

Alicia stirred but didn't make any sudden movements to draw the attention to her recovery. Her jaw hurt but she didn't move until the two guards had stepped back onto the slip.

"Once again, Deputy Stone, I bid you farewell and this time I'm afraid you can't be saved by the timely arrival of Ms. Carlsson or any of your cavalry. It seems she will share your same fate, and well there isn't anybody around here to come to your aid. Do have a nice life together. All thirty seconds of it," Conners said with a snide laugh to the motionless lumps in the stern of the boat. With his parting comment he lit an old newspaper he had found in a nearby trash can, and tossed the flame into the gas-soaked boat. It immediately burst into flames and the whole boat was engulfed in an instant.

"OK, let's get out of here before someone spots the smoke and us," Conners said and the three of them rushed out of the boathouse and Conners locked the door. "No sense in making it too easy to recover the bodies," he said laughing again. They walked quickly to their company S.U.V. and drove slowly out of the marina just as smoke started to roll out from under the eves of the boathouse.

"Good work gentlemen," he said looking back at the wooden boathouse now starting to catch fire. "We disposed of the NANOs they found and the meddling twosome at the same time."

As soon as the fire started, Alicia grabbed the back of Mitch's shirt and when she heard the boathouse door close she fought off the pain in her jaw and dragged Mitch with all her strength to the transom and pushed and pulled him into the water. Fortunately for her and for Mitch she had been a lifeguard and knew how to keep an unconscious person afloat. Unfortunately, that was twenty years ago and Mitch was slightly larger that some of the kids she had trained with. She kicked as hard as she could and tried to swim as far from the burning boat as she could. Alicia worked her way to the far end of the boathouse and held Mitch in one arm while she peeked her head around one of the boats to see if their adversaries had gone. When she felt the coast was clear, she swam to the next dock and up to the shore. She dragged the lifeless Mitch out of the water and checked to see if he still had a pulse. The wrist pulse was nonexistent and she pressed hard on the carotid on the side opposite the bullet wound. She felt a slight flutter and she started to cry in relief that Mitch wasn't dead.

People from some of the moored boats began running toward the burning building and Alicia called for help. "Hey, he's hurt, get an ambulance," she half asked half commanded to the first person who ran by. The next two people she pressed into service to help her carry Mitch to the marina office and onto a couch to await the paramedics.

CHAPTER 15

THE ESCAPE

*D*ispatcher Carol Vincent was working the Fire Control Desk on the 7-3 shift. Sergeant Faulkner had just delivered her and the rest of the dispatchers a cup of coffee. Whenever he had the chance, he always tried to bring the dispatch crew large cups of coffee and a few donuts. Even though the dispatch center had its own coffee machine, they always appreciated the gesture and Gary wanted to keep that important group of people very happy. Since they were his and every other road cop's lifeline to back up and help, he wanted them to be happy and very alert, even on the day shift.

Carol had just pulled the plastic lid off of the jumbo regular cup of coffee and was thinking to herself how peaceful the morning had been so far. She was working her rotation at the Fire Dispatch line this week and aside from a few early morning radio checks from some of the more remote departments in the county, both the radio and the phone lines were quiet and that was just the way she liked it. That bliss was about to end. Almost at the same instant, line one on the police dispatch phone started to flicker. Nancy Williams was doing her rotation at the main 911 control desk and was now frantically answering the flood of calls and redirecting them to the appropriate dispatcher.

Carol pursed her lips and blew some air across the top of the steaming cup of black coffee and was about to take a sip when line one on her phone lit up followed by line two. She quickly set her cup down and spilled some on her hand. "Shit," she said under her breath and reached for the phone and pushed the flashing button. "Fire Control, Dispatcher Vincent. What is the nature of your call?"

"We have a fire at the marina in Smyth's Cove. The boat house is burning."

"Yes sir, I have that. The boathouse at the marina in Smyth's Cove. Please stay on the line while I dispatch the fire department. Don't hang up," she instructed the caller in case she needed more information.

"OK, but hurry, it's really burning now," the witness said into her earpiece.

"Yes sir, please hold," Carol said and pressed the red hold button. She switched her head set from the phone line to the radio panel and pressed the button for Smyth's Cove Fire Department. The panel made a clicking sound as the switch activated the relays and the automatic radio beacons. At nearly the same instant the large siren mounted on a tower behind the Smyth's Cove Village Center building began to blare and scream out its summoning wail.

Everyone within five miles could hear the loud siren and in case a member of the volunteer department was somehow oblivious to that call for assistance each one had a pager keyed to the assigned radio frequency for all fire departments. These pagers were now sounding or vibrating simultaneously with the siren at the fire station.

Carol started her clear dispatch giving the now mobilizing firemen all the necessary details. "County Fire Control to all Smyth's Cove fire units. We have a report of a structure fire at the marina. Repeat. County Fire Control to all Smyth's Cove fire units. We have a report of a structure fire at the marina. Please respond." She released the mike key and picked up line two that was still blinking. "County Fire Dispatch," she said.

"Yes, we have a gunshot victim at Smyth's Cove marina. He's hurt bad and we need an ambulance fast."

"Did you say gunshot?" Carol asked and all of the other dispatchers alerted on that word.

"Yes, he's been shot and he's unconscious. Please hurry."

"Yes ma'am. Is the assailant still present?"

"No, he's gone."

"OK, please stay on the line while I dispatch the ambulance. Don't hang up."

"No, I won't and tell Sgt. Faulkner that we can make the meeting with him this morning."

"Yes ma'am," Carol said not understanding the last part. She was about to dispatch the ambulance when the first fire unit called out of service.

"Smyth's Cove unit T-One responding to the marina. Any more information? Over."

"Affirmative. The caller reported that the boathouse was on fire."

"Copy. Boathouse," said the fireman, "Unit T-One en route."

"Received T-One. Also be advised we have received a second call for the ambulance. Report of a gunshot, same location."

There was a brief pause. "Copy Dispatch. Please send out a second alarm and please dispatch the Harbor Department for assistance."

"Received Unit T-One. County Fire Control to Smyth's Cove Ambulance monitors. We have a report of a gunshot victim at the marina. Please respond." Carol didn't have to wait long. The ambulance crew was already en route with the first fire unit.

"Smyth's Cove Ambulance One, copy, en route."

"Received A-One," Carol said. The rest of the department called out of service and en route to the marina which was only six blocks away from the fire hall. Carol acknowledged each unit's call and proceeded to sound a second alarm and dispatch two more departments for mutual aid assistance to Smyth's Cove.

At the next console, Judy Anderson was beginning to dispatch a uniformed patrol to the scene at first to stand by in the event the fire was of suspicious origin. Now after hearing Carol dispatch the ambulance, she dispatched a second marked unit and the on call detective.

Gary was in the uniformed patrol office and heard the dispatches for both the police and fire units and he knew Mitch was involved one way or another. One of the uniformed officers just dispatched was in fact at the office and ran past the patrol office headed for his car.

"Hey Andy," Gary called after the blur past the door.

"Yeah," the Deputy said, "I've just been sent to Smyth's Cove, can it wait Sarg.?"

"Yeah, no problem, I just want to go with you that's all," Gary said grabbing his duffle bag and dashing out the door. The two men ran down the hallway and out through the security doors to the fenced parking area used for the patrol vehicles.

They wasted no time getting to Smyth's Cove and even with the morning traffic they pulled in behind the fire engines in only twelve minutes. The firemen were running back and forth grabbing hoses and equipment to battle the blaze which had now almost consumed the entire boathouse and what appeared to Gary, were most of the boats kept there.

Even though the marina owner was summoned and he lived only five blocks from the marina, he couldn't get there in time to save more than just a few of the twenty boats kept inside the boathouse. Once he arrived with the key, several of the other boat owners hurried to untie and push some of the boats out of their slips and across to another dock. Gary didn't see the county's patrol boat and from the looks of the building he figured it was at ground zero when the fire started. With that sudden revelation, he also figured that Mitch was somehow involved and the coincidence of the gunshot call didn't make him feel any better about the way the day was shaping up.

He walked over to the marina office and was stopped by an assistant chief of the Smyth's Cove Fire Department.

"Ah, Sgt. Faulkner, near as we've been able to determine at this point the fire started in or very near the county's boat."

"Great," Gary said, his suspicions confirmed by the fireman.

"We won't know for sure until we get it under control. It's still going strong on two boats and three more are being threatened."

"All the boats a loss?" Gary asked not happy with the prospect.

"No, a couple were pulled out when it started. A bunch of the boat owners swam in under the flames and cut the lines. They managed to push out about four or five big ones from the far end. There," the fireman said pointing at the end of the building farthest from the area of destruction.

"Thanks for all your good work," Gary said trying to smile for the volunteer firefighter, who Gary also knew to be the son of the owners of the small grocery store in town.

"Oh," the fireman added, "I hope your partner is OK. Didn't look good when we got here."

"Thanks," Gary said again and quickened his pace to the office. Shit, he thought to himself. That damn Mitch got his ass in a jam again. Gary opened the door to the office and was greeted by one of the road patrol deputies as soon as he stepped across the threshold.

"Hi, Sarg.," he said, "it's Mitch, he took one in the face."

"How is he?" Gary asked peeking over and around the half dozen ambulance and EMT workers.

"Don't know, but he regained consciousness as soon as they started sticking needles in his arm."

"Yep, that's Mitch. Never did like them," Gary said not looking at the deputy but trying to see through the crowd of emergency personnel. Alicia finally saw him and left Mitch's side and worked her way around the kneeling and stooping paramedics. She was all wet and her hair was matted around her face. She seemed to be covered in oil and various assorted and sundry marine plants and flotsam.

Gary wasn't sure this was the same beautiful woman he had met only a few days earlier. She was a complete mess and he wondered what her appearance had to do with the burning boathouse and a wounded friend.

"Oh, Gary," she started and then just couldn't contain herself any longer. The sight of Mitch lying on the coach in the marina office all covered with blood and the near death experience in the boathouse was a strain on her normally well controlled emotions. She burst into tears and threw her arms around Gary's neck as the torrent of emotional tears flowed down her face.

"Close friend," Gary said to the wide-eyed Deputy standing beside him.

"Oh, yeah, sure. I can see that," the Deputy remarked in agreement with a smile that said differently. "Anything you say Sarg."

Gary gave the Deputy a dirty look and hugged Alicia to give her comfort.

"Why don't we go outside and let these people work. He'll be all right. These are some of the best EMTs in the county."

"All right," she said nodding and sniffling and wiping her eyes with her dirty sleeve. She spread more oil on her face but Gary wasn't sure whether it was more or just a rearrangement of the black gunk already smeared on her beautiful face.

"What happened?" Gary finally asked when it seemed that she had regained her composure.

"He shot Mitch," she snapped angrily at Gary for not seeing the obvious.

"Yes I know but how? Who? What's going on?" Gary figured he better get all of the questions in at once of she started to lose it again.

"That bastard Conners," she hissed.

"Conners shot Mitch," Gary repeated in nearly the same contemptuous tone.

"Yes, and he torched the patrol boat. He tried to kill us both and dispose of us in the fire."

"That explains it then," Gary said. He reminded himself to get her statement on paper and forward the part about the fire to the Fire Chief. It would save them a lot of work in determining the cause. "OK," he continued, "go on."

"We were going over to the boat to get a sample of those NANOs when we bumped into Conners and his hired muscle. They had broken into the boat house and were waiting for us. I guess they must have searched the boat looking for the bags of NANOs."

"Did they find them?"

"No, I don't think so. I don't remember seeing them carrying anything when we met them. I guess the NANOs were still on the boat but," she paused and looked toward the destroyed boathouse, "now they've all been destroyed in the fire."

"Not all of them," Gary interjected. "I pulled a couple of bags from the well and it's at the office in storage."

"Oh, Gary that's just great," she said with a sniffle and the start of a smile.

"Go on," Gary prompted, "what happened?"

"Oh, yeah, well like I said, we were on our way to the boat and bumped into that piece of shit Conners. Mitch and he had a few words and then Mitch goes for him. I don't know what possessed him to do that except Conners was making some foul references to me and his good times."

"Good old Mitch," Gary said, "always defending the ladies."

"Yeah, well this lady didn't need defending, damn it. And besides, he almost got killed doing it for me," her tone changed and she started to cry again.

"He'll be all right," Gary said trying to comfort her again.

"Are you sure?" she said between more sniffles.

"Yeah, he's pretty tough and besides I've seen him a lot closer to death than this. Ask him about the scar down his cheek."

"He'll probably say it's a long story."

"Yeah, those are the best especially over beer and pizza."

"Or champagne and caviar," she said now nearly laughing and wiping away all the tears.

"That's better," Gary said now smiling himself. "OK, what's the rest of the story?"

"Mitch went for him, and Conners hits him with a round in the face. Mitch goes down and is out cold and all covered with blood. Conners just stands there all smug and tries to tell me that it was all in self defense and then I get really pissed."

"Oh, oh. What?" Gary asked almost afraid to find out.

"I raked his face with both hands. Dragged my nails down both sides really good. Then I went for his throat."

"Guess he couldn't shoot a charming lady like you," Gary added but Alicia just ignored him now.

"Anyway," she started again, "then his two goons grab me and try to pull me off of him but not before I plant my foot in his crotch. Conners doubles over in pain and I'm rather proud of my handy work and then that son of a bitch back hands me with the pistol."

"Oh," Gary said now studying the bruise on her cheek and jaw showing out from under the grease and dirt on her face.

"You better have the ambulance crew look at that. You may need a stitch or two. You'll match Mitch now."

"Yeah, except he has added a bullet hole to his collection."

"Go on," Gary said.

"After Conners hit me the next thing I remember is coming to in the boat on top of Mitch and as the main event at a barbecue. Apparently Conners thought that was the most spectacular way to destroy us and any evidence of the NANOs all at once."

"Yeah, good guess," Gary said watching the firefighters gain control of the inferno. "How did you get away?"

"As soon as Conners and his boys left, I grabbed Mitch and dragged him over the transom and swam like hell to the shore. Some of the local boat owners here helped me get him out of the water and into the office."

"That explains your new fashion statement," Gary said pointing to her wet hair and messy face.

The ambulance crew had Mitch all stabilized and wrapped up on the stretcher ready for transport. The deputy came out first and held the door open. Then came the stretcher with Mitch all wrapped, wired and sporting an armful of I.V. needles. Gary and Alicia moved closer to get a look at their friend. "Mitch," Alicia called.

"Hey, Mitch," Gary said as the stretcher passed them and then stopped at the rear of the large truck like ambulance. Mitch half opened the one eye that wasn't covered in bandages and as soon as he saw them he forced a half smile and was able to lift his left hand enough to give them a thumbs up sign.

"Meet you at the hospital," Gary said returning the sign. Alicia smiled and then started to cry again. Mitch tried to shake his head but winced in pain as the neck brace holding his head prohibited any movement. The ambulance crew carefully loaded him into the back of the rescue unit and climbed in after him. Gary took a few steps to the open door. "How's he doing?"

"Not bad under the circumstances. Under all that blood there's just a nasty laceration. Near as we can tell there's no bullet. It looks as if it just grazed along the side of his head from his left eye to above his ear. Head wounds bleed a lot but most of the time just look worse than they are. We'll know more when the hospital can get some x-rays but it looks like he'll live to fight another day."

"That's good," Gary said stepping away so the door could close. The crew backed the ambulance out between the collection of fire trucks and police cars. The beeping sound, the ambulance made in reverse, didn't seem to matter and the uniformed deputy had to run down the driveway and clear a path for the squad. "He'll be OK," Gary said reassuringly to Alicia as they watched the ambulance work its way up the access road to the main street in town. As soon as the ambulance made it to the street the sirens started to wail.

"Are we going to the hospital now?" she asked.

"Yes, after I talk to one of our investigators first," he said and walked past several fire trucks and over a spaghetti like jumble of hoses. "Hey John," Gary called to the detective standing next to another Assistant Chief.

"Yeah, Gary. How's Mitch doing?" he asked.

"He'll be fine or so the EMTs think. I guess they patch him up and do some tests on him at the hospital but it looks like he'll survive again."

"Good, I hate police funerals and especially for a friend. Any idea what happened here?"

"Got one eye witness over there to the shooting and the arson," Gary said pointing to Alicia who was standing rather forlornly and huddling with her arms around herself to either calm her nerves or ward off a chill. "She's kind of shook up and worried about Mitch."

"Can I talk to her now? John asked.

"Ah, no. She's a friend of mine and Mitch's and she saw the whole mess. In fact she was a target of the perp. I'll get it all on paper for you as soon as I can."

"Today," John pressed.

"No promises but I'll try," Gary replied trying to stall any further pressure.

"OK then, I'll just take a few photos when things cool down and then talk to the locals."

"We're talking arson and attempted murder here," John said rhetorically.

"Yeah," Gary said, "and we know who and hopefully where we can find the bastard. I'll put the info out on the air and in the computer."

"OK, thanks," John said. "Maybe we can close this soon with an arrest."

"Let's hope so," Gary said walking back to the shivering Alicia. "Cold? It's almost 80."

"Just got the shakes, that's all. Are we done here?"

"Yeah."

"Good. I need to get out of all this wet stuff. I want to change on my boat and I'll meet you back at the office in about fifteen minutes, OK?"

"Yeah sure. I'll just check and see if anyone has anything else on the fire. Back here in fifteen, right."

"Yeah, thanks Gary," she said walking toward her boat tied up at the end of the slip in front of the office. She carefully stepped onto the transom and then down onto the deck. She slid open the door and stepped inside. The blinds were drawn to protect her expensive and sensitive lab equipment from the sun and from prying eyes, but in the dim interior she just caught a glimpse of movement or maybe just sensed the presence. She turned to flee but was grabbed by the hair and yanked back. She started to scream but was cut off by familiar sounding voice telling her to keep quiet. He emphasized his point by shoving a gun into her already bruised face.

She struggled and tried to show the assailant some of her martial arts training but he had a handful of hair and he tugged it at regular intervals to remind her how really painful it was. "Let go you bastard."

"That's no way to greet an old friend, especially when we've meant so much to each other."

"Conners," she said nearly spitting out his name. "I figured a chicken shit like you would be long gone after what you did to Mitch and me."

"Yes, how is the dear Mr. Stone. Oh, I am sorry I keep forgetting my etiquette. I mean Deputy Stone or should I say now cold as stone?"

"You bastard," she snarled again and tried to give him an elbow in the stomach.

"Nice try Ms Carlsson, but please try to save some of that energy for later."

"Fuck you," she snarled.

"Exactly. But first of all please answer my inquiry about Stone. Am I to assume that since you are obviously alive that he is as well?"

"Yes, no thanks to you and for your information half of his department is up on the shore and all I have to do is scream and you'll find out just popular Mitch is."

"No, I don't think you'll do that," he said pushing the gun deeper into the discolored cheek.

"That hurts you shit," she said through clenched teeth.

"Of course it does and in case you haven't guessed by now I know lots of ways to inflict pain and, shall we say, I enjoy my work."

"Yeah well I know a few ways to inflict a little pain myself," she said still trying to get an angle so she could demonstrate her abilities.

"Please restrain your urges, at least for now. I would prefer not to have to kill you, but you must cooperate to prevent that possibility."

"Yeah, well you seemed pretty eager to kill me earlier in the boat house."

"An unfortunate miscalculation. I do apologize for my indiscretion."

"Not accepted," she said and tried to twist free. He held her hair firmly and slammed her hard into the cabin wall.

"Please Ms. Carlsson, do not force me to change my mind and kill you right here and now. I told you, you will live but you will have to cooperate. Do you understand that? You can be nice and live."

"What do you want?" she asked hesitantly.

"I'm sure you'll be disappointed but all I want is for you to carefully and slowly pull this boat out of the slip and head out into the lake."

"Where to?"

"Not your concern at this point. Just get out of the harbor and head west. I'll tell you after we clear the breakwater."

"OK, I'll help you out of here then you leave me alone, right?"

"You have my word of honor."

"How comforting," she said. "OK, I'll get you out of here but then you get out of my life ASAP."

"As you wish, Ms. Carlsson or may I call you Alicia?"

"Ms. Carlsson will be fine."

"OK, now, I'm going to release you but if you try anything or call for help I'll make sure I shoot whoever comes down the dock first then I'll put a bullet into your pretty face. Ooh, nice bruise," he added noticing his handy work.

"Yeah, I got it from a bag of shit."

"Not a good start to our arrangement."

"So let's just get on with it," she said in disgust, "then you can get out of my life that much sooner."

"Very prudent of you," he said and let go of her hair.

"Thanks," she said as he pushed her through the cabin door.

"Please keep in mind that I will kill you if you make any attempt to summon assistance."

"I understand," she said and slowly moved to release the stern lines. Then she walked along the side cat walk and untied the two bow lines. The boat just bobbed in the slip freed from its moorings. She walked back to the rear deck and saw Conners reappear in the door holding his pistol and pointing it in her direction. "Very good so far Ms. Carlsson. I've been watching and you've done exactly as we have agreed. Now just pull out slowly."

"OK," she said not hiding her contempt for her unwanted passenger. She went to the controls and turned the key. The engines turned over and caught and she let them idle for a few seconds.

"Do hurry Ms. Carlsson. We wouldn't want to draw any attention to us while we sit and idle."

"No, of course not."

"Fine then let's go," he said sticking his head out of the cabin.

Alicia slowly pushed the gear lever into the forward position and the boat began to slowly move out of the slip. She pushed the twin throttle levers and both engines revved and the large cruiser glided out of its berth and she steered it into the center of the harbor and headed for the main channel around the breakwater.

"You can come out of hiding now. We're away from the dock."

"Very good, Ms. Carlsson. Just continue out of the cove slow and calm."

"Hey Gary, isn't that your friend there?" the deputy asked pointing at the big boat moving away from the marina.

"What? Where?" Gary asked, somewhat surprised.

"There on that boat just pulling out. I thought I saw a man onboard for a second but I don't see him now."

Gary stood and watched as the cruiser pulled out of the marina and turned to port toward the end of the breakwater and the channel. "Shit," he said and started running down the long finger of land separating the open lake from the cove and providing a nice little harbor for the pleasure boats. "Get on the radio and see of the State has their boat anywhere near here," he yelled over his shoulder to the deputy. He made it to the end of the point of land just as the cruiser and Alicia made another port turn into the main channel. He stood and watched in amazement as Alicia guided the boat out into the main part of the lake and powered up. The boat planed out of the water and left a big wake as it headed west. "What the hell," he said to himself.

The deputy came trotting up. "Nope the State boat is up in Smugglers Bay doing Boating While Intoxicated patrol for the holidays."

"Damn, then we need to get another one somewhere," Gary said looking back at the now smoldering boat house. What the hell is with Alicia taking off like that, unless, he thought to himself then stopped. "Damn," he said again to the deputy. "I think she's got our shooter on board."

"No shit."

"No shit and we've got to get to her fast," Gary repeated and began looking around the marina at all the potential boats. "All these blow boats won't do us any good," he complained. "Doesn't anyone have power down here?"

"Don't you have a boat?" the deputy asked Gary.

"Yeah but it's a fishing boat with a 60-hp engine. We' never catch that twin engine monster."

"I know," the deputy said suddenly realizing a spark of inspiration. "Isn't there a Coast Guard Auxiliary unit here? Someone must have a power boat for rescue work."

"That's right," Gary said suddenly remembering about the guy Mitch had introduced him to last summer at the marina cookout and beer recycling party. What was his name, Gary said to himself trying to recall the name in the sea of faces that he had met that Sunday afternoon just before all hell broke loose in the lake and everyone became paranoid almost over night that the country was about to be invaded or destroyed. He could place the face and it was only a moment longer before he put a name with the image. "I remember now. It's Les Shepard," Gary said and ran back to the office. "Hey, where's Les Shepard's boat," he asked the started office manager who was busy trying to straighten up the small room after the invasion of the firemen and rescue personnel. She didn't hear or see Gary bound through the door and she jumped at the sound of a voice suddenly demanding information.

Once she regained her breath from the start, she gave Gary the information. "Down at the end of D dock."

"Is he around?"

"Yeah, he should be. I thought I saw him out there watching the fire a while ago."

"Great, thanks," Gary said and dashed out the door and across the gravel parking lot and out onto D dock. This was one of the permanent docks set on pilings driven deep into the lake bottom. The deck was attached to the vertical posts and unlike the floating docks on either side, it was subject to the variations in the water level of the lake. In the spring the winter runoff made the lake water rise to almost cover the dock. In the spring you might need a ladder to board your boat. Some of the boat owners would complain that they had to get their feet wet to get to their boats. By summer though the water had dropped low enough where you had to step down onto your boat from the dock.

In some cases the water was so high that the marina couldn't put any boats at this dock because they would be sitting higher than the dock itself. That of course made the boat owners very unhappy. This year however the water wasn't as high and most of the boats were already in their slips. Gary saw the long sleek green and white cruiser tied at the end of the dock and hoped that the owner was on board and not in town somewhere. Despite the inconveniences of the dock and the water levels most of the boat owners gladly paid the premium rental fees for a slip here. This was the only covered dock in the marina and during the often rainy weekends when the other owners were either hiding below decks or had given up and gone home, the boaters on D dock could enjoy an outside afternoon under the cover of a roof. The sailboat owners with their tall masted crafts were jealous but would never admit it.

D dock was where the minority of the power boaters kept their floating homes during the summer and Les Shepard was at the very end with his 45 footer. Gary stopped at the end of the main dock and called out. "Les Shepard, this is the Sheriff's Department. We need your help," Gary called into the rear of the large boat. He was more than a little envious of how nice it looked from the dock. He waited for a few moments and then a man appeared on deck. He was in his fifties with brown hair starting to go grey at the temples. He was in good shape and looked as if he visited the gym more than once a week. He was wearing a T-shirt that said 'Power boaters do it with more thrust', and a pair of khaki colored cargo shorts. As soon as he stepped out the cabin door he put on a pair of sunglasses that were attached around his neck by a black cord. "Yeah, I'm Shepard. How can I help you?"

"Mr. Shepard. I'm Sgt. Faulkner from the Sheriff's Office and this is Deputy Benton," Gary said pointing to the uniformed man who had just stopped behind him. "We know you're with the Coast Guard Auxiliary and we need your boat. It's an emergency."

"Certainly," he said. "Does it have something to do with the fire?"

"Yes," Gary said.

"I heard there was a shooting too."

"Yes, my friend. He's with our department and we think the perpetrator is on a boat that just pulled out of the harbor. The owner of the boat is also a friend of mine and she's in grave danger."

"By all means then, come aboard and we'll get underway immediately."

"What's going on dear?" a female voice asked from the cabin and everyone turned to look at the source. Both Gary and Deputy Benton just stood for a moment as a woman clearly twenty years junior to Shepard came up from below. She had long blond hair pulled back into a pony tail and was wearing a very small black bikini that didn't leave much to either Gary's or Benton's imagination. "Is everything all right, honey?" she asked Shepard.

"Yes dear. These men are from the Sheriff's Department and they need our help as part of the Coast Guard. I'm sorry," he said to the two visitors who were trying not to stare at the beautiful woman standing nearly naked in front of them. "This is my wife, Amanda."

"Glad to meet you," Gary said reaching out to shale her hand. "I'm Sgt. Faulkner and this is Deputy Benton." Benton took a step closer to the gorgeous lady and shook her hand and smiled.

"Yes Mrs. Shepard, we need your husband's help in an emergency matter and I'm afraid time is critical," Gary said.

"Oh yes," Shepard said, "honey will you get the bow lines and Deputy if you could take care of the stern for me we'll be out of here in two minutes."

"Ah, I'm sorry Mr. Shepard but maybe you didn't understand. I can't order you to come but as a member of the Auxiliary I can have you along even as a civilian but it is very dangerous and I don't think your wife will be safe."

"Not to worry, Sgt., she's an officer in the Auxiliary and was active duty on a cutter in the Caribbean for five years. She's seen more action probably than all of us. I wouldn't worry about her. She recruited me into the Auxiliary."

"Oh. Well then in that case let's go," Gary said sheepishly.

Shepard fired up the engines and when Amanda pulled in the bow lines he looked over at Benton. "All set there Deputy?" He asked.

"Yes sir, all clear."

"Good. Where to Sgt?"

"Out into the lake and probably west toward Society Island. We're looking for a thirty-five-foot Carver cruiser with two people onboard. They headed out of here about ten minutes ago."

"Ah, Sgt. I don't mean to interrupt but this guy may not want to go back to the island especially if he thinks that will be the first place we'll look. My guess would be Canada across the lake."

"You maybe right but now that means we'll have to cover a few hundred square miles of open water and we don't have a lot of time."

"No problem," he said, "this boat can out run almost anything I've seen in the Cove here and I've got radar. We should be able to spot something that big easily. Oh by the way Sgt. You wouldn't have any idea why my boat was sitting about eight inches lower at the dock this morning compared to yesterday? Usually the water level drops over the summer by that much but not over night. Somebody mess-ing with the dam down river?"

"Uh, yeah you could say that. We think the guy we're after on that boat had something to do with that to," Gary said trying not to go into any details that he wasn't sure of himself.

"No shit, well he'll have to answer to a lot of people around the lake and along the river. They depend on the water being at a certain level at least until Labor Day. Some boats are going to be nudging the bottom shortly, especially those in the slips closest to shore."

"Yeah," was all Gary said.

"In fact I may have trouble getting through the channel here. Most of the season I have only a couple of feet below the keel and now the channel is going to be shallow in spots."

"What about the sailboats?" Gary asked, "don't they draw more water?"

"Some do but I've got about five feet draft with the outdrives on this thing. Some of the newer sailboats draw only about four feet, less with a swing keel, but yeah they'd be in trouble if the water drops another foot or so."

"Brace yourself then," Gary said, "This shitbag released some kind of super small machine into the river that is dissolving the dam. In a day or two there will be a full breach."

"Holy shit," Shepard said, "looks as though the time frame is sooner." He pointed to the depth gauge and had a concern looked on his face. "See this. Yesterday this was a lot deeper in here. I think the lake is dropping fast."

Gary just watched the readout on the depth gauge. He knew that he, Mitch, and Alicia had done everything they could to save the dam but the reality of their failure was still hard for him to bear. The boat pulled out of the slip and into the Cove and followed the same route out into the channel that Alicia had. Amanda Shepard climbed back down from the bow and went below. A few moments later she returned wearing black biking shorts and a white T-shirt tied at the bottom to reveal her washboard tight stomach. "I thought I should look a little less like a beach bum," she said smiling at Gary and Benton and she nestled in next to her husband at the helm.

"Ah, how long have you two been married?" Gary asked trying not to stare at the shapely legs of the crew.

"About a year now," Shepard said.

Amanda gave him a playful poke in the ribs. "It will be a year next week," she said with a gallery perfect smile.

"Congratulations," Gary said still trying not to stare at her legs in the tight black shorts. "May I use the radio, Mr. Shepard?"

"Sure and it's Les."

"OK Les," Gary said and picked up the microphone. "Ah, what's the name of your boat?"

"*My Pleasure.* Amanda picked it out."

"Oh," Gary said nodding his head in understanding. "My Pleasure to Viking Princess. Come in," Gary said and waited for a few seconds. He repeated the hail and waited again.

"They don't seem to want to talk to us," Shepard said.

"Can't imagine why," Gary said and repeated the transmission again. Nothing. He tried again but this time changed the message. "OK Conners, you might as well answer. We'll be catching up to you soon," He said and waited again.

"Guess we better answer the man," Alicia said and reached for the mike.

Conners slapped her hand aside. "I'll talk to them," He said with an air of authority.

"Listen shithead this is still my boat and furthermore don't hit me again," she protested.

"Shut up and drive," he snapped back and grabbed the mike. "OK whoever you are. What the hell do you want?"

"First of all I'm Sgt. Faulkner from the Sheriff's Office and secondly I want you to turn the boat around and surrender yourself."

"Whatever for?" Conners said innocently.

"You know very well, just turn around. Don't be stupid enough to add more charges to the attempted murder and arson."

"My dear Sgt. you're mistaken, I acted in self defense when your subordinate attacked me."

"He's my friend and you can discuss that bullshit story of yours with a jury."

"Not a chance and besides I've taken out a little insurance policy that will protect me while I manage to avoid any further contact with you county cops."

"Gary help!" Alicia screamed into the mike in Conners hand and he kept the key open as he slapped her hard across the side of the face. She let out a groan and slumped into the seat and the boat veered to starboard. Conners almost lost his balance but regained his footing in time to block a kick from the stunned Alicia.

"Nice try Ms. Carlsson but don't do that again or our deal will be terminated and so will you."

"Bastard," she said holding her face and regaining control of the boat.

Conners spoke into the mike again. "I assume you heard that small outburst from Ms. Carlsson?"

"Yes, is she all right?"

"For the time being," Conners said, "but that is subject to her continued cooperation and your turning back to port."

"No can do," Gary said, "just give it up and no one else will get hurt."

"I'm sorry you feel that way Sgt. but I expected as much from a duty bound small town cop. I'm afraid then I'll just have to continue with my original plans. Good day." Conners unkeyed the mike, gave Alicia a 'don't even think about it look', and turned the frequency control knob to channel 55 on the radio.

"Conners to base, come in." He waited and the reply came in quickly.

"Yes sir," the male voice said.

"I'm about ten miles out on the same cruiser we stopped last week. I've got the locals after me and I'll need a pick up in about fifteen off the east end."

"Received," was all the voice said.

"There now Ms. Carlsson you'll be rid of me in about fifteen minutes."

"Not a minute too soon," she said without looking at him. "By the way why didn't you leave the marina with your two goons when you had the chance. Even a brain dead like you must have known the place would fill up with police."

"A weakness of mine. Actually probably the only one, but I'm afraid I have an irresistible curiosity to see my plans finalized."

"Sounds to me more like a penchant for the perverse," she said sardonically. "Then why did you leave us in the lab then?"

"An unfortunate interruption. It seems my employer wished me to deal with certain members of the company's backers on the Malthusian Project. The CEO seemed to have had an ideological dispute and wanted my particular negotiating skills to settle the matter."

Alicia just sat and steered the boat. "So what was the dispute that you were asked to resolve?" she finally asked.

"Well I wasn't completely privy to all of the information but if you feel you must know," he said a little self importantly. "The financial backers that started Millennium Eco-Technologies were all long haired hippie freaks left over from the 60's."

"If they were 60's flower children, where did they get the money to start a big high tech company?"

"I guess not all of them just did drugs and hung out in communes. Some of them apparently became successful business persons and made a few bucks here and there."

"OK, so a few rich old hippies start a recycling company. Sounds pretty logical to me and pretty responsible. Where's the CEO's beef with that and where do you thugs come in with your world wide extortion scheme?" she asked now trying to show some interest hoping to pump Conners for information she could use in her investigation.

"Yes the backers had a great cover plan."

"Cover plan?" she interrupted, "Cover for what?"

"Ms. Carlsson, have you never heard of a man named Malthus?"

"You mean Thomas Malthus?"

"That's right. Very good, I had to look it up when they told me."

"No surprise there," she said taking the opportunity to throw out the insult.

"I'll ignore that," he said.

"Yeah, I read some of his social commentaries in economics class in college. Don't remember much though. So what's that got to do with long hairs recycling garbage?"

"Those long hairs embraced Malthus and his philosophy like he was a god or something. They believed every word of his theory and wanted to turn it into a prophecy come true."

"I'm sorry," she said holding up a hand to stop him. "I'm a little fuzzy on his theory and ideas or whatever."

"To put it as simply as possible for you, Malthus believed that the resources of the earth would only support a finite number of people and that eventually those resources and the human population would reach an equilibrium. At that point no further population growth could be sustained. He acknowledges that certain advances in food production technology would prolong the inevitable but advances in medical science have far outpaced the food side of the equation and people live longer than they did in the eighteenth century. The equilibrium point is rapidly approaching, I'm afraid."

"OK, thanks for the sociology lesson but what does that have to do with Millennium Eco-Technologies and all the oldies from the summer of love?"

"I can't believe that you have grasped the concept, Ms. Carlsson."

"Indulge me, OK," she snapped.

"The hippies thought all humans were garbage. They wanted to recycle the whole world back to a point where only a few thousand or so could live as hunters and gatherers in peace and harmony with nature," he said and made a gagging sound.

"No shit," she said in wide eyed disbelief.

"No shit, exactly and no anything else. Just a few of them prancing in the fields and forests and living in tents or caves or wherever."

"That was the real plan for Millennium Eco-Technologies?"

"Precisely, except that the CEO and Lindquist are more pragmatic thankfully."

"Oh sure. Instead of destroying the world they merely extort money to stave off total annihilation. Same idea, different shitbags making the decisions."

"Now, Ms. Carlsson they are my employers."

"My point exactly."

"I'll ignore that remark as well," he said with a sneer.

"OK, so what happened and when was all this world recycling supposed to happen?"

"Well my understanding is that September 21 was the day the NANOs would be released worldwide. According to the computer projections the world would be back in the stone age by the first day of winter. As for what happened, well the CEO instructed me to eliminate all opposition and interference to the revised plans."

"Ah, are we in that category?"

"Yes, I'm afraid so. You have interfered at every opportunity and I must say it is getting rather annoying."

"Thanks, we try."

"Yes, but I am afraid your attempts have done nothing more than delay the fates of the backers. I was going to pay each one of them a visit but you and Stone kept popping up. No matter, I'll just be a little longer in wrapping up that's all."

"OK, so the hippies wanted to turn the world into a prehistoric paradise and your bosses decided they liked the world just the way it is with a little old fashioned protection racket on the side to keep the coffers full, is that it?"

"A little cynical, but accurate, Ms. Carlsson and as I said you and Stone and whoever else have merely been an inconvenient nuisance to the company and to me."

"Oh darn," she said, "and we were just trying to prevent a few megalomaniacs from causing a whole lot of death and destruction."

"I'm sure you are referring to the original backers. My employers and I are not nearly that delusional."

"Of course not," she said, "your motives are purely altruistic. Just pay up and everything stays nice and normal."

"Precisely."

"So what was the deal with the dam and the locks?"

"A demonstration of our power. Power perceived is power achieved someone else once said."

"Yeah, some other psycho like Hitler or Napoleon."

"No, Ms. Carlsson, we won't kill millions of people to make a point. We only threaten a few and the rest play along."

"Oh, I see. A compassionate psycho."

"Enough of this banter, we are almost to the island. Pull around to the east side and hold your position."

"No can do," she said.

"Don't make me have to persuade you Ms. Carlsson," he said handling his weapon.

"Save the macho shit. I'm telling you a fact. The water level is very shallow here and I can't get this boat in much closer," she said pointing to the depth finder.

He looked at the instrument on the cockpit wall, and then looked around at the shorelines of the far point of land. "I don't understand it," he said. "This is a lot farther out than when we first stopped your boat a few days ago."

"You're right," she said looking around and then suddenly remembering.

"You asshole. Those damn NANOs of yours breached the dam and now the lake is dropping. It must be down nearly a foot since yesterday."

"Damn," he said grabbing the mike. "Conners to base," he yelled.

"Base here sir. We've got a bit of a problem."

"Yea, well so do I. Just get out here and pick me up. I've got the cops on my ass and I need you to get me on a boat to Canada soon."

"Uh, that's the problem, sir, we can't launch any of the boats. Seems the water is too low all of a sudden and we can't get any of the boats away from the dock. They're all sitting on the bottom."

"Damn," he yelled again, almost loud enough for the men in the base to hear him without the radio.

"Yes," Alicia chimed in, "the dam. Seems your plans have left you high and dry so to speak."

"Shut up," he yelled. "I guess you'll just have to continue as my chauffeur that's all."

"You said you'd turn me loose when we got to the island. I can't help it of your NANOs screwed up your plans."

"Well one thing I have learned is how to adapt to changes and you must learn to do so as well. Now just head to the Canadian side and try to avoid any more contact with the locals."

"Bastard," she said pulling the boat away from the island and heading north.

"We really must work on your manners Ms. Carlsson. We'll be together it seems for a few more hours at least."

"Oh lucky me," she said and just looked out at the open lake.

"Yes it would seem that way," Conners said sitting in the seat opposite her.

She tried to think of a way to delay the trip and as Conners made himself comfortable she took the advantage when he was preoccupied with the view to slowly drop the engine rpms. She did it very carefully and slowly so that he wouldn't hear the pitch of the sound change but gradually the boat began to slow and thankfully Conners didn't seem to notice. Now if Gary could get here before Conners thought of something unpleasant to do to her.

CHAPTER 16

THE RECOVERY

*M*itch regained complete consciousness in the ambulance at the marina and as soon as the EMTs had the blood cleaned off his face he could see somewhat better although one eye was a little blurry. During the trip to the hospital, the EMTs had carefully washed away enough blood to fill a pail full of gauze pads but to everyone's relief they didn't find an entry wound in Mitch's forehead. What they did find was a nasty laceration and large contusion of the forehead. The laceration was about four inches long running horizontally from the center of the forehead, left to near the temple. Apparently the bullet had been fired at an angle and fortunately only creased Mitch's head. The resulting wound bled profusely but upon first examination the EMTs were reasonably certain there was no brain damage aside from a concussion.

"Don't try to speak and don't move," the EMT said as Mitch tried to focus his sight. The large bandage over the wound was partially obscuring his vision. He let out a low groan. The EMT wasn't sure if it was pain or an acknowledgment or both.

"We'll be at the hospital in about two more minutes," the EMT said and Mitch blinked.

The ambulance pulled into the emergency room driveway of the hospital and under the portico. Almost before the ambulance came to a complete stop, the EMTs in the back were out of the doors and had unlatched the stretcher from the clamps on the floor. The pulled out the stretcher and dropped the legs down so that Mitch could be wheeled into the ER. The ER staff had been put on alert by the ambulance crew and were ready and waiting for Mitch's arrival. Some of the nurses recognized him and put their hands on his as he was wheeled into one of the trauma rooms. Mitch made a feeble effort to grasp one of the nurses' hands.

"All right," one of the doctors said, "let's get him onto the table and start the full work up." The EMTs held their equipment, which had been placed between Mitch's legs for the transport, and four nurses and two doctors carefully lifted Mitch onto the examination table. As soon as he was attached to the hospital's monitoring equipment, the nurses removed the EMTs' gear and they gathered up their stuff and started to leave. "Good luck Mitch," they said, and Mitch just groaned again.

"Thanks guys," one of the nurses who knew Mitch said as they left.

"OK, I want full blood work and a complete set of skull and neck pictures," the lead doctor ordered and one nurse went to the phone on the wall and made two calls. "Now let's see what's under all that gauze," he said. He carefully pealed away the tape and pulled back the six inch square bandages. "Oh my," he said and the now conscious Mitch shot him a suspicious look.

"Deputy, if you can hear me don't try to speak but grip the nurse's hand once for yes and twice for no. OK?"

Mitch liked this part. One of the nurses who instantly grabbed Mitch's right hand was one of his regular drinking buddies after the long midnight shift. He had never asked her out on a date but maybe he would now. He wished his eyes would focus better so he could see her.

"Deputy, are you felling any numbness in any of your extremities?" Mitch squeezed once and thought about his nurse friend and an extremity he wanted her to hold. At least his mind still worked, he thought.

"Good," the doctor said. "Now how is your vision? Is it blurred?" Mitch squeezed twice.

"Now Deputy, from my initial observations here it looks like only an external laceration and a bad bruise. Do you understand?" Mitch squeezed once.

"I think you'll be fine but we'll get some x-rays and watch for signs of a concussion. A few stitches will fix the forehead and your vision should clear up shortly. You were very lucky." Mitch squeezed once.

"OK," the doctor said to the x-ray tech as he wheeled in the portable machine. "Full skull and neck series."

"Yes doctor," the tech answered and started to set up his machine. Mitch squeezed a couple of times just for practice and the nurse blushed.

"Seems he'll be back to normal soon," the doctor said smiling at the beet-faced nurse. She held Mitch's hand for a few more minutes then let go with a pat on his chest.

After the blood tests and the x-rays the doctor returned and set up to close the laceration. "OK, Deputy. I'm going to sew you up. I'm using a small needle and will try to keep the scar as small as possible, but you'll have one to go with the one on your cheek." Mitch only smiled and blinked.

"I'm going to give the forehead a little shot. Oh, sorry. Some Novocaine and you'll only feel a little prick," the doctor said and Mitch winced when he felt the needle above his eyebrow. He didn't move and the doctor seemed to take forever.

"There Deputy, all set. You took fifty-two stitches but I kept them close and the scar won't be too noticeable." Mitch just blinked.

"Just rest for a few minutes until the x-rays are done and then we'll get you upstairs to a room," the doctor said and left the room.

Mitch was just lying there staring at the ceiling and didn't even see the Lieutenant enter the room. "Hi, Mitch," the Lieutenant said quietly and Mitch looked in the direction of the voice but still couldn't get both of his eyes to focus.

"The doctor said you'd be fine. No holes."

Mitch tried to nod his head, then said in a whisper, "where's Gary and the FBI Agent?"

"You're not supposed to talk," the Lt. said.

"Where?" repeated Mitch with more urgency in his whisper.

"Gary called on the marine band. Seems he's in pursuit of the guy who shot you."

"Where's Alicia?"

"If you mean the FBI Agent, she's…," the Lt. paused.

"Where?" Mitch said now almost in a full voice.

"She's been taken hostage by the perp."

Mitch's eyes went wide and he tried to sit up but slumped back down onto the table and held his eyes shut to fight off the pain.

"Now damn it, that's why I didn't want to say anything. I knew you'd try to go save them. Now just forget it. We have every available man on this and the State is sending down their patrol boat. The Coast Guard is also involved."

"Coast Guard, they're on a boat?" Mitch choked out the words.

"Yes, he took the FBI Agent hostage on her boat."

Mitch tried to sit up again and this time made it but had to fight back the pain and brace himself until the dizziness subsided.

"Shit Stone, now lay back down and relax. You're out of this mess now. Let us take care of it."

"No, she's my friend and so is Gary unless you've forgotten," Mitch managed to say between deep breaths and waves of nausea. The nurse came into the room and saw Mitch sitting up and she quickly pushed him back down.

"What's going on in here?" she demanded.

"I'm sorry," the Lt. said but Mitch here thinks he's ready for duty.

"Not a chance. He'll be here for at least a week. More if he does anything stupid and adds to his injuries."

"Hear that Mitch? Now just do as the nurses and doctors say and we'll deal with the world out there." Mitch just clenched his teeth as he was helped back down. "Good I've got a department to run. I'll talk to you later when we have something."

"Yeah, make it soon," Mitch rasped. "OK, Lt.?"

"Yes."

"Where are they headed?"

"I probably shouldn't tell you, but the last report from Gary before the radio faded, he thinks they're headed across the lake and up the river to Canada."

"Thanks," Mitch groaned.

"Keep a close eye on him, nurse. We wouldn't want him to suffer a relapse," the Lt. said and left.

"There both of us have our orders Mitch," his nurse friend said. "Now just lay back and relax and I'll get you something for the pain if the doctor says it is all right."

Mitch did as she said until she was gone then lifted his head and checked to see if anybody was near his room. When he thought the coast was clear he took a deep breath and forced himself upright again. He sat there for a moment and winced at the throbbing in his head and tried to get his vision to clear. He closed his left eye and things became clear and the nausea seemed to abate a little. He'd have to work with only the right, he thought. But at least he could see.

Just as he was about to take his first tentative steps he was interrupted by a loud commotion. All of a sudden all the nurses began to run past his room but none of them even noticed him. Then the whole group of nurses and his doctors wheeled another stretcher past his room in the other direction, followed by another ambulance crew. Must be an accident, he thought and listened as the whole group went into a treatment room several doors down. Good timing, he said to himself as he braced for his next move. As soon as the ambulance crew walked past his door he slowly tried to stand.

He nearly fell as his knees buckled but he held onto the table and took a couple of more deep breaths. He wasn't sure but each time he took a deep breath he felt like he was breathing from a SCUBA tank. He seemed to get a lung filling breath and felt suddenly invigorated. Good, he thought, I need all the help I can get. He stumbled to the door and after two more refreshing breaths he stuck his newly stitched head out of the door and cautiously looked in both directions for any lingering staff.

Apparently, everyone was in attending to the accident victim and the only person between him and the door was the secretary. He waited for a few seconds and as hoped the phone rang and she turned away from the main door. Mitch seized the opportunity and stepped into the hallway and worked his way toward the exit using the wall to brace himself. He took several more deep breaths and each one seemed to clear his head a little more.

He was almost out the door when the secretary finished her call and turned around. "Hey, you can't leave," she yelled. Mitch took that as his cue to do just that. He summoned all his strength and dashed through the door and into the parking lot. Let's hope there are a lot of visitors today coming by cab. He looked around the lot and decided to keep going. The secretary was sure to have called help and his nurse friend and her buddies would be after him.

He ambled around the front of the building and thankfully a cab had just pulled up and a couple was being helped out of the back seat. The wife looked like she was very past due and the husband looked like he didn't know what to do. Mitch leaned against a parked car to fend off the dizziness again with some more deep breaths and waited until the nurse had wheeled the very pregnant woman into the hospital followed by the bewildered husband carrying the overnight bags. Good Luck, Mitch said to no one. He did his best to maintain his balance and walked as fast as he could and managed to get to the cab just as he started to feel faint and the cab was about to leave. Mitch opened the rear door and sort of fell, sort of slumped in.

"221 Morgan Street," he told the driver as he pulled in his legs and closed the door.

"Hey, you can't just," the driver started to protest and then saw Mitch in the back with his face all bandaged and still in the hospital gown.

"Go," Mitch commanded.

"You're not an escaped crazy patient, are you?" the driver asked putting the cab in gear again.

"I might be if you don't drive. Now move," Mitch almost yelled but the pain stopped any increase in volume.

"Yeah, sure buddy, no problem. Ah 322 Martin Street, yes sir."

"221 Morgan Street," Mitch corrected.

"Oh, yeah, right, sorry," the driver stuttered and the cab lurched out of the parking lot and down the driveway.

"Not to upset you or anything," the driver said trying to glimpse at Mitch in the rear view mirror and also keep an eye on the road, "but how are you going to pay for the ride?"

Fortunately, the hospital staff had only removed his bloody shirt and replaced it with a gown. He still had on his shorts but no shoes. He checked his pockets and pulled out a ten-dollar bill. "Here," he said handing it to the driver. "This should cover it. My place is only a mile away."

"Yeah, it'll cover the fare but what about my tip?"

"Your tip," Mitch said with a sneer, "your tip is don't piss off an injured man who's in a hurry and might tear off your head."

"Ah, ah, OK, yeah, good tip. Thanks," the driver said and returned his attention to driving. Mitch sat back in the seat and then glanced out the rear window at the gathering throng of medical professionals and hospital security all looking for the runaway gunshot victim.

"Shit, this day really sucks and it's only half over," Mitch said and all the driver said was "yes sir."

It only took about three minutes for the cab to pull up in front of Mitch's apartment house and the cab had barely stopped before Mitch was out the door. "Keep it," he said referring to any change that might be forth coming.

"Yeah," was all the driver said as he squealed the tires leaving in a big hurry.

Mitch reached into his other pocket and pulled out his door key and went inside the main door of the old Victorian house. Over the life of the stately home it had been partitioned off and instead of being a large single family home it was now an apartment house with four two-bedroom apartments. Mitch's, unfortunately today, was on the second floor and he started up the steps as fast as his wobbly knees and spinning head would allow.

Surprisingly though for some reason he wasn't out of breath even though it was a bit of an effort to keep from passing out.

He opened the door and quickly closed and locked it behind him. The A-H was still at the marina so he'd have to use his other car. He seldom drove it for fear of some moron hitting him or even worse it getting chipped in a parking lot by someone in an old rust bucket. If Mitch loved the old A-H, he was absolutely enamored with his other convertible. He put on a new T-shirt as delicately as possible over the head wound and slipped on an old pair of deck shoes. He wondered what had happened to the new pair he was wearing.

He went to his night stand and pulled out the second of his personal weapons. Although not the same sustained fire power as the .45 auto, the old .357 revolver would do the job. He grabbed a full box of shells and dashed out the back door with a set of car keys and a remote garage door opener. He made it almost all the way down the stairs before dizziness and nausea forced him to sit on a step for a moment and gulp in some air.

Once the wave passed, he slowly rose to his feet and walked across the driveway to the locked garage. He hit the transmit button on the remote and the door started up. He was glad the landlord had a locked garage and let him park his special car under secure cover even if it did cost him an extra fifty dollars a month in rent.

Mitch stepped into the garage now partially lit by the sun coming through the raised door. He ran his hand lovingly along the graceful curves of the midnight blue fender and up the frame of the swept back windscreen as the makers called it. He didn't have time to savor the moment though and he climbed into the plush sand colored leather seats, closed the door which latched almost without a sound and hooked the seat belt and shoulder harness. The key sliding into the ignition switch made more noise than the engine did when it started and Mitch had to constantly check the tachometer to assure himself the car was actually running.

With the confirmation of the V-8 operating, Mitch moved the burled walnut shift lever to the 'D' position and released the parking brake. If not for the notched positions on the console, Mitch again would not have known the car was in gear. The transmission was so smooth the change from neutral to forward gears was more like a reflex movement than a mechanical linkage. Now if he could manage to keep from passing out or having a major dizzy spell, he'd accomplish both his intentions of getting to the lake and not crashing his precious new Jaguar XKR convertible.

Once out of the garage, Mitch picked up the factory installed optional cellular phone and placed a call. He'd need a boat and since both his and the county's were now a part of history, he had to make other arrangements. He quickly made the necessary plans and returned the phone to its cradle. Now if he could get to the harbor in less than fifteen minutes, alive and in one piece, he'd only be about an hour and a half behind Alicia. He would need a small miracle or a lot of luck but he calculated their suspected course and figured he could cut them off if he moved like hell from the harbor.

He pulled to the end of the driveway and stopped for a second while he reached behind the seat and pulled out a light and hooked it over the rear view mirror. He pushed the power cord into the lighter in the walnut dash and the red strobe began to flash. The rear of the light was opaque and thankfully Mitch couldn't see the halogen strobe as it flashed in one second intervals or it would have nearly impossible for him to drive in his condition.

At least his brother police officers wouldn't immediately stop his car but in order to get to the Harbor in near record time he would have to exceed the posted speed limits by about 50 percent. Oh well, might as well see what she can do, he thought to himself as he wheeled out into the street and pressed the accelerator. The powerful V-8 jumped to life and he shot down the block in only a few seconds. No cars were near the intersection and he rolled through and headed for the main west bound street out of town. Traffic was a little heavier, but between his flashing red light and the convenient timing of the stop lights he was able to pass most of the traffic flow even though he seemed to spend most of his time in the center turn lane.

So far so good, he said to himself as he approached a red light and he slowed down to let the oncoming cars see him and to check the intersection himself. Mitch slowly worked his way into the traffic and had to stop for a minute to let a large truck keep its right of way. As he was sitting there, he glanced over at the car beside him and noticed that the occupants were a little awed by the sight of him and his car. He figured it wasn't every day someone saw a new example of the craftsmanship from Coventry let alone with a flashing red light driven by a man with a huge bandage on his forehead, grotesque discoloration of the whole side of his face and one eye closed.

Mitch left the gawking driver and his passenger sitting there as the truck cleared the intersection and no other cars were close. He pressed the accelerator and zoomed down the road catching all the remaining lights out of town. Now he was clear of traffic approaching him from the side but the cars in front of him either were ignoring the red light or just didn't believe it could be a cop in a convertible. Mitch flashed his headlights and honked his horn but most of the cars only pulled slightly to the right but the nearly instant acceleration of the Jag allowed Mitch to almost fly down the road and rarely take his foot off the gas.

Except for the tractor and hay wagon where he had to field test the four wheel anti lock disc brakes, the drive was smooth and quick and didn't draw any attention from a passing patrol car. Most of his department was at the island causeway or the marina fire and that left a thin contingent of State Troopers to cover the remainder of the county. Nobody would be just sitting looking for speeders this morning.

Mitch managed to cover the twenty-mile distance in just over thirteen minutes, which was an unofficial record even for the big police cars and some lead-footed deputies. Mitch decelerated to a more appropriate speed through the Harbor and pulled up in front of the local general store. This was one of the few places he knew of that could cater to almost any retail demand. It functioned as a post-office, grocery store, restaurant, bar, bait shop, hardware store and even a small hotel. Mitch figured Sam Walton must have gotten his ideas on retail from a place like this. Mitch parked the car, turned off the ignition and the strobe and hopped out as agilely as his head would allow.

In addition to all measure of services provided in the general store which was aptly named the Harbor Emporium, it was also the main office for the Village Police Department. The auxiliary office being at the home of his old friend and former State Trooper, Alex Brady. When Alex wasn't keeping the local drunks and rowdies in line, he was trying to keep the summer people from irritating the permanent residents and vice versa. Seems his job was mostly settling squabbles over boundary lines and dock space. But Alex liked it and there was seldom any serious crime aside from some drunk drivers. Between his State pension and village pay check, he and his much younger wife and two kids could live comfortably. That allowed Alex to indulge in his favorite pass time or hobby as he called it, which at times made some extra money and most times just allowed him to enjoy the peacefulness of the lake in the summer. Today Mitch would need Alex's assistance and would require Alex to mix business with pleasure. Mitch walked to the rear of the store and out onto the dock. He hoped Alex was there waiting after the phone call.

"Hey Mitch, in here," Alex called from the back door of the store, which for the fishermen and the customers of the small marina was in fact the front door. Mitch turned and fought off a wave a dizziness at the sudden movement of the head.

"Holy shit Mitch, what the hell happened to you?" Alex asked in astonishment as he came out of the screen door to greet his friend. "Oh man, you're the deputy that was shot this morning. I heard it on the scanner."

"In the flesh, so to speak," Mitch said reaching out to shake his friend's massive hand.

"You should be in the hospital not down here with the boats and the birds."

"I was until about a half hour ago."

"No way man. How did you get out? No, better yet, how did you get down here so fast?"

"Don't tell anyone, but in that," Mitch said pointing to the dark-blue convertible parked in front.

"I'd ask where but I'm afraid you'd say it was a long story."

"Your right," Mitch said, "but I can't start that now. I need you to get me out to the international buoy as fast as you can."

"OK, let me change into my fishing clothes."

"No, it's not for fun it's business. Your uniform is perfect. In fact you're just what the doctor ordered."

"Probably not," Alex said pointing to Mitch's rainbow colored face and the bandage nearly covering the half-closed eye.

"You're right and if it wasn't an emergency I'd be happy to lie around the hospital with all the nurses fawning all over me."

"OK, let's go then. What's the big emergency?" Alex asked as he led Mitch down the dock and onto the big motor trawler he used in his commercial fishing business.

"No, Alex not this one. You still have the water rocket?"

"Yeah right over there," he said and pointed to a sleek cigarette boat under a canvas cover. "You mean this one?"

"Yeah, we need to catch a boat heading to Canada with about an hour head start."

"Shit they'd be almost to Toronto at any decent speed."

"Not quite I hope but we need some greater speed and maybe we can catch them in this," Mitch said moving down the slip to pull the cover off the speedster. "Sure comes in handy to have something this fast."

"Yup, I can't believe the Town bought this for a patrol boat then a year later when the county marine patrol starts, they unload this for a song. I never would have been able to afford a new one of these," Alex said proudly, "but they dumped it for ten cents on the dollar. I spend more in gas than on the loan payment."

"Well this time the gas is on me. We've got to go find that boat."

"What's the big yank?" Alex asked giving the boat a quick visual check.

"Remember that gorgeous lady in the tight swimsuit making noise in my car the other day?"

"Yeah, the FBI or CDC or whatever agent."

"That's the one. She's been nabbed by the scumbag we were talking to in the parking lot. He's a major dirtball and he's the one that gave me this," Mitch said pointing to the new facial decoration.

"Then we need to get there yesterday and put this guy somewhere where he can make some new friends."

"Close personal friends," Mitch said.

"OK, you get the aft lines and I'll get the bow," Alex directed and Mitch pulled his end of the cover off and Alex did the same. Once the boat was opened Mitch and Alex undid the lines and climbed in.

Alex fired the engines and the through the hull exhaust system made the boat sound like a hundred of his sailboat auxiliary engines. Alex let the engines warm up a bit then backed the made for racing power boat out of the slip and then set the transmission into forward. Alex pushed the throttles a tiny bit and the engines started to rev, but he kept the speed down until he cleared he docks.

"What's the matter?" Mitch asked.

"Well among all of the other pieces of nice new electronic gear the Village equipped this thing with is a depth finder, and well we don't have much. I don't understand it. Yesterday there was ten feet in here and now it says we're down to seven feet. Must be the sensor is shot."

"I don't think so," Mitch said looking over the side. He could just about see the bottom. "One other thing Mr. Scumbag did was to sabotage the dam. My guess is, it has now breached and the lake is draining out just like in the winter only more so and quicker. There will be a lot of new beach front and very soon."

"It's only June. Damn the bastard. This will kill the season."

"One more reason we need to find this guy."

"No problem. What kind of boat are they in?"

"It's her Carver."

"Ooh, rich too," Alex said smiling.

"Nah, probably the Feds picking up the tab.'

"Yeah well, should be easy to find. The thing is shaped like a house and should show up on the screen almost as well as a tanker."

"Let's hope so," Mitch said, "and let's hope she's still alive and well."

"Right," Alex said and as soon as the depth finder told him he had lots of water under the boat, he pushed the throttles full forward and the engines screamed to their full potential.

They shot across the harbor and out around a few small islands and headed toward Conners' playground, Society Island.

"We'll have to cut wide around the island, Mitch, it's going to be really shallow but I'll head to the north side and it will cut our time down by ten to fifteen minutes."

"Great," Mitch yelled over the roar of the exhaust. He held on tight as the boat bounced over the slight ripples in the lake. If the wind was pushing the waves any higher, the boat would never have been able to move this fast without pounding the hull and the occupants into small pieces.

Mitch had looked at the charts for this end of the lake hundreds of times and went over the course of the two boats in his head. He figured even though Alicia's boat had good ninety minutes head start by now the fact that they had started from the Cove, which is a long way down a large bay from the main part of the lake, would add at least an hour or more to their reaching the open water. The Harbor however was on the main part of the lake and in direct line with the Canadian coast. He went over the two starting points and estimated the approximate speed of Alicia's boat and made an educated guess at the course of their target and half figured and half prayed that they would get to the buoy marking the border at about the same time as Alicia and her unwelcome guest.

From the buoy they could scan nearly twenty miles in all directions along the water boundary and hopefully easily locate something as large as Alicia's thirty five foot cruiser packed full of nice solid radar reflecting metal gear and equipment. Mitch chuckled to himself at that thought. He suddenly remembered the drunk driver he and Gary had stopped one night way back when they were working together on patrol. The driver had a nice new Corvette and was traveling at about ninety-eight when he and Gary had clocked him on radar. After a fairly interesting chase through the countryside they finally stopped the guy with the friendly help of a State patrol. The driver couldn't believe that his nice new car with a fiberglass glass body could even be seen on radar. Mitch took great pleasure in telling the guy that the fiberglass may be invisible by not reflecting radar waves but the big iron engine and frame of the car weren't. Now he was counting on the same fact to find a single boat in a large lake full of other boats.

Alex gave Society Island as much a wide berth as possible and kept and eye on the depth meter. Mitch just stared at the island and began to plan his payback for all his suffering and for Alicia. Once clear of the island and into deeper water Alex just sat back and let the boat fly over the blue green water.

"I figure at this speed we'll be at the buoy in about thirty or forty minutes and should be no more than fifteen behind them."

"Good," Mitch said now focusing his thoughts on Alicia and what he was going to do if they found the boat. "Just for practice," Mitch said over the loud exhaust noise, "how about turning on the radar and letting me look at some outlines?"

"OK," Alex yelled back and flicked on the power switch. The screen shown light green then changed to a darker green with a sweeping bright green line crossing diagonally from the lower right-hand corner. "There," Alex said pointing, "those are all sailboats," and he looked in the direction the radar was indicating. "There see," he said to Mitch who also looked.

"Yeah, OK, so we can find all kinds of boats but what about a specific one moving in an unknown direction?"

"Well," Alex said, "we'll just look for something the size of a bus heading in a northerly direction and check it out."

"Hope we get it right the first time."

"Me too," Alex said and swung the boat a little more to the northeast. He figured it would give them good coverage with the radar and cut down any intercept course. The two bounced over the water which was starting to turn into a chop. "If this gets any worse we'll have to cut the speed so we don't get bashed to bits," he informed Mitch.

"No, I can take it as long as the boat can."

"That's what I'm afraid of," Alex said and kept up the speed. Suddenly a large wave rolled into their path and Alex didn't see it until it was too late. The powerful boat was launched out of the water and as the propellers cleared the engines revved to the red line and gave off the loudest roar Mitch had ever heard. He managed to hold on and just as the boat apexed on its ride into the air, Mitch caught a glimpse of a large dot on the radar screen.

"There," he yelled over the still fully revved engines and pointed in a direction slightly starboard of their present course.

"There what?" Alex yelled back just as the boat splashed back into the water and they were tossed around the cockpit.

"There," Mitch said pointing and trying to get back into his seat as the boat's propellers caught the water and the boat climbed back to its original speed. "Slightly northeast, a big blip. I caught it when we were nearly in space there for a moment."

"Must be the antenna was up high enough to get a good look."

"Yea, can we do it again?"

"Ah, I'll pass," Alex said, "but show me on the screen where the blip was."

Mitch reached out and put his finger on the spot where he'd seen the point of light. "Here," he said.

Alex looked and then over at the compass. "OK, I've got a rough bearing," he said and turned the wheel a bit until the compass lined up with his estimation of the direction from the radar screen. "Keep an eye on the top of the screen now. You should see the same blip in about two minutes."

"OK," Mitch said and watched the screen and almost wished the spot to appear. Alex's estimate wasn't too far off. The blip appeared in one minute and forty-five seconds. "There," Mitch said again and pointed a little starboard again. Alex looked at the screen and waited for the antenna to come around again.

"I see it," he said and flipped a switch that changed the antenna's sweep from 360 degrees to about 120 degrees straight ahead. Now the blip would appear every two seconds instead of every six. The blip was almost constant now with one sweep passing as the next one began. Alex made a slight change in course again and the blip now appeared at the top of the screen directly inline with the bow and their direction of travel.

"How long?" Mitch asked eagerly.

"About ten minutes maybe less," Alex said without looking at the radar any more. He knew exactly where the target was heading now and exactly how much he had to compensate their course based upon the relative speeds of the two boats.

"Try for less," Mitch said anxiously and stood up to try and see Alicia's boat visually instead of electronically. "Do you have a pair of binoculars?" he asked Alex who now seemed completely focused on his course corrections.

"Ah, ah, yeah," he said after a moment. "Down below in the hanging locker on the right."

Mitch went down into the small cuddy cabin and opened the locker door. There hanging was a nice set of large binoculars. He grabbed them and climbed back up into the cockpit. "Where did you get these?" he asked admiring the large and expensive glasses.

"Uh, the village bought them. They think they paid for new uniforms."

"Uniforms, these would buy fifty uniforms," Mitch said knowing the little budget scam a lot of the small town departments played to get some special piece of equipment the politicians would automatically veto because of the cost. "You got them to pay for fifty uniforms for you and you bought these instead."

"Yeah, the supplier just wrote an invoice for shirts, pants and hats and sent the glasses. Only thing is I can't put in for a new uniform for a few years. Got to make this one last and look good for a while or I pay out of my pocket."

"So how did they end up on this boat?"

"The Village just sold the boat as is with all the equipment for one fixed bid. They just happened to be on board when the sale went down. No one ever asked about them?"

"Damn," Mitch said holding the glasses to his eyes and adjusting the focus. The bouncing of the boat made a clear sighting difficult but Mitch was able to spot their target. "There, straight ahead," he said without taking the glasses off the boat. "You're a pretty good navigator," he said to Alex who just had a little smile of pride on his face.

"In less than ten," Alex said and Mitch didn't respond, he just continued to look at the boat hoping to identify it as Alicia's. "That the one?" Alex asked.

"Yeah, I think so. we're at the wrong angle for me to see the name on the transom but it's a CARVER and it's big enough."

"Good enough for me," Alex said.

"Me too," Mitch replied checking his .357 just in case Conners wasn't in a mood to accept visitors. Mitch hoped he wasn't. He put on the shoulder holster he had kept in his car and adjusted the straps. Once he had prepared himself for any resistance on the part of Conners, he picked up the glasses again and tried to spot anyone on board.

"See anybody?" Alex asked.

"Ah, I think so but it looks kind of weird."

"Not a good word to use when we're headed into a confrontation with a nut case," Alex said finally looking over at Mitch. "What do you mean weird?"

Mitch didn't look at Alex but just gave him an answer. "Ah, I think I see Alicia but she's sitting on the transom and I don't see Conners."

"How do you know it's Alicia?"

"Trust me I'd know her a...," he paused to search for the right word.

"Yesss," Alex prompted.

"Hair anywhere. And besides that's the shirt she had on when all this started this morning."

"I'm not going to ask if you helped her get dressed."

"Good, don't," Mitch said now more concerned about what was happening on the cruiser. "Damn," he said now able to see Alicia better as they got closer.

"What?" Alex asked.

"She's on the transom and looks like she's tied up or something."

"Not good, where's this Conners guy? Can you see him?"

"Nope, but he's been known to be the hide and wait kind of asshole. He's probably using Alicia as bait to get us to focus on her while he takes advantage of our heroics."

"OK, so lets take the frontal approach."

"Sounds good," Mitch said, "how are we going to stop the boat?"

"Conners must be driving and he'll expect everyone to chase him. Alicia is just out there to keep everyone from shooting the S.O.B. He'll just lead them right to Canada and fight any extradition if he's arrested there. Nice guy this Conners."

"Yeah, real nice," Mitch snarled. "So how do we stop him and the boat?"

"He'll expect any rescue to come from the stern," Alex said. "We'll just plant ourselves in front and force him to stop."

"Kind of dangerous isn't?"

"Yeah you got any better ideas?"

"No. Let's do it," Mitch said not sure of the plan or his conviction about it.

"Relax, Mitch. Maybe he'll trade Alicia and the CARVER for this nice fast boat."

"You want to let him get away. In this?" Mitch asked incredulously.

"Might save your girlfriend and save a lot of wear and tear. Just let the Canadians pick him up. We'll get him back."

"Shit. I want this guy right here," Mitch said and made a gesture with his hands to show a choking action.

"I know but we need to worry about your friend first."

"You're right," Mitch said looking back at the boat again as they approached. He could see Alicia clearly and it looked like she was screaming something. "I think we need to do something soon."

"OK, OK," Alex replied and moved the speed boat into the path of the oncoming cruiser. "I hope this Conners guy doesn't like to play chicken," he added stopping their boat directly in front of the big cruiser.

"Naw, he likes the sneaky approach," Mitch said. They didn't have to wait long. The bigger boat just kept coming and made no signs of veering off to avoid a collision. Alex quickly engaged the transmission and the speed boat narrowly missed being hit by the oncoming cruiser. "Shit, this guy is crazy" Alex yelled as the CARVER plowed past.

"Told you so," Mitch said watching the boat pass over the spot they had just occupied. They had no sooner expressed their surprise at the failure of the boat to stop when they heard Alicia's screams as she rode past not moving off the transom.

"What the hell did she say?" Alex asked.

"Never mind that, why isn't she moving? She seems attached to the stern."

"Let's see if we can find out then," Alex said revving the engines and turning the boat around. They quickly matched the cruiser's speed and approached from the starboard astern. Mitch was on the port side of the speed boat and Alex was to his right. Both men had their weapons drawn and Mitch was holding his in a combat grip and searching across the cabin for a target he hoped would be Conners. "Come on you piece of shit, show yourself," he said under his breath as the boats came to within six feet of each other.

"See anybody?" Alex yelled over the sound of both boats and the churning water.

"No, not yet," Mitch yelled back.

"OK then, I've got to put my weapon down. I need two hands to keep us close, but not in the cruiser."

"OK," Mitch said, "but keep it handy."

"Always," Alex said and holstered the pistol but didn't snap the safety strap.

Mitch looked over at Alicia who was still sitting on the transom and was screaming up a storm, which Mitch couldn't quite hear yet.

"What's wrong? Where's Conners?" he asked.

"Gone," she yelled back, "and I'm tied to the anchor and…" the noise drowned her out and Mitch couldn't hear a word.

"What's she yelling? Can you hear?" he yelled at Alex.

"Hell no. I can barely hear you."

"Well I don't see anybody on deck and no one seems to be driving the boat. We've got to take the chance he's below just waiting."

"Not a good option," Alex yelled back.

"No, but we can't just ride along next to each other and wait either."

"OK," Alex acknowledged, "what's the plan then?"

"You're going to get us as close as you can and I'm going to jump over and try to stop the boat before he pops his head up. You're going to make sure he behaves himself if he does."

"Wait, wait," Alex yelled back, "I don't like the jumping over part. You're not in very good condition to be leaping between moving boats. If you miss you'll be through the propellers and fish food before I can help."

"Yeah, I guess I won't miss then."

"No, let me go you can steer the boat."

"Not a good idea. You're more familiar with how she handles and can get me close. I'd never be able to keep us tight without a collision."

Alex thought for a minute and weighed the choices. "I don't like either plan but your right. I'll hold the boats as close as possible. In fact I'll move us around to her port side so I can see better."

"OK," Mitch said and got ready to make the jump from one moving boat to another. Alex let up on the throttles a little and the speed boat backed off and Alex steered it behind the CARVER and increased the speed again to match the bigger boat's speed.

"OK," he yelled to Mitch who was crouching on the speed boats top deck ready to leap. "I'm as close as I can get. Whenever you're ready."

Mitch didn't wait for Alex's full statement, he leapt after the word ready. He pushed off as hard as he could but didn't really have a good foot hold and his feet slipped on the smooth deck as he took off. That reduced his flight path substantially and instead of landing on the deck and rolling to break his fall, he landed on the CARVER's gunwale and doubled over. He was now folded over the boat's side rail with his head hanging into the boat and worst of all his feet were now dangling over the side between the two speeding boats. Alex saw Mitch's plight and quickly tried to veer away but a wave caught the port side of the speed boat and pushed it into the side of the CARVER. Fortunately Alex and Mitch had the foresight to set the speed boats fenders along the starboard side to give some protection in case of a collision and when the two boats came together the fenders gave Mitch about eight inches of space between the hulls.

He saw the speed boat coming and tried to pull himself up and into the cruiser but didn't quite make it. Even though his legs were saved from the scissor action of the boats, the sudden nudge jostled Mitch and he lost his precarious balance over the rail and dropped completely over the side. Now he was holding onto the rail with his head looking over the side at Alicia and with the rest of his six-foot four inch frame hanging like the speed boats fenders.

He had to hold his feet up to avoid them being dragged in the water and increasing the pressure on his tenuous hand grip which was slipping with every bounce of the boat. Alicia was screaming and her eyes were wide with fear but Mitch was now more concerned with keeping himself out of the water and getting onto the moving boat. He decided to take a chance that would either get him on board or send him into the twin propellers and a future as a protein source for the local fauna.

He looked to his left and saw a rolling wave approaching. Just as the boat's bow cut through the wave, Mitch used all the strength he could muster to get a better grip on the rail. Just as the wave made its way along the hull, Mitch let his feet drag in the water. The momentum of the boat combined with the weight of the water to toss his legs back and up far enough for him to hook his right leg over the gunwale. He held that position for a second to catch his breath and then climbed over the rail and set both feet on the deck. Alicia was still screaming something to him but he held up his hand for her to wait and he drew his revolver and went to the cabin to search for Conners, who to Mitch's surprise and relief hadn't appeared while Mitch was hanging over the side.

Alicia just kept screaming something and Mitch came back on deck with a puzzled expression on his face. He put his weapon back in the holster and turned to stop the boat. It immediately coasted to a halt and Mitch turned to see what Alicia's screams were all about.

"Mitch, you ass, Conners is long gone. He was on the radio to the island and somebody showed up in an inflatable. The two of them took off toward Canada. He tied me to the anchor and set some NANOs on the rope holding it from dropping. They're dissolving the line and the anchor is in the water. When the line goes the anchor drops and so do I."

"Oh, shit," Mitch said, "was that what you were screaming about? I couldn't hear you."

"No shit, and while you were playing boat rodeo the NANOs have nearly dissolved the line. Oh and by the way, what are you doing here?" she asked.

"Ah, trying to save you and nice to see you too by the way."

"You know what I mean, you're supposed to be near death or something."

"So I'll try harder to accomplish that. I thought I was doing pretty well in that regard a minute ago."

"Mitch you know I'm glad to see you but the last time I saw you were in pretty bad shape."

"I'm a fast healer," he said and started to help her out of her predicament.

"Well get me out of here fast," she said struggling against her bonds. "He handcuffed me to the anchor chain."

"Shit," he said, "hold on."

"Funny," she snapped. "Just get me out of this before the NANOs finish."

Mitch looked at the line holding the anchor over the side and saw that it was only about 10 percent of its normal size. Just the weight of the anchor would pull the threads to the breaking point. "Damn," he said. "Hey Alex," he yelled over to the speed boat that was now just floating along next to the CARVER. "You got a cuff key?"

"Yeah," Alex said reaching out to grab the cruiser and tie off a line. "Here," he said and tossed it over to Mitch who almost caught it. The key hit the deck and slid into the corner under a collection of fender and dock lines.

"Mitch you clumsy oaf," she snapped again, "I"m about thirty seconds away from a fast ride to the lake bottom and you're all thumbs."

"Sorry," he said scrambling to find the key.

"Never mind the key, just pull in the anchor," she said sharply.

"Got it," he said holding up the key. He started to take a step toward her and suddenly she let out an ear piercing scream of terror and she was yanked backwards off the transom and hit the water with a splash.

"Oh my god," Mitch yelled and climbed up onto the transom.

"Mitch," Alex yelled as he saw what Mitch was about to do. "Your gun."

Mitch hesitated just long enough to hear Alex and he pulled out the revolver and tossed it on the deck. He took a couple of deep breaths and dove down into the lake in the spot where she had disappeared. He swam down as hard as he could and followed the air bubbles as he kicked and pulled at the water. He had no idea how deep it was here but he had to try to find her and hoped he wouldn't have to give up because of the depth. He put that thought out of his mind and kept swimming deeper and deeper chasing the rapidly diminishing bubbles. If the air was out here in the form of bubbles, it couldn't be in her lungs where it was needed. That plus the sudden jolt didn't give her much of a chance to get a deep breath.

Mitch swam harder and had to clear his ears a few times to equalize the pressure. He guessed he was past twenty feet and there was no sign of the bottom or Alicia. Just a dwindling stream of bubbles. After what he guessed was a minute he still couldn't see the bottom and suddenly the rising bubbles stopped. He didn't like that prospect and kicked harder and faster and kept going down. He cleared his ears one more time and almost as if someone pulled a curtain aside he caught a glimpse of Alicia's T-shirt in the murky water. He swam a few more strokes and reached out and touched her. She made no movement and Mitch saw the frozen expression on her face showing the last moments of terror and panic she experienced before the oxygen level in her blood dropped. He nearly panicked at the sight of her wide open sightless eyes and the auburn hair drifting in the current.

He swam around behind the motionless girl and found the keyhole in the handcuffs on her right wrist. He fumbled for a moment trying to get the key into the lock and turn it to release the latch. He pulled the cuff loose and out of the chain. She floated free but now with no air in her lungs she was only neutrally buoyant. Mitch's lungs were beginning to send out a message saying they were starting to demand fresh air.

CHAPTER 17

THE SAVE

*A*lex watched the spot of water where Alicia had been dragged in and where Mitch had dove in to follow and hopefully rescue her. He had both boats tied together and had climbed over to the big CARVER as soon as Mitch went into the water. He checked the depth meter on the cruiser and he shook his head in despair when he saw they were in forty-five feet of water. Damn long way to swim to have only one chance at saving her, he thought and went back to the stern and watched the spot of lake and hoped he'd see both of them alive again. He was startled back to reality by the sound of a boat horn. He looked up and saw a rapidly approaching power boat about the size of the CARVER but shaped more like his speed boat. Uncertain of who was approaching he drew his weapon and waited.

"He's pulled his weapon, Sgt.," Benton said looking at the figure on the stern of the larger boat. "Can't see who it is though. Got a uniform and a fast looking speed boat is tied up next to the CARVER."

"Maybe one of the hired guns for our Society Island friends. Better tell them who we are," Gary said and picked up the mike and turned the switch to P.A. "Keep an eye on him and if he takes aim on us give him a warning shot over his head," Gary said and then spoke into the mike. "Drop your weapon. This is the Sheriff's Department.

Drop your weapon and prepare to be boarded." Gary waited for a few seconds. "What's he doing now, Benton?"

"Just standing there pointing at his badge."

"What? Has he dropped his weapon?"

"He reholstered it and now he's waving and pointing to his badge again."

"Let me see," Gary said reaching out for the binoculars. He took them from Benton and looked out at the two boats and the man on the stern. "You haven't been with the Department long, have you Benton?"

"No sir, about eight months."

"Ever get down to the Harbor?"

"No, not yet. Why?"

"Well you should because the man in the uniform with the gun is Alex Brady and he's the local Police Department in the Harbor."

"Oh," was all Benton could say a little sheepishly.

"Well you'll have a chance to meet him shortly," Gary said, "but I wonder what he's doing out here and what he's waving his arms about. Let's get going Les."

"Sure Sergeant," Shepard said and pushed the throttles forward. 'My Pleasure' pulled in close to the 'Viking Princess' and Alex waved them to the starboard side. "Alicia is down there," he yelled over to Gary and his group.

"Diving?" Gary yelled back.

"No, she's tied to an anchor and Mitch dove in after her."

"I'm sorry, did you say Mitch? Mitch Stone, the Deputy?"

"Yeah, the one and only," Alex yelled back with a smile.

"What the hell," Gary said aloud to no one special.

"What's the problem Sergeant?" Shepard asked.

"Mitch is the one that was shot this morning at the marina."

"No shit," Shepard said.

"How?" Amanda asked.

"How indeed," Gary said. "Two hours ago he was being stuffed into an ambulance half dead and now he's out here ahead of us and swimming after Alicia."

"She the girl who owns this boat?" Amanda asked.

"Yes, and Brady says she's under water tied to an anchor. Can't you get me close enough to get over there?" Gary asked Shepard.

"Can do. I just need Benton to help Amanda with the fenders and lines."

"OK honey," she said scampering toward the bow.

"I guess I've got the back end," Benton said.

"Stern," Shepard corrected and slowly maneuvered his big boat next to the 'Viking Princess'.

As soon as they were within three feet, Gary leaped over and unlike Mitch's attempt at boarding, he landed on both feet in the center of the aft deck. "How long they been down?" he asked as he shook Alex's hand and looked over the stern at the few bubbles breaking the surface.

"About two minutes now," Alex said without taking his eyes off the spot.

"What happened, where's Conners?"

"Don't know about him. Nobody here except Alicia and she was handcuffed to the anchor. Mitch tried to unlock the cuffs but the rope holding the anchor out of the water broke and pulled her in. Mitch just dove in after her."

"He's supposed to be in the hospital with a gun shot wound."

"Yeah, so he told me when he showed up in that fancy ragtop."

"How did he get the A-H from the Cove?"

"It wasn't that old classic. The car he drove up in was a brand-new Jaguar convertible. Says he made it from the city in thirteen."

"Son of a bitch," Gary mumbled. "Damn, I just remembered," he said. "Alicia said she had some dive gear on board. I'll go get it." He ran to the cabin and brought out the gear and started to put it on over his clothes.

"Wait," Alex said, "I see something."

Gary dropped the tank and vest on the deck and ran back to the stern. All of them now focused their attention on the water to the rear of the CARVER.

"There I see them," Alex pointed.

"Yeah, looks like Mitch has her," Gary said and leaned out farther to see better. "Les, can you get on the radio and have an ambulance ready and waiting at the marina in the Cove."

"Wait, the Harbor is closer and I can get them there quick in my boat," Alex interjected.

"Yeah, you're right," Gary said. "Les, the Harbor instead. Tell the dispatcher that it is a water rescue and we'll need advanced life support."

"Right," Shepard said, "but Amanda can help with the first aid."

"Oh," Gary replied.

"Sure, I'm an ER nurse in Syracuse."

"Great, then get over here and get ready," Gary half asked half ordered.

She wasted no time in climbing over and leaned on the transom just as Mitch broke the surface with a very blue and very unconscious Alicia in a life saver's carry. Mitch gasped for breath and floundered. Gary leaped in and swam over to lend a hand. Gary held Alicia while Mitch spit out some of the lake and caught his breath.

"Quick get her up into the boat," Gary called to Alex and Amanda. Benton hurtled over to the CARVER and helped pull the lifeless girl from the water. As soon as they laid her on the deck, Amanda started CPR and Alex and Benton helped Gary and Mitch out of the water. Mitch almost collapsed from exhaustion. The swim and the rescue had managed to pop a few stitches and blood was once again streaming down his face.

Gary had gone over to help Amanda with the breathing while she did the chest compressions. Gary counted to five and blew a breath into Alicia's open mouth. Amanda kept up the regular pace of the compressions and Gary reached five again and gave Alicia another breath.

"Come on Alicia," Mitch said now breathing better himself and holding a handful of bandages that Benton had pulled from the first aid kit. "Come on you can do it," he said again as Gary gave her another breath.

"Wait," Gary said and Amanda stopped for a moment. Suddenly water began pouring from Alicia's mouth and Gary rolled her over on her side. When the water stopped he carefully rolled her back and tipped her head and started to breathe again. Amanda resumed the rhythmic compressions.

"Ambulance and paramedics will be waiting at the Harbor," Shepard called over.

"Good, four, five," Gary said keeping up the count and gave her another breath. He checked the area of the throat under the chin next to the Adam's apple for a pulse. "Wait, wait," he said to Amanda. "I think I've got something." He checked again and now started breathing into her faster. He watched to see if her chest expanded with his breaths and he saw a slight movement. He gave her a breath again then pulled away quickly as more brown green water poured up out of her mouth. As soon as the water stopped, he reextended her head to get a good straight airway and then started breathing into her again. After a few more breaths she suddenly began to cough and more water came out and flowed across the deck.

She coughed again and when Gary rolled her back her color was starting to return to a healthy living pink and she started to breathe on her own. Everyone cheered and Gary leaned back against the side and smiled at Amanda then at Mitch. "Let's get them both into your boat Alex and get them to the ambulance."

"Good Idea," Alex said and helped Mitch to his feet.

Amanda had found a blanket in the cabin and covered Alicia. Gary and Alex carefully lifted the still unconscious girl into the speed boat and set her into the cuddy cabin.

"I think I should go with her," Amanda said to her husband.

"Sure, OK, I'll meet you in the Harbor," Shepard said.

"No, I mean to the hospital."

"OK, I'll get there somehow."

"No problem," Benton said. "I'll take this boat back to the Cove and follow you, Mr. Shepard. I'll give you a ride to the hospital in my patrol."

"Thanks," Shepard called over.

"OK," Gary said, "that'll do it. We're going to the Harbor. See everyone at the hospital."

Everyone agreed and once Gary was on the speed boat he untied it from the 'Viking Princess' and pushed off. Alex had the engines started and as soon as they were clear he pushed the throttles full forward and the engines roared to life and they shot off in a spray of foam.

Mitch wasn't sure but he thought the trip back seemed much longer. Alex assured him that in fact they were making much better time since they weren't trying to find something and could just travel in a straight line. Amanda was still below keeping an eye on Alicia who still hadn't regained consciousness yet but was breathing on her own. Once in a while Alicia would cough up some more of the lake bottom but made no other sound or movement.

Mitch knew Alicia was in good hands and that he could do nothing more to help her and stayed out of the way. He was just sitting in one of the contour seats holding a bandage to his aching head trying to stem the flow of blood from the now fully reopened wound.

"You're insane you know," Gary finally said not being able to hold his anger back any longer. "You almost got yourself killed. Again," he said placing great emphasis on the last part.

"Yeah, but I managed to save Alicia," Mitch said in his own defense.

"Still no excuse for your leaving the hospital and then breaking who knows how many laws and rules to get out here ahead of us. How did you do that by the way?"

"I remembered the Harbor had bought this boat and I hoped it was still around after they downsized the police force a couple of years ago trying to cut the tax rate. Just a lucky guess. I just gave him a call and drove down to meet him."

"That's another thing," Gary said not hiding his frustration at Mitch. "Alex says you pulled up in a new Jag convertible. I didn't know you had one and I'm supposed to be your closest friend. What's with that?" Gary asked now going for all the answers.

"Ah, well, I, ah, bought it this spring," Mitch said evasively.

"Bought it," Gary said in disbelief. "It must go for eighty or ninety thousand new."

"Ah, more like one hundred ten, but I could pick the color."

"How nice, but where in the hell did you get $110,000 for a car? No bank on the planet would ever lend you that kind of money especially on your salary and with your child support."

"Don't remind me," Mitch said trying to avoid more answers.

"Don't try to change the subject. The car. Tell me about the car and for that matter you never did tell me where the boat came from either. What did you do, rob a bank on your day off?"

"Not quite," Mitch said, "and I'll tell you, but not here and not now. We need somewhere quiet without so many sets of ears."

"OK, I'll let it rest for now," Gary said, "but the first time we're alone I want all the answers."

"OK," Mitch agreed reluctantly.

"Now tell me how you managed to get out of the hospital full of doctors and nurses and not an hour after taking a bullet in the head."

"The hospital part was easy," Mitch said, "I just waited until everyone was busy with an accident case and then just walked out the door and grabbed a cab home. My car took care of the distance to the Harbor."

"Yeah," Gary said still wondering about the car. "And by the way, where did you get the cash for the A-H too?"

Mitch took a deep breath and was about to answer.

"No. wait. Don't tell me. It's a long story."

"Right," said Mitch and he moved to focus his attention on the island they were rapidly approaching. "We need to get those bastards," he said to Gary.

"We will, we will," Gary said reassuringly. "You think that scumbag came back here after he jumped ship off of Alicia's boat and set her up to drown?"

"Maybe," Mitch said not hiding his loathing for Conners and his crew. "We need to get them one way or another," he added under his breath.

"What?" Gary asked knowing what Mitch had murmured.

"Nothing," Mitch said as they passed the island and worked their way through the narrow and now very shallow channel between Society Island and some smaller and uninhabited pieces of rock with trees.

"It seems even shallower then when we came through here the first time," Alex said. "The dam must be about gone to drop the water this much."

"One more reason to get those people and get them good," Mitch seethed.

"About ten minutes guys," Alex said returning the boat to full speed once they were out of the shallow water. "There," he said pointing ahead. "I see the ambulance lights on the dock."

"Good," Gary said, "now we can get the walking wounded here and poor Alicia in a hospital where they belong," he said and nudged Mitch who had that 'who me' look on his multicolored face.

"We're almost to the slip," Alex said to his passengers who seemed to be preoccupied in their own thoughts.

"OK," Gary said.

"What can I do?" Mitch asked.

"Nothing. You're one of the wounded and not supposed to do anything," Gary said in a tone of voice almost like an order.

"Yes sir," Mitch said and sat back down while Gary handled the dock lines. Most of the Harbor had turned out and the ambulance crew was waiting on the main part of the dock. Several of the villagers came running out onto the slip and helped bring the boat into its berth. Once the lines were all tied the ambulance crew made their way out to the cockpit. Alex went below and with Gary's help lifted the unconscious Alicia out of the cabin and across the side of the boat into the arms of the paramedic. They set her down carefully onto the stretcher and strapped her in. They immediately placed an oxygen mask over her nose and mouth and turned up the flow. The crew wasted no time pushing her off the dock and some of the civilians who wanted to help or just watch were nearly shoved aside when the crew moved the stretcher.

"OK, Mitch old buddy, it's your turn and no complaining," Gary said. "Get into the ambulance with her. You're going back to the hospital too."

"But," Mitch tried to say something.

"But nothing. I can order you, you know."

"I know," Mitch replied carefully climbing out of the boat. "All I was going to say is my car is out front. I don't want to leave it in this crime ridden town," he said the last part just loud enough for Alex to hear.

"Hey, I resent the implication," he said smiling.

"Not to worry my friend," Gary said grinning from ear to ear. "I'll be glad to drive it back for you."

"Yeah, I'll bet you would," Mitch replied knowing he couldn't win this one. He reached into his still wet pocket and pulled out the key on an official Jaguar leather key fob.

"Ooh very nice," Gary said admiring the fancy key ring. "Now I see why the car costs a 110,000."

"Funny," Mitch retorted, "but that was extra."

"You're kidding. 110K for a car and they still clip you for a key ring. Incredible," Gary said shaking his head and escorting Mitch to the ambulance.

"You'll be really careful, won't you?" Mitch asked as if Gary was taking his only daughter on a first date.

"Yes," was all Gary said as he pushed Mitch inside the ambulance and watched as the crew closed and latched the rear doors. The ambulance pulled out and the spectators parted like some human sea. The siren sounded and Gary stood for a moment as the ambulance headed down the narrow village street.

Gary tossed the car key into the air and caught it. He walked over to the shinny blue land yacht and shook his head in amazed wonderment at how a man on a Deputy's salary could drive such a car. As he was standing there in amazement and wondering, a couple of the local young ladies came over. Gary looked up from his thoughts at the girls in very short tight shorts and bikini tops. "Is that your car?" one of them asked.

"Ah, no it belongs to the guy in the ambulance," Gary said now admiring the girls.

"We love this car," the other one said with a big smile and she gracefully rubbed her hip along the front fender.

"I'll be sure to tell the owner."

"Is he single?" the first one asked.

"Yeah, and his name is Mitch," Gary said throwing in a plug for his friend. Gary opened the door and sat in the exquisitely soft leather seats. I hate him, he said amazingly to himself.

"What does your friend do? Is he rich?" the second bikini top asked.

"Ah, he a Deputy Sheriff."

"Ooh," was all he heard as he fired the V-8. "Bye girls," he said and pulled out into the road. Gary was simultaneously filled with exhilaration and jealousy at the sheer power and beauty of the car his friend had never mentioned. Yes girls, he said to himself, he's rich but I don't know how. He reveled in the near sexual experience of driving the sports car to the hospital and he wished on several occasions that the hospital was a lot farther away at least for his sake. He arrived at the hospital only a few minutes behind the ambulance in a near euphoric mood after the drive in the Jag. He found Mitch sitting on an examination table with a nurse cleaning his blood-caked forehead.

"As soon as I figure out how you got one of these," Gary said holding up the car key, "I have to get one of my own."

"Nice huh," Mitch said between winces and a few ouches. "Careful," he said to the nurse, "I'm wounded not dead."

"No thanks on your part," she said and pressed a little harder on the open laceration. "Thanks to you I got reprimanded for letting you escape."

"It wasn't your fault," Mitch said, "I'll talk to the head nurse."

"Don't you dare," she protested, "you've done enough."

"That's for sure," Gary said in agreement. Mitch shot him a half dirty look and reached out for the car key. "Whoa, not so fast old buddy. I'm going to hold onto these until they cut you loose from here."

"May you develop a lingering and painful case of jock itch."

"Ooh, and you kiss girls with that mouth," Gary said now smiling with enjoyment and Mitch's helplessness. "How's Alicia?" he asked.

"I don't know. They won't tell me anything in this torture chamber."

"Careful with the insults," the nurse said and pressed a little harder on the wound again.

"Ow," Mitch yelled, "see what I mean. Comfort the injured my foot."

"Watch it buster or I'll have the doctor sew you up again but this time without anesthetic."

"You'd better behave yourself," Gary warned. "Relax, I'll go see how she's doing." Gary left Mitch's room and walked to the room next door. He peeked in and saw Amanda just inside the door.

"Psst," Gary made a sound and Amanda looked over.

"Hi," she whispered, "they let me stay when I told them I was an ER nurse."

"Good, how's she doing?" he asked.

"Better. She came to about fifteen minutes ago and now they're doing some blood tests and they want to do a C.A.T. scan as soon as she's stable."

"C.A.T. scan," he repeated sounding concerned.

"Yeah, they want to make sure there is no brain damage from being without air for a while. Pretty routine for near drowning victims."

"Oh," said Gary.

"Don't worry, so far they think she's just fine."

"Good," he said and looked over at Alicia laying on the exam table now all plugged in and full of tubes. She moved her head and opened her eyes and saw Gary standing in the door. She smiled and weakly raised her hand for a faint wave. Gary smiled back and said, "next door," answering her unasked question. She nodded slightly and Gary backed out of the room and closed the door. He went back to Mitch's room just as the doctor was about to start on the new set of stitches.

"May I come in Doctor?" Gary asked.

"I don't see why not," the doctor replied. "Seems like when this guy is around all the hospital rules go out the window. Just use one of those masks if you want to come closer."

"No here is just fine," Gary said. "I don't like needles much."

"Neither do I," Mitch added with a grimace as the first stitch went in.

"Then why do you keep getting yourself all banged and cut up?" Gary asked.

"Just bad luck, that's all," Mitch said.

"He going to be all right?" Gary asked the doctor.

"Don't know but if we can keep him here for a while this time we might know for sure," the doctor said and pulled another stitch tight as Mitch winced.

"He'll stay this time or I'll personally assign a deputy to watch him."

"Good, he needs at least a few days observation but my guess, after his exploits today, is he'll be just fine. A few more scars but otherwise just fine."

"Good," Mitch said, "then I can leave."

"No," both Gary and the doctor said at the same time.

"How's Alicia?" Mitch asked between winces.

"I got to see her. Amanda Shepard the woman from the boat is with her. Seems she's going to need some tests to make sure she didn't suffer any brain damage, but OK I guess," Gary said.

"She'll be fine with some rest too," the doctor said and pulled another stitch. "I examined her when she came in. No sign of permanent damage but another few seconds under the water and she wouldn't be so lucky. I guess we have you to thank, don't we Deputy Stone?"

"Yes we do," Gary said and Mitch smiled a little and the doctor finished the last stitch.

"Now if you don't pull these out, the scar won't be too noticeable," the doctor said. "I have to get back to your friend but I trust you'll still be here when I do my rounds."

"Yes doctor," Gary said for Mitch who just gave them both the innocent 'who me' look again.

"Good," the doctor said and left. Mitch looked over at his friend.

"Don't give me that look," Gary said. "Unofficially you did a great job today but officially you're in deep shit my friend."

"Yeah, we missed Conners."

"You know what I'm talking about," Gary said in his sergeant's voice.

"He knows," came the voice from the doorway. Both men looked and Gary saluted. Mitch raised his hand to do the same.

"Hi Lt.," Mitch said.

"Save the amenities Deputy. I'm not here to be friendly."

"No sir," Mitch said hanging his head.

"Like the Sergeant said, unofficially you did a great job today. We'll get your assailant. But, officially your in big trouble."

"Uh huh," Mitch said not looking up.

"Uh huh is right. Leaving the hospital, unauthorized involvement of another police agency, running your car all over the county at high speed and generally just causing me a lot of grief."

"Sorry Lt."

"Sorry won't cut it Stone. I'm placing you on administrative leave."

"For how long?" Mitch interrupted.

"For as long as it takes for you to get fully recovered. I figure a couple of weeks with full pay should help you regain your strength."

"Yes sir," Mitch said with a subdued smile.

"Oh, and by the way. Could either of you two tell a poor old public servant how a deputy has the money to have a car I hear you drive."

"Ah, well," Mitch started to answer.

"No, never mind. I don't want to know."

"I do," Gary whispered to Mitch.

"Oh, by the way Deputy Stone. The FBI is very pleased with your level of assistance and cooperation with their agent. I think they mentioned something about an official commendation. Good work Stone."

"Thank you sir," Mitch said.

"Now stay here and get better. I don't want to see you for a couple of weeks. Just relax OK."

"Yes sir, thanks," Mitch said.

"There you see even the Fibbies like you now," Gary teased.

"Big deal we still have that scumbag Conners out there loose somewhere."

"Not your problem now," Gary said. "We'll go through the proper channels and get him."

"Yeah, let's hope," Mitch said.

"Now you were going to tell me about all your toys, which by the way a couple of real nice looking ladies in the Harbor love your car."

"Oh, yeah, that," Mitch said hesitantly then changed the conversation. "What two young ladies?"

"Never mind them. I want to know about the car."

"Oh, all right," Mitch started again but was interrupted by a nurse and orderly with a wheel chair. "What's this?" he asked.

"Shit," Gary said at the interruption.

"I'm sorry are we interrupting anything?" the nurse asked.

"Yes," Gary said.

"No," Mitch said.

"Good," said the nurse. "Now Mr. Stone we're going to get you to your room."

"Sure," Mitch said and slid off the table and took a seat in the wheelchair. "Home, my good man," he said to the orderly and was wheeled away. "Later, Gary," he said.

"Count on it," Gary snapped back.

The nurse opened the hospital room door and the orderly wheeled Mitch up to the side of the bed and helped him up onto it. Mitch looked around and saw that the curtain was drawn between the two beds in the room and as soon as the nurse and the orderly left a faint voice spoke. "Hi, my name is Alicia, what's yours?"

"Hi, my name is Mitch, nice to meet you. You sound very beautiful." Mitch slowly got off the bed and walked around to the other side of the curtain.

"Oh Mitch I'm so glad to see you. Thanks for saving me," she said weakly but with a big smile.

"You're welcome," he said and bent over to kiss her. They held the kiss for a long time until she started to cough. "You OK?" he asked reaching for the nurse's buzzer.

"Yeah, fine. Just a little congested, That's all."

"OK," Mitch said.

She motioned for him to come closer and bent down as if to give her another kiss. She summoned all her strength and slapped him across the right side of his face.

"What was that for?" he asked a little shocked at her streak of violence.

"For dropping that handcuff key and letting me get pulled into the lake."

"But I saved you."

"Yes you did," she said smiling again and motioned for him to come closer again. Mitch hesitated a bit.

"It's OK," she said. "I won't hurt you."

He bent over her and she kissed him hard and long. There was a knock on the door. "Am I interrupting something, I hope?" Gary said and Mitch stood up fast enough to feel a little dizzy.

"Ah, no," he said peeking around the curtain. "We were just talking."

"I didn't hear any voices," Gary said with a gleam in his eye. "If you two can't behave I'll have you moved to separate rooms."

"That won't be necessary, Sgt.," Mitch said using his friend's title with a little sarcasm, "and since when did you join the morality police?"

"Honorary member," he said.

"Sure," Mitch said and Gary walked to the end of Alicia's bed.

"Hello pretty lady," Gary said, "how are you?"

"Fine," she replied but was suddenly overcome by a fit of coughing that left her gasping for breath.

"That doesn't sound too good though," Gary said, "I'd better get a nurse."

"Yeah," Mitch said now showing his concern on his face. Alicia coughed again and was still coughing when Gary returned with the nurse. The coughs subsided a little and the nurse tried to comfort Alicia and then turned to look at Mitch who was standing there looking helpless as his friend was trying to catch her breath.

"You're supposed to be in bed resting," the nurse said to Mitch. He didn't argue and went back around the curtain and got into bed again. It wasn't long before another nurse and a doctor entered the room and disappeared around the other side of the curtain. Alicia started to cough again.

"OK, nurse," Mitch could hear the doctor say. "We need to get her sedated to keep the coughing down and then I want a full set of chest x-rays, STAT."

"Yes, doctor," one of the nurses said and left the room. She returned shortly with an orderly pushing a gurney. The two nurses and the orderly lifted Alicia onto the cart and Mitch and Gary watched as they wheeled her out.

"Doctor," Mitch said as the physician started to follow, "what's wrong with her."

"Not sure, but I'd say pneumonia from all the lake water in her lungs. We'll know more after the x-rays."

"Thanks doctor," Mitch said as he left.

"She'll be fine," Gary said comforting his friend.

"Yeah," Mitch said but not too sure about his answer.

Gary left Mitch alone after awhile and it seemed more than an hour passed before they wheeled the now unconscious Alicia back into the room. Mitch strained to see her as they wheeled her past his bed but all he could see was her face with tubes protruding from her mouth. The team of nurses spent the next ten minutes hooking her up to several monitors and a flow of oxygen. Finally they started to leave and Mitch asked them if Alicia would be all right.

"We think so, but she's got a bad case of pneumonia and she suffered cardiac arrest in the x-ray lab. We were able to resuscitate but
we've got to watch her carefully for a few days."

"Oh," Mitch said sadly.

"As for you Mr. Stone, the tests all came back negative and unless
you have a relapse we're letting you go in the morning. We were
going to keep you for a few days but the doctors changed their
minds. They figure you'd only try to leave on your own anyway. You
seem to be more trouble than they want to deal with. You can rest at
home they said."

"Thanks," he said now concerned more about Alicia.

"You're welcome," the nurse said as she headed out the door.
"Don't worry, she's in good hands and we'll do everything we can to
get her better."

"I know, thanks again," he said.

He didn't sleep well at all that night. The nurses were in and out at
regular intervals to check on Alicia and Mitch was just too anxious
about her condition to sleep well. At around eight A.M. the resident
doctor stopped in to see him.

"Seems we can't do much else for you here," the young doctor
said. "Now you'll just have to recuperate at home."

"Good," Mitch said, "but I'm still worried about her." He pointed
at the other bed in the room.

"I know, but she made it through the night without a set back and
she's young. I think she'll be fine."

"Thanks Doctor," Mitch said and started to get dressed.

"I'll send an orderly up to get in a minute," the doctor said and
went around to check on the other more serious patient in the room.

"Thanks for all you've done doctor," Mitch said as the orderly
arrived and he took a seat in the wheelchair.

"You're welcome, and don't worry," the doctor called after Mitch.

The orderly wheeled Mitch to the elevator and then they went
down to the first floor. Mitch was wheeled up to the administration

desk and signed himself out. "Here you go Mr. Stone," the secretary said handing him the copies of his admission papers and his car key. "Your friend said your car was parked out front."

"Thanks," Mitch said and the orderly pushed him to the front door. "I can take it from here," he said as the orderly smiled and headed back into the building once Mitch was on his feet. He walked sullenly to the edge of the parking lot and looked for his car. Gary had parked it in a spot normally reserved for police or fire vehicles but apparently nobody complained because the Jag was still there and didn't even have a ticket on it. Gary even figured out how to put up the top and lock the doors. Mitch's mood was pretty gloomy even after he put the top back down and started his favorite toy. He pulled slowly out of the lot but he was beginning to formulate a plan that would improve his disposition immensely. He picked up his cell phone and punched in Gary's private number.

"Hello," answered Gary after a few rings.

"Yeah, it's Mitch."

"Ah, you'd better be calling from your hospital bed," Gary said sternly.

"Not to worry. They turned me loose."

"No lie," Gary responded a little skeptically.

"Nope. I'm free."

"OK for you but how's Alicia?"

"Not good, but not any worse either," Mitch said.

"Good, so what's up? You headed home?"

"Ah, not really. When are you going to serve the warrant on the folks at Society Island?"

"Uh," Gary hesitated.

"Uh, what?" Mitch pressed sounding angry.

"Well the D.A. says we don't have enough to get a warrant."

"What," Mitch yelled almost loud enough to be heard without the phone. "What's with that shit? With all that's happened the D.A.

won't seek a warrant on those people who want to hold the world hostage to their evil little machines."

"Nope. Says there is nothing to link any of the personnel with what's happened."

"Bullshit," Mitch exclaimed almost livid now. "What about Conners and his attempted murder of both Alicia and me not to mention the dam sabotage?"

"Nothing to link him or Millennium to any of the dam destruction and they deny any association with him or any of the assaults or the fire."

"Yeah, well let's just go down there and drag his sorry ass out and have a nice little chat with him."

"No can do. Our surveillance patrol hasn't seen him and Millennium will of course deny he's there. Without good probable cause we can't even knock on their door officially."

"Yeah, officially," Mitch said formulating his own plan to exact retribution for the events of the last few days.

"I don't like the sound of that," Gary said. "What are you planning on doing?"

"Nothing you need to know about," Mitch said mulling the idea over in his head. "You have any of those NANOs from the dam?"

"Yeah sure, we were going to use them as evidence remember, but there is no link between them and anyone at Millennium."

"Good then they should be disposed of, right?"

"Yes, but," Gary stopped. He didn't like where the conversation was leading and he didn't really want to know or find out what Mitch had in mind. "I suppose you know just how to dispose of them safely?"

"As a matter of fact I do," Mitch said riled at the failure of the system he worked for. "Meet me at the coffee shop with the NANOs," he said without giving a specific name or address for the well-frequented night stopping spot for all the cops.

"OK, but I should probably not do this," Gary said reluctantly beginning to guess what Mitch's plan might be.

"You're just doing the county and the department a favor by disposing of some very dangerous evidence and I just volunteered to help an old friend. That's all Sgt." Mitch said in a reassuring but slightly devious tone of voice.

"Yeah, so why do I regret this already and nothing has happened?" Gary said not comfortable with the way Mitch was starting to cover his trail. "OK, the coffee shop in ten minutes. Out back."

"See you in ten," Mitch said and hung up the phone and replaced it in the cradle on the side of the walnut-covered console. Now that both Gary and the Lt. had found out about his expensive toy he didn't have to be careful who saw him driving it around town. Up till now he had to be very clandestine about driving it and he would leave early in the morning and head straight out of town to another city to cruise in the open car. Now with the secret exposed he could drive it to his heart's content right here at home. Sooner or later he knew he would have to explain how he was able to afford such a toy. He hoped it would be later.

Mitch now drove down the main street to the coffee shop as if he was driving the Grand Marshall in the Fourth of July Parade. Nice and easy enjoying the smooth ride and the open air. Maybe he would volunteer to drive one of the dignitaries in next week's parade. Maybe the Dairy Princess, he thought. He put that pleasant thought out of his mind as he pulled into the parking lot of the coffee shop and then around back for his pickup. Thankfully there were no other cops in the shop at the moment who might see him and Gary and want to shoot the shit or worse start asking questions about the shooting or the fire while he and Gary were trying to load a container full of destructive NANOs.

As he pulled around back, he spotted Gary standing next to an unmarked department car. He pulled up next to the big domestic sedan and pushed the trunk release in his glove box. There was a barely audible click and the trunk lid raised up a small fraction of an inch. Mitch got out and walked around to greet Gary.

"How's the head?" Gary asked looking at the new bandage and the discoloration spread out across the left side of Mitch's face.

"Sore as hell. In fact sometimes I just can't think clearly for all the pain," he said with a wry smile.

"That's what I'm afraid of," Gary replied moving toward his trunk. He inserted the key and lifted the lid. There in the center of the compartment sat a thirty-quart cooler with the lid taped shut. "Think they're loose in there?" he asked carefully lifting the plastic box out of the trunk.

"Probably. I'll be real careful," Mitch said taking the cooler by the handles from Gary and setting it inside the trunk of the Jag. "Remember these things are programmed for iron and I wouldn't want them to start on the coach work of my nice new car."

"Yeah, and what about this car?" Gary started to ask again. "You said you'd tell me where it and all your high end toys came from. And I've been thinking. Not that Carol and I are ungrateful. In fact we are very grateful about the donation to Lizzy's college fund. Did that really come from the some rich aunt of yours who died or all of these big dollar items related?"

"I tell you later," Mitch said pretending to be in a hurry to leave. "Later, sometime," he said smiling and he gently pushed the trunk lid down until the automatic close took over and seated and latched the lid. "I've got to take care of these things right away," he said and got back into his car and started the V-8.

"I won't let this drop," Gary said.

"That's what I figure," Mitch said and he put on his new sunglasses and waved to his friend. He pulled out of the rear lot and back onto the main street and headed west. He had a delivery to make and since he was technically on administrative leave he wasn't really acting in an official capacity. Nothing would come back to haunt the department or more importantly him and Gary. He drove leisurely to the marina in Smyth's Cove and slowly past C dock which was where he had kept 'Cold Fortune'.

He was both saddened and angered when he looked at the empty berth. They'll pay for that, he said to himself and he pulled into the guest parking spot.

He checked over the line of cars to be sure his other prized possession was still there. He had left the A-H in the lot several days ago which now seemed like weeks. It was still there and still under cover. At least that was one thing that he wouldn't have to replace. He put the Jag in park, shut it off and climbed out. He needed to retrieve something from Alicia's boat but he didn't have a key and he guessed Deputy Benton had secured the cabin when he docked the boat.

No problem, he said to himself. Fortunately, the marina required all boat owners to leave a spare key in the office in the event of an emergency. If the fire had been a little later when the office was opened more boats could have been saved. He walked into the office and was greeted with congratulations and loud clapping. Everyone was glad he was all right. Only yesterday the staff had reported to work to find him sprawled out on the couch and covered with blood. Now here he was sporting a bandage on his head but seemingly no worse for the wear.

"Thank you," he said to everyone in the office and he answered a few questions about his wound and about Alicia. They were all saddened when he told them about her accident and condition in the hospital. He didn't answer the question about who might have set the fire. All he said was that the matter was being handled. As soon as everyone returned to their work Mitch asked the owner for the key to Alicia's boat. He said it was against policy but seeing that Mitch was a friend of the owner and a police officer he handed Mitch the key.

"Thanks," Mitch said and he waved to all the staff and smiled as he left. Nice people, he said to himself and walked down the dock and heard his name being called.

"Deputy Stone. Deputy Stone over here on D dock. On the end."

"Oh, yes sir. Wait, weren't you the ones who came out to help with our friend."

"Yes sir, That's us. My name is Les Shepard and this is my wife Amanda."

"Nice to meet you both, just call me Mitch, OK," he said. He couldn't help notice Amanda wasn't wearing much of a swimsuit. Micro is more the word, he thought.

"We're glad to see you're all right" Shepard said.

"Thanks."

"How's Alicia?"

"Not good. She caught a bad case of pneumonia, but the doctors believe she'll come through OK."

"Oh, that's good," Shepard said. "When you get the chance we'd love to have you over for drinks or dinner."

"Thanks that would be nice," Mitch said. "I'd like that."

"Good. We'll see you then," Shepard called back and they both waved.

Mitch waved back and walked down the dock and stepped onto the gunwale of the 'Viking Princess' and then down to the deck. He tried the door but just as he thought it was locked. Good man that Benton, he thought. He inserted the key, turned the lock and slid open the door. He stepped inside and turned on the cabin lights and looked around for a moment. He spotted his duffle bag and opened it pulling out the old leather and parchment manuscript and carefully unwrapped it on the navigation station. Thank god Conners had been more interested in his escape attempt and hadn't searched the cabin.

Before he started his research, he opened the cold well and looked inside. "Bless her," he said and pulled out two cold beers. He popped open the first one and nearly drained it in one long drink. He took a second swallow and finished the contents. After his refreshment he sat at the desk and opened the second beer. From the bag on the floor he pulled out the set of old charts dated 1952 and a new set he had purchased at the start of the season a few weeks ago.

The knock on the cabin door startled him and returned him to the present day world. He looked around and saw a tall blond in a tight pair of shorts and a bare midriff T-shirt. His mind was still on his research and it didn't quite register who the beautiful woman was until she spoke.

"Hi, am I disturbing you? I'm Amanda Shepard, Les' wife. We spoke earlier."

"Oh," Mitch said coming out of his daze. "Yeah, sure. Hi, come on in."

"Thanks," she said sliding open the door and stepping in. "We saw the lights on and well you've been in here all day. We wondered if you'd like some dinner."

"Oh, Yeah," Mitch said looking at his watch and remembering it was gone. "I've lost my watch and I guess track of time as well. What time is it anyway?"

"Almost eight P.M."

"Whoa. I didn't realize. I was doing some research and just got immersed."

"Well come on then, I've made a nice salad and Les has the barbecue going. We'll buy you a couple of beers and feed you a nice meal."

"Sounds good, and I can't refuse the invitation of a lovely lady."

"Thanks," she said smiling, "you really think so?"

Mitch didn't answer he just smiled back and turned off the cabin lights. He made sure the door was locked. He didn't want anyone to disturb his next rich aunt's death.

At about eleven o'clock, Mitch thanked the Shepards for the sumptuous meal and the more than a few beers. He walked carefully back to the 'Viking Princess' having had plenty to drink. The Shepards were great people, he said to himself. A few times he had to stop and catch himself as he walked the narrow dock in the dark. He tripped over a coil of line in front of one boat and nearly went for a midnight swim. After a few stumbles and missed steps he made it back to the boat and slowly climbed on board and made his way to the forward "V" berth where he and Alicia had spent the night a short time ago. He crawled in alone this time and fell asleep almost immediately upon hitting the pillow.

CHAPTER 18

THE LOCATION

*M*orning arrived and Mitch woke up with a massive head ache. He wasn't sure if it was the beers, the wound or a combination of both but he found a bottle of aspirin in the bathroom cabinet and swallowed a handful chased by a large glass of water. Breakfast was a bowl of dry cereal with no milk and a piece of toast. Alicia didn't have any tea and Mitch wasn't a coffee drinker. He'd find a coke somewhere for his caffeine fix, but the aspirin would kick in soon hopefully.

He packed up all the charts and carefully replaced the old log book. He also bundled his notes together, left the cabin and relocked the door. Before he returned the key, he thought he better put the duffle bag in the car first. He didn't want to answer any questions about what he was removing from someone else's boat. His concerns were unnecessary though, he found the office closed and he put the key into the night drop box. Must be before eight A.M. he figured and cursed the fact he didn't have his OMEGA SEAMASTER any-more. They'll pay for that too, he said to the locked door and his reflection in the glass.

Mitch walked to the Jag, started the engine and drove out of the marina passing the empty slip where he had kept his boat. He knew what he had to do and he drove on out the access road and headed west through town. About ten minutes later he pulled up in front of the Harbor Emporium and parked the car. Almost as if they had been waiting since yesterday two young girls appeared next to the car and began giving it an interested look.

"Hi," the blond said, "are you the one who owns this? We saw it down here yesterday."

"Yeah, I'm the one," he said climbing out and gently closing the door.

"We love it," the brunette said. "Can we go for a ride in it some-time?"

"Maybe sometime," Mitch said and smiled at the two car fanciers and went inside the store. "Is Alex around?"

"Yeah out on the dock," the clerk said. "Hey aren't you the one who was involved with that rescue yesterday?"

"I'm the one," Mitch said and pulled a piece of paper from his shirt pocket and handed it to the clerk. "Please fill this list and put it all in some cardboard boxes. Alex will tell you what to do with it then."

"Whose going to pay for all this stuff?" the clerk asked after Mitch who was already out the door.

"He will," Mitch yelled back. He walked down the dock and out toward the big fishing trawler Alex used for his commercial fishing business. "Hey Alex," he called.

"Yeah," Alex said from somewhere inside the big boat and then stuck his head out of the side door. "Oh hi, Mitch. What are you doing out of the hospital? You escape again?"

"Nope. Released by the doctor. I'm as cured as they'll be able to make me."

"What about Alicia?"

"She's not good but they say she's stable. Apparently the lake water in her lungs caused a bad case of pneumonia."

"Too bad," Alex said sympathetically. "I hope everything is OK."

"Me too," Mitch said, "but now I need a favor from you."

"Name it," Alex said stepping onto the dock and walking over to shake his friend's hand.

"I need your boat again."

"No problem. Where are we going fast to this time?"

"Not fast and I'm sorry not we. I need this one," he said pointing to the trawler, "and I need it alone."

"Ah," Alex hesitated and looked at the boat and then back at Mitch. "OK, but it's in the middle of fish season. The wife will be pissed if I lose a day's catch."

"Not a day. A week or two," Mitch said.

"Wow she's going to be really pissed."

"OK, how much do you make in a good day?"

"Oh, I don't know after expenses I give her two to three hundred."

"And how much do you give yourself?"

"Ah, never mind that."

"Well I need your boat for a while," Mitch said and pulled an envelope from his pocket. "Here's five thousand dollars for you and the wife and I'll fill it up with gas when I'm finished."

"Diesel."

"OK, diesel," Mitch said, "and here's another thousand. I have some groceries in the store and I need you to rent me a full set of dive gear and a couple of tanks. You still got that compressor on the boat?"

"Yes, and a couple of my tanks too. I just don't have any of the rest of the gear. I let my brother-in-law borrow it."

"No problem, thanks," Mitch said. "I've got an errand to run and I'll be back this afternoon. Can you have the boat and gear ready for me by say two o'clock?" Mitch asked looking at his watch and remembering again.

"Know where I can get a watch too?" he asked and said goodbye to his friend.

"See you this afternoon," Alex said.

Mitch walked along the side of the general store and back to his car. He didn't see the two girls but as soon as he opened the door they appeared from out of nowhere.

"Can we go for a ride now?" they asked almost in one voice.

"No, I'm afraid not. I've got some errands to run. Maybe sometime else, OK?"

"OK," they said together.

Mitch unlocked the trunk with his key and pulled out a carefully wrapped package about eighteen inches wide by twenty-four inches long. He had previously addressed it and now carried it into the Emporium.

"Yes, sir. I've got everything you wanted from the list already for you."

"Alex will stop in shortly and pay for all of it but I need you to do me a favor."

"If I can."

"I need this package delivered to a Mr. Lindquist at the facility on Society Island. Can you have it done today?"

"Ah, yeah but it'll will cost you."

"Doesn't matter. Just tell Alex and add it to the grocery bill. And give whoever delivers it a twenty-dollar tip, OK."

"Sure I'll do it myself then."

"Today!"

"Yeah, right away, as soon as I can get someone to cover here for me."

"Thanks," Mitch said and walked back out to his car. He got in, started the engine and backed out of the parking space. The two girls were still standing in front of the store looking at him or more accurately, his car. Things must really be dull in this town, he thought. Those two girls really need to get a life. He drove out of town and headed west around the end of the Harbor. In about five more minutes he pulled up to the red and white patrol car from his department. Deputy Greg Riley got out of the car and walked over to talk to Mitch.

"What brings you out here, Mitch?" Greg asked, "and how are you feeling?"

"I'm OK," Mitch said, "and I have some business to discuss with our friends inside."

"I thought the D.A. wasn't going to prosecute. Not enough evidence."

"Yeah, something like that," Mitch said unhappily. "Anyway you haven't seen anything of that Conners guy have you?"

"Nope, not a thing. A few of the big shots come and go but nothing of Conners."

"Oh," Mitch said a little disappointed.

"So what are you doing here?" Riley asked again.

"I'm going to join them in the recycling business. Except for the problems caused by Conners the company has a great idea and I want to contribute to their future."

"You want to make an investment with these people?"

"You might say that," Mitch said putting the car in gear. "If you can't beat them join them."

"Yeah, whatever," Riley said as Mitch pulled farther down the road and stopped in front of the guard house at the main gate just out of sight of Riley in the patrol car.

"What do you want?" came the surly question from the gate guard.

"I have an appointment with Lindquist," Mitch said back with his fake smile.

"I don't see you or any cops on my admission list for today and unless you've got a warrant you can just turn your fancy car around and drive back to your coffee shop or wherever."

"My, we aren't very cordial to guests are we?" Mitch said. "Now why don't you check your list again. I'm sure I'm there."

"I said get lost," the guard blustered and stepped out of the small house with his hand on his weapon.

"You shithead rental want-a-bes just don't learn, do you?" Mitch said still holding his fake smile and now pointing his .357 revolver at the man's genitals. "I told your buddies never threaten me with your sorry ass sidearms and now you've gone and done it. Just put your hands on your head and turn around."

"Hey, you can't do this you're a cop," the once tough sounding guard said almost crying now.

"I'm on administrative leave and well it looks like I am doing it," Mitch said and gave the man a shove into the building. He pressed the barrel into the man's left ear and took out the guards handcuffs with his left hand.

"What are you going to do?" the guard squeaked as the sweat started to pour out every pore.

"I might shoot you in the ear," Mitch said as the man began to tear up. "Or I might just cuff you to the desk here and tape your mouth shut. Now sit," Mitch pointed to the chair with his gun. "Oh and I'll take this popgun from you," he said and tossed the .38 out of the door. "Give me your hands," Mitch ordered and the guard held out his arms. Mitch hooked one wrist, threaded the free cuff around the desk leg. "Now bend over and stick your other hand in here. The scared guard did as he was told and Mitch clasped the cuff on the other wrist. "There now you won't cause me any trouble."

Mitch put his revolver into the waist band of his pants and then peeled off a long piece of tape from the dispenser. He wrapped it around the man's head several times crisscrossing his mouth. "There and quiet too," Mitch said pressing the end of the tape into the side of the guard's face.

"Um, um, um," the guard moaned.

"And a good day to you too," Mitch said now really smiling and he pressed the button to raise the gate and returned to his car. Just as he was about to sit, he caught himself and pulled the gun from the back of his pants. Don't want damage the leather, he said to himself and sat in the seat, closed the door and drove to the building containing the lab and, even though the D.A. couldn't or wouldn't be able to prove, the origin of the NANOs.

He drove past several buildings and turned left at the corner. As he drove down the road to the lab building, he noticed the sign on another structure. 'Administration', Mitch stopped and pulled up in front. It was next to the lab and Mitch remembered that he and Alicia had first been introduced to Lindquist in his office. This building must be connected to the lab, he thought. Good a place as any to start, he told himself as he popped the trunk lid and got out of the car. I wonder if anyone is in today, he mused, lifting the cooler chest carefully out of the trunk. He set it down and slowly closed the lid. Carrying the cooler into the front door, he walked up to the receptionist and sat it down in front of her desk.

"Where can I find the head of this place and Lindquist?"

"Do you have an appointment?" the young woman said trying to sound as if she were in charge.

"No, never mind. I'll find my own way, thanks. I was here a few days ago," Mitch said leaving the cooler on the floor and walking toward the large wooden double doors at the end of the room.

"Just a minute," she protested. "You can't go in there. If you don't leave, I'll call the police."

"No problem. I am the police and by the way where were you the other day to tell me I couldn't go in there when your boss was had me as a prisoner?"

"Ah, I don't," she stopped flabbergasted.

"You don't what?" Mitch asked sarcastically, "and if you want to call in more police, please do. There's a Deputy outside the main gate. My friends would love to be invited in here for a look around. No telling what they might find to help with our investigation of this place."

"Well I'll just call our people then and have you removed," she said returning to her desk and picking up the phone. She started to dial a number.

"That won't be necessary Ms. Norton," Lindquist called from the now open doors. "Mr. Stone or should I say Deputy Stone seems to want to see me so I guess we'll let him in. This way Deputy."

"Thanks," Mitch said and was led to the same office he had been in only a few days ago. Once inside Mitch fired off the first question. "You wouldn't happen to now where Conners is would you?"

"No, we haven't seen him for several days and in fact his assistant Jeff Steblin has disappeared as well."

"How convenient, and just when every police agency wants to link this place with the destruction of the dam along with arson and attempted murder and kidnaping."

"I'm afraid I don't know what you're talking about, Deputy. In fact our lawyers have been discussing something along those lines with your D.A. and since our attorneys have advised me not to say anything to you or anyone else I'm afraid we have nothing more to discuss on that point."

"Yeah, I figured as much. The only one who I can finger for all this is Conners and he has conveniently disappeared. Did he end up in your NANO goo like you tried on me?"

"Again Deputy I have no knowledge of any incident involving you nor am I aware of anything Conners did beyond private security for our facility."

"Then you deny instructing him to kill me and the FBI agent?"

"Of course. Once you left my office I was under the belief and in fact had given specific instructions that you were only to be removed from the property. That's all."

"Then Conners has a different meaning for removed?"

"I wouldn't know. You'd have to speak with him about that."

"Yes, and he's nowhere to be found."

"I'm afraid that is the only thing I can agree with you about. Is there anything else then before you leave, Deputy?"

"No, I guess you have all the damage control in place even though I know and you know your NANO machines destroyed the dam and are threatening thousands of lives and hundreds of millions of dollars of property and that your company is the hub of a conspiracy to extort money from every government in the world."

"Again I don't know what you are talking about."

"No of course not. Oh, by the way is this the only lab you have to make your recycling machines?"

"So far this is the only R and D facility for Millennium if that is what you mean."

"Yeah, I guess so, thanks, That's all I wanted to know," Mitch said and turned to leave.

Just as he started to open the door Lindquist asked a question. "Oh, Deputy, since your visit the other evening, I seem to be missing something."

"Oh," Mitch said without turning to face Lindquist.

"Yes, it seems that rare Viking manuscript I showed you is gone. You wouldn't know anything about that would you?"

"No more than you know about Conners, the NANOs and a lot of serious felonies, but if you would like to file a report I'm sure my office would love to come in and do a thorough search and investigation."

"No, no, that won't be necessary. I'm sure it will turn up."

"I'm sure it will, Mitch said to himself. "Thanks for your time," he said to Lindquist and pushed open the doors and left. He walked back to the receptionist's desk and picked up the cooler. "Thank you, you've been most helpful," he said and walked out the door.

Mitch walked across the front lawn and up into the lab building and stood inside the doorway. He tried a closed door and to his pleasant surprise it was open and the room inside was empty. Damn friendly of them, he thought and put the cooler inside. He walked down the hallway and just like a few days ago he pulled the fire alarm. The bell started ringing and he walked back to the small room and closed the door behind him. It worked before, he thought, and as planned a few moments later he heard the shuffle of feet and the main doors open and close. Mitch waited for a few seconds for any stragglers and then opened the door, picked up the cooler and walked quickly down the hall and into the lab, a quick look around assured him the room was empty. Once he was sure he wouldn't be disturbed for at least a few minutes, Mitch set out to exact his measure of payback for the events of the past few days.

Like most large ice chests this particular one had a plug in one end near the bottom to allow water to be drained without having to dump out the contents. In this case it also served as convenient method to disburse the NANOs. Mitch pulled the plug and the blue jelly like substance started to pour out of the drain hole. He picked up the cooler and walked around the entire perimeter of the large room leaving a trail of blue NANO goo along the walls and baseboards. At one point he got a little creative and ran a stream of blue goo up the wall and wrote his initials.

The image didn't last long as the stream started to run down the wall but he laughed at the subtle irony. He made it all around the room with some of the stuff still left in the cooler and he had an idea. He turned the cooler up on the opposite end to save the NANOs for another use.

Once he was happy with his distribution job he stepped over to the main computer terminal near the tank he almost disappeared in and he started to punch up all the NANO programs. There were too many but he saw that the terminal was connected to a large capacity storage drive. He found a tape, inserted it in the drive and moved the curser over all the NANO files and highlighted the whole directory. He dragged the entire set of files over the tape drive icon and released the mouse button. The computer hard drive started to whir and the tape drive began to record all the information.

Fortunately it only took a few minutes to copy the files. Just as the tape drive stopped and ejected the cartridge, Mitch heard the voices and footsteps approaching the lab. They seemed to be protesting the false alarm as the lab workers started to open the doors. Mitch just waited behind one of the swinging doors with his cooler until all of the techs were inside and he merely scooted out without anyone noticing.

Now for the second phase of his plan. He set the cooler back on the floor and the NANO gel began seeping out of the drain and Mitch just picked up the other end and dragged it the entire length of the hallway leaving a light blue trail of NANOs along the middle of the floor. Mitch emptied the cooler before he left the lab building and gave himself a mental pat on the back for a job well done. He walked back to his car started it up and picked up the cell phone. He punched in the telephone number off the business card he had removed from Ms. Norton's desk. When she answered, he asked for Mr. Lindquist. "I'm sorry he's not available, may I take a message?"

"No, Ms. Norton," Mitch said, "this is Deputy Stone and I think Lindquist is available."

"One moment," she said forcefully and Mitch was placed on hold.

"Yes, Deputy Stone," Lindquist said, "I thought we had concluded our business."

"No, not quite. I just thought you should know I just returned some evidence to your lab techs. We obviously can't prosecute Millennium so we had no need for any of the NANOs. I just delivered them to your lab."

"Oh, is that so. As I told you before I don't know what your talking about. Good day sir."

"Wait Lindquist," Mitch insisted. "I think you know exactly what I'm talking about, but no matter I just wanted to apologize."

"What for," Lindquist asked.

"Well I'm afraid I was just a little clumsy."

"Oh, how so," Lindquist asked but Mitch could hear the tension in his voice.

"Well like I said I was returning the NANOs that we believe were programmed to disassemble concrete and steel."

"Go on," Lindquist said his voice beginning to show the nervousness.

"Well I dropped them in the lab and seemed to have leaked out all over the place."

"Thank you Stone," was all Mitch heard before the loud click and then the dial tone. Mitch could only imagine the panic hitting Lindquist as the full implication of Mitch's deed took hold. Mitch hung up the phone and drove toward the main gate.

Lindquist abruptly hung up on Mitch and immediately switched his phone to intercom and pressed the button for the lab.

"Lab, Dr. Reynolds."

"Reynolds, you and your people must get out of there fast. I just had a report that some of those NANOs from the dam have been dumped in the lab."

"Not possible Mr. Lindquist. The tanks are secure and everything is under control."

"Listen Reynolds, I know what I'm saying, they have been spread all over the lab. You must get out now."

All Lindquist heard in response was a rumble and then the sound of falling debris crashing into desks, computers, and equipment. Reynolds dropped the phone and Lindquist could hear the panicked yells from Reynolds ordering his co-workers to get out and the shouts of some of the lab techs dodging the collapsing building. Mitch's phone call was in time to give the lab people a fair warning. Fortunately all of the workers escaped the collapse of the lab caused by the NANOs dissolving the lower parts of the walls. The weight of the building on top of the weakened walls provided all the destructive force Mitch needed to get his pay back at least part of it anyway.

Now the fleeing lab techs were running along the hallways to escape the crumbling building. With each footstep the lab techs picked up some of the NANOs from the trail Mitch had left and they carried the little machines to all parts of the complex. Mitch knew there wouldn't be enough NANOs left to do much damage, but they would create all kinds of small missing spots in the floors throughout the buildings. At moments like this, Mitch really liked his work.

Lindquist was just staring out his window, at the calm water of the lake not one hundred feet from his office, and trying to grasp the reality of the Stone's visit and the destruction of the lab, when Reynolds burst through the door. "What the hell happened?" he asked tracking in some dust from the ruins of the lab and a few million NANOs to add to Lindquist's decor.

"It seems we've had an industrial accident," Lindquist replied devoid of any emotion.

"That's it, an industrial accident. You called and said the NANOs were dumped. How did you know, who did it?" Reynolds was nearly screaming now.

"It seems our nemesis, Deputy Stone managed to acquire some of the NANOs before they reached the dam. He kindly returned them to us, that's all."

"Well then we've got to have him arrested or better yet sue him and the county for destroying private property."

"Shut up, you fool. Stone knows perfectly well we can't and won't do anything to him or anyone else."

"Why not?" Reynolds asked now almost in a rage.

"Because you idiot, if we make a complaint about him releasing the NANOs we'd have to admit they exist and that they came from here. Then they'd have the evidence to link us to the dam project and probably everything else."

Reynolds just let out a frustrated yell.

"Precisely, Dr. Reynolds, we seem to have been backed into a corner, and this Stone fellow has apparently won for now."

"Shit," Reynolds spat.

"Well we must find a new location for our research and development lab. You do have the files and records on our technology, don't you?"

"Yeah," Reynolds said barely controlling his anger, "it's all in the lab. Under a couple of tons of collapsed building. Maybe, just maybe nothing crushed the main computer."

"Shit," Lindquist said.

"Precisely," Reynolds replied.

"Do what you can," Lindquist directed, "and be prepared to vacate as soon as possible."

"Yes sir," Reynolds said and left in a full-blown rage.

Lindquist sat down heavily at his desk again and after a few minutes' reflection he picked up the phone and dialed a number he had long since memorized.

"Hello," came the woman's voice sternly.

"Yes, ma'am. This is Lindquist. We've had an accident at the lab."

"Most unfortunate," the CEO said without emotion. "What is the extent of the damage?"

"Total loss of the entire project," Lindquist said and listened to the long silence.

"Where was Conners when it happened?"

"Not here. It seems that the police are looking for him in connection with our demonstration."

"Can we be implicated?"

"No, I don't believe so."

"Good then we shall relocate the operation and continue as before. Our timetable simply has been set back. You do have the procedures for making the NANOs, safely in your control?"

Lindquist took a deep breath hoping he wouldn't get caught in a lie. "Yes, of course."

"Good. Prepare to abandon that site. We'll move to a more friendly environment."

"Understood," Lindquist said, "but what about the backers?"

"They have all ended their opposition to our project and any of its variations. Our plans will continue, albeit with a minor delay."

"Yes ma'am," Lindquist said hoping to end the conversation soon.

"Just make sure the files on the NANOs are safe."

"Yes ma'am," Lindquist said and hung up after he heard the click in his ear. He decided that he better check on the status of the NANO records. He walked out of the side door in his office and down the hallway connecting the Administration Building with the now destroyed lab. He stepped in a large hole in the floor and nearly twisted his leg and while he was rubbing the pain from his ankle he realized the hole was in the middle of the floor and it dawned on him how a part of the cement floor suddenly disappeared. Damn that Stone, he said to himself as he stumbled to the end of the corridor and was greeted with the sight of the entire roof of the lab now at ground level. He could only imagine everything that was once the lab was now flattened and crushed beyond salvage.

"Dr. Reynolds," he yelled over to the man who had just been in his office.

"What?" Reynolds replied indignantly.

"Can we save the NANO records?"

"Who knows under all this junk," the man said climbing over a pile of rubble near where his desk once was.

"We still have the backup tapes and files don't we?" Lindquist asked near panic at the potential catastrophe.

"Ah, we were using them in here today to backup our system and to refine the NANO instruction sequences. What or whoever caused this sure picked a good time. We had every disk and file in here for modification. All we have left is some of the production run of the stuff we used in our field test." Reynolds made his way over the pile of rubble and handed Lindquist a small vile of blue NANO goo. "These are the quality control samples of the larger batch that we deployed. Do be careful though they are still programmed for calcium and iron."

"Oh my god," Lindquist said and slumped against the wall. "Damn that Stone." He took the glass container which held about five hundred milliliters of gel. "This is all that remains of years of work and research?"

"What's the big problem? Just get those long-haired hippie engineers back in here and we can recreate the whole process in about a month or so."

"And without them?" Lindquist asked fearful of the answer.

"Then we're out of the nano machine business for a long time."

Lindquist nearly fainted at that last statement and he walked slowly back to his office making sure to side step the newly developed crater in the floor and being very careful with the last remnants of the Malthusian Project. He set the NANO container carefully on his desk and slumped heavily down into his chair. He picked up the phone again and pushed the redial button. He didn't want to make this call.

"Yes," the voice said sternly.

"Lindquist here. I have bad news."

"Oh," the voice said almost robotic.

"Yes, seems the damage is extensive and all the records have been involved."

"How did this happen?" the voice screamed.

"The lab was in the process of upgrading the files when the building collapsed."

"This is not acceptable. Why weren't those records in your personal care?"

Lindquist couldn't answer, but offered another response. "We could bring in the backers and reconstruct the project." Now he waited for the silence to break.

"We have eliminated the backers. They are all dead you fool. We used the NANOs on them. That's what I meant when I said there would be no further opposition."

Lindquist's heart skipped a beat and he set the receiver down on the desk and just stared out the window.

"Lindquist, you fool. Answer me," the CEO yelled into the phone but Lindquist was now deep in thought and mentally very far away from the phone. Finally the dial tone started to beep and he reached over and hung up the phone. He sat and now just look blankly at the blue gel sitting in front of him. He didn't know what to do about the lab but he did know what to do about the CEO and the project.

Mitch reached the main gate and walked back inside the small guard shack to see how the guard was holding up. It seems that he had managed to get himself onto the floor and was trying to lift the desk while pulling his cuffed hands out from under the desk leg. It wasn't working and Mitch went over and placed a handcuff key on the desk. He bent down and peeled the tape from the guard's mouth which gave Mitch a great sense of accomplishment but left the guard with a very painful looking red mark across his face. "I'm going to turn you loose," Mitch said, "but if you try anything stupid or macho I'll tie you up again where you won't get loose for a long time. Understand?"

"Yes," the guard said exhausted from his efforts at lifting the desk while bent over double.

"Good," Mitch said and pushed the key in the lock. "There, you'll be able to open them in a few minutes but after I'm gone." Mitch quickly left the small building and drove down the road in his Jag. He saw the guard appear at the door and start to run after him. Loser, Mitch said to himself and stopped at the parked patrol car to bid Riley a good day. Riley was engrossed in a book of some kind and the guard was just about to the cars. Mitch just waved and sped off leaving the irate guard with the one Deputy in the department that really didn't give a shit about any complaints about other cops.

Mitch smiled and drove quietly down the access road and just as he was turning onto the main highway he passed the store clerk heading to the island. He waved back as the clerk held up the package. Good, Mitch thought. Just like I told Lindquist. The book would show up soon. He kept the wide grin on his face all the way back to the Harbor. The Jag seemed to handle much smoother today, he thought and drove leisurely back to the Emporium.

Mitch pulled up in front of the store and stepped out of the car. He gave a quick look around to see if the two car fanciers were near but they must have found some other source of entertainment, he thought, not seeing them. He reached over the side and grabbed his duffle bag and set it on the ground and then reached over the door and put the key in the ignition and turned it to auxiliary. He pushed the button for the top and once it was up he secured it to the latches on the windshield and raised the side windows. He locked the car with the remote switch and walked around the side of the emporium and down onto the dock and out to the large trawler anchored near the end.

"Hey Alex," Mitch called out but there was no answer. He walked down the slip and climbed up onto the main deck of the boat. He looked around and saw a note attached to the main cabin door.

∾

Mitch:

Everything you asked for is below.

I paid the bill at the store. What the hell was the delivery charge? I stowed the groceries and the dive gear is in the front cabin.

Good luck with whatever you're up to.

Alex

"Thanks Alex," Mitch said to the note and opened the door and put his duffle near the main table in the cabin. Nice boat, he thought as he looked around. He checked to make sure he had everything he needed and found the galley fully stocked including several cases of beer. I hope he doesn't think I'm going to drink all this, he said to himself. Mitch checked over the dive gear he found in the front cabin. Four full tanks plus a wet and dry suit and an all new vest and the rest of the necessary gear. He knew the compressor was below and he didn't bother to look at it. Alex always kept his equipment in top shape, he reminded himself.

Once he was satisfied all was in order he pulled the engine key off the hook near the navigation desk and went up to the cockpit and fired up the twin diesels. He let them idle while he scurried over the side catwalk to release the bow and stern lines. Back in the cockpit he slowly pushed the transmission lever into forward and pushed the throttles just enough to move the boat out of the slip. He took it very slow, to make sure he didn't hit anything especially another boat, and because he wasn't quite used to a boat this size. Once away from the dock and clear of anything he might bump into and have to pay for he turned on all of the electronics. He kept a close eye on the depth finder.

The lake was really low now and he didn't want to find the bottom with the keel of someone else's boat. He had looked over the charts and maps so often over the last few days he just steered the boat by memory now and he relaxed at the wheel and watched the scenery pass by. He had to go way out around Society Island now that the lake had lost so much water. He regretted that he couldn't see well enough at the distance to admire his contribution to science. Mitch just smiled and said, "pay back is a bitch," to himself.

At the nice leisurely pace he maintained it took slightly more than two hours to reach his destination and then another hour to pin-point the exact spot he had determined from his research. The depth finder told him the boat was in more than one hundred feet of water but that only fifty feet to the starboard side the water was barely fifteen feet. He was over the main channel but was more interested in what should be on the shallow ledge. Mitch slowly moved the boat over the ledge and set the anchor off the transom. The bow of the boat was still over the deeper water but the stern should be in the shallow water. Once the anchor took hold, he cut the engines and went below to get his charts and maps. If he was right then he hoped that the boom and crane on the stern of Alex's boat would be used a lot.

From the bridge he surveyed the landscapes and the landmarks. He thanked Lindquist for having the old books translated even though now someone else was benefitting. The bad news about the events of the last few days was that a multi billion dollar dam and power plant were destroyed. The good news was that the river was back to its historic depth and course. He was almost positive at his findings and went below to get into his dive gear. The dark water engulfed him and he was at peace with the world. Alone and in the quiet embrace of the river, Mitch swam to the bottom and began his hunt. His research and now an educated guess made the search brief.

After several days of diving, Mitch pulled up the anchor and marked the coordinates from the GPS readout on his chart and headed back up the river but made a slight detour to the north shore and spent several days in Canada, drinking beer and making phone calls. He entertained several guests onboard his temporary floating house and after a few days he headed back across the lake to return the trawler to its Harbor home.

Once the trawler was safely back at the dock, Mitch packed up his possessions and locked up the boat. He walked back to the Emporium hoping to catch Alex but only the store clerk was inside.

"Is Alex around?" Mitch asked.

"Nope, he is out on a call somewhere. I think he's on that island. Apparently all the county cars were busy when the call came in," the clerk said.

"What call?"

"Think Alex said suicide."

"Oh really," Mitch replied. "Can you give him a message for me?"

"Sure."

"Tell him Mitch says thanks for the use of the boat and that he can have all of the rest of the food and supplies."

"OK, I'll tell him."

"Thanks," Mitch said exiting the front door and pressing the lock button on the remote. He noticed a message under the driver's side wiper.

"Hi, I'm Toni and I'm Mary. We are the ones who like your car. We want you to call us," Mitch read the note and didn't even bother keeping it, he just tossed it into a large trash can but it bounced off the edge and landed on the ground. He thought for a moment and then picked it up and put it in his pocket. He got into the car, put the top down and made a phone call.

"Sisters of Hope Hospital, how may I direct your call?"

"Is Alicia Carlsson still a patient?"

"One moment please," the line went on hold. "No, I'm sorry, she was released just this morning."

"Good thanks," Mitch said and backed the Jag out of the parking space. He headed back to Smyth's Cove but then turned around. He had some shopping to do.

EPILOGUE

Shortly after Mitch had left Lindquist's office several days earlier, the package had arrived and was delivered to the despondent Lindquist by Ms. Norton. Lindquist opened the package and to his amazement and shock found the missing log book of the Vikings along with a note.

Lindquist:

Thanks for the loan of this great book.

I was able to put it to good use and I am now certain of the exact location of that long lost Viking ship. Oh, and by the way I completed the translation from the notes in the book and have discovered that the ship's manifest contained at least a dozen chests full of the entire treasury of the Anglica settlement in Europe.

I figure it is worth about 20 million dollars give or take.

Thanks again for your help in dropping the water level to where it was a thousand years ago. Nice things those NANOs. They seem to have come in handy.

Lindquist read the note several times and became even more angry at the turn of events. Over the next several days he was under a constant barrage of calls from the CEO demanding he take action and do something about the loss of the project and all its assets.

Finally Reynolds informed him that not only were all the records of the project destroyed but that a search of the computer logs for the day when the lab collapsed showed that someone had made complete copies of all the files. Since none could be found on site, Lindquist could only guess that Mitch Stone had made the copies and was now in possession of all of the data on the Malthusian Project.

His whole world was now coming apart just as the lab had and the reappearance of the log book and the note from no one else but Stone was the last straw. Lindquist broke under the pressure on the day Mitch returned from his expedition. Lindquist took the vile of NANOs and drank the entire contents down in one swallow. As he sat at his desk and waited for the machines to follow their program he hoped that Mitch Stone would never have the opportunity to enjoy his new found wealth. That however was one wish that wouldn't be granted and Lindquist succumbed to the relentless activity of the NANOs. Ms. Norton looked for him at the end of the day and found only a withered mass of flesh in the chair. She called the police and reported a suicide but there wasn't much left to look at when the local police officer arrived.

Reynolds and the rest of the lab crew were quietly relocated to other facilities within the company and were reassigned to other projects, most of them legitimate.

The governments of both the United States and Canada acted quickly to the loss of the dam which served the economic interests of both countries. As a temporary measure they managed to erect a coffer dam to stem the outflow of water. They agreed that they would start reconstruction on a new dam and power plant within the next thirty days and hopefully they would have a good leap on the winter weather.

❧   ❧   ❧

Mitch stood proudly at the helm of the new forty foot sailboat. He carefully steered the boat down the exact center of the channel and around the point into Smyth's Cove. Although he knew the sailing characteristics would be reduced slightly he was glad he had opted for the wing keel. His old boat only drew about fifty inches of water and this new one although larger, drew only fifty-six inches. He slowed the forty horsepower diesel down and the sailboat slowed to a crawl. He rounded the point and headed for his slip. As he passed the 'Viking Princess' he saw Alicia standing on the deck. She looked angry, confused, happy and glad all at the same time and Mitch figured he would have to be very good at explaining this one.

As soon as he passed her, Alicia hopped off her boat and ran over to Mitch's slip. She was waiting for him as he pulled the bow into the dock. She caught the pulpit and guided it into the dock. Mitch cut the engine and quickly grabbed the stern line and jumped onto the dock to tie off the stern. He smiled when he realized his new toy was sticking out eight feet farther that the previous one.

"Mitch," Alicia cried running up to him. She planted a kiss on him that about rendered him unconscious. "Where were you? I missed you," she asked. Then her mood shifted to one of the other emotions she had displayed on her boat and she slapped him across the face. "Yeah! Where were you when I was in the hospital and where were you when they released me and…?"

"One where at a time," he said. "I promise to explain everything very soon."

"No. No more excuses. No more it's a long story. I want to know now," she demanded.

"I'm glad to see you too," he said, "and I see you're all better."

"Don't try to change the subject," she protested.

"I'm not, but we need to wait for a few moments until everyone is here. Gary, Carol and Lizzy are on their way. We're all going for a sail. Now go change into something more comfortable."

She shot him a pissed off look but walked back to her boat to change. Mitch stepped back onto his boat and waited for the rest of his guests to arrive.

The new boat handled well on its maiden voyage and everyone was cheerful but confuse. No one asked the obvious question until they had been out almost an hour and Alicia just couldn't hold her curiosity in check any longer.

"OK, Mitch, where did this boat come from and where were you for a week?"

"Yes, Mitch old buddy. We've been looking all over for you and now suddenly you pop up with this nice new boat and a lot more unanswered questions."

"Yes, and we won't take any more of your it's a long story excuses now," Alicia said sitting next to him and grabbing hold of his arm. She had changed into a black one piece that clung to her very closely.

"Uncle Mitch?"

"Yes Lizzy."

"Where did you find this nice boat?"

"OK, Lizzy since you've asked so nicely, come here and sit next to me," Mitch said. Lizzy giggled a little and moved in next to him. "There, now I have two beautiful women." Lizzy giggled again.

"Now Mitch. No more stalling. What's the whole story?" Alicia said poking him playfully in the ribs.

"Yeah, Mitch. Come on, give," Gary said with Carol giving him a look that said he would get no sympathy from her.

"Please now, Uncle Mitch," Lizzy begged.

"OK, OK," Mitch said and took a long sip of beer. Everybody was all ears now and he started to tell about all of the events of the last few days. "Like all good stories," he said to Lizzy, "we have to start this one the same way." He sighed and started. "Once upon a time…"

0-595-21481-9

CPSIA information can be obtained
at www.ICGtesting.com
Printed in the USA
BVOW09s1101230417
481970BV00001B/14/P

PINT SIZE

ADVENTUER

-

HOW TO

BECOME AN

AUTHOR

USING 7 KEY

PRINCIPLES

PAOLO BEN SALMI AKA
PINTSIZE ADVENTURER

UK Ambassador of the Borg Banking Group AND of Borg
University of International Skills, Award Winning Author, US Africa
Chamber Youth Ambassador to Global Diaspora United Voices for
Economic Empowerment Forum & Ambassador for Water-to-Go,
founded Sarva Education, Ambassador for VueBox, TruChallenge &
Choose Love

ADVENTUROUS
PUBLISHING

Publishing

DEDICATION

This book is dedicated to you the reader, I would like you to know that you have a book inside of you; in fact I believe that you have several books inside of you. I believe that you need to know this because the world is your stage; therefore, it is your choice to choose what you share on that stage. Afterall, there is always someone in this world that is either going through or has gone through what you are going or gone through; so why not share your story.

Remember you are and have always been a unique piece to the puzzle, why are you trying to fit in when you were born to stand out?

Go ahead and let your light shine.

ACKNOWLEDGMENTS

I would like to take this opportunity to acknowledge all the people in my life who have encouraged me to reach for the stars. I'm very grateful that I have had the privilege to have a soul army of people who support me with whatever do this soul army consists of members of my family, friends and even strangers who have taught me a host of life lessons that I will never forget, and I thank them for seeing the greatness in me.

CONTENTS

Introduction - Page 4

INTRODUCTION

IN THIS BOOK I WILL SHARE WITH YOU

"THE 7 KEY PRINCIPLES ON HOW TO BECOME AN AUTHOR"

This book is key if you desire to make the world a better place by sharing your story, in fact most of us have more than one story to share. A lot of the time we may think we are very strong because we train everyday physically, really what makes you strong is having a positive mindset and the story that you have; because everyone's story is powerful weather we had it easy or not, we always have something to share and something to learn. Once you choose to accept that your story is unique and that you are unique and good enough just the way you are.

Take a moment to think:

What if my past pains and experiences didn't happen?

How differently would your life be today without your past pains and experiences?

In life we grow to learn that experiencing contrast is an important part of our development.

For instance

How would you know hot without first experiencing cold?

How would you know happiness without first experiencing sadness?

How would you know up without first experiencing down?

The scars that you have acquired in your life journey is merely a reminder of your past pains and experiences and the journey that we have been on so that we can inspire others.

I'm asking you to publish your book and share your story with the world, because I believe that you are a true born influence. So, go on and share your story and really make a difference in your life and in the lives of others both locally and globally.

I would like you to start being the director of your own movie and instead of just being an actor in another person's movie. Please do not get me wrong, but just like anything in life it is always more fun when you can go to dinner at a friend's home and then also invite them to your place for a meal too. Not just go around eating dinner at all of your friends' homes without having the ability to host too. You deserve to manifest your deepest desires, you deserve to set yourself free so that you can not only leave the legacy, but also live the legacy too.

If you desire to write a book, then the time is now don't wait until tomorrow because tomorrow is not guaranteed, today is a gift that's why it's called THE PRESENT, tomorrow is a mystery, but not if we choose to start now by choosing to write your book today right now.

A book may open up closed doors that have been locked and buried for years. Writing is a way to unlock, each and every lock one by one so that you may begin to open up the gifts that reside deep within you. When you start writing your book you will discover things about yourself and life that you never knew.

Nowadays you can self-publish which is affordable and requires only basic computer skills you also get royalties from your book and you will become the CEO of your own destiny. when you hit the publish button you will become an Author. And you can earn a chunk of pocket money simply for your book existing and putting pen to paper.

And there's something that I can guarantee you is that life is infinite so share your story because the TIME IS NOW!! Never say you can't write your book weather it's too long or you don't have the time well if you don't have time make time if you share what you have to share you can save a life or change a life don't let that chance slip through your fingers like sand, please hold onto the opportunity of being in the present.

Trust me you will be an amazing author because you already are you are writing and living your story every day how you think I may know that is when you take a photo on your phone and you post it on social media you then write a caption around what is happening in your life.

Really and truly you have been writing for a pretty long period of your life as when you went to school or when you go to school your teacher might ask you to write a story that's exactly what I have done but all that I have done different is published my story so that I can share it with others like right now as you are reading this book.

Now is the time to start sharing your story. Your words are priceless, remember to start with why and write from your heart because if someone has to tell you what to write then it will no longer be your book, it's basically their book because it's not coming from you it's coming from them. It's the same way that, water can only be water if it consists of $H2O$, your book can only be your book if it comes from you.

If you know me then you will know about three options that I always talk about over and over and over again….

Option #1 – You can watch the movie

Is usually what hypocritical people do when something displeases them, and they would rather disrespect what they are observing instead of taking action.

Option #2 – You can be in the movie

Is usually what people do when they get hired for a job that does not resonate with them and they begin to fade away because they are not living their truth.

Option #3 – You can direct the movie

This is where you are able to plant your seed for your own dreams and this begins with having a fertile ground.

Thanks to a conversation that I had with one of our family friends called Travis .W. Fox a fourth option has now been added to my teachings

Option #4 – You can produce the movie

Once you publish your book you will become a leader and an authority figure in your industry.

Some people think that leadership is 100% of telling people what to do. However I believe that leadership is made up of integrity, vision, praising your team, self-awareness, listening first and speaking last, empathy, resourcefulness, developing and maintaining relationships.

CHOOSE TO TAKE ACTION NOW DON'T WAIT FOR TOMORROW!

"If not you, then who? and if not now, then when?
Well I am here to tell you that it's time to commit now, so just do it".
Paolo Ben Salmi.

PRINCIPLE #1

START WITH WHY

What is your WHY?

_____

_____

_____

The BIGGER the WHY! the easier the how. Find out what your WHY is, then the skills and knowledge will come to you easily. When we start with "WHY", we go from the inside out. Your "WHY" will fuel you and it will become the reason behind all that you say and do. This is like a car, when there is no power to start the car then you will not go anywhere, but if you do have power then you can pick a destination, and get from where you are right now, to where you desire to be.

I often overhear people saying that they would like to become an author to make money from their book, I personally believe that this is not a big enough WHY. Remember the saying the BIGGER the WHY the easier the how, and in addition to this Douglas Vermeeren often says

"When you make your goals specific and clear they will become attainable and near."

For example if your WHY may be money, then at least be specific about the desired amount. If your WHY is family, then at least be specific around what that would look like. If your WHY is to become a property investor, then at least be specific about the desired number of houses you would like to invest in. If your WHY is for a friend, then at least be specific around how you are going to go about that. If your WHY is to become debt free (contact National Debtline to discuss your debt: www.nationaldebtline.org), then at least be specific and clear about your vision for your ideal lifestyle. If your WHY is to become an athlete, then at least be specific about what that would look like. I truly believe that your vision is the postcode for your soul, therefore how will you manifest your dreams without first establishing a vision. In life people often fail to realise that we do not fail due to a lack of money, but merely a lack of resourcefulness.

The human mind is the most powerful tool that you posses, so once you give your mind a specific goal to achieve it will work wonders. A good example for this would be the world wide web, for instance if you were to type the word car into the search engine it would automatically generate pages and pages of results that relate to what you have searched for. When you give your brain something to focus on, it will always find the easiest and quickest way to achieve that very thing.

If you would like to write and publish a book the time is now, don't say, you can't because now you can. If you don't have time well make time because your words could save a life or change a life and never ever let opportunities like this slip through your fingers like sand, instead hold them so tight that you never let go. There are often times in life when we don't see things through and complete the task at hand. I have a method that I would like to share with you to aid you in getting things done. In life I feel that it is always a good idea to hire a coach, mentor and/or accountability partner. Set out daily tasks as action steps. Have fun, this is how I tend to complete things that I set out to do in my life. Just know that all your hard work will pay off in the end, for example when you publish a book you will earn royalties from each book sold, always remember in order to reap the rewards you first have to put in the effort.

PRINCIPLE #2

DESIGN A BOOK COVER THAT REPRESENTS YOUR TITLE

Design Your Book Cover - using a working title so that this book cover acts like a carrot on a stick inspiring you to publish your book.

What is your brand?

I'd like you to think about that, as when you define your brand you define your products, so that you know your audience, remember product + audience = brand so you need to define that before you really do anything.

You are the writer of this book therefore your design process must start with you. The wisdom of a forest is in a single seed.

I'd like you to take a moment to think about that and that should help you to create your cover, because if your book genre is about cars, don't you think that it would be a bit weird if your book cover had a picture of an aeroplane or something along those lines. So be sure to think about that when you are creating your book cover. Also think how can I create a cover that connects to whoever is going to read it. Also when thinking about connecting to the reader you always have to write as if you are the viewer and always think, what will they think, because the point of a book is to take a person from where they are now in time, space, this universe and reality and into your book because in order to connect you have to be on the same page, hehehhheh get it.

Did you know that each genre tends to have a standardised cover format?

For example thrillers, romance, fantasy, horror and science-fiction. These genres have cover design styles that were established decades ago. always remember that the goal of your cover is to sell books

Are you a young and upcoming author or are you an established and trusted author?

What are your three favourite book covers in the genre that you are writing on?

1. _____
2. _____
3. _____

What genre is your book?

Where will the book be sold?

_____

_____

_____

_____

_____

This is a very vital question, why?

I'd like you to close your eyes and imagine that you are writing a book about apples and your book will be sold in a carrot shop, well that wouldn't really work as you have to stay authentic as a brand and as an author at all times as the people shopping in the carrot shop they would see your book as an inconvenience so always sell your work in a place/setting that suits your book, because it not only helps you with regards to profit but also it helps your customers to define what your brand is and what it is that you do.

Where a book will be sold can have a great impact on its design. With the recent rise in e-readers, some authors choose an eBook only path, eschewing the printed format entirely. Design will be different if the book will only be sold on Amazon as a thumb nail. The text has to be bigger and much more eye-catching as someone scrolls through hundreds of different titles on a screen. A print book will live on a shelf in someone's home or bookstore where the consumer can pick it up, have a look through it, and have much more tactile experience.

A book cover is like the skin of an apple if it's bad on the outside you wouldn't want to eat it on the inside and that applies for your book if your cover is so bad that when its near people it pushes them away then you need to continue reading, so think what would suit this book, and remember this is a fun experience so play around with book covers until you find the right one for you, also feedback is only a stepping stone to getting better so ask around and ask others to give you their perspective around the book cover. Also when it comes to designing your book cover ask your book cover designer if your book cover can be used in print, eBook or both?

Also if your book will be printed, be sure to find out which format and size

This is very important as the size and format of your book will be what people see first and you would want to make it appealing ; with my books I have made them into an eBook and a book, but it's your choice, the pens in your hands and it's time for you to take action you could do one or the other.

Formats will include: a paperback, hardback or case bound. Hardbacks can be made with dust-jackets or with the cover images printed directly on the boards. Books can be almost any size any designer can dream up, but it's wise to really think about what's best for your book before selecting a size. The smaller the trim size the less words per page. A 300 paged book will get really thick if it is designed a bit too small, whereas a larger book needs to be a great length to not come out flimsy which is more like a magazine, or booklet because when people are reading your book they want the sensation to feel unique, and not like holding, reading and hearing of something they've already felt read and heard about ever before.

Also I'd like you to think about the size of your book because a book size of about 130 pages could mean you having your name on the spine, so size length and pages are a crucial and important thing to think about also, capturing your readers attention is a big thing so when people see you book you don't it to be so big that it intimidates people you want it to be just right for your genre so the reader not only reads it but they enjoy it because its practically your new baby.

Blurb

This section is about a lot of different things like about you an endorsement etc. When it comes to the about you section. You want to make sure that you write to the reader as if you've known them for years because it's not about a reader reading you book but it's really about the reader connecting with you.

Visualisation Time

I'd like you to close your eyes and imagine that you are at your first book signing event. Feel the pen in your hands signing all of these books and feel the pages of your book as you are signing your name for all of the readers, and one particular reader comes up to you and says......

"who are you"?... yes I know it's your book signing but they are asking you who you really are.

and you say your name and tell them that you are the author of this book and they say.....

"ok I know lot's about your book but I don't know anything about you"

And you say......

"but in the blurb I wrote all about me I'm a doctor I've got a PhD in physics I went to Yale University"

And they say.....

"yeah I know you achieved so much but I don't know anything about you, like who you really are on the inside"

And you say....

"I am a brother/sister a husband/wife a uncle/auntie and a storyteller both inside and outside"

And they say.....

"I know who you are I love it when I connect with the author and the book,"

"I really know you now"

How did that feel?

_____

_____

_____

_____

_____

Now do you really know the power of a reader knowing who you really are?

_____

_____

_____

Graphics

This ties into you're company logo your barcode and designs of front and back of your book and your publishers logo when you are about to hit publish on your book make sure to look at the quality of your book graphics because you may publish your book but it could be very blurry when it is in its actual book form and that is a big problem because in order to sell your book in many stores you will not be able to sell your book because they might not be able to scan the barcode of your book and encase you don't know a barcode is what makes your book known in a store so if you are looking for one of a book in a store but it has wrapping on top of the name, but you can see the barcode if you scan it the system will tell you the name and price if the book, so that is a main factor in creating your book.

Budget

This ties into how much money that you are willing to spend on your book, when it comes to the budget let your designers and publishers know how much you are willing to pay and how much they can do for you. this is really on of the first steps that you have to take because how do you know how much can get done if you don't know how much you can spend and if you are on a budget its ok to keep a tally on how much you spend and how much it will cost altogether.

When it does come to payment, don't be sad about it because it takes one to make one so to make money you have to loose money but its only for the better and this doesn't mean every time you make a payment go to a party and throwing money at people It just means you have to be excited about every payment, process and second of writing your book.

The Process of A Book Cover

The front cover also the back cover, which will be connected by the spine connected by the spine. A paperback book's pages which are glued together with a paper cover and then cut to size.

A paperback book's pages which are glued together with a paper cover and then cut to size. A hardback book's pages are either sewn or glued into a "case" made of cardboard which is then covered with cloth or paper.

The front cover also the back cover, which will be connected by the spine connected by the spine. A paperback book's pages which are glued together with a paper cover and then cut to size which will be connected by the spine connected by the spine the paper cover wraps around your book and includes flaps on both of the sides. When you open a hardcover book and see coloured or printed pages glued to the boards, you're looking at endpapers, a amazing extra set of pages designers can use to tie a book project together.

Market Research

Consider some guidelines: genre sells better in paperback whilst literary fiction, thrillers and biographies tend to sell well as a hardcover.

Think about a book where a person may be going weather on a plane or going on holiday to a friends house or on a road trip, most people would take a book with them.

Most libraries prefer hardcovers because they are delicate which suits readers.

Keep price point in mind: don't design a **(£40.00) hardback** for a Young Adult title (which tend to be priced around **(£10)** and max out at **(£18.00).**

Choose a design direction

Next, it's important to consider what your design direction will be and how it will fit the author's vision of her book. There are lots of beautiful books out there—but not all designs will work for every book. Consider input from the author or publisher. Make a Pinterest board of comparable titles with successful covers and book packages. Go to your local bookstore and handle books to get a feeling for the different paper thicknesses and materials. Make notes about what you like and don't like—that information could prove useful way later in the design process if you hit a wall.

Find out what your design needs to emphasize.

Think of the cover or front of the dust jacket as an extension of the marketing plan for the book.

What's the most important element of your story?

_____

_____

What makes your book unique?

_____

_____

Or is it a character in the book that makes it unique?

_____

_____

Or is it your style of writing?

_____

_____

Or is it your book cover?

_____

_____

Or is it the setting where your book takes place or topic
in history that it covers?

_____

_____

Or is it the font of your book?

_____

_____

If the book is similar to a hugely successful book, think about ways you can subtly evoke that title without creating a cheap copy.

Maybe the author is considering writing a sequel or plans on building the title into a series. Think about how future titles might be linked in design to the first in order to build the author's brand. If the author is well known the strongest piece of marketing might be their name. But for most authors, the book has to stand alone and make an impression among its competitors on a bookshelf.

Choose graphics and fonts

One of the great things about book covers is that there is almost no graphic style that *can't* work. Writers have wild imaginations, and it's the designer's job to create a cover that represents all of the wondrous worlds their pages create.

The downside of this is that narrowing down a style can be a challenge. Book covers can feature a photograph, illustration or abstract design. They can feature everything from cartoonish doodles to stark, modern typography.

Consider what message the graphic style sends to a book-buyer's brain. A photograph of New York City shouldn't be used for a book.

Find out what the printer needs

The final file for a book project will be one flat file that has all the pertinent graphic and text information for the front and back covers, spine, and flaps **(if your project has them)**. The printer will want this as one wide file that they can print and either cut or fold to fit the final book.

Most printers tend to use high-quality PDF's for printing.

PRINCIPLE #3

PUT SOME MEAT ON TO THE BONE

It's now time to put some meat on the bone - come up with 7-10 tips (tips will become the chapter names) within the subject area of your choice and then simply entitle each chapter using each one of the top ten tips, and make sure to Review your manuscript.

Don't make this process harder than it needs to be, because generally chapter titles are the easiest because they are just names or sentences that mirror your chapters, like a bat and a ball it's not hard to make a chapter for that because it's just a bat and a ball you don't have to make it complicated, like saying a round object and a cylinder that clash together at a top speed of 75mph woah wait a minute, calm down you lost me there, don't get too much into the zone that you forget that others are reading your book!!

Don't get me wrong whenever you are writing always get into a zone where you just process and download and insert them into your book but don't get into the zone so much that you forget that people are reading because you are not writing to yourself you are writing to the reader hence why some authors start their introduction with Dear reader/you, or whoever is reading that specific book so when you write you need to write to the reader the same way I am writing to you at this moment in time right here right now.

Also when focusing on writing to the reader remember that although you are writing to them not writing for them because as an author people will tell you to create a book around a certain topic and that's all good but when it gets to a point where you feel as if you have to do what they say well then its time to switch the tracks on the railway because if there are people who are constantly lowering your confidence you need not only to switch tracks but also your friendship circles because the people that you spend time with will have a massive influence on your development which can then equal who you choose to grow up to become so choose who you spend time with wisely.

YOU'VE GOT TO SAY THIS FOR EVERY CHAPTER THAT YOU COMPLETE

"GET IT DONE, THEN GET IT RIGHT"

AGAIN

"GETTING IT DONE, THEN GETTING IT RIGHT"

Why am I telling you to say this? Well it's because we sometimes focus too much on getting it right the first time, whereas we should be focusing on ……..

GETTING IT DONE, THEN GETTING IT RIGHT"

You may be wondering why should I say this well here's the answer even if your book is not perfect and you can see mispronunciations and defaults within your book then finish the book and then go over it and make corrections don't be too hard on your self because remember you have to write this book and if you discourage your-self then you won't have enough courage to finish the book remember you are your biggest bully even if other people are mean to you, are the one that beats yourself up after. But enough of that it's time to put some meat on the bone why because imagine that your cooking food and you put all types of ingredients like salt rosemary pepper cheese butter and you now get so exited because its time to eat you close your eyes while putting the food out because your just so exited you can smell the gravy all of the ingredients and that smoke goes swiftly from your plate and into your nose and it's time to eat and you open your eyes and you look at your plate and there's only a bone!

What all of that just for a bone wow this is surely not a nice meal a bone after all that work.

It's the same for your book you may have seasoned it so well with your eyes closed but really the magic happens and when you are watching you see your book getting bigger and better so keep your eyes open to really experience the process or by the time you think your done you'll just find yourself left with a bone and no meat.

Look at the stats of your followers and list them below......

What content do they watch?

_____

_____

_____

_____

Who do they follow?

_____

_____

_____

_____

What are their interests?

_____

_____

_____

_____

Who do they listen to?

_____
_____
_____
_____

Who do they watch?

_____
_____
_____
_____

All of these questions are fundamental to growing your brand and/or company and they are useful tools for writing your book because if you don't know what your audience wants then you cannot write a book without knowing what they do want because if that's the case I don't think your book is going to be very popular.

Plus, if you have tons of social media followers , you'll always have a huge source of ideas.
You could even ask your followers directly. Post a question on your Instagram story, and ask for replies. For example, let's say you have a brand related to the fitness industry. Ask your followers a question about their favourite unconventional workouts or what meals help them lose weight. And that information can be forwarded into your book and it'll be better for those who do workouts because they don't have to search online anymore because they have your book.

VIEW YOUR SOCIAL MEDIA COMMENTS

You may be wondering why I'm suggesting this and I know voices might creep in and say something like "ooh that's gonna take too long or ooh that's a long comment or ooh why do they have to talk so much….. but really when you close a door that only opens once waiting on a door step isn't going to open it again so when you have an opportunity to search through comments on your posts, just do it because you never know what someone has said or pointed out that can change, better and create something phenomenal so draft a schedule and plan out your day and make sure you make a spot for checking your social media comments weather its 20mins a day to a minimum of 5mins a day plan it out so that it works for you. View the comments on all your posts. You should do that even when you're not trying to come up with new ideas. Because your audience and followers might say something or comment on something that could take your book to the next level.

This gives you a chance to communicate with your audience. Always respond to their comments. Regardless of what your audience comments are about, I'm confident that you can generate at least one to two ideas from the comments in each post you publish. This great thing about this source is it's nearly never-ending. As long as you keep publishing new posts, there will always be new ideas hidden in the comments.

CONDUCTING SOME INTERVIEWS

Why well when you ask a question you will get an _____ and when you get an _____ your audience will get a better way of understanding your brand and your book, have you ever been to the supermarket? Well if you have there might have been a tasting section where you can sample a particular product they are selling so you know if you would want to taste the same food or product again, and it's the same for your book if you ask your audience what they like and what they would like to get out of your book then without a doubt your audience will buy your next book because they've already tasted the first book and now they want more… so you may be wondering "ok I know why to conduct an interview, but what questions shall I ask?"

Well the questions you have to ask are…

1._____

2._____

3._____

Hhahahahhaahaah look at your face, I tricked you! because it's your interview not Paolo's interview which means your own questions because you have to stay authentic as a brand and as an author.

Another thing you could do is to look at some of your competitors websites and look at some things that they have done wrong or something that they may have missed out and to convert those things into your book also look at their website comments and questions and include and expand on those comments and questions in your book because, "The biggest question is not a question that has already been asked but a question that no one has thought of." So where your competitors think 2 times ahead think 3 times ahead, if your audience asks 6 times ahead well answer 12 times ahead etc. the early bird gets the worm but the smart bird has enough worms to outlive the early bird, this mirrors a quote that I've heard of and it goes like this you don't have to work hard the only type of work you have to do is smart work.

YOUTUBE VIDEOS

It's 2021 and for that I believe that all businesses should have an online presence which includes having a YouTube profile. Use it to upload videos that can be related to chapters in your book, and then share those videos on all your social media platforms. Another suggestion is to record 3-5mins videos and Give your audience and followers a pretty clear reason for why they should buy your book because if you don't know why someone should buy your book then no one will buy your book. Various authors do promotions such as offering some special webinar to customers which they access by sending a receipt as confirmation of purchase.

PRINCIPLE #4

ACCOUNTABILITY

Just like anything in life, it can often be hard to just get started and this is exactly why a mentor, coach and/or an accountability partner is the key to your success. Having someone to be accountable to will influence your actions and results.

Ensuring that you set yourself up in such a way that makes you accountable is the difference that will make the difference to starting and maintaining focus on the task at hand. When we have someone to talk to and brainstorm with you will begin to feel more motivated to write. Accountability is all about being answerable to someone is a proven method for achieving your goals. Accountability buddies have been the secret weapon for so many success stories. As a writer you can be extremely imaginative and at times it can be a struggle to get focused long enough to get into flow. As we are all human these things happen but it's about now being accountable for things and showing up because maybe in your life people have let you down but its now about letting yourself soar no one physically mentally can let you down unless you let them let you down so on your list jot down being accountable for you and your book and create a plan for your days because the biggest mistake that we make is sitting down when we have work to do. Even if you spend 1-2hours on your book a day because in order to finish something you have to be dedicated to it and as always the same applies for your book. I also know that at times things may seem a bit overwhelming but you have to learn to motivate yourself even if someone sits next to you and encourages you or maybe a setting of something that inspires you weather it's photos of family friends your child/children or even your wife/husband the only thing that matters Is that you find a space/place person/people that inspire you to write this book and make sure that these people bug you about it why because

HOW TO BECOME AN AUTHOR USING 7 KEY PRINCIPLES

they have to remind you over and over again to finish/complete your book like I said in the previous chapters you can either save a life or change a life so never let that chance slip through your fingers like sand hold it tight that you never ever let go of it. When a door only opens once and you close it don't sit on the doorstep because it's never going to open again but if a door only opens once and you choose to embrace it go through it and help others which one would you choose, well I know that I would choose option 2 how about you option one or two circle one or two depending on which one you chose.

If you chose option two then please write your book now because your story is a key to unlock closed doors. By writing your story and sharing it you can not only save a life but possibly a generation and never ever ever let that chance sail away, say this with me and if you are reading this book alone call all family members to say this together;

I am the captin of my ship master of my fate,

and I am a storyteller that holds the most powerful weapon,

and it is so powerful that no one can destroy it, it is my story my story can never die, my story is immortal it lives on for ever.

My story is here as I am alive and here when I pass, my story is strong when I'm weak and powerful when I'm tired.

My story is invincible that no one can destroy it
my story is worth being shared.

My story is worth being heard my story is more
powerful than the most powerful, my story is
what makes me, me my story is my cool, my
story is my journey my story is powerful.

I am the captain of my ship and the master of
my fate......

I am a storyteller and my story is worth being
shared.

How did that feel?

_____
_____
_____
_____
_____
_____
_____
_____
_____
_____
_____

If you liked that exercise how about do it every day whether
you are getting out of bed or writing your book or even in the
mirror, make sure you say this at least 5 times a day because it
will empower you to write even more because your story is not

only needed but its powerful and it can either heal you or chuck you down a deeper rabbit whole and by the time that you realise how deep into the whole that you really are it will be too late because you'll be too deep to get out.

PRINCIPLE #5

PUBLISHING OPTIONS

As an author there are multiple publishing options that you can pick from. I highly recommend that you do some research around this and ask lots of questions to see which option best fits you and the book that you are writing.

1. SELF – PUBLISHEING EXPLAINED

Did you know that self-publishing is merely the act of publishing your book without the need of an established publisher. Self-publishing doesn't have the best reputation in the world of publishing, and the same goes for the self-published authors for a host of reasons. Some avid readers tend to not take self-published authors seriously as they would a traditionally published author.

2. TRADITIONAL PULISHING

Traditional book publishing is when you as an author is offered a publishing deal/contract and, in return the publisher will print, promote, publish, and sells your book through booksellers and other retailers. Be mindful that in this scenario the publisher essentially buys the right to publish your book and pays you royalties from the sales. It is absolutely vital that you comprehend the fundamental difference between Self-Publishing and Traditional Publishing. The fundamental difference is if the author owns the rights and royalties, then the book is self-published. If the publishing company owns the rights and royalties, then the book is traditionally published.

If you choose to publish through the traditional publishing option, it can be a slow and long process in some cases. For example this process can take up to 24 months which can range from editing the manuscript to showing up in bookstores. Compared to a self-publisher who could have written and published several books during the same time frame. In my perspective there is no correct or incorrect answer you just have to select the best option for you and the book that you are writing and factor in budget, skillsets, resources etc.

3. SETUP YOIUR OWN PUBLISHING HOUSE

Ned I say more as you get the best of both worlds whereby you are the owner and producer of your IP (Intellectual Property) so it is happppppy days. This is where Adventurous publishing was birthed and I am enjoying each and every moment and the fun aspect is that I get to publish as many books as I desire, I can publish books for others and I can also teach others how either self-publish or setup their very own publishing house. How amazing is that. I can help you when you are ready to take the jump of setting up your own publishing house.

CHAPTER 6

SHARE YOUR BOOK WITH THE WORLD

From the moment you become an author there are many ways to share your book for example:

Share your book with the world using many tools such as: book launch, podcast, media press release, public speaking, social media, webinar etc eBook, paperback or hardback interviews.

If you don't know how to do most of the above be open to invest in yourself by hiring a coach so that you can learn how you can make your book omnipresent in the world, so that not only the people in your village/town city or country can have access to it, but also people on the other side of the world. So that they can have access to it as well this is also a good way to make profit both locally and globally because the bigger the reach the more you impact, and that impact is obviously going to be a good impact not only in your community but also your country, society, villages, towns, cities, and the last destination is every corner and household of the world.

But before we take that big leap, all of the above fold into one thing, that we call marketing because if no one knows who you are how can they buy a copy of your book or even books if you've written more than one.

Did you know that a great way to share your book with the world is to set up multiple social media profiles on different platforms using the title of your book which make it easy for your readers and followers to find you. creating a book trailer is a fun and exciting way to share your book with the world. One of the best ways to share your book is through the power of brand advocacy and you can do this by simply asking your readers to send you some images of them with your book.

Another good way to share your book with the world is to comment on other peoples social media posts within your area of expertise as this will help to build your reputation as an expert on whatever genre that your book is about.

Write a press release for your book. Which is a extremely productive way to get some backlinks to your website and maybe even some press interest in your book.

Another is to do a presentation at a community meetup group. Don't 'sell', just give great information, and make sure to have some books to hand in case people ask.

A phenomenal way to promote is to do some give-away's which is one of my favourite ways to promote your book, which will not only generate some interest but will also help to get some reviews. The giveaways only work with print books although there are things you can do with your digital book. And it's good to know that the reviewers can be a little harsher than on Amazon but it's more than worth the effort.

You may want to consider creating posts about your book on your social media business pages and pin them at the very top so that as soon as people go on your page the first thing they see is your book and they would be able to find out more.

Start posting some content like quotes or words of inspiration from your book on social media which is great for exposure and gaining more followers as when they see snippets of the book they would want to read more.

If you haven't already, start giving talks at local schools if your book or genre that you are writing about is appropriate this will expand your reach because when a child hears about your book and he/she likes it they would share it with their friends so this is a very vital and important.

Another suggestion is to create a social media ad but make sure it's closely themed around time or an event. So if its Independence Day and you have written a book around independence theme your advert around that so it not only links to something but if someone is searching independence on their device your book ad will pop up.

You should consider starting to create some social media hashtags Ask questions, engage users. If you are keyword savvy then use keywords in all of your posts titles and content so that it will show up on the search engines and give you ongoing promotional returns. Ask your followers for some reviews and some testimonials as when a reader shares their perspective of your story others will do the same monkey see monkey do. Create a URL that you can forward to people that take people to your Amazon page. Use this as your "main website" in your book and whenever you're talking about any of your books.

Start a podcast or better, get on someone else's podcast. This is something that I have done I have my own podcast called life according to Paolo where I interview people from all around the world around their life journey. Write on a topic related to your book, and then link to your book in your post. Start a social media group around your book. These are really valuable places to connect, get ideas and even get amazing content ideas for your next book.

Host an event around your book and what it talks about. Or set-up a launch event. Make sure you have enough critical mass to do this otherwise the event can look very empty. When you have a huge audience of loyal followers and readers who buy and read your book it would be a good idea to organise live events that will enable your fans to meet you and get to hear readings of your book.

CHAPTER 7

YOUR BOOK IS YOUR BUISNESS CARD

Your book is your business card therefore now the journey truly begins so buckle up because it is about to get exciting. One of the things that I really love is the ability to turn your book into a workshop, webinar, seminar, coaching, mentoring, flashcards set, wristband, badges, public speaking presentation etc – the possibilities are endless. When you become an author, you instantly become an authority in the industry that your publish in. You instantly become more credible in the eyes of your clients, prospects, family, and friends etc. Your author status can radically increase revenue streams and catapult you and your business to levels that were previously unimaginable.

Becoming an author is the difference that will make the difference because your book will set you apart from your peers in both a business and/or personal capacity.

NEW DOORS ARISE WHEN I CLOSE MY EYES AND WRITE

You can use your book to open doors that may have previously been hard to get into. For example, my book and "published author" moniker has helped me land contributor roles at various outlets. It also helped me to speak at different events and I was even more privileged to host one of my own events at virgin money lounge thanks to a dear friend called Sunil Chuni I also held my own event at Chelsea FC thanks to Karl Southwell I also got to attend a Brunel Engineering master classes for children in year 9 in which we done 3D printing, we learned about genes and cells within the body. We had the pleasure of attending thanks to Lesly Warren and the STEM team at Brunel University I also am one of the ambassadors for VueBox thanks to Anoir Houmou founder of VueBox.

YOUR BOOK CAN OPEN MULTIPLE DOORS OF OPPERTUNITY

Your book is not only a big thing with pages and words on it is also a business card because a book Is a steppingstone to something bigger and better not smaller, and remember a seed doesn't grow into a tree after a day it takes time the same applies to your book It will take time to grow so enjoy the process and always remember throughout all stages of this book that you are writing make sure to smile be happy and have the greatest time of your life because your book is not here to hurt you it's to heal you and to let go of all barrios that may have been holding you back because it's time to let

Goooooooooooo!

YOUR BOOK IS YOUR BUISNESS CARD

Your book is a strong marketing tool. Your book is basically your business card why do I say that well its because if you hand someone your business card they are less likely to keep it but if you give them a book they will read it and love it because you are a born storyteller and don't think that it will be seen as you being bias if you are at an event or getting interviewed and then you mention you book no way. You wrote it to share it so don't be ashamed to share it with others.

You can give copies to contacts when you meet with them, send copies to potential clients and mail them to other influencers you're hoping to connect with because they will be inspired to see hear and read your book what I would like to share with you is that…..

"We are the authors of our own life stories."

BONUS CHAPTER: BERNARDO MOYA

I wanted to gift you a surprise chapter and Mr Bernardo Mayo was kind enough to contribute a chapter to my book

Bernardo Mayo's Bio:
http://www.thebestyou.co / http://thebestyouexpo.com/
http://bernardo-moya.com/
Inspiring People - Inspiring Stories - Inspiring You

Bernardo is the founder of The Best You. A platform that is in the business of helping people achieve their dreams. The Best You care, we listen to, and provide our customers with skills, tools, knowledge, wisdom, and experts to enhance and improve their lives. We help people discover their true purpose.

Bernardo is an author, mentor, coach, speaker, businessman and Entrepreneur. He manages the largest NLP Training company in the world, and promotes seminars for Richard Bandler, Paul McKenna and John La Valle. www.nlplifetraining.com

He is an NLP Licensed Trainer and loves to see the results that our seminars and products have on people and organizations.

He is interested in Linking up with people who would like to market his unique seminars and distribute his personal development content.

I encourage you to send a LinkedIn invitation any time, or email me at bernardo.moya@thebestyou.co

Specialties: Publishing, Magazine, Personal Development, Seminars, corporate Training, selling, marketing and

networking. Promoter, author, producer and distributor of
personal development content.

Bernardo helps speakers and authors set strategies to increase
and generate income from their IP.
More information on Bernardo http://bernardo-moya.com/

Interview with Bernardo Mayo:

Q: Introduce yourself and tell audience a bit about what it
is that you do
A: I am Bernardo Moya and I am the founder of The Best
You and I am also the CEO of NLP life training I am an
author, I am a speaker, I am a promoter I've been in this
business of personal development for 10/11 years. I have
many hats, I started reading books and attending all sorts of
courses like everyone else and eventually I became well what I
do now for The Best You promoting more than 700 speakers
I have had more than 70,000 people attend all different
workshops and seminars and we are now doing expos all over
the world so that is what we do. The Best You helps people
achieve their dreams and we provide these speakers authors
leaders an opportunity for them to share their expertise, so they
can inspire others

Q: What is your why and why do you do what you do
A: Well my why I think it is additionally to being a promotor
what I personally want to do is I coach and mentor people and
I want to work with more and more people so my why is
providing learning possibilities through workshop seminars,
online content and really in any format to provide people with
ideas through these live events and all my different platforms,
but my personal why is to is to coach and mentor people in
helping think and helping them become aware of their
thoughts and thinking bigger and understanding that it is never
too late and making sure that they ask themselves empowering
questions that would be my why

Q: Do you like to go on adventures

A: Yes, indeed I do in my downtime what I love to do is I like to ride my motorcycle, so I have a couple of bikes and have to go to different places. I have down South Africa, I've done Vietnam, I've done Madagascar, some places in Canada so that is what I love doing and those are some of the adventures that I have been on, but I find with bike rides, the longer the better. I would say that Vietnam would have been one of my best adventures we did around 2900 km 12 days riding over the most beautiful scenery as challenging as it was it was amazing

Q: Who inspires you and why

A: Well a load of people inspire me, I am inspired by lots of speakers and authors I mean Brené Brown, Brendon Burchard and I have many other inspirations as well but obviously the greats I love Les Brown, Brian Tracy, Jim Rohn. They were the people I really read an obviously I had been influenced by the work of Dr Richard Bandler through working and promoting him for 10 years, so it is safe to say that he has helped me to become who I am

Q: What were the 2 most pivotal moment in your life and what did it teach you

A: Well my dad died when I was 15 that was difficult so overcoming that and having a set of responsibilities that I have never had before and stepping up really and then losing my money the first and second time, but the second time would definitely have been a lot tougher. Having to start all over again I was in real estate and had to start again so from real estate I became a promotor I started getting into the world of personal development so its safe to say that I re-invented myself and started all over again at the age of 40 those are my 2 most pivotal moments

Q: What are the 3 biggest that you learnt from life and what is the difference that makes the difference

A: Well I have learnt many, many things and I think I have obviously well what I normally talk about in my book "The Question" is about obviously being resilient. Being resilient now is something that I appreciate now that I am now capable of. I've been very strong in getting through things when I put my head to something I normally see it all the way through at least big projects and things like that its not that I have completed and everything and anything I've done is a success because it is not but I have always taken it to where I could and it became a reality in a big way. So, resilience and reinventing yourself is pivotal in order to stand out and change/revolution. I think welcoming change and understanding why change is important has been a big lesson for me and something I preach and recommend people to embrace change and see it as something good that allows, you to grow and it is what life is all about

Q: What is your dream adventure and why
A: Again, they are around motorcycles maybe me doing a long trip all the way down south America I would love to do that I would love to get lost and do some retreats and really just dig deep into meditation and spending more time thinking and being creative instead of working as much as I do that would be my dream adventure

Q: What has been the biggest challenge that you have faced in your life
A: It would have had to be when I lost my money losing my dad and I just lost my mum recently so that has been my challenge recently and those have been my biggest challenges and I am looking forward to coming out on the other side and keep going

Q: What was the reason behind your last adventure of self-discovery and outdoors in the wild
A: To get away really to disconnect is something that I love doing there's something about riding a motorcycle that is

special as you're in the moment you're in the now there are no distractions because if you get distracted it could be dangerous, so I love that

Q: Would you agree that children my age should spend more time outdoors if so, why

A: Yes, I do I believe children should spend more time reading, watching videos that can help them become more inspirational learn and model people that have been more successful learn from people that have done some amazing and inspiring things there are some many great auto-biographies out there I would definitely forget spending so much time on games, spending so much time on social media. I think they estimate an average of 4 years that the average person spends on there in their life. I think the younger generation will probably be around 6 or 7 that's a long time to spend on your phone so absolutely get out there.

Q: What was your first adventure

A: I don't remember it was so long ago it is probably in black and white. I used to do a lot of thing and have done a lot in my life I was a DJ, I worked in night clubs so kind of a lot of the things I do now is with life you learn skills that you can then bring on to your next you but my motorbike adventures have been the most exciting things I have done and you know just feeling connected with the wild life and where you are in nature

Q: Has this interview shifted your perspective, if so how will   you   change   going   forward

A: I've been interviewed many times and there is always something that you learn every time and every question that you are asked obviously that helps you to trigger new ways of thinking so I encourage people to keep an open mind I encourage people to think about what they think about and making sure that they have good strong internal dialog and making sure that they ask themselves empowering questions. I would recommend anyone and everyone to read my book "The Question – Find your true purpose" It has great reviews its all about trying to teach people skills which I think are essential, basic but people don't usually follow.

Q: What message would you like to share with the people
A: Well what I would say to you young ones is get out of the mindset that you will live forever because no one knows how long they are going to live having experienced losing my mum recently I am even more determined to do more help more achieve more and be more and to do that by pushing and constantly pushing forward because our reality ladies and gentleman is our mortality that is our reality so focus on the now. I actually shared a quote today on my Instagram that said, "If you woke up breathing this morning its already a good day." So, I'll leave you with that. People can find me my brand TheBestYou.co that is my brand The Best You Expo that is related to my big events wherever and whenever we are running an event. My webpage Bernardo-Moya or Bernard/Moya I am also googleable, so you can find me anywhere. On social media you can find me as Bernardo Moya and then my book is thequestion.co Thank you so much mate I am very proud of you and keep going you are an inspiration keep going lots of love.

GIVE YOURSELF TIME
JOURNAL

GIVE YOURSELF TIME DAILY JOURNAL

Writing things down is an effective way of remembering and reflecting on all the amazing things that happen every day and it can transform your mindset.

No matter how much you write or how little you write take the time to really think about your day, at the end of your journal you can then go back and treasure those memories.

Date: __/__/____ Today I am Grateful For…

_____

_____

_____

_____

_____

What Would Make Today A Great Day?

_____

_____

_____

_____

_____

During the evening just before going to bed take a
moment to reflect on your day then List the 3 best
things that happened…

1) _____

_____

_____

_____

2) _____

_____

_____

_____

3) _____

_____

_____

_____

Date: __/__/____ Today I am Grateful For…

_____

_____

_____

_____

_____

What Would Make Today A Great Day?

_____

_____

_____

_____

_____

During the evening just before going to bed take a moment to reflect on your day then List the 3 best things that happened…

1) _____

_____

_____

_____

2) _____

_____

_____

_____

3) _____

_____

_____

_____

Date: __/__/____ Today I am Grateful For...

_____

_____

_____

_____

_____

What Would Make Today A Great Day?

_____

_____

_____

_____

_____

During the evening just before going to bed take a
moment to reflect on your day then List the 3 best
things that happened...

1) _____

_____

_____

_____

2) _____

_____

_____

_____

3) _____

_____

_____

_____

Date: __/__/____ Today I am Grateful For…

_____

_____

_____

_____

_____

What Would Make Today A Great Day?

_____

_____

_____

_____

_____

During the evening just before going to bed take a moment to reflect on your day then List the 3 best things that happened…

1) _____

   _____

   _____

2) _____

   _____

   _____

3) _____

   _____

_____

_____

Date: __/__/____ Today I am Grateful For…

_____

_____

_____

_____

_____

What Would Make Today A Great Day?

_____

_____

_____

_____

_____

During the evening just before going to bed take a
moment to reflect on your day then List the 3 best
things that happened…

1) _____

_____

_____

_____

2) _____

_____

_____

_____

3) _____

_____

_____

_____

Date: __/__/____ Today I am Grateful For…

_____

_____

_____

_____

_____

What Would Make Today A Great Day?

_____

_____

_____

_____

_____

During the evening just before going to bed take a
moment to reflect on your day then List the 3 best
things that happened…

1) _____

_____

_____

2) _____

_____

_____

3) _____

_____

_____

_____

Date: __/__/____ Today I am Grateful For...

_____

_____

_____

_____

_____

What Would Make Today A Great Day?

_____

_____

_____

_____

_____

During the evening just before going to bed take a
moment to reflect on your day then List the 3 best
things that happened...

1) _____

   _____

2) _____

_____

_____

_____

_____

3) _____

_____

_____

_____

Date: __/__/____ Today I am Grateful For…

_____

_____

_____

_____

_____

What Would Make Today A Great Day?

_____

_____

_____

_____

_____

During the evening just before going to bed take a moment to reflect on your day then List the 3 best things that happened…

1) _____

_____

_____

2) _____

_____

_____

3) _____

_____

_____

_____

Date: __/__/____ Today I am Grateful For…

_____

_____

_____

_____

_____

What Would Make Today A Great Day?

_____

_____

_____

_____

During the evening just before going to bed take a moment to reflect on your day then List the 3 best things that happened…

1) _____

_____

_____

_____

2) _____

_____

_____

_____

3) _____

_____

_____

_____

Date: __/__/____ Today I am Grateful For…

_____

_____

_____

_____

_____

What Would Make Today A Great Day?

_____

_____

_____

_____

_____

During the evening just before going to bed take a
moment to reflect on your day then List the 3 best
things that happened…

1) _____

_____

_____

2) _____

_____

_____

3) _____

_____

_____

_____

Date: __/__/____ Today I am Grateful For...

_____

_____

_____

_____

_____

What Would Make Today A Great Day?

_____

_____

_____

_____

_____

During the evening just before going to bed take a
moment to reflect on your day then List the 3 best
things that happened...

1) _____

_____

_____

_____

2) _____

_____

_____

_____

3) _____

_____

_____

_____

Date: __/__/____ Today I am Grateful For…

_____

_____

_____

_____

_____

What Would Make Today A Great Day?

_____

_____

_____

_____

_____

During the evening just before going to bed take a
moment to reflect on your day then List the 3 best
things that happened…

1)   _____

              _____

              _____

              _____

2)   _____

              _____

              _____

              _____

3)   _____

              _____

_____

_____

Date: __/__/____ Today I am Grateful For…

_____

_____

_____

_____

_____

What Would Make Today A Great Day?

_____

_____

_____

_____

_____

During the evening just before going to bed take a
moment to reflect on your day then List the 3 best
things that happened…

1) _____

_____

2) _____

_____

_____

_____

_____

3) _____

_____

_____

_____

Date: __/__/____ Today I am Grateful For…

_____

_____

_____

_____

_____

What Would Make Today A Great Day?

_____

_____

_____

_____

_____

During the evening just before going to bed take a
moment to reflect on your day then List the 3 best
things that happened…

1)   _____

_____

_____

2)   _____

_____

_____

3)   _____

_____

_____

_____

Date: ___/___/_____ Today I am Grateful For…

_____

_____

_____

_____

_____

What Would Make Today A Great Day?

_____

_____

_____

_____

_____

During the evening just before going to bed take a
moment to reflect on your day then List the 3 best
things that happened…

1) _____

_____

_____

_____

2)   _____

_____

_____

_____

3)   _____

_____

_____

_____

Date: __/__/____ Today I am Grateful For…

_____

_____

_____

_____

_____

What Would Make Today A Great Day?

_____

_____

_____

_____

_____

During the evening just before going to bed take a moment to reflect on your day then List the 3 best things that happened…

1) _____

_____

_____

2) _____

_____

_____

3) _____

_____

_____

_____

Date: ___/___/_____ Today I am Grateful For…

_____

_____

_____

_____

_____

What Would Make Today A Great Day?

_____

_____

_____

_____

_____

During the evening just before going to bed take a
moment to reflect on your day then List the 3 best
things that happened…

1)   _____

_____

2) _____
   _____
   _____
   _____
   _____
   _____

3) _____
   _____
   _____
   _____

Date: __/__/____ Today I am Grateful For...

_____
_____
_____
_____
_____

What Would Make Today A Great Day?

_____

_____

_____

_____

_____

During the evening just before going to bed take a
moment to reflect on your day then List the 3 best
things that happened…

1) _____

    _____

    _____

    _____

2) _____

    _____

    _____

    _____

3) _____

    _____

_____

_____

Date: __/__/____ Today I am Grateful For...

_____

_____

_____

_____

What Would Make Today A Great Day?

_____

_____

_____

_____

During the evening just before going to bed take a
moment to reflect on your day then List the 3 best
things that happened...

1) _____

_____

_____

_____

2)   _____

_____

_____

_____

3)   _____

_____

_____

_____

Date: __/__/____ Today I am Grateful For…

_____

_____

_____

_____

_____

What Would Make Today A Great Day?

_____

_____

_____

_____

_____

During the evening just before going to bed take a
moment to reflect on your day then List the 3 best
things that happened…

1) _____

_____

_____

_____

2) _____

_____

_____

_____

3) _____

_____

_____
_____

Date: __/__/____ Today I am Grateful For…

_____

_____

_____

_____

_____

What Would Make Today A Great Day?

_____

_____

_____

_____

_____

During the evening just before going to bed take a
moment to reflect on your day then List the 3 best
things that happened…

1) _____

_____

2) _____
_____
_____
_____
_____

3) _____
_____
_____
_____

Date: __/__/____ Today I am Grateful For…

_____
_____
_____
_____
_____

What Would Make Today A Great Day?

_____

_____

_____

_____

_____

During the evening just before going to bed take a
moment to reflect on your day then List the 3 best
things that happened…

1) _____

_____

_____

_____

2) _____

_____

_____

_____

3) _____

_____

_____

_____

Date: __/__/____ Today I am Grateful For…

_____

_____

_____

_____

_____

What Would Make Today A Great Day?

_____

_____

_____

_____

_____

During the evening just before going to bed take a
moment to reflect on your day then List the 3 best
things that happened…

1) _____

    _____

    _____

    _____

2) _____

_____

_____

_____

3) _____

_____

_____

_____

Date: __/__/____ Today I am Grateful For…

_____

_____

_____

_____

_____

What Would Make Today A Great Day?

_____

_____

_____

_____

_____

During the evening just before going to bed take a moment to reflect on your day then List the 3 best things that happened…

1) _____

_____

_____

_____

2) _____

_____

_____

_____

3) _____

_____

_____

_____

A MESSAGE FROM ME TO YOU

I believe in you…

Be yourself no matter what and know that you are your biggest fan, always remember that life is a journey of market research and what you choose to do with it is up to you. take responsibility for your actions and word and surrender to the internal journey of self-discovery and the external journey out in this beautiful world that we get to call Earth.

Trust your highest thought, your clearest words and your grandest feeling? Your highest thought is always the thought which makes your feel good. Your clearest words are the words which contain truth and honesty. Your grandest feeling is LOVE
Paolo Ben Salmi

ABOUT THE AUTHOR

AS SEEN OF TV, RADIO & NEWSPAPERS

Paolo is also UK and African Ambassador to Global Diaspora United Voices for Economic Empowerment Forum

Advisor at SoulJah Kingdom Rise

UK Ambassador of the Borg Banking Group AND of Borg University of International Skills www.borgglobal.com

Podcast Show Host of Life according To Paolo: https://paolobensalmi.sounder.fm/show/life-according-to-paolo

Paolo is the youngest ever Water-to-Go Ambassador: WWW.WATERTOGO.EU/PARTNERSHIPS/ PAOLOBENSALMI

Paolo and his family are the UK Associates for 360Wise Media www.360wisemedia.com

Paolo is founded of SARVA next generation education turning learners into leaders

LinkedIn profile: http://linkedin.com/in/multiple-award-winning-author-paolo-ben-salmi-aka-p-573145194

11yr old Paolo Ben Salmi aka Pint Size Adventurer is not is not your average 11yr old.

Paolo was chosen to develop UnLtd application process together with his mother, big brother and big sister

Paolo works in partnership with Brunel University alongside his mother and four siblings aged 20, 16, 13 and 7 (who's the youngest ever STEM ambassador for Brunel University)

Paolo is the youngest ever member of the Wisdom Council:
https://www.facebook.com/990806777731137/posts/2128059590672511/?d=n

Paolo is proud to be a brand Ambassador for VueBox, Choose Love and TruChallenge

My family and I have been acknowledged in the credits of a NEW movie called: How Thoughts Become Things movie promotional link:

Bit.ly/HowThoughtsBecomeThingsMovie2020

Paolo and his family held their signature 2 Day Family workshop called Dreaming Big Together - Mamas Secret Recipe at The Hub Chelsea FC

Water-to-Go blog about Paolo:

https://www.watertogo.eu/blog/meet-paolo-water-to-gos-youngest-ever-ambassador/

Paolo is the founder of his own publishing house called Adventurous Publishing.

Paolo hosted his signature program called Pint Size Adventurer - The Abundant Adventure Creator™ at the prestigious Virgin Money Lounge: London Haymarket: Pint Size Adventurer - The Abundant Adventure Creator - My Virgin Money

Paolo has interviewed people like Harry Hugo, Travis W Fox, Douglas Vermeeren, Bernado Mayo, Bob Doyle, Meagen Fettes, Udo Erasmus and Dr John Demartini to name a few.

Paolo Ben Salmi is an award-winning author of the book series called Pint Size Adventurer - 10 Keys Principles to Get Your KIDS off their iPads & Into the Wild.

Paolo is an Award-Winning Public Speaker (who has spoken at eleventh such as Mercedes Benz World and Virgin etc.)

Paolo has participated in brand campaigns for Sainsburys, Legoland, Matr, Warner Bros, Sony and Made for Mums to name a few.

TruLittle Heros Award - U12 Entreprenur 2017, Guest speaker at The Beat You Expo:

https://youtu.be/Fz9mErjC8rA where there were 15,000 attendees

Mercedes Benz World, Official Judge for Made for Mums Toy Awards 2018 via Team Trouble, Former International Radio Show host

Thanks to Douglas Vermeeren back in 2017 Paolo made history by being the youngest to interview Dr. John Demartini: https://www.facebook.com/350400542063654/videos/363072487463126/

Paolo has spoken on stage alongside people such as: Dr John Demartini, Douglas Vermeeren, Dr Toby Bailey, He Amb Arikana Chihombori Quao, Prof. Chimezie, Ambassador Koomson was appointed by His Excellency Flt. Lt. Jerry Rawlings as Ghana's Ambassador to the U.S., Dr Debbie Bartlett, Amb.(Rtd) Robert Perry, Robert Barnard-Weston, Col Brian Searcy (Rtd-USAF), Lamido Umar, Keston White-Marin, Evelyn Okpanachi, Prof. Abraham Osinubi, Alison Hall, Gunter Pauli, Steven Fern, Kanayo O. Kanayo and Hon. Kizito Ikenna to name a few.

Paolo is a personal developments coach and founder of Pint Size Adventurer who is here to help you to plant the seed toward self-discovery, exploration of the internal and external world and adventurer in abundance via a variety of products and services to assist you to create a brighter future

Paolo desires to encourage as many children as possible to go on adventures both internally and externally to activate their natural curiosity.

The question is are you watching the movie, in the movie or directing the movie?

Book:

Pint Size Adventurer: Mindset Is KEY
https://www.amazon.co.uk/dp/1913310337/ref
=cm_sw_r_cp_api_fabt1_.AdVFbHXR201J

Pint Sized Adventurer: The Abundant Adventure Creator
https://www.amazon.co.uk/PINT-SIZE-ADVENTURER-ABUNDANT-ADVENTURE/dp/1913310183/ref=tmm_pap_swatch_0?_encoding=UTF8&qid=1585959464&s r=1-1

Facebook page Pint Size Adventurer:
https://m.facebook.com/paolobensalmiakapintsi zeadventurer/

CHECK OUT MY LATEST BOOKS ON AMAZON

BEN SALMI FAMILY MANTRA

"BEN SALMI TEAMWORK MAKES THE
DREAMWORK

We believe that there is no such thing as failure only
feedback.

We also believe that the journey of one thousand miles
begins with a single step in the right direction

FAMILY ANTHEM

If you want to be somebody,
If you want to go somewhere,
You better wake up and PAY ATTENTION

I'm ready to be somebody,
I'm ready to go somewhere,
I'm ready to wake up and PAY ATTENTION!

The question is ARE YOU?

Printed in Great Britain
by Amazon